THE BOOK OF MRS NOAH

Michèle Roberts is the author of eight highly acclaimed novels including *Daughters of the House* (1992) which won the WH Smith Literary Award and was shortlisted for the Booker Prize. She has also published a collection of short stories and three collections of poetry. Michèle Roberts lives in London and Mayenne, France.

ALSO BY MICHÈLE ROBERTS

Fiction

A Piece of the Night
The Visitation
The Wild Girl
In the Red Kitchen
Daughters of the House
During Mother's Absence
Flesh and Blood
Impossible Saints

Poetry

The Mirror of the Mother
Psyche and the Hurricane
All the Selves I Was

Michèle Roberts

THE BOOK OF MRS NOAH

VINTAGE

FOR JOANNA DEFRIEZ AND HELEN WALTON

Thanks to Howard Burns, Sarah Lefanu and Anne Morgan
for reading and criticizing early drafts.
Thanks to all the friends who sustained me with encouragement and hot
dinners, and to those who helped me find rooms to write in. Thanks to
Salvatore Camporeale and Melissa Bullard for sharing with me their inter-
pretation of the Annunciation. Thanks to all at Methuen and in particular
my editor Elspeth Lindner.

Published by Vintage 1999

2 4 6 8 10 9 7 5 3 1

First published in Great Britain in 1987 by Methuen London Ltd

Vintage
Random House, 20 Vauxhall Bridge Road, London SW1V 2SA

Random House Australia (Pty) Limited
20 Alfred Street, Milsons Point, Sydney
New South Wales 2061, Australia

Random House New Zealand Limited
18 Poland Road, Glenfield, Auckland 10, New Zealand

Random House South Africa (Pty) Limited
Endulini, 5A Jubilee Road, Parktown 2193, South Africa

Random House UK Limited Reg. No. 954009

A CIP catalogue record for this book
is available from the British Library

ISBN 0 7493 9773 X

Printed and bound in Great Britain by
Cox & Wyman Ltd, Reading, Berkshire

'That floating Colledge, that swimming Hospitall–'
John Donne, *Elegies*

1   Noah died last night. Surely I should have prevented it, but did not.

We stand on the riverbank, quarrelling. Our bare feet share the same patch of silky mud that squirts between our toes as we shift back and forth, towards each other and away again, and his brown fingers hold mine until I pull them away from him, and the rain beats on our shoulders and on our hair. The green rags of the palm trees bend under the water that pours from heaven as though the sky is a split skin, and the bright grey clouds are reflected in the gleaming puddles on the ground.

I argue that it is time to board the Ark, to make the voyage. Noah promised to accompany me. Now he says he has changed his mind. It is too soon. He is not ready. He's not sure he'll ever want to come with me.

In the end I leave him behind. I teeter across the slippery gangplank into my wooden shelter, hastily closing the door after me as thunder and lightning begin to surround me with flashing blue zigzags of light, long low growls like sheets of corrugated iron being shaken up and down. From one of the hatches I peer out, seeking Noah's figure on the shore.

A silver pin sizzles down from the heavens, fallen from the quiver some god of destruction rattles at us so viciously. It strikes Noah between the shoulder blades with a fizz of blue light, and cracks him in two. Flames burst up from what was his spine and is now a long split, gaping emptiness. Flames form him: flesh and bones and hair are drawn in leaping fire. For a moment he wavers, and is still upright, and has shape; and then he crumples, sinks to the ground, a small heap of black ashes that the wind lifts and scatters on the river.

Noah has been wiped out. There is no dead body to prove he

has ever been alive. I am alive, and he is not. I put my hand to my side, which is seared and raw, as though my skin has been torn off, as though Noah has been unpeeled from me by the fire. I am burning too. Loss is more than absence: it is the fire.

I open my mouth to begin screaming, and wake up.

Noah lies asleep beside me, his round face peaceful, his black hair sticking up in spikes, his mouth open. I touch his cheek with my finger. I should ask for forgiveness. But I can't. Not yet.

2   My story begins in Venice.

Noah and I travel there on the little local train from Verona. We jolt along, stopping at villages that seem to consist only of a church, a scatter of pink concrete villas. It's a steamy, sticky day: the mountains on the horizon are misty blue shapes against a golden sky. The ditch running alongside the railway brims with purple mallow, pink campion, lavender thistles. Light blooms in the grass. Green light, that pours onto the glassy twists of the olive trees, onto the tobacco-coloured hilts of the swords of maize stuck in rows, onto the vines spreadeagled and sagging on their wires. The tall maize, ear-high, rustles all about us, stretching away across the vast plain, an ocean of green and bronze.

Our compartment, empty apart from us, is fitted out in silvery aluminium. Our seats are of maroon leatherette, the elbow-rests fat as aubergines, a strip of white linen antimacassar running behind our heads.

Noah is sitting opposite me, his attention on the newspaper in his lap. His hair is standing on end as usual. His blue eyes are screwed up against the sun. His hands caressing the smudged newsprint are brown flags defying me to approach him too closely, to say what's on my mind. He sighs, sags, looks tired. I wear him out with my demands. The air between us bristles with outrage.

Don't start again, his silence pleads: I know what you want to say. We've been through it all before. Every month for the last two years.

Walking on the water. I stand on the deck of the *vaporetto*, packed in amongst Venetians serenely going about their

9

business with briefcases and shopping bags as though immune to this miracle, and I laugh and laugh, staring unbelieving at the façades of palaces gliding by like theatre sets on the greeny-blue waters of the Grand Canal.

Our room is in a *pensione* behind the Accademia, on the wide Zattere waterfront facing the Giudecca. The walls are washed salmon pink, and a pink glass chandelier frilled and floppy as a giant squid hangs over the huge bed with its brocade-covered headboard in blue and pink and turquoise. The bedside lamps are cut from amber perspex and wear black and gold masks, and the radiator has cream accordion pleats. Below the window a narrow canal slaps at the weedy stone wall, and, opposite, a walled garden is full of flowering trees and stone statues. The air is as milky blue as the water in our bath. We sit at opposite ends of it, washing each other's feet, tickling each other with soap. A truce.

The city smells of cats' piss, yeast, rotting rubbish, coffee, fried fish, blossom. Noah leads me out into it, taking my hand and drawing me along. He's been here many times. He knows every path through this labyrinth of water, and so I allow myself to become passive for once, swept along behind him. We measure the city that floats, the city of carved pink islands and oily green canals. We travel through burning streets of yellow and rose façades, glittering churches, small blackened palaces. We plunge down crowded passages that twist and turn and double back. I lose all sense of direction. Venice loses me. Hanging on to Noah's hand.

Noah leads me, certainly and repeatedly, back towards our bed. Through courts and alleys striped by black shadow and sharp sun, up and down narrow stairways, over tiny humped bridges, along water corridors. Our bed is a four-poster sailing along the canals through the afternoon, and we on it are lulled by the rocking of the water, the swinging and clanging of the church bells, sweaty and hot and languid, our bodies taking and taking their holiday. But I can't abandon myself completely. Noah has betrayed me, and now I'm on guard.

We go down to supper in the dining room below. Noah's conference doesn't start until tomorrow morning, so we've got this evening to ourselves. Green light from the canal just beyond the ornate arched windows ripples in green waves

10

across the white walls and floor. The waiter is detached and severe, a priest saying Mass. He bends over silver trays, he flourishes silver cups, he flaps linen napkins, scrapes and bows and sweeps through the watery green room.

We eat chicken. I remember how I took Noah's flesh between my teeth, biting him gently, licking him, teasing him with lips and tongue, sucking up his juice. Spirals of black hair pattern his chest, arms, legs. I groom him, comb him with my fingers, pretending to search for fleas, pulling each curly black hair until he yelps and grabs me. His fingers sidle into me, a longboat riding my canal. He tells me I can have whatever I want, that he will give me whatever I ask for. (Except . . .) I don't know what to say. I drink wine in the *pensione* dining room, swirling the yellow liquid in the shining cut glass.

We walk out again, into the sparkling dark city. The night pulls us, unresisting, down tunnels of lights and laughter, past open-air restaurants where red mullet crackles on grills over beds of charcoal. We find a café in a small *campo* lit by flaring torches, and sit down outside and order coffee. The air laps at us, as warm as the sea, a black deep through which glide strings of lights, strolling people, gondolas, on which the churches sway up and down, docked for the night. I stretch out my legs in front of me and look around at the golden and black plane trees, the stone benches under them, the well in the centre of the little *campo*.

Then I see her. My grandmother, walking rapidly past us, her head down. There's no mistaking her face, her shape. Even as I turn my head and stare after her, she's gone, gliding down a narrow passageway.

– That's Nana, I exclaim, getting up and knocking my chair over in my hurry: what on earth is she doing here?

– How can it be your grandmother? protests Noah: you know she's dead.

He glances at his watch.

– Time for me to get back to the hotel. I want to put in a bit more work before going to bed.

– It *is* her, I insist: I *must* speak to her.

Ignoring his protests, I run across the *campo* into the shadows under the plane trees. There are seven exits; I counted them when we sat down. The *campo* is a kaleidoscope, shifting, turning, offering seven times seven ways of experiencing it, seven ways in and seven ways out, a crystal constantly changing, linked to all the other crystals that make up Venice. How can I be sure which way my grandmother has gone? I stare down the black mouth of a *calle*. Was it this one?

Behind me Noah is calling me to wait. I run.

I fly, full tilt, after the sturdy figure always just in front of me, whipping round corners just ahead, her face resolutely set forwards though I cry out her name and, behind me, hear Noah call out mine. I increase my speed until his voice dies in the distance. I knock into strolling people and send them stumbling. My heart beats in my throat.

She leads me towards the Grand Canal. I skitter through an archway, down a greasy stone ramp, and onto the bobbing raft at the end of it.

It's very quiet here, the palaces behind me closed and shuttered, noises and lights far away across the dark water. There is no one about. I can hear the creak of ropes, as the invisible gondolas moored by the stakes stuck into the mud tug at their fastenings and the ropes grow taut and then slack. I can hear the slap-slap of water on stone, my own harsh breathing.

My grandmother is not here.

I peer at her absence, the pitch-black night at the end of the raft. The Ark is moored there, way out somewhere in the lagoon. I know it.

I strip hurriedly, tearing at buttons and fastenings. Cotton frock, underwear, espadrilles drop, a crumpled heap of darkness.

A cry. My name called.

Noah stands, panting and dishevelled, at the top of the ramp.

– Don't do it, he shouts: don't be stupid. Come back. It's dangerous to swim in the canal. You could be killed.

He is starting down the ramp.

– Keep back, I yell: or I *will* jump in.

He halts.

– I know you're upset, he shouts: we can talk about it. Let's go back to the hotel. You need to rest.

Under my bare feet is the cracked splintery wood of the raft, dry and warm. The night air, fragrant with the smell of ripe fruit, caresses my skin. I shiver.

I stumble forwards to what I judge must be the edge of the raft, one foot pressing into the night in front of the other. When my left foot comes down on nothing I teeter, almost fall in. I stop, balance myself, raise my arms above my head. No moon, no stars. Just this cloudy blackness.

I launch myself forwards and down. Noah's cry behind me is cut off as I enter the water. It smacks my ears but can't hold me back.

3   If I have my grandmother's blessing I can leave for
     the Ark without too much fear. I need my ancestor at
     my back.

This is the way I imagine it.

I take the lift down inside myself, pressing the button marked
Help. I drop past floor after floor of memory, down past death,
down to the bottom floor of the unconscious. I step out into a
large square room. The sign over the door reads *Ladies*.

I have arrived in a veritable college of grandmothers. Seated
in rows on old-fashioned commodes are scores of stern old
women with bright eyes and white hair. I start laughing. These
are real thrones all right.

Here's my own grandmother, sitting in the middle of the
room, filling in her football coupon.

She frowns at me, holding my hands.

– Get on with you, you storyteller. Become a journey-
woman. Build your Ark. Sail off in it. Get going.

Then she smiles.

– When I'm on my own, she says: I make whatever I like.
She shakes her biro as I kiss her soft cheek.

– Hop it. Be off with you. You've got to invent your own life.
It's up to you.

It could also happen like this.

The lift carries me very high, up through layers of white
cloud. I step out onto a terrace walled in glass. Up here it's
night, the darkness pressing cool and moist on my skin.

My other grandmother is perched on a stool, eyes clamped to
the telescope she has trained upon the distant stars. She swings
around to face me, and sighs irritably.

– Well? What do you want?

She's as remote and indifferent as snow piled on a Himalayan peak that no one has ever climbed: that's the cold place she's won for herself in her old age. She's left us messy and emotional young ones in order to dwell in a fastness of prayer and ice; it's an effort for her to readjust her eyes and focus on me rather than on wheeling empty air, on stars. Her face is austere: all neediness has long since been scoured away from it by the winds she lives amongst and loves.

– I've no time for children and grandchildren any more, she remarks, frowning: young people today are graceless, ungrateful and spoiled rotten. I've spent my life in the pursuit of wisdom, but none of you cares for that, or listens to me. Too difficult for you, isn't it? You're still children, all of you, playing your silly games of sex and politics. Why can't you grow up? Why can't you leave me alone? Why must you still come running to me and expect me to do it all for you?

I open my mouth to speak, but she shrugs me into silence and goes on.

– I know what you're going to say. I've heard it all before. I can read your thoughts. They don't interest me. I'm weary of the world you still choose to live in. I have nothing to say to you except this: you are naïve and stupid and ignorant; you have never listened to me or taken my advice; and so now I wash my hands of you.

Now she glares at me.

– I don't *like* you very much. So get *out*! Get *out* of my house!

4   I swim out along the Grand Canal, towards the Lagoon.

How shall I recognize the Ark when I reach it? It's certainly no good relying on Arkitects to design it for me ready-made. They all disagree on every aspect of it and spend their time squabbling over how to interpret the specifications laid down by the great Client in the Sky.

For example, the great Origen imagines the Ark as a sort of truncated pyramid, a classification system in three dimensions of the hierarchies in the natural world. On the top deck there is a cabin for Man, and beside that, space for Woman and their three sons and their wives. Below this comes the deck where the clean beasts are kept, and below this again a deck for the carnivores and reptiles. Origen draws a horizontal line through the middle of the Ark at this point, to demonstrate the need for a strict division between Above and Below. Under the dividing line is a storage deck, where food is kept, and under this, the place of offal.

St Augustine is convinced that the Ark should be built according to the proportions of the human body, and St Ambrose agrees with him, at great length. St Augustine points out that there is no need to have a deck full of fish tanks on the Ark, since the fish can swim alongside through the waters of the Flood, and that it's unlikely God means Man to take the insects on board since they breed on putrefaction and will be catered for by all the corpses floating about. St Augustine also thinks that Man can feed the carnivores from his stores of fruit and chestnuts rather than tackling the problem of preserving fresh meat on a long voyage.

Hugh of St Victor designs an Ark with stalls on the outside

16

for frogs, seals and sirens.

The poets Prudentius and Avitus both imagine the exploits of the raven to be sent forth from the Ark to see whether there is dry land in existence. Prudentius and Avitus reckon that the raven can perch on floating carcases and gorge himself for the duration of the Flood. They do not, however, tell us much about his hutch or cage. I think this must be the same raven who turns up on the battlefields of the Anglo-Saxon heroic poems, picking out the eyes of the dead.

Tertullian is terse, but he reminds us that the Ark will be built before the founding of cities and is therefore unlikely to look like one.

Buteo remarks that no special arrangement is needed for the reptiles, actually, because they can easily just twine themselves around the beams and the rafters (presumably on the third deck).

Tostado describes a higgledy-piggledy of animal arrangements, with Man walking between the asps, dragons, unicorns and elephants at feeding time; thanks to God they will not harm him.

There is no consensus on whether the centaurs, sirens, satyrs and fauns will actually be on the Ark with special living quarters provided for them.

On the other hand, everyone agrees that the Babylonian Sibyl will certainly be on board, for she has been commissioned to write a long poem about it all afterwards.

When we come to visual representations there is even more confusion.

The Ark is an enormous chest, banded with iron.

The Ark is pretty much like an ocean liner.

The Ark is a longboat with a prow carved like a dragon's head.

The Ark is a floating castle, a small city of wood and stone with towers and turrets and gates.

The Ark is a detached suburban house.

These are the main types I have been able to detect.

I'll add a few of my own.

The Ark is a huge seed, tossed along by the waters, carrying its cargo of new life.

The Ark is a bestiary, of beasts domestic and fabulous. Here are, preserved for ever more, not just the Unicorn, the

Dragon and the Bonnacon, but also the Phoenix, the Loch Ness Monster, the Bearded Lady, the Siamese Twins, and many more. The Ark is a series of allegories, a Sunday newspaper, a zoo.

The Ark is a coffin bearing dead bodies out to sea.

The Ark is the coracle in which the hermit saint sets out for paradise, rowing away from this earth, which is the condition of exile from the city of God, towards freedom and the enchanted isles with their mountains of glass, their talking birds.

The Ark is a sieve.

The Ark is the cradle of Moses, the basket caught in the bulrushes, and it's the manger in which Jesus sleeps. On second thoughts: I didn't make this one up. St Augustine probably did.

The Ark is the nuclear shelter of the survivalists, defended by machine guns.

The Ark is an inner-city neighbourhood fighting back against poverty, unemployment, racism, police raids.

What kind of Ark do *I* want?

I depend on books to help me out when I'm stuck. I dive between the covers of a novel, my foldaway house that travels in my pocket, my cool tent that I can put up wherever and whenever I choose. I trained as a librarian thinking it would give me time to read, but I spend most of my days, in the public library where I work, checking that books have been correctly re-shelved, showing readers how to use the catalogue on microfiche, chasing enquiries and loans.

I've taken two months off work to travel around Italy with Noah while he researches his book on the Italian health service and attends various conferences. My bibliographical skills have come in useful; I help him organize his card index, classify his hills of files and notes.

But in the evenings, when Noah pores over statistics in our hotel room, time hangs heavy, tugs my empty hands. I've already finished reading all the novels I brought with me.

I need work to do. I need books. I'll invent a library.

5 The cabin smells of dust, leather, furniture polish. I pick my way across it in the dark, fumble at the catch of a porthole, swing it open.

Sudden white light, hurting my eyes. I blink, refocus on walls lined with wooden shelves behind glass doors, packed with maroon boxes labelled in white. *Mazzo* LIII. *Mazzo* LIV.

In the centre of the archive a baize-topped table on wrought-iron legs bears two large open volumes of manuscript, two brass lamps with parchment shades, a paper press, various lumps of rosy marble. A leather sofa with a ripped yellowing seat and a carved back is set against one wall, flanked by two shabby velvet-covered armchairs. A spotted china globe dangles from the ceiling, which is painted with four female figures, faded and flaking, representing the seasons. The wooden deck is scattered with worn rugs.

I seat myself at the mahogany desk I have placed underneath an enormous oil painting of Judith slaying Holofernes, donated by Artemisia Gentileschi. Deep soft armchair upholstered in cracked battered leather. In front of me is a pile of cataloguing slips in blue cartridge paper, a green blotter bound in half-calf, a flowered china inkpot with a quill pen balanced on top of it, and a plastic tray heaped with nibs, rubbers, a bottle of glue, a pair of scissors, and a stapler.

I try out my signature on a piece of blotting paper. Mrs Noah, Arkivist of the Ark.

I draft notes for the brochure outlining the Ark's function and services.

The Ark of Women is the Other One. The *Salon des Refusées*.

Des Refusantes. Cruise ship for the females who are only fitted in as monsters: the gorgons, the basilisks, the sirens, the harpies, the furies, the viragos, the amazons, the medusas, the sphinxes.

Where shall we go, the women who don't fit in? Those of us who are not citizens but exiles? Those of us who are not named as belonging, but as outcasts, as barbarians?

Into this Ark of Women.

The Ark of Women has been founded by an international committee of sibyls in order to guard and encourage women's creativity. Every women who has ever lived has deposited here her book: her story or novel or collection of poems or autobiography. On the Ark time doesn't work normally and nor do clocks: all the stories, from past present and future, are here, rubbing shoulders in the dark. Some composed at home, some dictated to friends, some written during the writer's stay on the Ark. The Ark is not only an archive: it is a rest-home that swims, a workshop that floats, a bubble of temporary retreat for women who need time to write away from their families and domestic cares.

The Ark's bookstack, extending over many decks, contains all the varied clashing aspects of women's imaginations expressed in books. These can be called up by a classification system of great subtlety, based on the crystalline thought processes of the unconscious, designed by a committee of poets. Men's books are of course available, on inter-library loan. Please see the catalogue.

Aids to study on the Ark include comfortable cabins, beds in the reading room for those wishing to rest or dream, food and drink always available (supper, however, prepared on a volunteer rota basis), and a crèche for those needing to bring their children.

Writing materials on offer include knotted strings, circular seals, blackboards and chalk, wampum belts, message tallies, tablets of clay and ivory and wood, oracle bones, slabs of gold and silver and wax, shards of pottery, strips of cloth and papyrus and paper, sticks of bamboo, palm leaves, bits of birch bark, leather scrolls, rolls of parchment, copper plates, pen and ink, palettes and paintbrushes, sticks and dust-trays, printing presses, typewriters, tape recorders, word processors, etc.

Women come on board the Ark for a bit of peace and quiet in

which to think about their lives and question them.

Women come here to develop their craft, to discuss work in progress, to give and take criticism and advice on redrafting, to share fears, failures, ideas.

Women who hate the very idea of writers workshops come here to get away from other women, to live in cells of silence and isolation, to be as selfish and unsisterly as they like.

Women come here to find out what it means to be a woman writer, whether in fact that matters, whether we aren't all just writers.

Women come here to free their imaginations, to learn to play again, to destroy.

Some rush home again. Some leap over the side in rage and despair. Others enjoy themselves. You can read all about the Ark in our records. Please ask at the main desk for further information.

I get up, and prowl along the bookshelves until I find the leatherbound brass-cornered volume that is the index to the sibyls and their works. Soft thick pages: rag paper, lovely to touch. The entries are written in my clear neat hand, wide margins left around them, each name underlined by flourishes in faded brown ink. I'm impressed by my handiwork: no blots or crossings-out. I run my index finger down the columns, pausing over particular names. The Nubian Sibyl, the Persian Sibyl, the Bombay Sibyl, the Guatemalan Sibyl, the Brixton Sibyl. I know them quite well, have read their works in a tumult of sorrow, laughter, rage. They've come, in the past, to give talks at the public library where I used to work. But I see that opposite their names I have scribbled *Gone out of town*. So. What about some of these others? The Babble-On Sibyl, the Correct Sibyl, the Deftly Sibyl, the Forsaken Sibyl, the Re-Vision Sibyl. I'll try them. I scribble down the shelf-marks of their works, then hunt along the shelves again until I find the corresponding numbered boxes which I lift out and put on my desk.

Inside the boxes, under each cardboard lid, are masses of tightly rolled parchments, some no bigger than cigars, each one tied up with string and labelled in black ink. I select at random, undo the strings and unroll the parchments, flattening them with my fingers and weighting the ends with the lumps of marble I fetch from the centre table. I browse. Some odd titles here. Unmemorable. It's a biggish book, people say, coming up to the desk in the public library: with a red cover, you know? But these sibyls will do. They are the companions I want.

6   This morning the Deftly Sibyl has woken up hating her husband. Lying rigid, a foot away from him, she feels her heart pump with anxiety. His back is turned to her, only his shiny bald patch visible. She shudders. She'd better get out. Run away.

She has an escape fund. A secret building society account, added to monthly. Rarely touched, in fact, except to buy clothes for the children, Christmas presents, birthday gifts for family and friends. But it *is* her money, produced by scrimping and saving on the housekeeping, working odd nights as a barmaid when her sister will baby-sit, writing reviews and articles for magazines she despises. It's there for her if she ever needs to run away. Enough for a ticket to Newcastle, where her best friend Emily lives. Single.

This morning she decides to run away into the field backing onto their (George's) little house at the end of the village street. She effaces herself in sweatshirt and jeans, ties her hair back. Slips out of the back door, down the path, over the stile.

Early morning is cloudy, the grass smelling fresh and moist. She would like to walk barefoot in it, to lie down in it, to rub her face on the earth, to stuff it into her mouth. She starts to run round the edge of the field, the hedgerow a blur of olive green, the cold air stinging her cheeks. She wants to be a good person, loving and unselfish. But at the moment she is possessed by hate. If she runs fast and long enough, perhaps she can sweat out the hate, trample it underfoot and leave it behind, return to the house a kind mother and wife with a sense of humour.

She wants to leave her husband and children. She wants to live in a house that is *hers*. That she pays for with her own money. A place in which only she lives, where no one else enters

23

unless invited to do so. George has the power in this house: he earns twice as much as she does. Living with George, in George's space, at George's rhythm, it is impossible to concentrate properly on her writing. He's so proud of the elegant avant-garde novels she writes, but nonetheless his needs have to come first. Since he works freelance, his hours are unpredictable. She can't start working until he's left the house, left her in peace. She has to stop as soon as he comes home and re-possesses the kitchen where she writes. She can never plan her own work, can never be sure of a long stretch of hours ahead into which she can slowly sink, submerge herself, reach that level, far down, where she makes contact with what wants to get written today. She hovers on the brink, head raised, unable to let go, waiting for the crash of his step on the path. Then the children. Off at school all day now, giving her clear limits of time, but still needing to be fed cleaned up after cared for listened to played with accommmodated. Oh yes she loves the children and George but that's not the point.

She slows down as she passes the gate and sees the bullocks in the corner. Old friends. They lumber towards her, eager and curious, bawling, some of them with coats of black satin, others auburn and ruffled like doormats on stocky legs. They push their snub heads at her caressing hands, lick her with rough tongues. Tired of the game, she smacks their backs, waves her arms at them, and they lumber off. She pads on again.

If she lived alone, meals would not be such a fuss. She'd eat if and when she was hungry, a bowl of pasta and a salad, her elbows on the table, no need to talk to anybody, a book open beside her. None of this searching the supermarket for economical cuts of meat, searching the recipe books for a hundred exciting things to do with mince. Once she heard a man complain that women on their own don't dine, don't know how to. We don't always want to dine, you poor fool, she screams into the wind: it makes a change, not bloody dining. *Dearie*, she addresses a thistle as she gallops over it.

George's face at dinner last night. Sulky, cold. Yes, she admits it: she had too much to drink, lost control, poured herself out like spilled wine onto the white linen tablecloth. Which she'll wash, dry and iron. It will take longer to launder things with George. His disgust at her as she sat pounding the table with her fist, blethering on about her need for uninter-rupted work, for silence and solitude, not letting him talk back, interrupting him, speaking to the soup tureen not to him. She slid into bed as a criminal. Unreasonable, rude, unkind, surprising herself as much as him with her carping, her complaints. Bad bad bad. She knows it, even before he tells her.

Which is why she is out here this morning, racing the devil around the muddy track circling the field, her lungs burning, her throat raw and dry, her legs aching and shuddering as she urges herself on.

She's begun to need to complain. Better to do it out here, where no one can hear her, where she can't hurt those she loves, won't let them down.

Around and around she runs.

Running away. Around and around.

The Re-Vision Sibyl needs to be careful. Don't quarrel with Jim when he forgets to send three maintenance cheques in a row then points out how hard up he is with a second family to support. Don't let on how interested she has recently become in feminism, how her current lover, to her own surprise, is a woman, lest Kitty be taken away from her, in her best interests of course. Work hard, yes, get on with her writing, yes, but never forget to put Kitty first, prove to the school and the social workers that single mothers can cope. Just. Provide the child with adult male company, uncle figures, to ensure she won't turn out queer; on the other hand, don't let them stay the night lest snooping neighbours report you and you're seen to be doing it for money. One day someone will find out that she augments her meagre maintenance and social security payments with writing stories for women's magazines under a false name, and then she'll be for it.

Today it's her birthday. Her mother, bless her, has sent her a cheque for twenty pounds and she's blown the lot on food. Rarely able to get out at night, she misses her men and women friends; but tonight she's having ten of them round for supper, and for the rest of the week she and Kitty will survive very well on the leftovers.

She's stuck in the middle of a story. Doesn't know how to end it. What a relief to put her pen down and take up a knife instead.

25

She's going to make a real French meal, posh food, the sort she cooked when she was married and bought all the newest cookery books.

She starts with the apple tart.

The table top is white formica, cool to touch. On her right, the basket of apples. In front of her, the wooden chopping board; in her hand, the savage black knife. To her left, the blue-rimmed china dish.

She pares the apples, one by one. The sturdy russet coats, rough-textured and scarred, all colours between yellow and red, fall off as the ragged edge of the worn blade reaches under them. The peel slides over her fingers, sticky with juice. She eats a sliver, licks and wipes her hands. Then she chops the round white bodies of the naked apples into quarters, and halves these, and then scoops out the core, the black shiny pips. Now the apples lie in the china dish, rows of crescent moons.

She melts butter to a pale gold foam in the big frying pan, lays the slices of apple in it, sprinkles sugar over them, pokes them gently with a wooden spoon. They start to take on a deeper colour, a rich yellow. Scent of butter and apples and caramel.

Another slab of butter into the white china mixing bowl, quickly cut into small pieces with the tip of her knife. Swift snow of flour, a little sugar, gritty, glistening, rubbed together to make sand. Egg and water mixed in with a fork, the crumbly mess rapidly gathered into a plump buttery ball she tosses from hand to hand before rolling it out into a thick circle she picks up and flaps like a pancake, tosses into the aluminium tin which she shoves into the oven.

She switches on the radio while she makes the *crème patissière*. Evensong from St John's College, Cambridge. The voice of a male priest invokes God the Father and God the Son. The male choir, so hushed, so reverent, murders successive antiphons with a prissy breathing in and out of notes, a cricket team masquerading as coy nymphs. Hefty boys in frilly white drag, she imagines them, massed solidly in the safety of their oak pews and choir stalls, high-faluting, up up up and away their voices intone, deliciously shivering at how precious and right their prayers are. No women here.

She breaks egg yolks into a bowl, whips them with sugar and flour, boils them with milk. Beats and beats with her wooden spoon to remove lumps. Lumpy female bodies. Lumpy bellies and breasts. Eggs breaking and splattering, warm mess of sweetness on the sheets, warm flow of sweat and blood. We can't have *that* in our nice Anglican chapel. Only male chefs please.

She composes the tart. Layer of crisp pastry. Layer of cognac-scented egg cream. The apples on top, arranged in overlapping circles brushed with apricot glaze. It is ready. Her devotions are over. She takes off her floury apron.

Tonight they will eat it. The labour of several hours will vanish in ten minutes. Rather like her stories, she supposes, read in the hairdresser's under the dryer and then discarded. What would it be like to produce great novels? Real art? She shrugs and laughs. She's a good cook, anyway. Perfect results every time. She wishes she could say the same for her stories.

Soon they will all be home from church, stampede of parents-in-law, nephews and nieces, Neil and his brothers. The Babble-On Sibyl smiles to herself, the cats stirring around her feet as she stands at the sink washing parsley in the tin colander. In the meantime, she has the whole house to herself, the stillness of the empty room scoured by light, the white curtain lifting at the window.

The glass doors of the dresser swing open at her touch. She pulls out a red and blue paisley cloth, spreads it on the round table, places a vase of bright leaves and ivies in the middle. She loves coming to stay with Neil's family. Image of unbroken happiness she hasn't quite found in her own life so far, that she worships in this kitchen shrine. Now she has it for her own. Now she has Neil.

Departing up the path to the car in a flurry of silk headscarves, leather handbags, walking sticks, white socks, they exclaim how good she is to stay home and make the lunch, releasing them to the pub on the green, after sermon and hymns, for gin and tonic, cheese squares arranged on saucers, air thick with plummy voices and cigarette smoke, the children bribed with crisps to run and squabble in the garden outside.

What she had meant was, she would stay behind and *write*. But it is inconceivable to Neil's mother that a real woman could ever do such a thing on a Sunday morning. Real women either

27

go to church, or get the dinner on. Preferably both. And the Babble-On Sibyl very much wants to be loved by her mother-in-law, very much wants to be a real woman. So she will cook the lunch. Her new family regard her hobby with affection, amusement. She's an authoress, you know, they say at drinks parties, pushing her forwards: quite a civilizing influence on our Neil here, eh? Neil's eyes signal: don't be upset; I love you. So she smiles. Yes, two collections of stories, slim ones, published, despite her youth. No, it doesn't bring in much money, writing. Good thing Neil's got a steady job, yes.

She's glad, anyway, to have got out of going to church. Only Neil knows how churches frighten her, that cold space between nave and chancel which holds nothing for her now, since Fanny's death, but a tiny wooden box set between tapers and stiff white gladioli. She fought Neil's parents for that, insisted it mattered that there was a funeral, that the dead baby had a name. The cold, coffin-shaped space is inside her still, a year later. Womb frozen, so that no sick baby can grow. Cervix clenched, so that no baby can slip out before time. She hasn't told Neil he's loving a wife with ice inside. She still can't talk about it. He's very patient. He makes love to her often. She knows he wants her to know how loved, how safe, she is.

How often she dreams of death, getting it muddled up with life: Fanny bursting up through the flowerbed with a hideous grimace and wizened limbs. She whisks an egg yolk with a drop of wine vinegar, adds oil drop by drop, beats at the thickening mixture, the cold glassy pleats of mayonnaise, greenish, smelling of olive. The dead salmon lies on its silver bier, parsley at head and tail. She has laid him out between the flowers and the candles. Now she anoints him with her home-made chrism.

Car tyres skidding and crunching on the gravel outside. The dogs (who terrify her) barking. Rattle at the latch as the door opens. Neil's footstep in the passage outside, his cheerful voice upraised.

– Where's the worker, then? Where is she? Curled up in a corner, I bet, with her head in a book. Where are you, Ba?

Her mother-in-law's voice, brisk, complacent.

– She won't have much time for *that* when the next baby arrives.

28

She snatches up the cut-glass decanter of sherry, swings it wildly above her head as though to throw it. Puts it down, shaking, just in time, as the kitchen door bursts open and they all crowd in about her.

On her way to the conference, the Forsaken Sibyl cycles past the park. Its colours draw her in. Irresistible. She dismounts, wheels her bike through the gate onto the asphalt path. Why worry if she is late? Being here is suddenly more important. She needs to calm down, anyway. Too churned up by last night's telephone conversation with Julia to concentrate on political theory.

She's strolling along a wide avenue edged with ornamental maples turned into translucent clouds of yellow sharp as lemons, fine as glass. The trees glitter like metal in the intense light of the sun, yet their colour is also soft, the yellow of chemicals, shiny as butter. The oval leaves of a cherry dangle, single flames, strange hot pink fruits. The trunks are a clear black, wet licks of paint. Luminous yellow. Splashes of rose, sour lime.

I'm afraid of loving you too much, Julia says, and laughs. Her olive eyelids cast down, her beckoning glance. Then her hands outstretched, forbidding contact; rapid talk of male lovers. Then the midnight phone call, newly seductive. I can't stay away from you, you know?

It's Saturday morning, nine o'clock. Few people about yet. She patters along in the troughs of dry leaves at the side of the path, lifting her cold face to the glare of the sun. Gold handcuffs. Gold chain around her neck. Runny gold light, leaking from her eyes. Leaves whirl about her, one by one surfing down from the blue sky, crackling under her boots, under her bicycle tyres.

She halts, to draw in the sweet smoke of a bonfire. November is bitter medicine in her mouth: the taste of chrysanthemums' cold russet hearts, the spicy burning smoke. A squirrel flows across the olive grass, waves of movement passing from body into long fur tail, rippling it. The brown of beeches separates into glowing scarlet, bright apple-skin, then blurs back into bronze.

I won't press you. I won't make demands. I'll keep my

29

distance, the one you indicate. I'll tie my hands behind my back, gag my open mouth. I just want to be with you sometimes.

This must be the last day of autumn, this radiant spending of colour, this transfiguration by light, this nail of sun banging the cold treacle of the air and smashing it to splinters. Tomorrow there will be rain, and sodden leaves squelching, dark mush underfoot, cold torrents of wind sweeping the last leaves from the trees. But this morning she treads, forgetting Julia at last, along a gold tunnel, no different in herself now from the sealskin tree trunks, the fresh earth of the flower buds, as the yellow park fringes her, then enters her, and she takes it inside. No more difference between outside and inside, no separating skin; just this flow of goodness, sweetness, self and words gone.

You can't control these moments; they lift off swiftly as they come; however much you long for their return. She sits in the conference hall, filling the thick notepad on her knee with abstract and technical words. Loss. Loss.

Walking back to her shabby flat after delivering the two children to school, the Correct Sibyl decides to stay outside. She, the old pro, famed among her friends for her capacity to stick at it rigorously, to write her thousand words a morning come what may, to produce a meaty piece of social-realist fiction every two years, is admitting defeat. The empty white space of the paper rolled into the typewriter terrifies her. She has nothing to say. She has dried up.

But she cannot afford this self-indulgence. Packets of words circulate in the bookshops like packets of Cornflakes in the supermarkets. She must stay on the production line, produce this season's new variety, special offer. Or she will be discarded, obsolete. No new Correct this year? Well, switch to Weetabix. Spot the difference. Correct drops to the trash can. No recycling in the Grub Street economy.

Clicking along the busy little road between the Victorian tenements gradually being prettied up for the influx of gentrifying home-owners pushing out poor tenants like herself, she wards off panic by reciting the litany of shops. On the far corner is the off-licence run by Mr O'Ryan who drinks in the Three Compasses next door and who is to be seen on Sundays buying a bunch of tulips from the flower stall to take to his mother. Next comes the Spanish deli, spice cave from which Mr and Mrs Garcia and their teenage daughter dispense chorizos, olives, honey-cakes, glutinous sweets. The West Indian restaurant opposite doubles as mini-cab hire office and as breakfast parlour: families hire beaten-up limousines here for weddings and funerals in their local church, the sumptuously panelled Tabernacle painted with apocalyptic texts. Next door is the Turkish fish and chip shop selling Jamaica patties and Chinese spring rolls; the Scottish grocer stocking everything from plimsolls to lemons to brillo pads; the chair-mender who works amidst enormous gilt-framed looking-glasses and broken chaise-longues; and the tailor whose window is adorned with a portrait, wreathed in plastic roses, of his mother, Kathleen O'Donoghue Tailoress, propped by old dress patterns from the forties. And lastly, just underneath the flats where she lives, the West Indian video hire shop, outside whose windows the local children gather for free film shows, and where the police come screaming up to investigate Black men in parked cars, to accuse them of theft, to turn the boots inside out, to search their pockets.

Unemployed youths and children skiving off school have turned the paved space in front of the Anglican church into a piazza for running races, for playing hopscotch and riding bicycles and skateboards. A lone roller-skater executes a figure of eight backwards with swooping grace, ears plugged by music muffs. The Correct Sibyl lingers to watch. Perhaps that is the way to do it; turn it the other way round.

I belong here, she reminds herself: this is my home. Out of this emptiness, somehow a story will come.

7   Outside the porthole, gulls loll on currents of air.
     I scribble, on a blue cataloguing slip, the message
     I want to send.

Dear Sibyl: this is an invitation to join me, Mrs Noah, on board the Ark. The purpose of my voyage, though not necessarily of yours, is to solve a problem: to discover how other women survive; to sail towards, and explore, the Western Isles, in order to arrive at a solution. I need companions. I'll leave you free all day to get on with your writing; I simply suggest that in the evenings we could get together and tell each other stories. I need to hear your stories. Will you come with me?

Now I need to send out my invitations.

I open the deep drawer in which I keep my collection of *ephemera*: bits of printed matter I am convinced will soon become obsolete. I preserve them as museum relics, memory of the time before paper is replaced by plastic in all its forms.

Bus tickets, *vaporetto* tickets, entry tickets to churches, the zoo, art galleries.

Squares of tissue paper, picked up in markets, used for wrapping oranges and lemons, printed with exquisite fifties and sixties designs, stamped with gold. Similarly, labels off tins of tomatoes and bottles of olive oil, and butter papers printed in old-fashioned typefaces with blue designs of cows.

Holy pictures picked up in churches: pale pastel represent-ations, wreathed in flowers, of swooning saints, with prayers printed on the back, details of indulgences, tiny inset relics.

None of these will do.

Here's a stack of old airmail envelopes, fragile blue paper boats striped in red and green, stuck with large glorious stamps franked with wavy black lines and circles, adorned with prints of red pointing fingers, eagles, aeroplanes, wings. Artifacts giving pleasure to the ears hearing the rustle of the flap, the tongue licking the sour-sweet gum, the eyes feasting on the words *Espresso* and *Via Aerea* in bold scarlet, the nose scenting the fresh ink, the fingers smoothing the grain of the delicate, almost see-through paper. Soon these will be replaced, I'm convinced, by spools of tape; we'll marvel at the absurdity of sending words as physical objects in packets from hand to hand. So I hang on to them. Sentimental? Reactionary? I suppose so. I console myself in advance for the time when the surreal poetry of addresses, written in words, will be replaced by rows of dreary numbers. Postcodes are bad enough, but things will get even worse.

Here is my collection of antique London telephone directories with their beautiful plain pastel covers: dusty pink, banana, olive, sky blue. The details of exchanges are given in words: PRImrose, BLUebell, SPEedwell. Of no use any more to anyone but me. I shall flip through them in the evenings as a change from reading the dictionary.

They won't do either. To send out my invitations I'll rely on an old technique that's coming back into fashion, newly granted scientific respectability.

I shut my eyes, and concentrate.

8   The Re-Vision Sibyl is swimming through sleep, rolling over and ducking, gliding along on her back, easy, feet flicking up and down in the water. A knobbly sack is lying across her legs, a burden weighing her down, bringing her head up from dreams.

– Mum. It's me. Let me in.

Feet treading her ribs. Kitty wriggles under sheet and blankets and down by her side. Small warm body pressed against hers. Head laid on shoulder, silky hair lapping face and neck. Kitty's hand pats her cheek, dances along her collarbone, flicks her ear lobe.

– Mum. Wake up. Cuddle me.

She shifts, slides an arm out under Kitty's body, pulls her closer. Kitty buries her face against her mother's skin.

– You smell nice.

– So do you.

Sleepy satisfaction. Powerful perfume of their naked skin released by the night, soap gone, sweat in the creases, pores breathing warmth. She draws it in, sour-sweet, milky.

– Mum.

– Mmmm.

Now Kitty's on the move again, propping herself on one arm under the heave of blankets. Fiddling with her hair, stroking and lifting it with her fingers, separating the strands. She starts to twirl it, plait it. Slow shivers along the back of the neck and down the spine, her bones pouring away, trickles of pleasure starting up all over as her daughter's hand caresses her head.

– There. You're done now.

Hot breath blowing in her ear. Sensation of sweetness dissolving in her throat, dissolving her.

That reminds her. For once, she has not been dreaming about her overdraft. Sleep-fuddled, heavy, she considers, clambering after the memory up a swaying rope stair.

– I had this dream last night, she tells her daughter: I was on board Noah's Ark with a bunch of friends.

Kitty's sucking her thumb and the edge of the sheet, both at once. Not interested. She lays her head back on her mother's breast, pulls her arms around her. They fall asleep again.

Morning. The Correct Sibyl walks around her room with no clothes on, enjoying the brush of the rugs on her bare soles, letting her stomach relax and flop out, plump and wrinkled. She's got a dirty face and she swings her arms to the music in her head and feels the sun on her skin and hair.

She lies on the unmade bed and looks at the green and gold tangle of the maple tree outside the window, the sharp jigsaw of its leaves, points jagging the blue sky. The light slides, sliced into oblongs, through the bits of stained glass Tom has propped on the windowsill: plum, orange, strawberry, apricot. Light lies like water on the fat blue arm of the chair, on the bits of carpet on the white painted floor.

She picks at her toenails and scratches her head. The sheets are full of the crumbs left from her long, lazy, uninterrupted breakfast. The tray of dirty dishes is still by the bed. Greasy thumbprints on the newspaper.

Twelve noon, and she's still lounging about. Delicious. With Tom and Jessie away at their father's for the weekend, she's having a morning off work goodness cleanliness godliness. Just as well, since she's got writer's block. Daydreaming. Doing nothing of any value whatsoever except pleasing herself. To hell with the muse.

She decides to take a bath. The window in the bathroom that she shares with the tenants downstairs is cut low, just beside the bath, so that she can turn her head and look out at the thrashing green branches of the maple tree through the open casement. Baby in a glass womb. She floats in the water she has scented with prodigal handfuls of bath salts, dissolving mauve grit. Cool air blows in from the window around her neck and shoulders. Lapped in wetness and warmth, fragrant steam, she joins two worlds: the air and the clouds and the racing green

35

leaves, and the deep enclosure of white enamel. She swims in and between both. She lies in her bath imagining she is the Ark plunging through rain and oceans, and the wind sweeps over her and through the house.

The Deftly Sibyl adjusts the straps of her pale blue nylon swimsuit, pads across the dimpled rubber tiles of the changing room and out into the great domed hall echoing with the shouts and splashing of the schoolchildren having a lesson at one end, lowers herself down the little aluminium ladder.

Now she's in her element of sloppy turquoise, legs and arms propelling her through liquid glass, chlorine smarting at the back of her throat as she dips her chin and the water slaps in. Above her, a wooden sky, and below, navy lines that wobble and loop. She keeps to her traffic lane, doing a neat breaststroke up and down, timing her lengths by the clock above the diving board. Important to keep fit. To keep things in perspective. George is working at home today, so she's taking time off. For herself. She will *not* worry about money.

Besides the youngsters at the shallow end, the pool is full of other fish. Girls streamlined and silver-bellied as mackerel stroke past, white arms lifting in a shower of drops. An older woman in a pink turban. A youth doing butterfly, head and shoulders darting absurdly up and down, eyes goggling on rubber stalks. A narrow-waisted man with a pointed black beard flexing his muscles before dropping his goggles into the deep end and diving to retrieve them, waving them above his head, looking around to see who watched. Now they're nicely wetted, he dons them, does a showy crawl to the far end, dispersing the little ones with the spray he raises. He does like to make a splash, this one.

She forges through the blue water that is both translucent and opaque, marvelling at the lightness and ease lent her body, the closest she can come to flying, her thighs and arms flexing with a power that pleases her, stomach sucked in by her movements, wet hair in a heavy dollop on her neck. Then she relaxes, rolls onto her back, glides idly, just twitching her toes and fingers, letting the other swimmers' currents carry her through the choppy pool and so to the ladder again and out back up.

Standing naked under the hot hiss of the shower, she bends this way and that, the steamy jet of the water hitting her like darts. At first, shy, she keeps her eyes on the cream tiles of the wall. Then, bolder, she glances at the other women in line beside her, each twisting and turning, skin gleaming under a lather of soap. Smooth outlines, each one different, some curved and rippling, some lean, some fat. Each one naked and uncaring. She peeps at the triangles of hair, black and brown and golden, the slump and slack of bellies, the swing of breasts. Watches a face upturned, eyes closed, for the stream to rush over, hands smoothing back shiny black tails of hair, wringing the last drops out, reaching for the thick towel. They're nymphs, she thinks: or mermaids, swimming around the Ark. She surprises herself, feels gently amorous. Shocked, cross, she stomps into a formica-walled cubicle and bangs the door.

Once she closes the shabby front door of her squat and steps outside the white stucco block, the Forsaken Sibyl is walking in morning air blue and shiny as porcelain. Her determined steps crack it. Then relief takes her over: she's shut the eviction notice away behind her. She's out. The world touches her: cold air tangy on her lips, the sun hot on the back of her neck, relaxing her body. She skims along the pavement, caught up in a wave of green light as pure and clear as glass, as water, veined with yellow. Antique-shop windows display oil paintings in gold frames, Chinese jars in red and blue, ebony cabinets inlaid with mother-of-pearl.

She will *not* torment herself with longings for Julia. She will exorcize them. She needs a treat. She buys tulips from the man on the corner by the cinema. He sits among orange plastic buckets packed with flowers whose colours glisten fresher than wet paint. A water-sprinkled rainbow hedge. A wall of perfume: she is eating white narcissi petals. One bunch of tulips is tawny and striped, an armful of red and yellow tigers splitting open pale green sheaths, and the other is a collection of pearly pink eggs. She buys fat rosy hyacinths too, juicy trumpets toppling above fleshy stalks, and a scarlet geranium shooting away from its frilled fan leaves, and a cyclamen violently pink as a flight of flamingos over a pond.

That's this week's gas and electricity money almost gone. To

37

hell with it. To hell with Julia. Today she's going to be a lily of the field.

Today she wants chaos: every possible combination of colour and form whirling together. She stopped painting at puberty, when she grew frightened of colours. That red Flood swept her towards the knowledge of death. All the colours got mixed up, no boundaries between them, blurred into each other and lost their names, a dark smear on the palette. She wanted to enter the dance of colours, to go beyond the severe line traced by others' words around that white space, her female body, to explode it. That way lay madness. So she drew back, stopped painting, used words instead, unravelled the wild complex whole into limping lines of words that belonged in time and space and could only say one thing at a time.

She fills her room with the flowers she has bought until it looks like a funeral parlour only waiting for the corpse laid out in the middle. Hers?

Now she is able to let herself remember her dream of the night before.

She meets her own ghost.

Asleep. The room grows first chill, then icy. Body jerks with fright. A cold hand on her naked back, waves of ice, a glacier forcing itself through an unwilling valley. Words spoken.

– Remember the dead woman artist.

She has lined up a row of jugs containing tulips, hyacinths, geraniums and cyclamen. She will learn to live in the rainbow. To find the end. She wants rain. An Ark.

The mountain falls, sheer, down to the sea. Picking their way down it, hopping from slab to slab of white rock carved into the semblance of steps, they keep well into the lichened wall. The heat beats up at them in waves. The Babble-On Sibyl licks her cracked lips, imagining salt on them, shifts her smart scarlet holdall from one brown hand to the other. The dry flowers of the seaside, gorse and pinks, fringe the way plunging ahead, and umbrella pines lean over them, scant shade.

There's no beach at the bathing place. The rocks have been levelled out under a platform of concrete, just enough space for the café thatched with grasses and bamboo, a strip of blue wooden beach huts with yellow shutters fronted by an emerald-painted verandah with a lime canvas roof, two rows of mats and deck chairs in scarlet and indigo, sun and shadows striping the wooden staircase leading to the tiny jetty.

Fifty yards out from the shore, looking back, the water is navy, dancing with figures of eight and circles in bright blue as it catches the sun. Then, when she swims nearer the landing place again, and dog-paddles along the steep rocks she climbed down earlier, the water is transparent green, the seabed lit up as though there are lights hidden in the coral. At first the heavy flippers she has borrowed from Neil cumber her, the goggles clasped too tightly to her wet head, the eyepiece misted by sea water. Then she gets the hang of it, beats her rubber fins up and down, takes a deep breath, and submerges herself.

The underwater world is illuminated, magnified. The mountain sheers down, knobbled and weedy, in a sharp slope she bumps against. She hangs in blue space, can see her legs dangle, rounded and pale brown. Far below her, a bright carpet: a play of broken crystals, gold bits, fragments of sapphire, emerald, jade, turquoise, all flashing and changing as the water gently moves over them. Neil swimming in front of her looks as though he is flying in a vast blue sky high above this jewelled earth, his skinny white legs kicking lazily above a flowerbed of white coral.

Back on her red cotton mattress, skin basted with cocoa butter and coconut milk, she roasts, the sun licking the water off her with a scorching tongue, drying her harshly. She lifts an eyelid, contemplates her scarlet satin bikini with pleasure, her deepening tan. They have saved for this holiday for three years. Oh, to stay here always. To live on an Ark, to dive off it daily into this sparkling sea, to drop down through it to that iridescent bed. She reaches for Neil's hand.

9   I design a chapel for the Ark.

It's a non-denominational one, available to anyone or any group wanting a quiet place in which to pray or think or write. Not everyone uses it. The Buddhists, the Hindus and the Daoists have built their own temples at the other end of the Ark. From time to time processions wend their way along the deck, as the devotees of different faiths visit each other and attend each other's ceremonies. The Muslims have likewise erected their own place of worship. The Sufis don't need temples or churches and prefer to dance and sway aloft in the rigging. The Theosophists use the saloon. The Quakers meet all over the place, building soft walls of silence and attention around themselves.

It's mostly the Protestants and the Roman Catholics who use the chapel. Like a theatre, it adapts itself to the requirements of the different rituals enacted in it. It can be stripped bare for the Methodists, filled with flower arrangements and Mothers Union banners and Pre-Raphaelite stained glass for the Anglicans, packed with plaster Sacred Hearts and lacy altar cloths for the Papists. Sometimes it shudders with the exaltation produced by Black Gospel choirs; sometimes a spiral of plainchant coils up through a smoke of incense; sometimes brass band and organ together blare out their praise; sometimes jazz, skiffle and rock music pound and thump in the aisles.

Today, the chapel has been reconsecrated for use by the Roman Catholics. Although I no longer practise the religion of my childhood, I still find Catholic churches holy places in the way that Protestant ones are not. There is an absence in a Protestant church, an emptiness. It is not marked with the

40

presence of God as I was taught to understand it: the winking red light in front of the tabernacle of the Blessed Sacrament. Nor does a modern Protestant church testify to the action of God in creation through the presence of works of art. It is the statues, the altar-pieces, the sculptured tombs, the decorated walls, doorways and roofs, created by the struggle of human minds and hands to express the relationship of human beings to food, sexuality and death, that brings God into a church. The Catholic churches I have seen in Italy, however tacky and over the top in their decoration, hush me, make me reverent, fill me with pleasure. In fact, the tackier the better.

I am not disappointed. Today the chapel's gloom is dispelled by bursts of light from the black iron racks of candles before the shrines flanked by tall columns clothed in red brocade leggings bound with fringed gold cords. I recite the litany of ornament; I catalogue church furniture. Here are baroque lanterns on poles, monstrances wreathed in tarnished golden leaves, dusty red velvet cushions edged with gold braid arranged on elaborately carved prie-dieux. Here are magnificent black oak confessionals with bolted doors and windows, domed tops, iron grilles, and purple silk curtains. Here are walls hung with silver ex-votos: hearts and legs and stomachs and arms. Here are floors chequered in rosy marble and planted with memorial tablets, ceilings offering a glimpse of heaven swagged with flowers, ornate doorways alive with saints perched on the spandrels swinging their long legs as though out on a picnic. Here are altars dressed in lace and satin skirts, set out with candles and books and gilt cookery utensils.

Here is Our Lady with a freshly painted wax face and silk robes embroidered with gold thread, a ruff of tin lace at her neck, jewelled rings on her fingers, her thin blonde locks streaming from under her white muslin veil and spiky crown, and all of humanity sheltering under her upraised arms. Here is Our Lady again and again: with her china face contorted by grief and her long hands lifted lamenting over the dead son in her lap; with a black skin and coiffure and glittering gold eyes outlined with black kohl; with a pasty-faced porcelain baby in her arms. Here are dead bishops incorrupt in glass cases, dead virgins scattered with crepe roses, dead nuns cruelly crowned with thorns. Here is the cold scent of dust and myrrh, and the

41

slow heavy speech of the organ, and a flaming heart transfixed by an arrow of gold.

I sit down in one of the pews. The Roman Catholics are singing the Litany of the Blessed Virgin Mary. They are praying that our voyage may be fruitful and safe.

Holy Mother of God
Holy Virgin of Virgins
Mother of Christ
Mother of divine grace
Mother most pure
Mother most chaste
Mother inviolate
Mother unblemished
Mother worthy of all love
Mother most wonderful
Mother of good counsel
Mother of the Creator
Mother of the Saviour
Virgin most wise
Virgin worthy of all reverence
Virgin of renown
Virgin of power
Virgin of mercy
Virgin of faith
Mirror of justice
Seat of wisdom
Cause of our joy
Shrine of the spirit
Shrine of honour
Betokened shrine of devotion
Mystical rose
Tower of David
Tower of ivory
House of gold
Ark of the covenant
Gate of heaven
Morning star
Health of the sick
Refuge of sinners

Comforter of the afflicted
Help of Christians
Queen of angels
Queen of patriarchs
Queen of prophets
Queen of apostles
Queen of martyrs
Queen of confessors
Queen of all virgins
Queen of all saints
Queen conceived without original sin
Queen assumed into heaven
Queen of the most holy rosary
Queen of peace
pray for us

I want to join in. I want to worship, to praise. My own mother. All mothers.

I want everything: I want to be virgin, amazon, lesbian, mother, lover of men, artist, friend.

Here are the feminist Roman Catholics opening their mouths wide to praise the Great Mother.

bright goddess
black goddess
companion of sibyls
lover of difficult daughters
truth-teller
ark of all life
hunter of meanings
sister of sisters
moon-swallower
blessed black triangle
blessed black O
precious vessel of blood
hill of sweetness
dark cave of becoming
maker of God
secret pearl
virgin of silence

whore of wisdom
mother of many words
juggler of atoms
land of milk and honey
house of warm flesh
gate of paradise
be with us

I am holding a lit candle between my hands, as are all the women around me. Pearls of transparent wax fall down it, harden, grow cloudy, thicken. One by one we are blowing the candles out. Moment by moment the darkness encroaches. All of us go on together now, our voices thin and hoarse.

preferrer of sons
despiser of women
breast of marble
lover of patriarchs
blocked ears
blocked mouth
blocked shout
jailer of daughters
bag of emptiness
transfusion of bitterness
tongue of ice
spine of rigidity
fearer of chaos
fearer of darkness
hood of loss
foot binder
soul binder
let me not become that

10   I say hello to the five sibyls as, one by one, they enter the chapel. We introduce ourselves to each other. Then we push back the front pews and arrange a circle of chairs. Perhaps some of the sibyls might consider a chapel a strange place in which to hold a writers meeting? It will do for our first session, I decide. We can switch venues for the next one. Just to make my position clear I pop my typewriter cover over the tabernacle on the altar.

We seat ourselves, and I survey my new companions.

The Babble-On Sibyl chooses a basket chair packed with fat silk cushions. She wears a faded blue dress of Indian cotton in a swirling paisley design, flowing and loose in the sleeves and skirt and gathered in at the waist by a tasselled gold cord hung with tiny gold bells. Her straight brown hair drops over her eyes and down her back. Ornate gold earrings, which don't suit her at all, dangle from her ears, and her arms are laden with heavy gold bracelets. She plays nervously with these, twisting them round and round and pushing them up and down her slender arms. Her round face is young and unlined, and her bare feet are shod in Indian sandals of plaited brown leather. She twists her feet around each other, ankles and calves into a tight knot.

The Deftly Sibyl sits upright on a canvas director's chair with her name stencilled on the back. Her knees are pressed together, in exact alignment with each other, and her hands are clasped over them. Her hair, dragged back and fastened in an untidy coil at the nape of her neck, reveals the alert expression of her face, the crease above her brows, the lines drooping from nose to mouth. Her eyelids are painted pale blue, and her lips pale pink, like her fingernails, and her nose is dusted with

45

translucent powder. She wears a trouser suit of flowered green and purple corduroy, green slingbacks, and a wedding ring.

The Forsaken Sibyl ranges to and fro, picking at her fingernails. She has cut her hair short, in two different lengths; one side of her head bristles in a crew cut and the other sprouts with curly red tufts weighted with amber and turquoise beads. Her green eyes glare out from her pale bony face, and her wide mouth opens over strong teeth. Her ear lobes are hung with loops of silver wire from which dangle black feathers, and her long fingers are braced with fluorescent plastic rings. Tall and thin, she wears a floppy black jumper, skinny black slacks, and big black crepe-soled shoes, and she pads up and down, up and down, watching.

The Correct Sibyl hides her eyes and most of her face behind a large pair of red-rimmed sunglasses. Short curly fair hair, a delicate mouth with tightly compressed lips, high cheekbones with hollows under them; not much else can be seen. Her small hands fiddle with the notebook in her lap. She wears a grey wool jumper, a well-cut grey flannel skirt, a shawl striped in brilliant red and orange, and knee-high leather boots in shining chestnut. From the embroidered shoulder bag slung over the back of her plain wooden chair there peeps a grey manila folder and a large desk diary.

She glances at her grey metal watch.

– Shouldn't we get going? If we're all here, which I assume we are? Let's make a start.

She looks pointedly at the Re-Vision Sibyl who is scrabbling around on her knees on the floor, picking up the clutch of gaily coloured felt-tips she has allowed to spill out of her white plastic carrier bag.

The Re-Vision Sibyl looks up.

– Sorry.

She seats herself hurriedly in the only remaining chair, a rocker made of pink steel tubes. She is wearing a brown linen fifties jacket tightly nipped in at the waist and decorated with cream lapels and cream pocket flaps, a long tight skirt slit at the back for easy movement, cream cotton lace stockings, brown schoolgirl's lace-ups. She settles herself, pulling at her padded shoulders, twitching at her stocking seams. Then she looks around.

46

– Right. I'm ready.

I utter my carefully rehearsed speech of welcome, repeating my desire for the voyage, its proposed function, and my need for the sibyls' help. Everyone nods, apart from the Forsaken Sibyl.

– Aren't *you* going to tell any stories? she asks me: how can we function as a real group if you hold yourself apart and just listen to what *we* say? I think it would be better if you joined in.

– You're assuming, points out the Babble-On Sibyl: that we're going to function as a collective, in the traditional feminist way. I'm not sure that I want to. I met plenty of feminists at college, I was quite interested at first in going to their meetings, but I ended up feeling completely rejected by them. Feminists don't like women like me. That group at college were a really hostile bunch, I can tell you. They didn't approve of my need to wear pretty clothes and make-up and do my hair nicely. They didn't give me their support at all, when I needed it so badly! It's so unfair. The trouble with the women's movement is that they don't like heterosexual women. Women like me, who really like men, who really like being women, we're made to feel we don't belong. Why *should* I be a lesbian? I just don't feel that way about women. I'm heterosexual through and through. My husband's not sexist, yet when I took him to a feminist bookshop to choose me a birthday present, he wasn't even allowed into the café! I *did* decide I would like to be in this group, because as far as I know you're all professionals and I wouldn't want to be in with a load of beginners, and I could do with more support for my writing. I'm feeling completely stuck at the moment. But I wouldn't mind at all if there were some men involved too.

– Quite right, says the Deftly Sibyl: I must say I'm rather irritated by the fact that there aren't any men here. I call that sexist, excluding men. I felt that attending a writers group might help me, since I'm also blocked right now, but why do we have to be all *women*? What matters is simply being a *writer* and striving for excellence. We're just creating a ghetto if we don't join in with men. If women want to be taken seriously as writers it's the quality of their writing that decides it, not their sex, and certainly not membership of a movement or group.

47

She looks severely at the Forsaken Sibyl before going on.

– I have to admit I'm rather disappointed by the quality of the work produced by the so-called feminist writers. It's hard not to feel that, first, they are more concerned with a political message than with the fact that they are working with language, and second, that they are limiting themselves unnecessarily by concentrating on questions of gender. I'd be the first to admit that women haven't always had equal opportunity and so on, but once they become writers they can be as good as any man. The imagination is a liberating force, don't you see? The writer, as Virginia Woolf said, is androgynous. Quite honestly some of these feminist writers would be better called hysterics, the way they fulminate on in the most angry and unpoetic way about their own bodies all the time. We simply can't have a horde of strident whining frustrated neurotics pushing into Parnassus and claiming that they are writers. Quite frankly, not everyone can make it. There's not enough room at the top. One's got to preserve standards after all.

She pauses to draw a breath. True to ourselves as would-be sisters, we wait for her to finish.

– Some of my best friends are men. Writers. They don't call themselves *male* writers. Why should they? And they treat me just like one of themselves! Not as a *woman*. That would be patronizing, if they judged me by anything but their most exacting standards. It's a mistake, I'm afraid, to demand special treatment for women. A weakness. And d'you see, in any case, it really is so boring, what so many women write about. Themselves. The small world of the home. Whereas in fact, one's just as capable as a man, if one has a good home help or an au pair, of thinking and travelling about and going to pubs just like men do. And, if I may say so, writing about *real* oppression, if one wants to write committed works, rather than going on about being a woman. That's rather self-indulgent, in this day and age, what with war, and poverty, and the Bomb, and totalitarianism, and so on. Those are the *real* issues. It's nothing to do with being a woman if you see your children dying of hunger, or if you have mice put up your vagina in prison, or if you're a Black maid raped by the son of your white employer. One's simply a human being. Not a *woman*.

48

Out of the corner of my eye I notice a red-faced middle-aged man peering around a column, a sheaf of papers under one arm. No one else seems to have seen him. They're all too intent on the discussion.

The Forsaken Sibyl hisses and spits.

– Neither of you should even be in this group. You're traitors to your own sex. I may be the baby in the group, seeing as I haven't had anything published yet, but I'm absolutely clear about what we should be doing. Men have dominated literature with their fantasies and lies about us, they've invented their phallic language to silence us and put us down, they've constructed a ridiculous grammar based on male subject and female object, denying the body and repressing the female point of view, and all you can do is say how wonderful men are! Men with their cold rational minds and their dreams of genocide and their pornography, they are dangerous I tell you. What we've got to do is forget their literature and write our own. And that means inventing a whole new female language. Incoherence and irrationality and syntactical violence and multiple word-orgasms, that's what we need.

– Excuse me, says the Re-Vision Sibyl: sorry to butt in and all that, but I really haven't any idea what any of you are talking about. Do you think you could try and use ordinary language? It leaves me cold, the way you go on.

She looks at us.

– What's the problem? We're all lucky enough to have been able to take some time off and get down to some writing, and here you are wasting your time scoring points off each other. I came here to work, not to talk about it. All right, I admit, perhaps I don't take my writing as seriously as you do, because I don't suppose you'd think of what I write as proper writing, anyway. Not like yours. I can see you've all got fancy ideas about being real writers. I just write stories. I do it for the money as much as anything. I just get on with it. Well, I used to. Recently I haven't been able to write a word. I *would* like to try something longer, a novel maybe, which is why I'm here. I could use the free time. And I'm quite happy it's a women's group. It's women who read what I write, after all. But I can't see the point of this sort of discussion before we've actually done any writing. Let's get down to it! Let's get *going*.

– Don't you think, the Correct Sibyl replies: that it's rather simplistic to talk as though common sense were all we needed? Will that really help us bridge our differences? How, for example, do you propose we should set about judging each other's work? What are our criteria? In what terms should we discuss our problems with writing? I may be unhappy at being told that some of us have this mysterious quality called talent whereas others haven't. I'm equally dismayed to hear that the biological fact of being a woman automatically produces good art. My own writing is going really badly at the moment, as it happens. I could do with hearing some properly rigorous arguments on what constitutes creativity. Somehow, I'm sure, gender and the imagination are linked, but I don't think any of you have theorized it correctly as yet.

– Who cares about theory? yells the Forsaken Sibyl: I'm not a bloody academic. I'm a writer. If you're going to wait to write until you've formulated a theory on how to do it, you'll never get anywhere.

The middle-aged man, who can clearly bear it no longer, rushes out from behind his column. He halts in the middle of the space between our chairs and holds up his hands in protest.

– Ladies! Ladies! Let's not get too excited. Let me give you *my* point of view. You shouldn't have started without me.

– I never invited you, I exclaim: who on earth are you?

– What are *you* doing here? chokes the Forsaken Sibyl: this is a *women's* group. Get out!

– Aha, murmurs the Babble-On Sibyl: a man. Things are looking up.

The Correct Sibyl stirs, and opens her notebook.

– What is *your* position on this question? she asks: I'd be interested to hear you define it.

– Do come in, says the Deftly Sibyl: we've only just started the meeting. Your point of view is crucial. Do take a seat.

The Re-Vision Sibyl begins to rock her tubular chair back and forth. The creak of the rockers is a calming sound. We all watch her, as she considers what to say.

– I was dead scared of coming here, she informs us: I was sure you'd all disapprove of what I write and think it's a sell-out of your politics. Well, now it seems to me that we've all got quite different views on what the group should be like, whether it should even exist, and that's a relief. So why not let a man in, as an experiment? It might be interesting, to match our writing against his, and to see to what extent they're different. As long as he promises to behave properly and has some work he's seriously interested in doing.

She looks at him sternly.

– Please, begs the middle-aged man: let me stay. I need this group, I'm sure of it.

– Tell us all who you are first, I burst out, furious at his interruption of *my* project: go on, introduce yourself.

He draws himself up.

– I am the speaker of the Word of God.

– All men think that, scoffs the Forsaken Sibyl: pull the other one.

The Deftly Sibyl leans forward in her chair, studying our visitor closely.

– I don't see, she declares: why you shouldn't be allowed to explain yourself and your narrative theory. As a modernist, of course, I've never believed in omniscient narrators, but I hope I'm tolerant.

– I think we should take a vote, growls the Correct Sibyl.

– No, I insist: let's ask for inspiration.

I point at the brazier which I set up earlier in front of the altar on a tripod. At its foot is a wreath of laurel. I pull a spray of leaves out of the wreath and cast them onto the glowing coals, causing smoke, a sweet stench, to eddy forth.

– I don't accept inspiration coming from anyone but God the Father, grumbles the middle-aged man: sheer idolatry.

– Be quiet, I snap: if you want to take part in our group then you must have the courtesy to abide by our rituals.

I turn to the others.

– Who wants to be priestess? Who will consult the sacred fire?

The Forsaken Sibyl's voice is unexpectedly confident.

– You, Mrs Noah. You must become a sibyl too, like the rest of us, as I told you before. After that we'll all take turns.

The others all agree, silencing my protests. So I approach the tripod.

They are all quiet and still now, watching me. I tremble, not knowing what god I shall summon up.

I lean over the tripod, and breathe the fumes in deeply. My body starts to shake, to jerk, and then a thick cloud of smoke pours from the bitter burning leaves and hides the sibyls from my view. My feet dissolve, or the floor does, and I'm falling, down into the pit that's opened up beneath me. Someone is holding my hands lightly and whispering to me: let go, let go. And then I'm off, cutting downwards through the whistling air. My voice leaves me. I hear it talking to the others, hoarse and gasping.

– Hear me. This is the story of the burning laurel leaves. This is the story you may have read in the library, in the books written by men.

The god Apollo, who was poet and musician, loved the beautiful nymph Daphne. She did not return his ardour. Fleeing from his embraces, she prayed for help to Mother Earth, who transformed her into a laurel tree. Disconsolate, Apollo made himself wreaths from its branches, and so the laurel became the emblem of poetry.

Hear me. This story has an earlier version. Rewritten, it has been almost erased. Its forgotten words, trampled in the dust of the male scholars' sentences, yelp in their elegant pauses, poke through the gaps between their graceful lines.

Grasp the laurel branch, you women, the laurel named as Apollo's sign (the male poets are crowned with laurel wreaths). Sit under the laurel tree. Put your ear to the trunk and press it to the bark, which is Daphne's book, Daphne's body, and hear her speak. The girl stilled in the tree. The virgin with a heart of wood.

I want to get out, she cries: I want to get out. My mouth is full of green sap, of green words.

Pick up your pens, and transcribe the creak of the branches, the rustle of the leaves. Hear me.

Daphne, fierce priestess of the women's mysteries. Daphne, with a knife in her hand and her face daubed with blood. Daphne, who leads her troop of maenads up to the hills outside the city, in the grey smoke of dawn.

They cut young shoots from the laurel tree, and chew the fresh leaves. The sour juice tips down their throats and sharpens their senses and their minds; the sap of the laurel darkens their eyes and quickens their tongues.

52

They are poets now, hunting their meanings across the high wooded slopes, on the stony mountain-tops, along the dry beds of streams, through flowering meadows and fields full of wheat. While the drug of the laurel works in them they are frenzied, eager, fast.

At evening they carry back down to the city the poems and stories they have captured, and sing them to the waiting people. They go home with bloodstained mouths, and their husbands and lovers walk warily around them.

Every month they repeat the rite, chewing on the tough laurel to release the fierce spirit, to find their power, express it; hunting for images and tales, dipping their fingers in blood and painting their mouths, then singing. Who does not fear them, envy them?

Apollo has stolen Daphne's laurel branch to make his own crown, has locked up her version of the story inside his, has pretended she is captive and silent inside the tree, has claimed that women do not make poets and storytellers, that poets and storytellers make women.

Hear me, you women. Hear the laurel tree speak. Let me seize you too, and infuse you with my power. Pity the male god, who searches for the woman he has lost, for her harsh magic, for her healing words. Pity him. Do not be bound by him.

– Me? shouts the middle-aged man: searching for a lost female? What nonsense! I can get a woman any time I like. Women adore being fucked by writers, especially women with aspirations to write themselves. You trying to accuse me of impotence or something?

His crimson cheeks puff out with rage.

I feel sick. Laurel-leaf sickness. Seasickness. This is our first real squall. I wouldn't mind morning sickness. If it were a baby heaving up and down in me, doing a sort of dance, I wouldn't mind. But not this pulse and swell of anger.

– You and your interruptions, I shout back at my uninvited guest: you'll spoil everything.

He subsides, looks at me pathetically. I know his type. All he wants is that I should match him in passion, join him in his arguing which is his way of showing he's interested in what I've said, be as ferocious as he. He's not a bully. He just likes a good fight. So do I, but marriage with Noah has shown me the dangers. Once I get angry and start shouting I say things that wound deeply, send him white-faced from the room. Then silence for two days. So it's better to keep a rein on my temper.

– You behave yourself, I warn our visitor: and then we can talk. For a start, I'm not addressing you by this ridiculous title you've assumed. Voice of *God*. Who d'you think you are? As far as I and this group are concerned, you'll be known as Gaffer from now on. Meaning one who makes gaffes.

– People keep telling me I'm dead, he complains: twice over, once as God and once as Author. But I'm damned if I'll lie down and hand over my creative function to any pipsqueak thinking that her garrulous confessions or streams of consciousness constitute a proper act of creation. They don't! You need talent and craft and enormous patience to be an artist. As I should know, none better. Didn't I end up creating a near-perfect account of an entire world? It's true that I had to destroy what I wrote, more than once, and try again. I admit that. There's nothing wrong with redrafting. It's necessary. First I invented a world and some action, then I wrote it all down. I did have some secretarial help, a few scribes who took dictation. But *I* am the Creator! I take responsibility for the whole thing. I've never pretended to be less than dedicated. You can't combine creation with a whole lot of other hobbies. All these silly people going to creative writing classes. They don't understand that you've got to give up everything else if you want to be a serious artist. It's all a question of imagination, you know. And mine's the best.

– So what's brought you here, then? I sneer: why bother trying to join our writers group?

He looks sheepish.

– Actually, he admits: I'm having a few problems with my writing right now. I did all right when the Bible first came out: I collected a lot of royalties and retired to a tax-free haven. Heaven. I was read by everyone in the old days. I was on the curriculum at universities, critics squabbled over my message and my prose style, other writers copied me, I was rewritten countless times by people inspired by my story, people even named their children after my characters. All very flattering, even if I disagreed with a lot of the reviews and thought that half my fans hadn't got the point. But now, having published one big blockbuster going from the beginning of the universe right through to the end, I'm not sure how to go about writing a sequel, whether I've left myself anything to write about. To put it frankly, I'm stuck. Writer's block. People always say the second novel is harder than the first, don't they? So I thought I'd attend a writers workshop, see if I could pick up a few tips. I was just passing and I saw the notice saying *Writers group this way*. So I nipped on down. I do think you could have waited for me, though, before you got going.

– You weren't supposed to come, I mutter: I never thought of asking *you*. Now you're here, I suppose you should stay.

– Good, he beams: now, tell me, which of you is the tutor?

– There isn't a tutor, I yell at him: this is a *group*.

– Don't be too hard on him, the Babble-On Sibyl rebukes me: he's not used to our ways yet.

She smiles at him.

– Come on. Tell us what you think about this whole question of women's writing.

The Gaffer coughs, and looks around.

– Well, he begins: I'll have to tell you the truth. I am truth incarnate. I'm incapable of lying.

– You can tell us *your* truth, sneers the Forsaken Sibyl: but I'm afraid you'll find it's partial.

The Gaffer looks pained.

– Listen, he says: some of you aren't going to like this, but I'll have to say it. That's how you operate, right, saying what you think? Well, my problem is that I don't know any women writers, for a start. Where I live there aren't any. So of course it's never crossed my mind that women, and certainly not *mothers*, could create whole new worlds. I *do* sometimes think of my imagination, the Holy Ghost as I like to call it, as having a female aspect, in a purely allegorical sense of course. To that extent I think of the writer, ie me, as androgynous. But I've never needed to imagine women creating because I can do it all by myself. Women are *receptive*, yes. They're great at listening for my Word and taking it in. Take Mary, for example, this girl I knew years ago. She was this terrific incubator of my ideas. She gave them a nice warm place in which to grow. But she was empty to start with. I mean she couldn't have done anything

55

without me. I had to sow the seed. It's the *male* who represents humanity, creativity, spiritual quest, after all. How could a *woman* possibly do that? How could a *mother* know anything about human growth? Any fool can give birth. Writing a book is *labour*.

He lowers his voice.

– I have to admit that the thought of what goes on inside women turns me right off. Women writers, well, they're like leaky wombs, aren't they, letting out the odd stream of verbiage, the odd undisciplined shriek. They don't *create*. They just spill things out of that great empty space inside. It's babies they hold, not books. It's only frustrated neurotic women who write, women who can't have children, or who are scared of their normal feminine fulfilment. I'm sorry, ladies, I'm sorry. I'm sure most of you are planning to do sterling work. But I'm convinced you can write properly only when you rise above your bodies and forget them, when you get to the proper height from which you can survey the whole human race and speak for it, when you become, yes, androgynous. More like me. To put it bluntly, when you are *virile*. Of course I like to think of myself as having a womb. But it's *imaginary*. A real one can only get in the way.

I howl with laughter. I can't stop. I can feel my face turning red, tears coursing down my cheeks as I rock from side to side and then fall on the floor and pummel it.

– You see the danger? the Gaffer sighs: this unfortunate tendency to overstate? to overreact? to exaggerate?

– Please, the Deftly Sibyl says to me: control yourself. You'll give us all a bad name.

She turns to the Gaffer.

– Mrs Noah is not a writer. She's a librarian.

– You shouldn't judge *us*, adds the Babble-On Sibyl: by *her*.

I'm surprised. It's the Correct Sibyl who comes to my rescue, helping me off the floor and onto my chair again.

– I'm sorry, I mumble: I'm feeling a bit sick.

– Don't be sorry, snaps the Forsaken Sibyl: you should be *angry*.

– Let's call a halt for the moment, I suggest, wiping my eyes: I think we've got as far as we can for today. Let's go and have supper. I need an early night. I'll be all right in the morning.

But I can't sleep. I'm too confused.

Here I am, returning to a nice warm womb full of the nourishment and sweetness of women, a fine safe place in which to grow and change, and what do I find? Not only disagreement and conflict (women's groups? give me a coffee morning any day) but also untruths. To speak is to lie. To over-simplify. I don't believe in that conversation we've just had. The taking up of positions as in a war, no ambiguity allowed. Ambush of the images streaming up along the narrow pass, polemical boulders dropped on them, crushing them. I spoke more truth when possessed by the inspirational leaves. Who are the sibyls and the Gaffer? I don't know yet. I'll have to find another way of getting to know them.

I prowl the dark passages and companionways of the Ark, nightmare tangles of decks and steps, identical layers. No numbers. No signs. I can't tell which deck I'm on. From time to time, through a closed door, I hear snores and mutters, my sister dreamers mapping their sleeping worlds. From far below me, many decks down, in the depths of the bookstacks, the bowels of the Ark, come muffled roars, screeches, bellowing. The utterances of hysterics. Their crazy complaints, pre-verbal. I refuse them. I escape up a ladder, towards a higher deck. The hold is safely locked, and it can stay that way.

Here's my cabin at last. Falling onto my bunk I bury my head in my pillow, press my fingers into my ears, will myself towards oblivion.

11   The first thing the Deftly Sibyl does, once the Ark has left the Venetian lagoon and is heading out to the open sea, is to fall ill. To fall, down onto the deck of her cabin. Bending to find her slippers under the bunk, then straightening up again, she is gripped by violent pains in the lower back, and falls.

She staggers up. Someone is sawing her in half; she's the lady in the circus trick only it's real. She lacks backbone; a section is missing. When she tries to walk a step, her bones melt in heat, pain at the point of collapse, the base of the spine. She is a ruined column, toppling. She lurches towards a chair, sobbing, unable to stop the tears washing out of her eyes and down her face. Crying does not stop the pain nor ease it, just accompanies it. Her hips grind. Her bones wrench apart.

She shouts for help. The other sibyls come out of their cabins along the companionway and carry her into the sickroom.

She invents it, according to what she wants: a quiet place. The white walls are bare. Thin white curtains drift against the open portholes, letting a breeze stir about her aching neck. The wooden deck is painted pale pink. A bamboo screen hides the door, shapes the sickroom into a hollow of privacy and rest. No clutter of ornaments, pictures, books. Just this enclosure of bare wood.

The Deftly Sibyl lies flat on her back, staring at the ceiling, and remembers the sickbay at convent school. Mysterious place that she entered only once, after fainting at early Mass. Tiled red floor, folded white counterpane at the foot of the high hospital bed, tall window blocked by red serge, smell of disinfectant. Coolness and peace; a picture of the Virgin on one wall. The kindness of tiny wizened Sister Joan, the infirmarian, after the sternness of the other nuns in the classroom.

Is the Ark a floating convent then, full of sisters? Is she on retreat amongst them? Sisters are the last thing she's ever wanted. Not her style, those gossipy female friendships, hint of Lesbos with the grumbling about men, the threats to a safe, well-ordered marriage. Yet the other sibyls behave as though she's invited them to be her nurses: lift her up and down, carry her to the lavatory, wait outside the door while she grips the cold enamel edge of the washbasin and tries to lower herself onto the pan without screaming. Agony. She sweats. Then the women's hands raise her again, cart her along the companion-way back to the sickroom. She refuses a bedpan, that humiliation. One of the sibyls has remade her bed. Even though it hurts so much to sit down, lift her legs in, lie back, shove herself lower down the bed, the clean sheets feel wonderful: cool scratch of ironed cotton and the light floating weight of the quilt like a cloud settled on her stomach.

The sibyls leave her alone, as she asks them to.

Am I being ill, she wonders to the yellow afternoon: simply in order to be taken care of?

It is extraordinary to lie in bed, not in too much pain as long as she does not move, and wait for dinner, lunch, breakfast to arrive. She marvels. Meals she has not cooked herself. For the first time in twenty years.

She has not been ill in bed since she had chronic tonsillitis as a child. Once she stays off school for two whole weeks, and her mother takes unpaid leave from work to look after her. Her mother is pinned to her bedside for half an hour at a time, reading to her, telling her stories. The late dark afternoons of that winter illness are the worst, when her mother's downstairs catching up on housework, and the grisly radio play she dare not switch off tells of murder, and her bed and body are too heated, flush of fever swilling the room, her fear lying panting in the corner, and not enough lights on, and her brothers and sisters have all gone away and left her alone. Fourteen days like that she passes, throat aflame, head bowed by concrete weights, eyes rolling over the ceiling like escaped marbles, arms sometimes long enough to scrabble on top of the wardrobe, and once her self floating high above the bed and looking down at the body tossing on it.

One time her mother's ill with a bad back. Not for long; she has too much to do, is scared of losing her job, can't leave the running of the household to her husband for too long. The children surge into their mother's room, never wondering for a moment whether she wants peace and solitude. They've got her, pinned down again; she's still theirs, there for them to love and cuddle, no escape.

The Deftly Sibyl stares at the walls, grateful for their lack of demand. At home it is impossible to be ill. The children wouldn't understand, would fret. George wouldn't be able to cope. She wouldn't be able to cope with him not coping. Bad mother. Bad wife.

She likes it here in bed. She doesn't have to hold everything together. She doesn't have to hold anything. One by one the burdens topple to the floor: shopping, cleaning, cooking. All the responsibilities. She has nothing else to do but lie here and watch how the light filters between the white curtains into this empty space which she does not fill or disturb. When something is empty then you can see its shape.

Into the emptiness swims the meaning of her illness. She invents it. It may or may not be true; impossible to know. What matters is that she's found it, believes it.

She's finally got herself a room of her own, which no one enters without her permission, which belongs to her alone.

The home of her childhood is all bustle and movement. She shares a bedroom with her two sisters. Inside her rounded bedside cabinet lives her doll, the curved cupboard her room where she sits peacefully alone. From time to time she opens the white door and peeps in at her, then closes the door again quickly, not wanting to disturb her solitude for too long. What does the doll do behind the closed door when she can't see her?

It is necessary to have a secret, and a secret place. The houses in the suburb where she lives are not designed to accommodate mystery, the unconscious. Downstairs is open-plan, every corner visible, large plate-glass windows on two sides hiding nothing of the garden's bland flowerbeds, cropped lawn, concrete patio. Upstairs, the bedroom is filled with her elder sisters experimenting with make-up, new hairdos. This house, this suburb, make her ache to be unseen, to be able to invent a movement incorporating both display and retreat, both silence and speech: *choice*. The suburb is too public, too falsely communal, too bright white clean glaring hygienic.

Diligently the child invents her escape. She clears out the coal hole, furnishing it with wooden boxes, chipped mugs rejected from the kitchen, a strip of old carpet. She makes dolls' rooms in cardboard boxes, a chair a chestnut on pin legs, postage stamps for pictures, chest of drawers of a stack of matchboxes. She squats in the cupboard under the stairs between the massive hoover and the old sunburst bakelite radio. She buries treasures under the trees in the park. None of these retreats lasts. She's unable to stake a lasting claim.

When she gets married and acquires, through her husband, a home of her own, she doesn't realize at first that that doesn't give her a private room, and that she hasn't, as young wives are supposed to do, grown out of needing one.

But now, at last, she can sleep by herself in this single bed, for as long as she wants, without feeling guilty, without betraying her marriage. Hours to spend as she likes, daydreaming, dozing, being a child again. Illness has given her the power she was unable to claim when well: the power to refuse others' demands sometimes, to go away by herself, to be free to do what she wants, which is to be still, and dream.

The pain has been useful. It's made her slow down, stop, be silent. It's let her withdraw from her family into this retreat. It's absolved her from guilt about not working hard enough finishing her next book, not earning enough money. It's forced her to admit, grudgingly, her gratitude to the others for looking after her when she needed it.

She starts to get well, and to want to write. Images begin to emerge, diving up from the deep to break the surface of her mind, turning over and lolloping in the green waves, showing the flick of a fin, of a tail. She's fishing for them, casting her line, waiting patiently for a bite, a tug, a kick, reeling in, rod bent taut, uncertain what she's hooked: an old boot, a lump of seaweed, a mermaid.

Quilt pulled up over the head, a soft cave. Bed is a good place for writing: why did she never realize that before? Hesitant scratch of pen on paper, the loose sheets scattered across her stomach as she tries out two words at a time, rejects them, starts again, a fresh sheet each time so she can see properly what the words look like. Haul them in gently, coaxing, a net of words sprawling. The deepest pleasure there is, this certainty that the words are there, hidden underwater, and will come when she calls, when she stops still and listens for them. Four hours of alert concentration, the music in her head sounding stronger and clearer as she goes on, led by its rhythm to shape one phrase, one sentence at a time. A paragraph gathers form and speed, leaps forward shedding silver adjectives, sinewy, bony.

She stacks the pile of scribbled-over sheets together, her sieve of words: two words on the top one, a hundred on the bottom one. Later she'll re-read and sort and discard her gleaming catch. She's tired now, needs to sleep, to dream her way into the next shoal of images. It doesn't do to hurry, or you lose it, that new meaning that gleams, phosphorescent, in the ocean lapping her body, her bed. She floats between her scrawled drafts, sinks down to the seabed of words, lets sleep quench her and turn her loose.

12   When I'm seven, I'm given an Advent calendar for the first time. The four weeks before Christmas are represented by numbers printed on the doors and windows of the façade of a paper house, one opening for each day, the whole design framed in glittering silver holly leaves. The calendar hangs in the sitting room above the side table where we shall build the crib later on.

Each day I pull open a new door or window, carefully moving around the house according to the dates on the paper casements. Inside each one I find an image printed: a lamb, a star, a shepherd's crook, a bunch of grapes, an angel. And so on through the month. When at last I open the door marked 25 December I find the Child inside.

I am a house with many windows and many doors. Each day I must pull one open and peer inside. This is my time of Advent, of preparation. I have work to do. If only I knew what that work is.

I'll start with today's door. I'll reach for it.

It bursts open.

Memories of my last conversation with Noah, on the train going to Venice, leap out.

– In any case, he asks: what makes you think you'd be able to be a good mother? Are you really sure you want a baby? It's not just a passing whim?

In the archive I discover an ancient volume of riddles dedicated to the Sphinx. She may be on board with us but I haven't seen her yet.

When is *a confinement*, I read: *not a confinement*?

13 At sunset I climb to the very top of the Ark, open the trap door there and peer out, watching the sun fall heavily into the sea and disappear. At dawn I watched it struggle up again out of the deep. What happens to the sun when I can't see it, sunk in darkness, traversing the land of the dead, the underworld? I want to find out. Tonight I want to reverse time, and follow the sun.

I climb out onto the roof of the Ark, the guidebook which I have found in the archive clutched in one hand. It doesn't tell me much. A scanty volume. I dive into books and fish greedily for treasures. At primary school, having read all the books in the school and hungry for more, I was put to reading the Bible. To slow me down a bit. Very well then. A plunge back into Genesis; into sub-plots and sub-texts.

I dive into cold blackness. I part the steep hills of water on either side of me. Down and down I fall, to the deep seabed.

My bare feet touch gravel. The sun rolls along far ahead of me, a wheel glowing in the darkness. In its muffled light I see bright fish dart upwards in wriggling shoals. I walk in slow motion, my hair floating up in the water like weeds, my arms stretched out for balance, my legs pulled along by currents of curiosity.

I halt. In the distance, shining through the green screen of the sea, is a palace as vast as a city, hidden behind gleaming battlements, scales of mother-of-pearl.

The way in is by water.

To Atlantis: also called the house of memory and of forgetting; the fossil of the old world.

I come closer. The thick walls are pierced by a colonnade

faced with marble. A high doorway claps its wooden tongue behind twin red columns.

Once through the main entrance I cross a courtyard, weedy and barnacled, now an aquarium for slow-moving fish, and come into a great hall set with obstacles of white coral, twisted white branches bursting up through the marble pavement, delicate forests of knobbled whiteness dancing underneath my feet in the clear water. And now the palace discovers itself to me, a labyrinth of revelations turning over and sliding like the inside of a Chinese puzzle box carved in ivory, as one saloon opens out of, and into, another.

I find interior gardens slung one above the other, a waterfall of courtyards planted with roses and lilies still impossibly blooming and set with pools once stocked with carp. Now the bright carp are everywhere about me, exclamation marks in gold and red. Orange trees launch up from earthenware pots; vines twist along gilded lattices; red persimmon fruits dangle from black branches. Each of these gardens is a secret and a surprise: I come upon them unexpectedly, as they open up at the end of a gallery or a corridor. As I climb higher and higher in the palace, so the gardens tumble past me, a rain of scents, of butterflies and ferns and bees.

I float through a loggia of creamy stone into a tiny court, the fountain at its centre half buried by a drift of sand, broken shells, polished white bones. These must be the gardeners, I decide, looking at the clean dislocated skeletons: this is their tomb.

I swim through a low dank tunnel, its walls painted with *trompe l'oeil* landscapes of the outside world, and emerge into a grotto. Water slides over the white pebbles underfoot, over silver gravel, over the creamy cockleshells decorating the walls in patterns of arabesques and fans. From niches of mossy stone satyrs peer at me, their long mouths curled up and grinning. Lady satyrs too, with muscular legs, little breasts peeping out of their thick fur, and big pointed ears. One of them looks rather like me.

In the beginning, I remember: as in the end, the waters covered everything, and all kinds of creatures flourished in them.

I bounce slowly through a passage hung with mirrors and

painted with all kinds of fish and waterfowl leaping in lakes and streams, stags and boar and deer chasing each other across the ceiling and around the door at the far end.

Now I come to the room of metamorphoses.

Here all the rules are broken, joyfully. Here chaos reigns for the sheer pleasure of it. Here are men turning themselves into gods and gods into men. Here are creatures that are half-beast and half-man, with pink naked feet and thick swishing tails.

Here are male gods, disguised as bulls, dragons, showers of gold, attempting to seduce women. A fleshy hand grips a delicate white chin, forcing it up. A great phallus waggles. Shrieks and laughter. Games of kiss and chase. Gestures that beckon and repulse.

Here are nymphs, hiding behind rocks, in the depths of streams and pools, combing and plaiting each other's hair, riding on the backs of dolphins, blowing sea-music out of conch shells, playing with each other in a tangle of breasts and necks and knees. Here are goddesses bathing in the company of their maidens, tipping water from silver basins over their heads, or striding the hills wearing gilded helmets and kilts, a froth of hounds at their ankles, long-haired women running behind them with outstretched arms, darting over the dewy grass.

Here are heroes and heroines, legs entwined, falling back, gasping and sweaty, onto gold couches. Hands part plump thighs; tongues plunge into dripping wet openings; clever fingers make the juice run, the heat mount, the flush spread. Beside them, lovely athletic boys wrestle, oil each other, lick and fondle each other, give each other voluptuous slow massages. Reclining on silk mattresses, ringleted girls spread their legs wide, admiring each other's cushiony lips and springing triangles of hair, enjoy each other's display. One woman puts her mouth to another's, touches her all over.

You may look, you may touch, you may tease, you may bite. You may experiment with being held down and tied up with strings of coral beads, with being blindfolded, with being fondled by strangers. You may invent any game you like, for three or four or more to play.

God the Father didn't approve of this state of affairs, so he sent the Flood. It's all there, in chapter six of the Gaffer's novel. God the Father wanted order. So he invented heterosexuality, monogamy, and the family.

Into the hall of the giants now, a vast, dark, windowless place whose walls are painted with images of enormous grotesque figures cowering, terrified, under boulders and broken columns and thunderbolts being hurled by the king of heaven. I escape up a staircase so narrow it seems to have been made for dwarfs. I bend my head; my knees brush my chin. I catch glimpses, as I squeeze past low openings slit in the stone, of thumb-sized chambers and chapels, of throat-like corridors branching off. The miniature palace within the palace. A new crystal growing, a new cluster of cells. A pregnancy flowering in the stone.

I push open the golden door at the top and enter the hall of the expectant mother. This is a long gallery with tall arched windows on one side reaching from ceiling to floor, tall mirrors between the windows throwing back the images of the frescoes painted opposite, other mirrors tilted to reflect the swags of fruit carved on the bosses of the high ceiling.

A naked goddess is painted in the centre of the long wall, her arms outstretched towards me as I enter. As I walk down the gallery, and past her, never taking my eyes off her, her arms swivel and stretch after me, as do her eyes. How's it done? I can't believe it. Laughing, I swim back through the cool green waves, and watch the painted beauty turn and languish after me. It is not possible to be other than desired by her, sought by her, reached for by her: she turns, and turns, and turns, keeping me always in the circle of her arms and eyes.

Further, and higher, into the twelve-sided zodiac room, to scrutinize the baffling chart of the stars, of the child I want to bear. The domed ceiling peels back in a welter of vines and flowering boughs to reveal the night sky, curved expanse of deep inky blue, sea trawled by nets of golden constellations, each knot a star. Gods and goddesses in faint gold outline move across the blackness, starry profiles. The depth and reach, the unfathomable time and space of the universe, is caged in gold wire, unimaginable distances flattened out into two dimensions, the human body patterned onto the night and patterned by it.

A narrative is simply a grid placed over chaos so that it can be read in descending lines from left to right, if that's what you want to do. Some writers prefer the chaos, prefer simply to record, rather than to interpret, the interlocking rooms and staircases and galleries of this palace, this web of dream images that shift and turn like the radiant bits of glass in a kaleidoscope. Others, like the Gaffer, make a clear design, slot incident onto a discernible thread.

I understand the Gaffer's point of view, because now I want to retrace my steps and find the way out. But which way did I come? There is no sign saying Exit, no red arrow pointing.

I choose a door and plunge through it. This isn't right. I'm in a vast saloon, draped in crimson silk hangings, that I haven't been in before. I go back, but I can't find the zodiac room, or the long-mirrored hall. Passage after room after staircase beckons me, mocking, only to present me with a dead end, or an unfamiliar suite of lavishly decorated chambers whose doors give on to yet more splendid corridors and galleries.

The palace broods over and around me, tightening its grip, chuckling: I've got you now, and I'll never let you go. Panic whistles up in my throat, and I let go of my last vestige of a sense of direction. I'm running, but I can't escape the palace: it's swallowed me up, and I rattle in its dark belly. I'm alone. I could die here, and never be found, my body withering to a pile of scattered bones like those of the gardeners in the courts far below.

Is this the mother, then, this horror? This hold? This great gloomy imprisoning embrace that hangs on, that won't let the child step out free? That sits, and waits, implacable as death?

How could I ever become a mother, let myself become that embodiment of possessive power, fortress jangling with locked gates, sealed windows? Never. I'm the child running away from home, from the enormous voracious controlling mother, drumming my fists on the bolted door: *let me out*.

Mothers are not free. A woman entering pregnancy is entering time, and history, process whirling her inexorably towards the moment of giving birth, that long road of mothering, her life altered irrevocably and utterly, no going back, no returning the baby to the shop, sorry, I've changed my mind. Women who do are monsters.

To become a mother is to become unfree; tied down; committed, as to prison. A confinement. Leaving the crossroads, the myriad beckoning possibilities; choosing just one not hovering over many.

To become a mother is to own up to having a female body and the social consequences of that: invisibility. Mothers exist only on mother's-day cards, on telly ads for margarine. Mothers don't have jobs, do they? Mothers have no money.

Therefore mothers are boring and unsmart and have tiny minds. Mothers are cabbages buried in the mud of suburbs.

Therefore motherhood is a woman's mystical destiny, her fulfilment that puts her in touch with the rhythms of the cosmos, a glory men can't aspire to. Therefore any woman not choosing motherhood is not a real woman. Therefore any woman not choosing to have children is taking the easy way out. Therefore mothers don't need to be paid and should not complain. Therefore mothers distrust women who are not mothers. Therefore women are scared of mothers. Therefore it's the mother's fault. Therefore mothering comes naturally.

Therefore a mother's life is already over. Therefore mothers can't invent their own stories. Therefore mothers can't live their own lives. Therefore mothers should not want paid jobs.

Therefore it is better not to be a mother but to remain a child and remain free. Therefore it is better to imitate men. Therefore it is better to dream of a thousand possibilities, to fantasize omnipotence, to deny death.

Therefore to become a mother is to accept death. Therefore it is better not. Therefore men preach the resurrection and eternal life. Therefore women are not men. Therefore women are not.

Therefore I will not become a mother. Therefore I want to become a mother. Therefore I cannot find the way out.

– You left a lot out of Genesis, didn't you? the Forsaken Sibyl remarks to the Gaffer once I'm back on board the Ark and telling the others, over breakfast, what I've seen during the night: there's almost no description there, if I remember correctly, of Atlantis, of what the world was like before the Flood.

He looks pleased.

– So you *have* read my book. I wouldn't have thought it would have appealed to you, somehow.

– It was a set text throughout my childhood, the Forsaken Sibyl growls: I couldn't avoid it. It was there, like Mount Everest, so I climbed it.

The Gaffer reflects.

– You could say I discarded a chapter. I don't approve of pornography, you know. My book was written for a family market, after all. I didn't want to encourage youngsters to try out perversions, all the wrong things. I wanted to show the purity and beauty of married life. I saw the Flood as a sort of correction fluid, blanking out all the bad bits, the parts of creation that had gone wrong. In later chapters of my novel, of course, I stressed how perverts always come to a sticky end. Torn apart by dogs, stoned to death, killed off by plagues, and so on.

– Censorship! exclaims the Correct Sibyl: I can't possibly accept that. It may well be useful sometimes to divide writers into progressives and reactionaries, but things should *not* be taken further than that.

– Censorship can be enforced, the Gaffer says, coughing: rules and regulations, you know. Acts of Parliament. Zealous police and customs officers.

– You'd censor male writers, wouldn't you? the Babble-On Sibyl taunts the Forsaken Sibyl: if you had the power? I bet you'd be the first to demand that male pornographers should be punished and their books and magazines burned.

– You'd like to censor other women writers sometimes, wouldn't you? the Deftly Sibyl insists to the Correct Sibyl: you pretend to be a liberal, because it looks good, but you'd write damning reviews of bad girls who wrote things you didn't like. If they experimented with pornography, for example, or criticized feminists as puritanical and sentimental. Oh yes, you would.

– But why should you want to read what I left out? asks the Gaffer: why try to rewrite my story?

– Perhaps this is the moment, I say: for someone to *tell* a story?

– Someone tell a story, the Forsaken Sibyl suggests: about one of the characters the Gaffer completely forgot to put in? Fill in one of his gaps?

14 I am a wanderer. The soles of my feet are yellow with callouses, my body is lean and muscled, my brown face is polished by the sun and wind. It is the changing seasons that are my constancy. I and my people are always on the move. We drive our sheep and goats along in front of us, as we trek from one watering hole to the next. We butcher them for our food, make cheese from their milk, and our tents and bed-coverings from their hides.

We travel through the wilderness, seeking water. A parched riverbed spells death, an oasis life. Always in my mind I carry the image of the shimmer of light on a deep pool, green grass at its edge. Fresh water trickling over my dry tongue, loosening it to prayers and songs. My life is a long thirst.

Linked together by our need for water, my people are also linked by blood, the ties of kinship which separate us from the other nomads wandering this harsh world. Blood is spilled when we defend our claim to pitch camp at a particular watering hole, a particular spring. We slaughter our animals with clubs and knives. We kill our enemies. We offer blood sacrifices of lambs and kids. Our people are stern with wrongdoers. Robbers and murderers, who add to the weight of suffering we carry, have their hands cut off, are stoned to death.

Blood also separates women from men. When my monthly bleeding begins, my mother gives me a bundle of rags and tells me to sew them to make my bandages. I sit and do it so proudly, outside, where anyone can see me, my father, my brothers, my uncles. My mother hits me and hits me.

I am afraid of growing older, of the years of hardship stretching ahead, of a painful death that will perhaps come

71

early. I tell no one this. There is no point.

I accept leaving my people and being given to Jack as his wife. He watches me from behind a tree one day, when I sit in the shade of a rock and wash fleeces. I pretend not to notice his eyes running over me, measuring my strength, my youth, as I swirl the heavy wool in the green water at my knees. I know him: his route has often crossed ours.

He is kind to me. He does not beat me. He is anxious that I stay with him, for his children have been killed by thieves, and his wife has run away into the desert, crazed by grief. He wants more sons. When I bear him three in five years, he treats me with respect. In bed at night he becomes more gentle, less desperate, and I start to like being with him there. He says it is our duty, that his God wishes it, and I certainly don't mind.

Raising our children, preparing and cooking our food, making blankets and clothes, caring for our livestock, all this carries me through my life. I cradle my sons, one by one, in my arms, then have to let go of them, slap them into shape, watch them grow. Not exactly pleasure but a sort of satisfaction arrives for me out of my work. I am creating the survival not just of myself but also of my children. So far I am winning against the cruel nature stalking us with the threat of death. And so I gain the courage to go more deeply into my life, and start to feel less afraid, more capable, more powerful. I start to reflect on the world around me through concentrating intently on whatever it is that I am doing. I flow out of myself and become pot, hide, fish, earth, leaf. I worship the creation of the world day by day by letting myself become part of it, by working. God is in my hands as they scrub, wring, knead, scour, caress, sew, carve. I act, I create, and God pours through me. At these times I am not-myself, I go into a strange country. Sometimes I come to with a shock, to find myself kneeling, my forehead bowed to the ground.

When Jack catches me at my wild prayers one day he is worried I have fallen ill. I reassure him, but after that he watches me secretly, not wanting a second wife to lose her wits.

For Jack God is different. He is a mighty father in the sky, who punishes us when we do wrong, and sends us diseases and plagues and famines to show us his power. I can't understand

72

why that's necessary when the terrible beauty of God shimmers as close to us as the raindrop on the end of a twig, burns in the grass. You only have to sit still and *see*.

Jack walks and talks with his God. Sometimes, in the evening, at sunset, he goes off out of sight and stays away for a whole night. In the morning he comes back and announces that we have to offer a sacrifice or else we're in trouble. It's confusing for the boys, I think, Jack telling them one thing and me another. As they grow older, though, they decide to follow their father's example.

– What does your God look like? I ask Jack.

– I don't *see* him, he replies: he's too magnificent for that. I hear his voice sometimes, like the ringing of cymbals and harps and trumpets. Or he comes veiled in a golden mist, like the smoke of a heavenly fire. He wraps himself in the clouds and holds the sun in front of his face. His eyes are stars. And yet he is greater than all of these. His splendour is so great that if I looked at him I would surely die.

Jack's God is up, and mine is down. That seems to be one of the differences between the two. I wonder whether there are in fact two Gods, and whether they know each other. I wonder whether without knowing it Jack and I worship the same God. I don't think of God as a person but I might be wrong. My God is all over the place. I keep tripping over God at the oddest times, and not always in secret holy places or when I am by myself. Sometimes God is in bed with us.

– There is only one God, Jack repeats to me: and he lives beyond the sun and the moon and the heavens and sees everything we do and wants us to obey him and love him and behave properly.

– Well then, I reply: he'd be pleased, I'm sure, if you gave me a hand with the milking.

I have a picture in my mind of Jack's God as out to get us. Ready with his thunderbolts. He frightens me. Whereas when I meet my God in the middle of doing something ordinary I am flooded with happiness like sweet fresh milk. Jack says mine is a childish vision. I am not sure.

Time passes. My sons reach manhood, and take wives. I slow down a little, stop counting the silver strands in my black hair, feel restless. When my monthly bleeding lessens and then finally stops, I feel like a girl again, skinny and nimble. I am not sad. I rule over three fine sons and their wives. Jack and I still make merry at night. But I catch myself thinking: so what now?

One night I have a dream. The earth appears to me as a woman groaning and arching in labour. She twists her hands in the tops of trees, which are her hair, and bites hard on the mountains, which are her arms, while her belly shakes, threatening earthquakes. Her waters breaking are a great flood. For nine months she has carried the seed of new life safely inside her, letting it float on her waters. Now it rushes out on a flood-tide of water and blood, while she heaves and shouts. And then the waters subside, and the waves are stilled, and the new child lies on her breast.

In the morning I tell Jack my dream. He is troubled by it, and goes off at evening to commune with his God. On his return he is white-faced and shaking.

– A great disaster is on the way, he tells me: God has warned me that he is about to destroy the world. People are so wicked that he is sorry he ever created us. There will be a great flood, and the whole race of mankind will be wiped out.

That night I have a second dream. This time the earth again appears to me as a pregnant woman, but this time at the beginning of her pregnancy. Inside her womb she holds the whole of creation, all forms of life dancing and growing within her. Jack and I and our children are there too, swimming on the waters inside her belly until we are ready to be born.

In the morning I again tell Jack my dream. Again, he is troubled by it.

– If your God is serious, I say: and he really intends to destroy us all with a great flood, we could escape if we built a boat with a roof. A house that could float. These tents would be no use in a really bad storm, they're far too flimsy. But a covered wooden shelter that could go with the storm and ride it, that might save us.

– I'll go and ask God what he thinks, Jack says.

He comes back next morning.

– God is willing for us to be saved, he announces: since we are less wicked than the rest of mankind. What we have to do is

74

to build a big wooden Boat with a roof and go into it with our sons and their wives and all our animals and livestock. That way we can see it through.

That was *my* idea, not your God's, I think. But I hold my tongue. This isn't the time for a quarrel.

Building the Boat is a real problem. Jack is handy at building sheds and cages for the animals, of course, and fences around our tents, since whenever we settle anywhere we always make ourselves secure against winds and robbers and storms. Our buildings, such as they are, are light, being woven of saplings and plastered with mud. Similarly, our rafts, whenever we settle for a time near a river or a lake and want to catch fish, are simple light craft, woven from lashed saplings like floating carpets.

We scratch pictures, in the dust, arguing. In the end we copy the shape of the closed earthenware pot we use for baking fish in the fire.

The people camped nearby help us. We pay them in sacks of wool. They laugh at us as they work. They declare that they would rather die than be shut up in a wooden box. They are used to the touch of wind and sun on their faces, and they are frightened of the dark. In the end I hold my peace, just thinking: they'll be glad enough to be saved when the time comes.

First of all we build the skeleton of the Boat, a spine with ribs arching above and below, and then we fit curved planks over it, making a large door in one side and rows of windows high up under the eaves of the roof. We paint over the entire vessel with a special waxy paint we make from tree resins mixed with egg white.

Inside we construct three tiers, the lowest one of stables and cattle sheds, the middle one of poultry houses and bird-cages, and the top one of living quarters for us. I paint the walls of our rooms with pictures of the world we are about to leave. I dip my brush in the pigments I have mixed from berry juices and earth and I paint tents and water pots, the sun rising over the purple mountains, the flowers waving in the grass. I think that perhaps the Boat will be our burial place, our coffin, and so I also paint pictures of people dying, falling sick, drowning. To give myself courage. I lay our best rugs on the deck, and hang others on the walls, and I bring in our mattresses and pillows and cushions. I stack cooking utensils in a corner, and I help my three daughters-in-law carry in sacks of dried fruits, grains and flour, casks of oil, barrels of water.

When all is done, we gather on the riverbank and pray. Jack kills a lamb and offers a sacrifice, calling on God to be our good shepherd and take care of us, his faithful flock. The smell of the blood turns my stomach, and so I look away towards the green weeds under the fast-flowing river, the sand and rocks at its edge, the bushes and grasses dry and dazzling in the sunshine. I pray too, keeping my eyes averted from the bowl of blood at Jack's feet and putting my fingers in my ears so that I can't hear the sizzling of the burning lamb. Then I crouch down on the dust of the earth and commit us to her care, begging her not to be barren but to deliver us, to bring us through.

Then I pack my own private goods: my best linen robe, my blue eyelid paint, a bracelet of shells, a game of spillikins, a basket of embroidery threads. At the last minute I stuff a basket full of herbs, flowers and vegetables, I am not quite sure why, and then I am ready.

The weather changes. Violent storms by night, sticky heat by day. The earth is shaken by tremors stronger than we have ever experienced before, and the big mountains to the west begin to smoke a little. It is a sign. We know it, even before God tells Jack it is time to board the Boat. God is scolding and impatient, urging Jack to get a move on before it is too late.

Then the rain begins to fall, and does not stop.

We visit all our neighbours in turn, begging them to join with us. They sit tight in their tents and refuse to budge. They have never seen weather like this, they admit, but they see no reason to believe it won't clear. They can't hear God speaking the way Jack does, so they have no inkling of what is going to happen and don't believe Jack when he tells them. In the end we leave them. I am sick at heart, but I can't see what else we can do.

In the afternoon of that day an arch of colours appears in the sky, a bridge between heaven and earth. It twinkles in the rain, with the sun behind it, like strings of polished stones. One end of it touches the roof of the Boat and the other is hidden in the grey clouds.

– It is a rope, I declare, gazing at it: with God holding the other end. We shall be safe.

Jack goes off to ask God what it is all about.

– It's a sign, he says on his return: that God won't let go of us. He is our father, and he has put the arch of colours in the sky to show us that he will save us. It's a sort of heavenly rope.

– That's just what I said, I retort: your God is just copying me.

Jack goes as pale as sour milk.

– Don't blaspheme, he cries: or you'll be cursed and thrown off the Boat.

He looks so fierce that I decide to keep my opinions to myself. Two of my daughters-in-law are whimpering and blubbering with fear, and I relieve my feelings by turning on them and telling them to be quiet. Sara, my third daughter-in-law, tosses her head at me, and I slap her, I am that upset.

In one way I'm not at all sorry to have to go on board the Boat. I am fed up with hardship, with cleaning and cooking and scraping a living, with the constant battle against flies and dirt and illness. Don't ever let someone try and convince you that living close to nature in tents in the open is some sort of picnic. It's not. Either we are wading through seas of mud when it rains, or we are being bitten to death by insects when it's hot. The milk is always going off, and the tents leak, and I am forever washing and tidying and mending, forever making do, always trying to keep my self-respect by keeping a nice home. What for? I think to myself sometimes: why bother?

Sometimes I dream of running away, just going off and leaving them all to it. On my own I could live as I like, eating when I want to, skipping meals if I feel like it, sleeping and getting up when I want. Sex? What you don't have you don't miss. I know how to give myself pleasure, anyway. Sometimes that's all that's necessary, the quick solitary hand up the skirt and as many shudders of ecstasy as you feel like.

What I really want is a Boat of my own. I want to sail off all by myself, to abandon myself to the seas and the winds and go exploring, with no worry about where I will end up. But Jack thinks it's our duty to save the world; we have to try and entice all our neighbours on board, let alone our family and all the animals. He won't hear of our building two Boats, and I can't build my own without his help. So I have to drop my plan and go along with his.

We fight about which animals to take.

– The fewer the better, I say: who'll clean out their pens and cages? Me, of course. So let's leave most of them behind.

Jack is horrified. He's a kind man, and he can't bear to think of our cattle drowning.

– No, he insists: we must take two of each sort, so that we can mate them afterwards and be sure of a renewed stock.

– Just like us, one man and one woman? I say: we've done our mating. By your logic we're too old to be saved. We should just put the youngsters on board. And let's not forget to take as many nasty creepy-crawlies as possible, two cockroaches and two mosquitoes and two spiders and two fleas.

What a strange way to live, I suddenly think to myself: couples couples couples. I want to live on my own.

I shut up about all this because Jack is getting upset. But when the heavy rains come, and turn into the Flood, I feel relieved. More than that: I am excited and pleased. The world is getting washed and scoured and rinsed for the very last time, and then God pours it all away with the dirty water, as sick of it all as I am. The world is a stack of pots I shall never have to scrub again. I enjoy the prospect of destruction. I don't get on to the Boat feeling like one of God's elect, some sort of holy being. I am escaping from a life that wearies me.

The noise, once we are on board and have shut the big wooden door, is terrific. The animals down below are bellowing in misery, not used to being cooped up in such a small space, and the birds are squawking as though they are being torn to pieces. They quieten down a bit after we feed them, but it makes me realize how difficult the voyage is going to be. I don't want to think of it.

None of us sleeps that night. Jack pretends he does, to set the rest of us an example, but I can tell he is awake because he isn't snoring. I lie listening to the rain drumming on the roof, and think about the neighbours we have left outside. Just before dawn the swollen river bursts its banks and takes us and sets us free with a great lurch and a bump. Trapped in the dark, we all shriek and hold on to each other, while the animals below set up their noise again.

When morning comes, Jack and I decide to climb out on to

the flat space we have left, as a sort of observing post, on the roof of the Boat, to see what can be seen. The moment we open the trap door we are drenched. We give up the idea of climbing out any further and just stick our heads out into the gale.

There is nothing there. The world has vanished. All around us, as far as I can see, straining my eyes in every direction, are the waters of the Flood. I can't see where sky ends and water begins. The horizon, if there is one, is grey mist. The Boat is a child's toy made of straw, bobbing helplessly up and down on the waves. I peer downwards, thinking of my neighbours with the water first creeping into their mouths and then filling them up. They are below us now, sinking down onto a cold bed. We have not heard their cries in the night.

For the rest of that day, and the next one, we slump in despair, only rousing ourselves to feed the poor beasts below and to swallow a bite ourselves. We fall sick with guilt and remorse. The will to survive leaves us, just as we have deserted our neighbours. The tides of the Flood enter my soul and drown me too. Welcome, death, I say to myself: I am no better than the slayers of animals I used to despise.

My daughter-in-law Sara saves us. I do not like her much, have never done. She has a sharp way of looking and speaking which bothers me, especially when I think it is aimed at me. She is a restless girl, bitter and dissatisfied, and she never bothers to hide how she feels. I am angry with her when I remember my own struggles, as a young woman, to become a good wife and mother, to put up with Jack's ways, to learn to suffer in silence. Sara makes me remember these things which I would rather forget. When I explain to her the best method of making yoghurt, or bread, she looks at me with a sort of veiled insolence, her hands demurely clasped but mockery darting from her eyes. I dread that look of hers, so I speak sharply to her always, just to keep her in her place. My other two daughters-in-law cause me no such trouble, but they are no company either, with their meek and mild ways. Sara, for all her sauciness, at least has a mind of her own.

On the third day she saves us.

– Mother, she says to me, giving me that awful sly look of hers: you didn't shut the trap door properly when you came back down from the roof, and it's leaking. Just look at the mess on the floor.

I jump up scolding. Seizing a rag, I begin to swab the puddle I am sitting in, and then Jack groans and get up too, and re-closes the trap door and makes it properly fast. Then I realize that I am both hungry and thirsty.

– Come on, Sara says: I'll make you something to eat. A real meal. And you can tell me whether I'm doing it the right way.

She feeds us. She kicks us out of our gloom, and goads us back into living. Every time she sees us ready to drop back into weakness, she mocks us back onto our feet. We dislike her for it, but it works. She organizes us. She makes us all take turns, Jack and my three sons included, in preparing our food and feeding the animals, in clearing up afterwards, in washing our dishes and clothes.

– This is women's work, not men's, Jack and my sons protest: this is the end of civilization as we know it.

– That's right, Sara says: if you want to survive, do it.

Sara becomes our leader. She is mother and father to all of us. A strict parent, always ready with the whip of her tongue. We know that without her we would die.

Time passes, passes. Days, weeks, months.

Sara looks less restless and dissatisfied. Nowadays she walks about with lighter steps, humming, and sometimes she sits with me in the afternoons when all the others are asleep, and we talk. We mellow a little towards each other, recognizing our need for one another. I notice how she is beginning to stand in a new way, with her belly thrust a little forwards and her hands resting on it. She has a new smile, very different from her old one. Still secretive, but pleased.

– You'll have to take things a bit easier, I remark to her one morning while we are forking filthy straw out of the sheep pen: with the baby coming. Save some strength for him.

She turns scarlet.

– I didn't think it showed yet.

Then she looks at me in her old way.

– How do you know it won't be a daughter? That's what I want. A daughter. If it's a boy I'll throw it over the side.

I am shocked. She looks down, and I am shocked again to see that she is crying. I can't bear this. I have never been able to endure the sound of my children crying. Something tiny and

80

monstrous and dark within me wakes up and joins in, and then I have to slap it back down, slap the children to stop them crying. I hold my hands together in my lap, itching to slap Sara as she goes on weeping, her face ugly and red, and that terrible sound coming from her.

– You didn't welcome a daughter, did you? she says: you were happy with your three fine sons, and you've never thought much of the worth of daughters-in-law.

We spread the clean straw on the floor of the pen in silence. Then, exhausted, I sit down in it to rest. I want to tell Sara to go away, but I'm unable to do so. She sits down beside me. I fear her now. She is my accuser, my judge.

– When I came to live with you all, she says: I was so lonely. I missed my people so much I could hardly bear it. I wanted my husband to love me and to be loved by him, but he took little notice of me. Except at night when he would climb on top of me for a few minutes and then fall asleep. All day long it was nothing but work work work. I wanted kindness from you but you kept scolding me. Everything I did was wrong. I felt stupid and useless. So I gave up trying.

I am struck by how young she is. Younger than I when I married Jack. Cautiously I grope my way back to that time and try to remember what it was like. I expected so little. That was what saved me from too much sorrow.

– What about God? I ask her: isn't God a comfort?

– I don't believe in him, she says: I want my mother.

She starts crying again. I want to shake her. I stop myself, and take her hand. I expect her to withdraw it, but she doesn't.

– We had a song, my sisters and I, she sobs: handed down from one of our ancestors who was stolen away into captivity and made to marry her captor. She sang how she was as lonely as a water lily whose stem is gnawed by a beetle. That was how I felt. Living with your son, before the Flood came, I used to sing it to myself every day, for comfort.

She blows her nose on her sleeve and looks at me defiantly.

– I want a daughter, she says: I'll love her properly. The way no one loves me. And then I'll let her go. I'll let her leave me. I know it's got to happen.

81

She's on the verge of tears again. I can't bear it. I search hurriedly for something to say that will stop her.

– You're my daughter now, Sara, I say: please stay with me.

We haven't any choice, anyway, I think. We just have to make the best of it. But I promise her in my heart: you have looked after me, and now I will try to look after you.

We begin to rely on each other in a new way. Sara is someone I can really talk to. Jack is depressed, and isn't much good to me. He doesn't tell me his thoughts in the old way, and he stops coming to me at night. I miss him.

– What's your God thinking about things? I ask him one day.

His face grows even more miserable.

– I can't hear what God's saying any more, he confesses: there's too much water in the way.

I find this odd. To my way of seeing we are surrounded by Jack's God. I believe in his power and anger as never before. Whereas my God seems to be sleeping or dreaming. I have to take it on trust that the earth will deliver us again out of her womb. There is no sign I can see that this will be so.

We have to wait. We have to be patient. It isn't easy to stay cooped up in a small space with the fear of death tapping at your shoulder night and day, after a lifetime of running about outside and going pretty well where you want.

We remain in the Boat for nine months in all; for the length of a pregnancy. When we are not working we sit and gossip, or we play at spillikins, or we try to pray. I embroider linen for the new baby, or I just sit in silence. That feels good.

I need nothing now but this water surrounding us.

I develop eyes of piercing vision, capable of seeing down through the wooden hull of the Boat, through the fathoms of ocean underneath us, right down to the stones and gravel and sand that once formed the earth, the dry land. I build a new world there, one of my own choosing. A childish vision, idealistic, impossible. I know that. I fill it with people who are as fluid as water, flowing past each other in peace and letting each other alone.

My world allows people to choose how they will live: by themselves, or in groups, or with one other person. People are allowed to be flexible, to change, to change how they live. There are no rules about having to get married and have

82

children, having to leave your mother if you don't want to, having to live with a man if you don't want to. In this deep-sea place Sara and I can keep house together, and no one minds. I give us fins on our backs and tails, like fish, and I build us a cool cave decorated with coral and shells, with a floor of silver sand, and green weeds waving around the entrance. The water slides all over my body as I lie in it and am carried along by it. Water is my mother, my lover, my bed. My element, which gives me the freedom to swim off wherever I want to go. Water is my food and drink. Water is my god.

I've had enough of being a woman, with being confined in a clumsy body, with being defined by men. Yearning and suffering and dying on the harsh earth. Just as when I am a child I yearn to escape upwards and join the birds in their airy element, when I pretend I can fly, so now, as an adult woman, I am reborne from the Boat into water. I become fish. Untroubled by the Flood, which, after all, is merely my home. I go with it.

We carve a tally of the days we spend afloat, using Jack's knife to notch slashes in the doorpost. Every morning one of us marks the wood in this way, while someone else peers out through the trap door to see what the weather is like. We invent a lot of new words for different sorts of rain.

After nine months have passed it stops raining. We look at one another. Without saying a word, Jack goes down to the middle deck and fetches out a raven and a dove. Opening one of the casements he lets them go. That evening, only the dove returns. It bears a sprig of olive in its beak.

Next morning, when we wake up, we find that we have been put ashore in the night. Perhaps Jack's God has pulled us from above and mine has pushed us from below. I don't know. But here we are, wedged between two enormous rocks. At first, looking out of the trap door, we assume we have landed on an island. Then, when we emerge, we discover that we are balanced on the tip of a mountain. Fancy that, I think: a Boat on a mountain-top. How ridiculous. I start laughing so hard I can't stop. Not until Sara shakes me. Then I begin to weep.

We clamber out of the Boat onto dry land. There, shining above us in the grey sky, is the arch of colours. A thin sun

83

glimmers behind the clouds, and the air on our faces is fresh and damp. Way down below us we can see the tops of trees.

The waters, ebbing and receding from the mountain, have left a trail of litter. The rocky ground is sticky with slimy green debris, rotten vegetation. Bones, clotted with lumps of hair and gristle, poke up out of it. Here and there are the corpses of men and animals, bloated and stinking, whose rotting flesh has turned all manner of bright colours, as though it reflected the arch of light above.

How does a baby feel when it is born, propelled from the safety of the enclosing waters into the enormous dry world? Beside me Sara is being sick all over her feet.

I want to go back on the Boat. I don't want to see the ruin of the world, these scraps of clothing caught on the rocks, this broken baby's rattle a body's length away. Jack has his face turned away from mine. I know he is trying not to weep.

– Wife, he says, gripping my hand: we should offer a sacrifice. Go and fetch a lamb from the Boat.

– No, I say.

I point at the band of colours hanging over our heads. One end hides in the clouds, and the other touches the roof of the Boat, just as before.

– The earth is a hard mother, I say: but she has delivered us, just as I dreamed she would, and we've been born onto this mountain for good or ill. She will cut that shining cord in her own good time. When she does, it's up to us to get on with living. There is no need to kill an animal. I want no more death.

Jack stares at me, his face wretched and uncomprehending. Then his shoulders sag.

– I can't bear this. I'm going off to find a clean place in which I can pray.

He blunders off, crying.

The rest of us bury the dead. We dig one large shallow grave as best we can, and roll the bodies into it, then cover them with earth and stones. A little way down the mountain we find a big puddle of water. In silence, we strip off our filthy clothes and wash ourselves, all of us going in together. It doesn't seem to matter, that we show our exhausted naked bodies to one another. It is a kind of prayer for the dead, and for ourselves, to

84

pour scoops of water over each other's heads. It confirms us as a family, as survivors. Then we go back on the Boat to feed and water the animals, and to prepare a meal. It smells too bad outside to stay there for long.

Jack comes back after dark. My sons and daughters are eating supper, but I can't touch a thing. The meat stew nauseates me. As though it were boiled up from dead babies.

Jack stands in our midst and raises his hands, palms upwards.

– God has spoken to me, he announces: he is very terrible, but he is also merciful. He is our shepherd, and he has brought us here, through the waters of the Flood, so that we may know his might and tremble before him. He has put the arch of colours in the sky as the sign of his pledge to us, of his new alliance with us. He wishes us to offer him burnt meat as a sacrifice, so that he may enjoy its pleasant odour. And he commands us to go forth and be fruitful and multiply. We shall become the masters of the earth, and hold sway over it. We have dominion over all the animals and birds, over all the fruits of nature, over the fish that swim in the seas. Everything that lives will serve us for food, and will tremble before us and be filled with fear at our approach.

– This way of talking is a disaster, I retort: what good can come of our setting ourselves up like lords? The animals have suffered just as much as we have, and have been reborn just as we have. It's wrong to make them our servants again. We need to treat them differently now. They are our companions, not our slaves.

– God has decreed it, is all Jack will say: as the rule of our new life.

I heave myself to my feet and raise my arms just as my husband has done.

– Then I too, I declare: have a rule for my new life. I swear that I shall never kill an animal again, shall never shed blood again, shall never eat meat again. I am sick of killing, and so would your God be if he had any sense.

This argument confirms the division between Jack and me. I still love and respect him. How can I not? We have come through so much together. But our opinions are leading us along different ways.

85

After supper, the others fall asleep. I stay up, unable to sleep for worrying about what will happen to us next. The wooden ceiling above my head shuts me into a space of sour breath and sweat, of torment. I open the trap door and clamber out onto the roof.

The cool evening wind has swept away the foul stench of the day, and the darkness has blotted out the ugly view. I sit cross-legged, the breeze fanning my face. I listen to the silence of the night and throw myself into its untouchable blue distances. I look up at the stars, my eyes walking amongst them, hopping from one to the other as though they are stepping stones. Perhaps we are not alone, after all. Perhaps there are other living creatures on those stars. Perhaps all this business of living and dying goes on all the time among the stars. The earth is only one place among so many.

Night has cut the bright cord, and set me upright. Now I need a name. I need names.

I decide to give the earth and all her creatures new names, as you do with a baby when it is born. I jump up, and begin to pace up and down on the roof. I think first of the arch of colours we have seen twice, once before the Flood and now after it. It links our new life to our old one, ties heaven to earth, knots us to God.

– God's bow in the rain, I call out: God's rainbow.

For the rest of the night I wrestle with words, trying to find new ones. The names are a string with which I tie together my understanding of the God I know in this new creation, my way of connecting us all with each other and with God, humans and animals and birds and plants, none of us superior to the others however different we may look. Naming the names is a form of worship. I grow drunk on it.

– God's rainbow, I chant to myself: God's knot, God's promise, God's-not-forgetting, God-not-forgotten.

Also I mourn. This work of renaming includes contemplating all that I have lost: the old world with all its beauties and sorrows. The people we knew and travelled and laughed with. The drowned beasts. Also my hopes for a new and better world which would not include killing, the ruthless mastery of nature. Jack said to me before he slept: it is necessary to dominate nature in order to live from it; how, otherwise, shall we start

86

our new life and survive? I had no answer for him. I dream of a harmony between all created things, a state of peaceful growth, of unity and kindness and no killing. I know I shall not see it.

In the morning I take Sara aside and tell her I've renamed the world while she was asleep. She looks astonished at first, then worried.

– No, no, I'm not ill, I say: just listen, will you?

In the end, perhaps just to humour her crazy mother-in-law, she agrees to teach the new names to her baby once it is born. She is doubtful about how many she will be able to remember, when she's no longer looking at the things I've named, or should illness or death prevent my being there to remind her, and so I start thinking of a way to help her do it.

I go back in my mind to the time when we started building the Boat, how we drew pictures in the dust on the ground of what we thought we wanted.

I take dollops of wet mud in the palm of my hand, and shape them into little slabs. I sharpen the end of a stick into a point. Then, with the stick, I draw pictures on the mud slabs, one by one, of all the new words I've made up. I keep the pictures as simple as possible: a few strokes and curves. Some of them are just straightforward drawings of things, or part of a thing, as I see them in my mind's eye, like *bee*, or *leaf*. *God* is a circle. Then I work out I can use sound as well as sight. So *belief-in-God* comes out as a circle holding a bee and a leaf. I enjoy myself doing this, playing games again. An aged child I am, squatting on my haunches getting my hands all clotted with mud. When I've finished, I lay the slabs on the roof of the Boat to dry in the sun and grow hard. Then I collect them up in my apron and give them to Sara. And I give a name to what I've done: I call it *writing*.

– See, I show her: this mud brick is a *word*, and it means *my-love-for-you*. And it will replace me when I'm no longer with you. It will survive our separation. It will survive my death. This is my gift to you, daughter, and to your children and to their children.

I laugh at myself. I wanted to save and change the world, yet all I've been able to do is make up a new kind of toy.

That's more or less the end of my story. I decide to stay on the mountain-top and end my days there. It is no longer unpleasant to me, now that the filth on the ground has been dried by the sun and wind and the bodies have been shovelled into the earth where they belong. I am filled with weariness. Perhaps I just lack the courage to struggle on. The weather is turning colder, and the others want to get down the mountain with the livestock and find shelter, found a settlement. No more wandering: we are all agreed on that. Sara wants a wooden house, like the Boat she's grown used to, not a flimsy tent, to shelter her baby in. She wants to stay in one place, to become a farmer, to plant the seeds we have brought with us, to see them grow. She wants crops, and a harvest, and a barn full of wheat, and an end to wandering.

So they leave me, as I ask. They build me a little hut near the Boat with a few provisions stored in it, and they tether a couple of goats nearby to keep me in milk and cheese. Then they take the rest of our goods and animals and move off down the mountain to find the place where they will build a home.

My parting with Sara is as sad as that with Jack. Both of us weep.

– I shall return and visit you very soon, Sara promises me as she embraces me: after the baby is born. I'll bring her with me.

I don't want to lose my newly found daughter so soon. I begin to love her, then have to tear her from me. She talks of staying with me, but I pack her off. I drive her away, using some of my old harshness, complaining that all I want now is to be left alone. I know it is right that she goes with her husband and family. Hers is the last human face that I see. She waves goodbye, then drops out of sight behind an outcrop of rock. What hope would she have, staying with me? That is what I say to myself when I find myself missing her.

A strange time begins for me. For the first time in my life I am free to do what I like all day long. My increasing weakness means that I can't get about very much, so I stick to my little patch of mountainside near the Boat. I like being surrounded by nothing but wind and sky. I sit for hours watching the changes in the clouds, the shifting of the light, the play of sunsets and dawns. Daily I witness the creation of the world. When I pray, it is not with words. When I talk, it is to praise God, by which I mean the action of creation. I don't try to draw a picture of this. Sara will need to break the circle I drew in two, and find a new word. But I don't need words any more. I'm alone, and I've given my words to Sara, to do as she likes with.

I don't last long in my solitary retreat. Cold white pieces of sky fall down day by day, smoothing out my world, blotting out my thoughts. God's silence wraps me up, hushing me, putting an icy finger to my lips. I open my mouth and the whiteness of the sky falls onto my tongue, dissolving, pouring down my throat like sweet milk. Welcome, death. In you I drown. Until I'm reincarnated, born again into the next story. I'm the ghost in the library, cackling, unseen, from between the pages of the sacred texts, waiting my chance to haunt a new generation of readers. I'm what's missing. I'm the wanderer.

15 The Babble-On Sibyl sits tugging a comb through her hair in the communal bathroom that she has dreamed up on the Ark: cavern of red brocade encircled by pink-tinted mirrors and red and gold shaded lamps that is set with Art Deco vanity tables and red plush pouffes and sofas, and crowned with a jingly crystal chandelier swinging from the gold-encrusted ceiling. Her source of inspiration is the Ladies Boudoir in the Lyceum Theatre on the Strand, but she has added a couple of touches of her own: enamel baths behind red brocade screens; free-standing wooden towel-horses bearing piles of fluffy white cotton and linen.

She has always loved other people's bathrooms, loves seeing what they keep there. Visiting new acquaintances for the first time, she makes for the bathroom as soon as possible, opens the cabinets to discover secrets: the packets of hair dye, the ladies' razors, the laxatives, the discreet bags in flowered cotton containing rubber domes and tubes of foul-smelling cream. Her voyeurism is a mark of love, an effort towards intimacy she cannot always make in a sitting room. Using her hostess's hairbrush, patting on her moisturizer, sniffing at her cologne, inspecting her range of eye-shadow colours, she gets close to this woman she does not yet know. Back in her armchair, sipping a cup of tea, she is cool, watchful. A woman may be a rival for Neil's attention; she cannot afford to relax her guard.

One Italian couple she knows have a bathroom each, all black tiles and gleaming chrome, and special men's and ladies' toothpaste. She and Neil, moving hastily in their need to find a home together, are stuck with pale orange vinyl bath and bidet, always a little greasy to the touch, chocolate and orange-flowered plastic shower curtains, camel tiles around the washbasin, and wallpaper jazzy with enormous cream and orange lozenges. She doesn't mind: having to use a bathroom of someone else's choice means she's not responsible, doesn't have to reveal her own taste, commit herself. No one can snoop in her bathroom and secretly claim to know her. She hasn't plunged for baskets of ferns, china dishes of pretty pastel soaps, hanging bamboo shelves, like some of her friends. She hasn't gone all bohemian, with the radiators painted gold and hung with old bead necklaces and grotesque raffia masks dangling from the high lavatory cistern, like Neil's ex-girlfriend. Nor has she not bothered at all: stained cork mat, yellowing bath with brown streaks under the taps, piles of old copies of *Private Eye* in a corner, plastic beakers crusted with toothpaste, wastebin overflowing with bits of used cotton wool and empty cardboard lavatory rolls. She has seen beautiful bathrooms, too: one walled in plain shining mahogany, a man's room this, with his silver-backed brushes of pure bristle lined up next to his silver-topped bottles of eau de Cologne and aftershave under the thick square mirror secured with silver studs. She could never afford anything like that; useless to dream of it. And that bathroom she saw once in a house in the country: enormous, carpeted, with armchairs and pictures, bath proud and nude in a corner on curled feet, long windows open onto a view of lawn and flowerbeds. Better to stick to her tangerine vinyl suite; like her clothes and hairstyle, she suddenly thinks, safely sweet, tasteless and out of date.

She crumples a fistful of pale frilled cotton. Her curiosity begins not in bathrooms at all, but in her mother's bedroom, clean shrine in the afternoon, the bed looking as though it's never slept in, net curtains hazy at the window, clear space full of light, of absence. She tiptoes across the furry carpet to the little antique chest of drawers, pulls out, one by one, the shallow tiers. Handkerchiefs, ironed and folded monogrammed squares, kept in an embroidered linen sachet, a sprig of lavender laid on top. Petticoats in pastel nylon with pencil straps. A drift of silky nightdresses, pink and blue and lemon. One black one with red bows. Row of sturdy cotton bras, cups reinforced with circular stitching. A pink corselette with hooks and eyes gripping the elastic, wrinkled suspenders dangling. A fragrant pile, interleaved with ribboned bags of lavender, of knickers, enormous they seem to her, like shorts, the legs edged with lace, little pleated nylon skirts with cotton gussets. There is such order here, such spotlessness, such care taken with this store of underwear whose quiet arrangement no one will ever see. The daughter sighs, running her fingers through orlon and silk, lifting each pile out, then replacing it.

When she is older, she confines herself to other women's bathrooms. Hard to explain if you're discovered going through a wardrobe.

How is it that other women have the confidence to make such clear-cut choices about their clothes, their possessions? She knows, from her delicate rummaging here, that the Forsaken Sibyl has a secret stash of powder and lipsticks, that the Deftly Sibyl sometimes takes sleeping pills, that the Correct Sibyl uses washing grains to remove blackheads, and that the Re-Vision Sibyl travels with a child's slimy flannel bearing the picture of a panda. She herself carries a neat zipped plastic case, free from Elizabeth Arden once sufficient purchases have been made, stocked with lotions, creams and make-up bought from a chainstore combining quality with low cost. Anyone might have such a blandly pretty outfit of conventional equipment; it gives nothing away.

She is so eager to please; not to shock. The two collections of stories she has published were written before she met Neil and fell in love. She has written hardly anything since. Why?

She grimaces at herself in the mirror. Suddenly she hates her face, smooth screen which she has defied time and experience to mark, whose bones she has not allowed to emerge, whose lines and crows-feet she has worked tirelessly to erase. What's behind her face? What cries, what laughter wait there to be expressed, to carve a personality onto and out of her round pink mask, to give her her own distinctive individual beauty?

Her mother uses Nivea Creme, cupping the shallow blue tin in one hand, prising off the round lid with its elegant fifties logo in swirling white lettering, peeling back the thin disc of silver paper with a fingernail, digging her fingertips into the glistening surface of the cold cream, roughing it up, scooping up a fingertipful which she dabs onto her face, around her eyes. Her mother's eyes are brown, deep-set, sunk into shallows of

92

bone, surrounded by webbed lines. Eyes that look unflinchingly at her husband's minor cruelties, at her own yearnings and silences, at her children's squabbling. Tired eyes sometimes, beautiful eyes, eyes holding an infinity of knowledge.

The Babble-On Sibyl is frightened of writing honestly about her own sexuality; about what she has learned about men after loving, and therefore studying, quite a few of them; about what can happen, spoken and unspoken, between a man and a woman. Things a woman can be ashamed of, in herself and her man; things she is confused or embarrassed by. Things which, if she admitted their burning existence inside her, might force changes in her life. Things she has discussed with no one. Things which could hurt her lovers, her family, her friends.

So why talk about them? Better to write about sex in conventional feminine terms, discreet and romantic, giving nothing away, nodding towards received wisdom and common sense. Or to write about sex in the rip-roaring way some women writers use, objectifying herself, seeing herself through men's eyes, in their terms and language, thrusting nipples, wet cunt, taut breasts, a lover no more than a cock driving like a piston, a woman's response the echo of his. No doubts, no fears. None of those moments in between, which carry perhaps the truth of the experience but which are so hard to catch, to put into words, flickering just out of sight, glimpsed from the corner of the eye, off-canvas.

Most male writers do not seem to have this problem. They expose their nearest and dearest in the frankest way without worrying whom they hurt, true to the dictates of their art which transcend those of ordinary bourgeois morality. Is that really true? What do *they* leave out? Plenty, she's certain. Or else, *pretending* to be frank, they reproduce the conventions which enmesh her: man as intelligent ironist, woman as sticky fly-trap; husband as adulterer, all those campus novels, young students his prey and so flattered to be so. Boring silent frumpy wife. Nothing changes. Pursuit, gratification, boredom, pursuit. Female characters complying. Of course. Let's not be sentimental.

Why write about sex at all? Every novel with its obligatory sex scene, hero's fucking odyssey in between his thoughts on life money death god irony. Sex as decoration in the twentieth-century novel. Sex put in as spicy ingredient because it sells.

Fantasy sex for consolation of male readers, character armour of machismo left intact, the women characters either a projection of a feared and repressed part of the author or dream figures plucked from the childhood level of the unconcious. Where are the modern male writers who write honestly about their own sexuality? She can't think of one. Stendhal, Balzac, Sterne, all did better.

Isn't it rather neurotic to write about sex, to isolate it artificially from the rest of life? Shouldn't sex be just one aspect of a well-ordered well-balanced life, and so, in context, not really that remarkable? Why all the fuss?

Sex seems to be the dominant contemporary emblem of the psyche. To explore sexuality seems to open the way to exploring what makes people tick. If the psyche is part of the universe, there need be no shame in exploring the 'inside' as opposed to the 'outside' of the great realist writers? But 'outside' remains more respectable. If you want to write about 'inside', better project it, put a man on the moon, on the Russian frontier, on the seabed?

Why is it that she wants to talk about what is called perverted sex, sinful sex, immature sex? Is the writer's finger that of the masseuse, the doctor, unerringly finding the wound in the psyche, the bruise, and so, in the examination, bringing healing, restoring wholeness? No; that begs the question; too romantic. Who defines health anyway? Why is one form of love sick and another not?

The feminist group at her college believed that women wrote about sex in self-defence. Tired of men's ignorant fantasies, they wrote 'the truth'. What words are capable of doing that? Start by exploring, perhaps. Take that word *woman*, and squeeze every last drop of meaning out of it? That will take her a lifetime.

She throws away her comb and stands up. Sheds her clothes, the crinkled dead leaves of several seasons back. Dons a bathrobe she selects from the rack by the door, voluminous garment in heavy checked wool, comfortable, warm. Then she picks up a pair of scissors, blades like two legs dancing. Flexes them. Begins to cut her hair off. It's too long, almost down to her waist; a child's hair, not a woman's.

She shears her fringe. Startled face springs out at her in

94

the mirror. Clips the tendrils curling on her neck, delicious shivers of pleasure as the cold steel grazes her skin. She leaves one long lock, plaited, to remind her of what's gone. Her make-up looks wrong now, too pink and blue. She soaks a sponge in soapy water, clears it off. Not nakedness, not true self, not essential core: just a new image. To start with. She picks up her pen and writes.

Her pen is a dagger. Her father lies dead at her feet in a splatter of blood. She is a murderess.

Hand shaking. Dip your pen in your father's blood and write another line. Watch your husband's face tighten with bemused pain as your nib jabs at his soft secrets, the most vulnerable parts of himself; the places he let you see because he trusted you. You have betrayed him. You have destroyed his trust in you. Is this really what you want: to ruin your marriage? to expose how nasty you yourself are?

She needs to find another way. Truth is not obvious or straightforward. Sneak up on it, sideways, from behind? Tell the truth but tell it slant? Confessional writing, the belief in truth found through simple straightforward outpouring of feeling, won't do, if it reproduces the sinner in the confessional, the accused in the dock, the madwoman in hospital. Speak not to your enemies, your judges, the snoopers and voyeurs with power to arrest, punish, define, drug and prevent you, but to your allies, your friends. Discover a language that *they*, listening intently (you hope) for your words, will understand, take in, recreate, give back to you. So that true conversation can begin. Sabotage the enemy's language, disguise yourself in it if you must, play spy at the enemy's dinner table. Observe him. Make up your own code under the enemy's nose, pass your secrets in the images he is conditioned to find banal and absurd and therefore undetectable, uncrackable. Send up metaphor flares which he will think are just decoration not urgent complex signals of desire, intent. Smuggle your weapons under aprons of gossip, your diplomatic bag. *Begin*.

Her words make such a clatter. Who goes there, friend or foe? Password!

She sweats. What shall she say?

Start with a few lies?

To invent simply means *to find*. What's inside.

16 When I was twenty I started my librarianship training, in the Department of Printed Books in the British Library.

My bunch of keys enables me to unlock the hidden doors in the walls of the public galleries, to swing back a section of bookcase and vanish behind it, to disappear into books, parting their pages and walking into them. I am Alice. My bed has paper sheets.

The unconscious of the library is held in the bookstacks. Iron ladders thread through it; I peer down through the open grille-work rungs at the floors falling away under me, six layers, a transparency of books. I clamber about Western culture's brain. I find the locked room of uncatalogued, inaccessible and forbidden erotica, and I read these books too, poring, in musty dimness, over excited guilty tales of whipping and slit-silk knickers and maids giving their all on back staircases for a few pence stuffed up their cunts.

The conscious mind of the library is contained in the Reading Room, vast circular space under a lofty glass dome. Rows of desks and armchairs radiate out from the centre like threads in a web, and the superintendent, black hairy spider, crouches in the middle in a glass cage. Around him curve the stands of catalogue volumes, labyrinth that the alphabetical order of author entries unravels. James Brown, Murderer, precedes James Brown, Pederast, and James Brown, Poet.

No classification system. Just a subject index: more alphabet.

Here on the Ark, in my Arkive, I can search through B until I come to Baby.

– But the world's such a terrible place, Noah complains: why bring a child into it? That's irresponsible.

I consult the book of riddles.

Does *want* also mean *want*?

17 On our seventh day out in the calm blue sea, we spy land. An island, sprawling in a froth of breakers. We see its palaces from far off, glittering and crystalline against the clear sky, the sun bouncing off their marble domes and porticos and flashing us a message: come closer. I fetch the guidebook from the archive and study its maps closely. I don't think this is the land I'm searching for. Nonetheless, no harm in having a look.

We moor in the tiny harbour. Leaving the sibyls scribbling in their various hiding places and the Gaffer sunbathing on the roof of the Ark, I go ashore and walk into the city down streets lined with buildings of a severe beauty, a restrained grace, their classical portals and windows flanked by elegant columns flowering with leafy capitals. Some of these palaces are in a good state of repair; many others are crumbling, mutilated by weather and corroding time, their stone decoration blurred and broken, cracks in their façades, roofs gaping open. A programme of restoration has clearly been started, and then abandoned.

I reach the main piazza, an enormous rectangular room. On one side is a basilica, a Renaissance stone veil thrown around a medieval building and pierced by a double tier of *loggie*, a pattern of white arches and columns in clumps like the stalks of giant flowers. On the other side, forming a large squared-off corner, is the wide terrace of a café. Away down the other end, past the elaborately decorated façades of churches and palaces, is a tall clock tower, and two statues, one of a lion and one of a dragon, set on top of two lofty slender columns. Under my feet is a carpet of white stone, and above, the ceiling of blue sky.

It's utterly quiet. No dogs barking to break the hush. Nothing stirring in the sharply cut shadows. The basilica floats across the piazza as serenely as our Ark has sailed across the sea, but there is no sign of life behind her high windows. Not the flicker of a handkerchief. Not the sound of a single footfall coming down the long external staircase under its arched canopy. The siesta hour.

I move out of the white dazzle of the sun into the cool darkness of a colonnade, and sit down on the stone pavement, resting my back against a column. I unfurl the Italian newspaper that someone has left lying there, and laboriously push my brain through its closely printed columns. Leaping over words and phrases I don't understand, leaving gaps in my reasoning, I make my own translation.

I am a citizen of this proud city; and my ears are clotted with wax. Better that way. Then I can't hear what the wind is saying. The sirocco blows in on its way around all the continents in the world, and covers the cars with a fine layer of red dust brought all the way from Africa. A strong, harsh wind, whirling in from the sea, bringing whisperings and mutterings from lands I have never seen, insistent warnings hinting at the imminent outbreak of yet another war rooted in the spiralling greed of the great empires for money, profits and power. More lands and villages bombed and burnt, more women raped by soldiers, more people starving and thirsting in refugee camps, more corpses riddled with bullets, fried by napalm, poisoned by gas. Sooner or later will come the war to end all wars. One last great ejaculation of fire, the world crumpled and burnt out, our rulers emerging from their shelters to sift our ashes. If one green leaf pokes up through the cinders and grows into a tree, I shan't be there to see it and nor will you.

The wind scratches the heart, strikes the breastbone, whimpers down chimneys and coils around the cots where children sleep. Sometimes it chuckles. Sometimes it sobs. I mourn too, reading the newspaper's list of the dead, the dying, the about-to-die. I'm a hypocrite. I'm a citizen of the First World. I'm responsible. What have I ever tried to do to prevent the rulers of my country from waging war and death?

I want to go on living my nice comfortable life. If I read the newspapers every morning, the complacency of that life is destroyed. I can't bear it. I clap my hands over my ears, rush indoors, seal my ears with wax, great gobs of brown glue sticky as burnt sugar. I am beginning to forget how to speak, because, with my gummed-up ears, I can no longer listen. I am beginning to die, because I am no longer listened to. I can't write: the only word I can spell is *death*.

Folding up the newspaper, I shiver. The afternoon sun paints the inside of arches a dark gold. It is conceivable that the world will suddenly end, that the Bomb will fall. It is conceivable that all these peaceful streets of palaces will burn to ash.

How could anyone let herself have a baby once she knows it's likely that the world will be blown up in that child's lifetime? The shadow of the Bomb falls across my ovaries. I shan't conceive. Death, the guerrilla, has got me, scuttles through my dark interior, booby-trapping my desires for a child, setting mines to kill the life that stirs in me every month. He's winning. He's captured my territory, and my hands are lifted in surrender.

I never wanted to come here. I'm in the wrong place. I turn to flee. Then I remember. Before I go, there is one more monument I must visit here.

I go out of the piazza and down a deserted and colonnaded street, into the great church at its end.

It's cool and peaceful inside, out of the blaze of the street. Smell of damp, old stone, incense. The rosy floor is slippery. The door in the side aisle has been propped open, letting in brilliant light. Just outside is a fountain, a single jet of water tinkling into a basin of white marble set on green grass.

I sit down, in one of the front pews.

There she is, the Queen of Heaven. Seated, cradling her divine child, on a low stool which her draperies flow over and almost conceal. Her pale oval face is grave and sweet, and her head is bent a little to one side, reflectively, her eyes glancing towards the spectator. The veil covering her hair and shoulders and sweeping down around her feet is of a blue so dark it is almost black, edged with gold and lined with olive green. Her dress is crimson, stencilled with a pattern in gold. She is very grand. Around her head shines a gold halo, flat as a plate, and she is seated against a splendour of dark gold streaked with orange. Within this fly two burly cherubs with

100

blue wings, dressed in green frocks, holding a triple crown above her head.

A flying carpet carries her up, and separates her from a tranquil landscape painted in soft blues and greens that shows this city with the harbour in front and the dumpy blue mountains behind. The clouds extend upwards and surround her, so that she flies up inside a mandala of whiteness framing her gold radiance. And on the clouds, and in them, almost part of them, are angels and cherubs, looped together in a tangled necklace of legs and wings. A school of them, lively as dolphins, playing flutes, harps, cymbals and dulcimers, and their mouths opened wide and singing. These cheerful babies are all colours: red or blue or green faces and wings, tunics of pink, plum, lime, violet, lemon. So round and soft are the contours of their faces and limbs that they are like plump fruits hanging in a woven garland, ornamental swags, bearing bright peaches and nectarines, flung about the Queen of Harvests.

Then I suddenly see it. The rope of cherubs is the rainbow, arching, in all the rainbow's colours, entwined with the white clouds, around the Madonna and her Child, enclosing them.

So the rainbow signifies the rebirth of humanity. Not just once, as the Old Testament has it; or twice, as the New Testament commentators argue; but over and over again.

The Madonna in this church feeds her baby from a tiny white breast pointed like a pear. The sixteenth-century artist is in no doubt that the new birth which will save the world is that of Christ.

But perhaps renewal has to be achieved repeatedly, by each of us, by each community. The divine child has to be born, with labour and struggle, in each of us: the discovery of how to create a world of freedom and justice, how to live fully, how to stop hating and killing, how to prevent the planet from being blown up.

I sit and look at the Madonna and her bambino and feel doubt rise in me, as green and bitter as bile.

18 Back on board the Ark I cook supper for us all. The Ark as crammed larder. At least one sensual treat a day aids the creative process. So I serve the others with *bigoli*, a local speciality I have brought back from the market on shore: thick yellow spaghetti made with egg, with a hole down the middle. Next, *baccalà* with *polenta*, cod soaked in olive oil, and maize pudding. I shan't learn the word for meat: the sight, smell and taste of it have begun to disgust me. Though reading meat recipes used to be my form of pornography. I still kill mosquitoes every night, smashing them, with a wetted handkerchief, against the cabin wall, in a splatter of blood (my blood). But I don't want to eat meat any more.

– The imperialism of cookery books, I say to the others: with the words of exotic recipes we invade the Third World yet again. Rich whites knowing the names of Javanese dishes pluck money from wallets, food from shops, while the Javanese peasants starve and do not discuss anorexia or vegetarianism.

Clatter of scraped clean plates.

– Eat up your meat, the nuns used to tell us, says the Correct Sibyl: think of the starving millions who'd be glad of your leftover scraps of gristle and fat. Mortify your body. Spoon up the food that revolts you: the slime of tapioca lumps at the bottom of the soup bowl; the tinned sweetcorn, tasting of polish, that you choke on; the glutinous jam congealed like blood on dry pastry. Get a holy soul out of purgatory with every flaking butter bean you swallow, every gob of vomit you hold back. Eat this spoonful for me, darling. This is my body and my blood. Do this in memory of me. The blood and body of the mother nourish the child inside. That is the true holy communion. We're sailing past butter mountains over an

102

ocean of milk, while babies die safely out of sight.

– The meat market, says the Forsaken Sibyl: is marriage. Virgin cattle branded in red. My mother failed the test. My adoptive parents *chose* me. Picked me out. Plenty of white babies available in those days before the abortion law was loosened. My mother was damaged goods. Bruised like a fruit in the gutter tasted once then thrown away.

– My mother started married life in lodgings in Fog Street, Manchester, says the Re-Vision Sibyl: she wasn't used to such cold. All through that first winter, she told me, when it rained every day and got dark at three o'clock, she sat in the kitchen wrapped in her overcoat and cried. For her mother, for the apple orchards of her native Normandy. Love lugged her across the water and made her strong. Her first child, a boy, died at three days old. She was alone, among strangers, my father away having to travel on business. She endured her grief and pain all by herself, taking them into her, stoically. They became her framework, a second skeleton. She survived, to have more children, to find a job, to make a home. As I hoped to do. As I wanted to do.

– A woman I know, says the Deftly Sibyl: went through the marriage ceremony while having a miscarriage, standing upright in her white brocade tent while the blood coursed through layers of sanitary towels and seeped into her satin shoes. She stumbled to the hospital, not to the reception. A man I know left the registry office with his finger swelling up around the platinum wedding ring. Later he was discovered in the bathroom with a woman friend and a tube of KY Jelly. In the end he went to a jeweller's and had the ring sawn off. Then at last he went to the reception.

– A woman I know, says the Babble-On Sibyl: had an affair with her butcher. At noon he pulled the iron shutters down, then fucked her on the tiled floor among the heaps of sawdust, in the cool gloom, the taut red carcases swaying above. Her husband found a brown paper bag in her knicker drawer, containing her photo and that of the butcher placed face to face, two kissing squares of celluloid. So he beat her up. When I got married I wanted a wild pagan ritual with me in a low-cut silk frock and my friends dancing and singing. I checked out Kensington registry office. No one could call that a holy place,

103

with its red flock wallpaper and bouquets of artificial tulips and officials in bulging satin ties. In the end I got married in a little Anglican church in the country, wearing a wreath of lilies, a veil, the lot. I mourn for the ceremony I did not let myself have. I mourn for the fact I can't marry all my women friends. No public ceremonies to celebrate the passionate love between friends. Our real wedding was in bed. We held each other's ears and whispered into them the words we made up. Neil's idea. I love him for that.

– What is a husband? asks the Gaffer: the one with too much power. I don't understand why you women want to get married. What's in it for you? Status? Money? Security? You itch, you get married. You do your mating dance, produce your children. What then? Those years stretching ahead. Dryness, no passion. I know this. I've pressed my face against the bedroom windows. Better not to marry, and not to burn. Better to be safe. Better not to have that power. Better not to hurt the women. Better not to let your needs out. Better to be like me.

I serve green salad, pears, more wine.

– Time for a story, the Deftly Sibyl suggests: about a woman who's *not* married?

19   Death. Think on it, as I have been instructed to do.
Hovering above the bed, I shall take leave of my body,
the spittle-flecked lips, the thin cropped hair sodden
with sweat, the wasted scarred limbs, the rolled eyes. Then up,
into the night, and up, further up, past the chapel tower, above
the realm of moths and bats, up the staircase of the stars, to the
place where there is no night and no crying out and no hunger
for kisses.

If I am sent to hell. I have seen pictures of it. I remember the
one painted on the right-hand wall of the apse in our old parish
church. The doors of hell are open, and I peep inside. I meet
two naked women, both of them graceful and fair, with
gleaming silky flesh and unbound golden curls. They wear
ropes of pearls about their necks, rings on their fingers, jewels
in their ears. One of these ladies is held down by two scarlet
devils, while a third tears off her breasts with red-hot pincers.
The other lady, tied to a gridiron, is having her eyes put out,
and a glowing poker thrust between her legs. Swirls of smoke
obscure the other tortured souls; it is these two naked ladies
only who represent the torments of the damned. As a child I do
not understand why this should be so. Our parish priest, a holy
man who does not keep a housekeeper-whore as so many clerics
do, explains to me that women's beauty evokes men's lust, and
drags them down to vileness, away from their search for God. I
watch these ladies in their agony. Every Sunday for sixteen
years. My father has told me how pretty I am.

I shut my eyes in order to meditate and to prepare for sleep
by thinking of the Four Last Things: death, judgement, hell,
and heaven. I open them again, unable to bear the horror. I am
an exile from heaven, beating on its closed doors. Will they

remain closed to me when I die?

God is not here with me. I see only furniture. This bed, my prie-dieu. I don't like the crucifix; it dominates my cell, but I won't look at it. I won't be responsible any longer for his pain, my poor torn brother. Nor can I console him. I have abdicated my position at the foot of the cross. For me, now, Jesus is only one more wretch condemned to death by a cruel Father-God in the name of a corrupt religion that crushes the spirit rather than freeing it. Crushes the body. Maims and rips it in the name of love. I can't love a God who requires such suffering, who wills his son to be tortured to a slow death. I can't purchase salvation that way. I have given up that God. My visions over my years in this abbey have taught me different truths, and I trust them more. But the God of the priests does not let go so easily. I shall be punished, I know that. Tomorrow morning, when I kneel in the chapter-house in front of our Abbess and all the Ladies of our community here I shall learn what my punishment is to be. I am a heretic who refuses to recant. I do not expect mercy from him whom I have abandoned.

On my sixteenth birthday, I walk to St Paul's to attend Mass, with my sister Joanna and our aunt Dame Alice. It is a spring morning. May. Our Lady's month, and mine. The city rises about me, roofs and tiles and thatch washed by the cold light, the stone of the great church scrubbed by the sun to the colour of milk on oatmeal. After Mass, I kneel in front of the Virgin Mother and light a candle and pray. A lay brother pushes a twig broom across the wide flags, and the dust dances up in golden grains. The choir, practising for vespers, uncorks a sweet and piercing music that explodes in a froth of spine-tingling sound over my head where I kneel at the Lady altar and see the light splash in, red and green and blue smudges on the clean stone floor. The columns arch above my head, whippy and thin as young willows in the fields. God swings about in the sculptured air like a child on holiday.

The cloud of gold dust hangs between me and the Virgin's kind face like the pillar of fire the Israelites saw as they tracked across Egypt searching for the promised land. I close my eyes, and see a pillar of gold smoke against my eyelids.

We stand outside the west door, enjoying the sunshine. The

yard smells of fresh-cut grass, manure, baking bread. Seagulls and pigeons hop and peck, seeking crumbs in the cracks between cobbles. Joanna dusts her palms together, beats her hands on her heavy skirt and laughs as the birds scatter upwards. They make a flashing pattern of white embroidery, glossy linen threads looping and darting and then settling on the grass again, stitches in an orderly row.

Then the three men come into the courtyard, beating drums and crying out in a strange tongue I cannot understand, and we, with the rest of the strolling crowd, turn to watch them.

They are friars, I think at first, for they wear rough habits of brown wool, and deep hoods drawn forwards over their faces. On the back of his robe each man bears a red woollen cross, and in his hand each one carries a scourge. The sun flashes on the hooked metal barbs embedded in the leather thongs that swirl up and down in the air as the men march forwards, shaking them. At first I think only how pretty they look, like bright ornaments, like the thorns of rose bushes when raindrops hang on them and they glitter.

The three men circle the courtyard, their sung prayers issuing in hoarse cracked voices from thin lips. They limp, and their bare feet are dusty and scarred.

Then they halt, quite near us. Without speaking, they throw back their hoods in a single gesture, and wriggle out of the top part of their habits, so that they stand naked from the waist upwards, their brown robes hanging down over their girdles. For a moment they stay thus, in silence, and they kneel down and raise their flails.

They have their backs to us. We are too close not to see. I hear Dame Alice and Joanna gasp in the same breath as I, and we clutch each other's hands simultaneously. Each of those poor penitents has a back covered in unhealed wounds, the flesh torn and red in layers of pus and suppuration. Patches of dried blood crust around places that are open and raw and still bleeding. As we gape and watch, they begin to whip themselves. Steadily, methodically, the black snakes of the scourges whistling over their shoulders, first to the right and then to the left, as they take up their chant again. Each metal hook bites and grips the edges of wounds, and tears them a little wider, raking across fresh undamaged skin at the same time and ploughing it into channels of blood.

– Come away, my aunt chokes, tugging on our hands: come away, children.

I cannot. I am taken by the harsh music of the flagellants, the song of their whips in the air, the hiss of leather, the rattle of the metal tips clashing together and then descending onto red meat. I believe I can hear the harmony of the black barbs as they drag across bleeding wounds that are open like ecstatic mouths. And the men keep up their singing, their high complaint, whose rhythm orders and measures the pace and fury of their strokes.

I wrest my hands out of the hold of my sister and aunt, and move sideways. I need to see the men's faces. I want to know how much they hurt.

I know death already, of course, and corpses. I hear my mother's shrieks as they try to pull the stuck baby out of her, and I see the sopping red mess she lies in as I am hurried in to say goodbye to her. Her bed is like a butcher's shop, and the dead baby lies on a cushion like a joint of meat waiting to be carried home. Also I have seen animals slaughtered, and beggars rotting in the street, their flesh stinking, and my aunt's husband before he died, with the bone sticking out of his gangrenous leg. I know suffering.

I know suffering as a blow to be resisted, by cursing, by yells. At the most, endured. The chicken pinioned on the chopping block by my aunt's hand, the fish still wriggling in anguish in the basket, my mother arching her back and thrashing on the bed. I understand that for all of them a moment comes when struggle ceases and the spirit seeks only to be released. But this voluptuous abandon to torture is new. These three men bend forwards into their pain, inviting it, supplying it. And so in turn I bend towards them, wanting to understand.

Two of them have their eyes closed, sweat and blood running in white and red rivulets down the grime of their faces. They are sealed off; their ecstasy is private. But the third has his frenzied eyes wide open, and stares at me, and salutes me with them as one who is kin to him. He summons me, his little sister of the precious wounds. Though my sister and aunt snatch me away and bear me home with them, angry and scolding, his message stays with me, inscribed on my flesh in letters of red.

*

My father has been teaching me to read, and in the evening he sends for me as usual. I am his favourite child, being the elder and more closely resembling my dead mother than my sister does. He is a man who greatly loves learning, and at night, when he has shut up the shop at the front of the house, he retires to his private room at the back and is transformed from apothecary into wizard. He calls me his little scholar. Already I know Latin, and some French. Along with new words he feeds me sweetmeats made by my aunt, little balls of paste flavoured with almond and rose-water. Learning is no hardship, for it means time alone with my father, his finger guiding me along the brown loops and curls of the page, his palm offering me my reward. Language tastes of frangipane and peppermint and sugar, and I roll it over my tongue, the words dissolving into me. My aunt mutters that I am lazy and spoilt, and my father laughs and pulls my hair.

At the moment we are reading an encyclopedia listing the properties of precious stones, plants and planets, a work that knots the universe together into harmonious music. Naming is power: the hidden world yields up its secrets when you link the right names in nature together, when you trace the correspondence, taut as a fishing line, between star, herb, season, humour and beast. I see God as a doctor and philosopher, as a teacher like my father. I trust my father, that he will sew up the jagged edges of the morning, wipe away the blood with a dry maxim, cover the torn flesh with the cloak of scholastic truth.

There is a new lesson this evening, with no sweetmeats to follow. Instead I taste bitterness. I swivel around on my stool and stare at the great bed in the corner, and imagine two heads laid on its pillows. I look at the wooden clothes press, and see it full of the new wife's things. I see her fur slippers tumbled on the floor, her cup of spiced wine set next to my father's, her fat arse resting on my stool, in my place, next to him. I see myself outside the door in the dark, pressing my ear to it, hearing their laughter, the disgusting noise of their kisses, the creaking of the bed. Perhaps there will be a new baby, a new bloody mess on the sheets, more screaming. Another death.

My father's hasty words tear strips off my heart, but I keep my back as straight as the flagellants'. Like them, I kneel down.

Like them, I apply lashes of hate to myself.

– I shall never marry, I blurt out: I wish to dedicate my life entirely to God.

My father raises me from my knees and sends me to bed.

– We will speak of this in the morning, he says: after I have talked to your aunt.

Joanna and I discuss the news in whispers, mindful of Dame Alice snoring in the other bed. My sister is not disturbed by our father's intention to remarry. She expects an indulgent stepmother who will give her new clothes and caresses, who will allow her to have a pet dog of her own, who will be different in every possible way from our strict aunt. I despise Joanna for these simple wants, but I keep silence, thinking: she is only twelve years old, after all. My sister wriggles her plump body closer to mine and blows her hot breath into my ear, telling me of the other things she also wants, giggling. A doting husband, a house of her own to order as she pleases, servants to skip to her whims, mornings of lying abed dandling her little dog. The secret delights of the night.

I have seen our dogs engage in their hasty, indifferent coupling. I have seen the pictures of devils on the walls of our church, with female faces painted over their private parts. I have heard our priest describe, many times, the shameful itch, the hot allure of women for men. I am familiar with the half-naked idiot youth who sits at the end of our street and begs from all who pass. Once or twice I see his wrinkled purplish member, ugly and comic, dangling from the rags around his waist. I want to touch it, in case it is as soft as a rotting rose. Once, while I look at it, it rears and swells into an enormous rod, and Mad Jack puts his hands on his hips and smiles at me.

My father. Joseph's flowering rod. In the bloodied bed, with the new wife. I do not know what a woman is supposed to do when a man smiles that particular invitation. Mad Jack stretches out his arms to welcome me, and my father feeds me sweetmeats, and my insides dissolve to wet sugar.

I try to pray. Joanna is fast asleep, her head on my shoulder, and Dame Alice breathes heavily next to us, her mouth open. I cross myself and call on God.

He comes in the shape of the three flagellants. They stand in

110

a row at the end of the bed, their scourges neatly rolled up and tucked under their arms, and they nod a greeting to me.

– Little sister of the precious blood, they whisper: we will teach you the true ecstasy of the flesh, the dance of numbing and forgetfulness, the high song of pain. We will show you the strait and narrow way to perfection, the bliss to which only the pure of heart arrive.

They shake out their scourges in a single beautiful coordinated gesture.

I have already been taught to meditate on the passion, wounds and sacred blood of our Saviour Lord Jesus Christ. I have spent hours in church kneeling under the enormous crucifix, gazing at the thick nails driven through his hands and feet, the gashes torn in the soft flesh. I have learned to enter his suffering, to share it. So it does not seem strange to me that my new brothers show me the way further in.

At first their whips only tickle me. Then they drive me up a red spiral of agony. Only the chosen, they whisper to me: can follow this path, can trust that God is surely at the other end. The lashes sting my flesh and make my feet nimble. But I faint before I reach the top. I wake to find Joanna shaking me and Dame Alice standing by our bed holding a lit taper. Someone is screaming, and I do not at first recognize my own voice.

Two months later my father accompanies me to the Cistercian abbey at Bidewell in Kent. My eyes dry, I strip off my velvet mantle, the gold ring and chain he has given me, my embroidered coif and girdle, my silk purse with silver drawstrings. I pile all these items into my father's arms, asking him to sell them and give the money to the poor. My sister does not need more finery, I assure myself. Better to cover Mad Jack's nakedness. Then I go through the door into the enclosure. I have forgotten to ask for my father's blessing, but I do not look back.

I follow the Mistress of Novices along the cloister as eagerly as my sister will go, when her time comes, to meet her husband. Behind me is colour and glitter, the changeability of weather and affections, the surge of pleasure and pain. Henceforth the Office and the Liturgy will provide me with seasons, will mark off day from night, each hour ordered by the Rule, each minute taken care of by Mother Church, my time divided by her into passages of work and prayer, study and contemplation. I throw myself into my future as though into a bottomless sea. Safety as the waters close over my head and I die to the world, to time, to the flesh.

God plucks me from drowning and baptizes me with the sea of my sorrow. God sets me in this abbey, which is an Ark of Ladies sailing towards salvation.

In the centre of this Ark is our cloister, the place where I most often meet God. He wears a red robe and is borne up by four pairs of fiery red wings. He hovers above the grass of the cloister garth, and I look at him out of the corner of my eye, for I do not dare approach him face to face. He is warmth, and great sweetness inside me, and steady light, and he breathes on all the plants growing in the garden so that they flourish and bloom. Even in wintertime the air of the cloister is fragrant with the scent of balsam and roses, lilies and cedar, jasmine and frankincense.

But when the bell in the chapel tower rings, summoning me back down into time and duty, the gates of paradise close against me and I drop, disconsolate, into God's absence. Hurrying along the cloister, to the chapel or the refectory or the chapter-house, I hear snickering laughter behind me, the flick and click of metal on the tiled floor, and I smell foul air, as though the devil has farted. Then I choke and freeze, while icy invisible hands grip mine or pull at my habit. Sometimes they lay themselves around my ankles so that I am obliged to stand stock-still and rigid, listening to the voices that hiss in my ear and whisper to me to lash myself until the blood comes.

The other Ladies, seeing me suddenly stop rigid and then jerk my body from side to side, think that I flaunt myself as some sort of visionary, that I am rotten with spiritual pride. I am often late for the office in chapel, or for meals, and so I have to perform constant penitences. I dare not confess my trouble lest I am charged with possession by demons, and though I know this to be true, I fear that exorcism will not help me. I am already lost.

All of the Ladies practise mortification of the body. We keep Lent twice a year, and in addition we fast every Friday. We sprinkle vinegar and bitter herbs on our food. In the fresco painted on the wall in the refectory, Our Lord eats supper with

112

his friends, smiling, passing baskets of cherries, flagons of amber wine, dishes of nuts and fine white bread. Our supper is spread below: thin gruel or porridge, hard salty cheese. We wear spiked chains twisted about our arms, and hairshirts, and we scourge ourselves once a week in the privacy of our cells.

I have three male helpers in mine. One brother deftly strips me of my habit and folds it neatly on my bed, then caresses my naked limbs with his cold hand. I like his touch; I shudder with pleasure, waiting for what will come after. The second brother takes me in his arms and hugs me to his breast, holding me so tenderly, making sure I cannot break free. I do not want to. I tremble in his embrace, my head on his shoulder, my face smelling the dirty wool of his habit. Then the third brother lays on the whip.

The pain is my consolation for the time I cannot spend with God. I can tell no one this. But my three brothers know it. They know how to touch me delicately as though with tongues, until all my flesh tingles and cries out for more, more, harder, harder. They know how to turn me round and pinion my arms afresh and tickle my breasts with their thongs, how to send the lash whispering around my private parts and between my legs. I grow to need them holding me down, holding me back, and I plead with them in ashamed and disgusting language that they will go on and hurt me more. Then they do. They hurt me and hurt me, and I sing and sob along with the pain until the tide of pleasure rises in my running blood, in the urine I cannot stop myself from passing, and overwhelms me, and I drop to the cold floor, panting and crying out. Then the three brothers mock me, calling me their vile animal, their little sister of filth and excrement, and I roll and grovel at their feet.

This goes on for five years. God slips away from me. I can no longer rise above my throbbing and tormented body into that high pure place where God flies gaily in the green sweet-smelling garden. I live only in my dreadful body. I punish it, through redoubled fasting and mortification. I become very thin. My monthly bleeding stops. I set exquisite stitches, in gold and silver threads, in a white silk stole our Bishop will wear. Is not this sacrilege? I live in hell, no longer daring to appeal to Our Lady and the saints for help, for have I not betrayed them, and my vows? I cannot expect them to visit me

113

in my house of foul delight. Trying to expiate my longing for my brothers' company, and for that of my fourth brother and lover the whip, I grow sick. And by now I know my brothers' names. Our Lady Abbess has warned us against the blandishments of the heretics spreading their contagion through our country as they arrive from the Low Countries and distribute their message through their disciples and their books. There can be no mercy for a nun convicted of following the Fellowship of the Atonement.

One December, in the season of Advent, my sister Joanna comes to visit me. The trees are leafless and black, the earth rigid with frost, the days short and dreary. It is the long night of the year. Snow falls, and melts to dirty slush, and falls again.

On that particular afternoon I am walking, as usual, in the dark cloister, making my cold legs move me around and around. A cloister is a kind of prayer in stone. I cannot pray; I let the force of the cloister pray me. I stumble along under the vaulted painted roof, looking through the repeating slender columns at the little garden and at the well set in the centre of the grass.

I am awaiting the birth of the Christ Child. I believe he will lighten my darkness, and loosen the grip of winter, and plant me with new green shoots of hope. I hope I believe this. I need him to be born. I need to hold him, the new fire, to the ice in my soul. I need him to melt me, to free me.

The iron handle of the well is very black against the white square of snow that blots out and redefines the little courtyard. Whiteness replaces black. White lines spell out the curves of the opposite side of the cloister, and white wedges and triangles and squares are its jutting roof and the cell windows above it. I need blackness, the darkness in which things germinate and grow. The world is spoken through white, and I need it to be balanced against black, set against black, the one giving a shape to the other. I watch a sparrow hop through the snow to the well, leaving a trail of tiny precise black prints. I am clothed all in white. I want to be both the snow outlining the dark shapes of stone, and the stone that the snow clings to. I want to be both the cloister encircling the garden, and the space thrusting out

114

against the pierced stone walls.

One of the lay sisters, muffled up in a thick mantle and felt boots, stumps towards me, her frosty breath hanging before her in the air. She pulls at my sleeve, and then gestures with both hands, signing to me that I have permission from the Abbess to break enclosure for an hour in order to speak to my sister and her husband, who have travelled out from London to visit me.

Joanna sits by the parlour fire, wrapped in furs. Her cheeks are pink, and her eyes sharp and brown. Her husband, the merchant, who stands behind her chair, looks to be a kindly and prosperous man, but after our brief salutation I have no eyes for him. We Ladies are not supposed to touch people, but I kiss my sister's cold face, and hold her hands in mine, and then drop to my knees in front of her. The warmth of her presence thaws me. I burst into tears. I feel her recoil from my noisy grief, and from my sick, emaciated body, but I cannot stop. I burrow into her lap. Unlike me, she smells so good, of fresh sweat and cold fur and wood-smoke. I snort at her like a pig rooting for truffles, I eat her and drink her in, and I go on sobbing until she pushes me away.

– All this snot and tears will ruin my clothes, she reproves me: I have enough of that already.

I look up, gulping, as the nurse comes out of the shadowy corner and puts a plump white bundle into Joanna's arms, turning back a corner of the silken wrappings so that I can see the tiny face.

I am astonished by my meeting with this child. He is already himself: delicately formed, all his features clearly marked. His dark blue eyes stare gravely at me from under the black tufts of his hair, and his brow wrinkles as he considers me. I do not know what to say to him. I am silent in front of his questioning eyes.

– Go on, Joanna urges me: hold him.

I wrap my sleeves around him, for greater protection from the whistling draughts, and sit back on my heels, looking from my sister to the child and back again. The child's eyes seem to me full of wisdom, and experience. Yet his tiny rosy mouth, opening and closing as he sucks the air, and his little fist darting out from his bindings and waving, make him nothing but small

115

new animal.

– It's a miracle, I breathe.

Joanna bursts out laughing.

– I remember how unpleasant you once considered it, she mocks me: all the business of making babies. You never said a word to me about it. But I knew from the look on your face how you felt.

Her husband looks a little sorry for me, and bends forward to touch Joanna on the arm in reproof.

– Of course we thank Almighty God, he declares: for his goodness in giving us this child.

My sister tosses her head at him. I see how she pleases him, how she has mastered him. I imagine their deep soft bed, its curtains drawn against the cold winter night, and their two bodies riding and tumbling over each other. I understand, suddenly, their kindness to each other, their courtesy, their pleasure. Then the baby vomits a thin stream of milk into my lap, and his nurse snatches him away.

Joanna helps me wipe myself. This establishes some friendship between us, some calm. I settle myself on a stool, and wave her husband into a chair on the other side of the fire. I sit between them, warming myself in their company, and we talk. Master John tells me something of his life as a merchant, his travels to the Low Countries, and what he has seen there. He tells me of the communities of holy women called Beguines whom he has visited in Flanders and Brabant. He interests me particularly by his description of their goodness, their prudence and economy, for I have heard of them only as loose women, as heretics, and he insists instead that they are lovers of God and sisters to each other, bound by no vows, submitting to no rule except that of friendship, and collectively earning a living.

– I wish I could be a Beguine, I blurt out: my life here constrains me too much. It is full of too much pain and hardship.

Joanna and Master John exchange looks.

– Be careful, Master John cautions me: what you say aloud concerning these matters. Many of the Beguines, though not deserving it, are arraigned for heresy, especially when they travel to beg for their alms. They are suspected by many, and suffer for it. You too will come under suspicion if you speak freely of your admiration.

– I will pray for them, I say, sighing: I wish them very well, poor ladies.

– You should pray for yourself a little more, my sister retorts: you look so thin, so ill. What has happened to you? I never thought to find you so pitiably haggard, so wretched. I suppose you have been mortifying yourself with penances. What good does that do? Surely it is far more worthwhile to praise God through a healthy life, with a healthy body. A soul who truly loves God has no need to fear the body's desires. Why have you been tormenting yourself?

Master John's upraised hand checks her. I am so surprised by her blunt words concerning my physical welfare that I do not take in the rest of what she says. Not until I am alone again in my cell when I have time for slow reflection. But now the Office bell is ringing, and I am rising to my feet and hurrying towards the door.

They leave the following morning. While Master John supervises the loading of their horses, Joanna leaves her son in the care of his nurse and insists on coming with me to see the guesthouse garden.

– There is something I must say to you, she says: where no one can hear me. It is better to go outside.

The lay sisters have shovelled the snow off the path the day before. Now it sparkles with a sheen of frost in the pale sunlight, its yellow sand overlaid with silver bits of ice which crunch under our wooden soles. The pleached apple trees trained along it are gnarled plaits of pale green and grey, and I stroke the cold roughness of their trunks as we pass between them. I drink in the clean chilly air, holding it in my mouth like a swallow of the Moselle wine my father used to let me taste from his cup. The brick wall separating us from the Ladies' garden glows red, the moss and lichen in its cracks as bright as turquoise and jade. One of the lay sisters is burning rubbish, the smoke of her fire as thick and sweet as incense in my nostrils. She smiles and nods to us as we pass, and I am filled with shame. I am lacking in charity. So long involved with my private misery, I have not made friends here, have not loved the women I live among. Yet this nun still smiles at me.

117

I have not loved my own sister properly, either. I know it. I understand the reasons for her reserve with me over the past five years, I think, the lack of letters or visits. Her coming to see me now, her soliciting this final interview, means that at long last she has forgiven me. Happily I seat myself next to her on a stone bench set at the end of the path in the shelter of the garden wall.

– Before our father died last year, God rest his soul, Joanna says, crossing herself: he asked me to come and visit you. He had had no news of you for a long time, and he was anxious. I sent you the news of his death by a servant rather than coming myself because I had only recently begun to carry the child and was very sick. I told myself that I preferred to wait until my baby was born and that I would come to see you then so that I could show him to you. But there was another reason that made me delay my visit. I have only come at all because Master John said it was my duty to do so.

I can hardly bear to listen, but I force myself. I am afraid that my sister's words will summon up my three brothers to punish me again as I deserve. It is better to stay quiet, for I can think of nothing to say.

My silence drives Joanna to further anger.

– Of course you were always the one our father favoured. I suppose you thought I neither noticed nor cared. I wanted to learn to read too, but there was no chance of that. You stood always in my light so that I was merely your shadow.

She sits with averted face. I make myself speak.

– Forgive me sister, I say: for all the times I wronged you in the past.

Now her voice is quick and harsh, like a cartwheel jolting over loose stones.

– You think it's so easy to be forgiven, don't you? You think you just have to ask and it comes to you. You holy Lady wrapped in proud purity! When I sent messages telling you of Dame Alice's death and then of our father's, you sent none back. Did you imagine my husband too could not read? Could you not imagine we needed word from you?

She kicks at the gravel at our feet with her fur boot. Furiously, so that the small stones skip in all directions.

– You did not love me, she accuses me: you scorned me. And

118

now you expect me to forgive you. Tell me why I should forgive you after all the times you have neglected me. Even after our mother's death, when I cried myself to sleep every night, you never once tried to comfort me. You sat with our father in his room instead. Why did you never think I might be grieving for our mother as much as you and he? You thought I was too little and too stupid to feel anything. Only you were allowed to have feelings. You left me alone, when I needed you.

Her face still turned away from me, she draws her feet back close together and thrusts her hands more deeply into her fur sleeves. We both sit very still, but the air between us crackles.

Black earth and green grass are closely fastened under transparent ice. A blackbird strikes its beak against the silence of snow, the garden a forge for his silver notes. My sister's words touch my skin, enter me. My mouth is sore with the need to speak true words, not to lie, to acknowledge my sister in the angry place I have driven her to and from which she reproaches me so bitterly. I am trying to make reparation, and I do not know how to do it. I have been stuck in the mud of despair for so long. Joanna's passionate cry tugs me out of it, breaks me open.

– All those years I hurt you and failed you, I say: I am very sorry for. I can hardly tell you how sorry.

– What's done, Joanna mutters: is done.

– Will you forgive me? I ask her: I have punished myself arrogantly and uselessly for my sin rather than try to mend things with you.

I can see the struggle in her face now, as she turns to me and I see that small crying child missing her mother, uncomforted. I have learned the pleasure there can be in not forgiving, in not allowing oneself to be forgiven. In refusing that grace. Have I not inflicted that on myself for the past five years?

– I suppose I do forgive you, my sister murmurs at last.

Her kiss is formal, dry brush of lips. She touches my hand. Pauses, then puts her face close to mine.

– With Master John, she whispers: I have begun a new life. No, not just the married one. A spiritual one, a rebirth. He has converted me to the true faith. I am happier than I have ever been.

I stare at her in shock and unwilling comprehension. She

119

hurries on, telling me what I have already begun to suspect, that she and her husband have secretly become adherents of the Brethren of the Free Spirit, in so far as, being a married couple, they can.

My own sister a heretic. Therefore in danger of death. But she shrugs off my anxious questions. Back straight, eyes gleaming: she is the beautiful one now, the strong sister, the clever one.

– Do not betray us, she says: and do not fear for us.

She gabbles to me of incomprehensible doctrines. How humans can attain a sinless state, in which sensuality is so guided by the soul that the body can be allowed any gratification it likes. How these liberated souls are not subject to ecclesiastical authority, being blessed in and by themselves. How free souls can enjoy heaven on earth. How the carnal act is not a sin, but, on the contrary, a route to God. How the perfect have no need of the Eucharist and the Mass, nor of the Passion of Christ.

– Why are you telling me these things? I ask, full of terror: how can you speak thus in this place dedicated to holiness?

My sister's grip on my wrist tightens. Her eyes flash scorn.

– I am offering you freedom and consolation, she breathes: the happier life you spoke of yesterday. Can't you see?

Her husband calls from the other end of the garden, startling us both. Such a confidence in his voice that he will be listened to. Such assurance that she is here, waiting for him. I am envious.

– Listen to me, Joanna hisses: will you? Before I go I have a present for you.

She fumbles inside her furs and extracts a velvet bag laced with leather which she lays on my lap.

– Don't let anyone see it. It comes from our father's library. Our new mother has sold most of his books. Master John helped her. He kept this one, thinking it safer. I am not able to read it, and so now I want you to have it.

She gets up. I clutch the little bag.

– Our father made his own translation into English of the *Miroir des Simples Ames* of Marguerite de Porête, Joanna says in a voice sharp with excitement: in secret, for his own use, and now for ours. He must have meant to tell us before he died. It is not too late now. He was one of *us. He too.*

– But who is Marguerite? I ask: how do you know her?

– Marguerite was burned alive in Paris thirty years ago, my sister says: in 1310, as a heretic who would not recant. Also she was a Beguine.

Then she is gone, tapping down the path in her wooden-soled boots, to rejoin her husband and her child.

The three flagellant brothers do not visit me again.

I stop using my scourge, and hide it under my bed, along with my hairshirt and my spiked chain. I stop sprinkling bitter herbs on my food, and eat with relish, savouring the taste of bread, of milk, of the pure water from our well. I grow breasts again, and I begin to bleed again every month. I no longer meditate in front of the crucifix. That bloody flesh hanging from the nails disgusts me. I do not need it for my salvation. My own blood is fresh and sweet.

Spring comes. The orchard is thick with pear blossom, the bare trees suddenly flowering, rods dipped in white stars. I ask permission, for the sake of my health, to work outside, with the lay sisters, in the fields and the kitchen garden. I kneel on the earth, smelling it, crumbling it between my fingers, breaking open the moist clods and digging my nails into them. At first my back and legs ache, but this is pleasure not pain. And now, rather than pleading with God to listen to me, I begin to listen to God. So my visions arrive.

In the first vision I find myself in a basilica shaped like one of the beehives in our garden and made of rosy bricks fitted closely together, bricks baked onto a thick rope which coils around and around. Bricks coiling to make a basilica, a beehive.

Columns, sturdy as the bodies of women standing in a circle with joined upraised hands, support the upper gallery. Between them are arches as tender and fine as the place at the back of a knee, the dip in the shoulder, the turn of the neck.

The small church closes around me like a second skin, closes not around empty space but around fullness.

A staircase hidden in the thick outer wall takes me up to the circular gallery. I pace it, around and around. I find God here,

121

God quickening in this kiln of dark pink bricks. Just above my head is the vaulted roof, whose curves repeat, loop, arch away and back again, divide each other, join each other, intersect. Fans of sinew and muscle, balancing of bones, warmth of flesh. Clear limits and edges of stone, but not sharp.

On my right the leaping columns open onto the deep interior space of the church. I can float out into it, fly in it, turn over in it. On my left is another circle of columns bracing the outer wall. In their recesses are empty niches shaped like egg halves, shaped as though a huge thumb has gently pressed itself into the inner rim of a clay pot, decorating it around and around. Pinpricks of light in the centre of each recess let fall lozenges of gold onto the tracery of cracks in the pavement. Darkness except for these tiny diamonds that are the windows.

The little basilica is blown like a bubble in stone, rounded and airy, swelling upwards, suspended, caught. It holds me. I can play in it, roll around in it, pray in it, dance in it, sleep. God is born here. This place enables God to be born: crouches, squats, pushes God out, embraces God. These bricks are woven together to make God's basket, God's Ark.

This church is the woman's body, where God begins.

In the second vision I stand enclosed by a box made of dark blue glass, opaque and shining, a slippery and precarious container, with nothing for my outstretched hands to hold on to. The glass box, and I inside it, hang suspended in a deep shaft, down which we suddenly start to fall at great speed.

The blue glass walls surrounding me become transparent, so that I can see the pictures, incomprehensible and bright, painted on the wall of the shaft. As I drop past them, these pictures run together and blur, forming the image, in white brilliance, of a tall shape. An angel? A human being? The image detaches itself, passes through my blue glass wall, and enters me, mixing its substance with mine. It is my soul.

My soul: a necessary word. My soul: meaning the memory of myself in my beginning. How I became. How two struck and fused, how a seed of life sprouted.

Our great Doctors teach that the woman's body is merely the bed of earth which receives and grows the seed of the man, merely the container for his power. He gives her a baby, they say. But they are wrong. The seeds of new matter spark in the woman's body as well as in the man's. They mix their seeds together. Thus I too began.

My soul is my remembering how at that time what I call I was not I, how I was kin in my being to earth, rocks, sea, trees. How I leaped and grew from being that towards being female, passing through thousands of years of change, living two times. How I might have become a mackerel or a dandelion or a man.

My soul simply holds my memory together, is the knot tying me into the dancing web of creation. Through my body I am part of the universe in its constant becoming and changing and dying and transformation, and my soul is the word that tells me that.

Creation happening. Now. Creation happening over and over again, unceasingly. Seven days and seven nights! I could laugh out loud. A thousand thousand years, and nine months, and a single second, and I am in all of these and I dance.

The soul is born as the body is, down the birth canal. The channel joining heaven and earth. The slippery bridge. The rainbow. The sign of birth, when the waters break and the sun shines in all its radiance, the fire in the sky, the joining of the elements anew as the child is born.

It is the woman who reminds the child of the soul, by giving birth to the child. That struggle of creation. That labour. The new body delivered in its wet shining memory of connection to everything else that has been and will be and is. The dancing.

In the third vision I see Lot's wife looking back. Looking back at what lies behind her, at what she has lost: that great fair city of infancy, the strong mother-city holding the child and keeping her safe.

Lot's wife turns her face away from the present, towards the past. Her feet are stuck. She is too frightened to move. Frightened of change, of newness, of suffering.

Her mother is gone. She weeps, and she beats herself because the mother she would like to beat instead is not there. And her tears, flowing copiously, harden and set, until she has turned into a pillar of salt.

She is alone now. A rock in the desert. Her husband and

123

family, losing patience with her crying, have gone on without her. Dogs sniff and lick at her, and raise their hind legs and piss against her. She leans into the wind, which carves her a face, a body, the semblance of a woman.

Now she can't cry any more. She is dried up and hard. She can't feel.

Yet salt can melt. If the Flood comes again. If water surrounds her and overwhelms her and lets her dissolve in it. Sea water. Salt tears. Swimming strongly on them to a new life.

I am Lot's wife. Learning to mourn.

In the fourth vision a woman whose nightgown is soaked in blood clutches me by the hand, and won't let me go. I struggle to be free of her red embrace which stains my white robes. I turn my face away from her and the stink of the blood streaming down her legs and puddling at her feet.

– Daughter, she reproaches me: don't you know me?

Holding her at arm's length, I look at her.

– Mother, I cry out: let me go. I never wanted to be like you!

She drops my hand and pulls her tangled hair forward to hide her eyes. I suppose she is crying, but I'm already moving away from her. I must not look back.

Her voice follows me.

– I am Lady Wisdom. Who else should I be? You have spent your whole life searching for me, and yet I was close by you all the time.

Aghast, I turn round, ready to run back towards her and to kneel at her feet. Too late. She has disappeared.

I have no more visions. I should have burned Marguerite's book, instead of keeping it in my cell where it could be found, and produced in evidence against me. I did not trust Marguerite's words enough, that they would stay in my heart if I let the parchment they were written on go from me into the fire. I could not bring myself to burn her book. Any book.

Marguerite has gone through the fire before me. I have this one night left to me before I find out whether I am to follow her there. I want to use this night for prayer, but I cannot. I have no time. It has been more important to me to write this account of my history. I have bribed the nephew of one of the lay sisters

124

with the promise of a rich reward from Master John if he can get this writing safely out of the convent and into my sister's hands. I want her and her husband to know my thoughts. I want their child to know. I want my life, with all its errors, to have been of some use. Perhaps its use is simply that now I have earned death, and am ready to die. I pray that my words will reach the ones I love even if I have to die. I pray that my life has not been one long mistake.

I wish I had been able to leave here, to spend time with my sister talking; to find those other sisters, the Beguines. It is too late now.

I am a stranger in this world. I am an exile from heaven, beating on its closed doors.

20 The Re-Vision Sibyl sprawls in the Ark's kitchen, finishing a late solitary breakfast. A sit-down affair, leisurely, no Kitty to get ready and rush to school.

The kitchen is the sort that the heroine in one of her stories might choose. A slightly romanticized version of her grandmother's kitchen in France. The table, spread with a yellow oilcloth stencilled with wreaths of red and pink and white flowers framed in dark blue, bears a double-decker tin coffee pot marbled in pale green, a chipped white coffee bowl banded in navy and decorated with stylized clumps of blackcurrants, a basket of glossy croissants, a gold-flecked china dish full of apricot jam, and a red and white checked napkin. No plate. Crumbs on the cloth, a cat sidling at her ankles, a tin pitcher of milk.

Above her, the smoke-blackened ceiling, and high shelves bearing iron cooking pots, this year's supply of jams, the brass pans of the heavy kitchen scales, their golden weights marching alongside. Lower down, the row of china canisters, white glaze stamped with blue squares, bearing flour, spices, tea, coffee; and the racks of metal ladles and whisks. A tiny basket, shaped like a holy water stoup, holding boxes of matches, hangs above the gas stove. Frilled muslin curtains at the windows, floor tiled in stiff arabesques of yellow and blue. Clutch of brooms in a corner, tower of aluminium buckets, boxes of string, old jam jars and carpentry tools cluttering the little tin table near the furnace and the ancient washing machine.

The Re-Vision Sibyl dawdles her spoon in her bowl. Swirls of milk scum, coffee dregs. She could happily stay here all morning rather than getting down to some writing, feasting her eyes on the carelessly exquisite still life on the dresser of those onions tumbled into a wide shallow basket, brilliant brown skins nestled against tissue paper of a thrilling indigo, the creases glistening and darkly blue, and, catching the light from the window, transparent and rich as stained glass.

Language is as changeable and delicious as food, coming from outside her to inside. Many times as a child she puzzles over this, trying to discover why certain sounds, certain words, fascinate her, and why she wants to make them part of herself. *Carpet*, for instance. How, why, does the sound manage to convey the meaning? No other sound, she is convinced, could get its essence across so well. Then, in French lessons at school, she learns the word *tapis*, which carries an equally mysterious weight of truth (the close-cropped pile that, brushed the wrong way, sets her teeth on edge, the oblong shape, the geometric pattern of faded scarlet and blue), and becomes confused. She discovers the opposite: that words dissolve into absurdity if she repeats their sound over and over again, their shape and colour detached from their context of meaning. *Biscuit*. She chants it, sings it, looks at it, and the precise meaning crumbles, a blur of yellow, into incoherence, and she's bitten, eaten the word; and her body, her self, is as fluid as carpet, biscuit, meaning as little, as much.

Playfulness vanishes during years of English lessons in primary school. Write a poem, the pupils are urged: about spring, about autumn, about Christmas. Sharp, eager to please, she discovers that the poem is a gift to the teacher, a gift to the mother. Like the sampler produced in sewing classes, the bean sprouted in biology lessons. It's meant to be pretty, to confirm her as the good loving daughter, and she's encouraged to decorate the borders of her words with little pictures of ladies or holly leaves or snowmen. She conjugates the verbs of her pleasing: crazes for collecting miniature teddy bears, ornamental soaps, glass jewels in matchboxes; desklid decorated with pictures of pink ballerinas, kittens, puppies; poems about roses, that rhyme, in regular rhythm. It all comes so easily. The knowledge she had before about words slips away under an avalanche of pink niceness. She is grateful, veiling herself, during the march up to puberty, with signs of a pleasing femininity (pleasing others); veiling her fears, the boy in herself, with images of cute curly-maned ponies.

127

Blank years until she is fifteen, when a heaven-sent English mistress (a dyke – she knows that even when she has no words except *spinster*, *eccentric*, *desirable*, *fiery*, *demanding*) rescues her with poetry. Poetry snatches her out of the banalities and deprivation of her everyday speech based on self-repression and polite dishonesty. The poetry of Donne and Hopkins (no women – she's never heard of a woman poet) sings to her, wakes her up, makes her grasp that she could *live* if she could ever invent a language to speak her like this. She could spend the rest of her life searching for words.

She starts to write stories and poems, in secret, trying to recapture the lost world of her childhood in France. Is it just the sound of the French language, or particular words spoken in it, she's never sure, that catches at her heart, that transports her to a place that is simultaneously a state of mind? A street in Toulouse, early morning, cobbles under the plane trees swept clean by rain overnight, now speckled with sun chasing shadows, the green leaves blowing, the rosy church washed by light, cool wind on her neck and warmth on her face ... No, that's wrong, those words aren't quite it ...

Is it that the French language summons up a particular relationship between, say, *sun* and *stone*? Is it that the words spoken in the French language reassemble that particular beloved landscape of place, of the heart (*France* meaning *mother*) and fill her with consoling joy for its loss? Certain words give her back the mountains, cold bony austere, give her back herself measured by the wind against their slope, their shape. No, that won't do either ...

Simply by chanting certain words to herself, or by coming across others unexpectedly in a book, she can re-evoke the sensation of *being-in-France*, *belonging-with-mother*, and that conjunction of language/place ravishes her with pleasure yet as though she's dying, a shivering all over and then orgasm felt in the throat, fountain of sweetness overflowing.

Leaving her mother in order to love her husband (no of course it's not that simple) she abandons that language, that usage, picks a way out: stay inarticulate about desires and feelings that don't fit the romance of marriage she's dreamed, that she talks her way into; sweep gritty rebellion into a diary dustpan; write stories of a galloping naturalism that are clear-cut about *he* and *she*, *he-and-she*, yet hide the longed-for body of the mother under Regency buckskin breeches and caped greatcoat; endure her husband's gentle jeers at what she writes; pick up a romance to read and see *him* become the baby, furious at her lack of attention; forget how to speak French.

She goes on making her childish gifts of pretty words, which upset nobody and which cloak her conflicts just as they did when she was a little girl, which are despised just as the collecting crazes and reading habits of little girls are despised even as they are encouraged as suitable. And she makes her gifts of food, which are necessary; soluble art.

If she is a good wife and mother then she is like her own beloved mother; feminine, a real woman; and will be loved by her.

She cherishes the tools of her trade, picked up at junk stalls in the market, keeping them clean, polished, sharp: the wood and bristle basting brush; the tiny nutmeg grater; her 1930s apple corer and potato peeler with their fine red wood handles; her collection of bizarre egg whisks all spirals and loops; the metal lemon squeezer; the plywood flour sifter with its fine mesh. It is her trousseau. Her mother adds to it, giving her treasures from the old home in France; blue and white lace-edged napkins she hemmed herself; heavy teacloths with a thick red stripe down the middle; a damask tablecloth. Her mother loves to give to others, to fulfil their needs; her mother practises the generous, unselfish arts, cooking and sewing for others. Oh the pleasure of this receiving; of this being given to; of being loved by her. Do nothing to break the beautiful cords of this love, this definition of yourself; for without it you are outcast, dying, monster, bad daughter. Done for.

When she is first married, she scorns machines in the kitchen, convenience foods: no, she will do it all herself, like her grandmother and mother did, and enjoy.

Then she discovers she can't cook well for people she doesn't know as friends, doesn't join in inviting. Jim's business associates, at first feasted on home-made puff pastry and pâtés and pasta, are now fed grim gourmet meals concocted from packets and tins. And when Kitty arrives, she buys a liquidizer for those endless purées of spinach and carrots. She buys chocolate biscuits as bribes, fish fingers, crisps, instant caramel whips, takeaway hamburgers and chips. The food Kitty likes.

She starts to revise her opinions as she starts to revise her writing. Her precious kitchen tools lie in the drawer, blunted and dulled. The kitchen table is littered with papers and typewriter ribbons. She worries about white sugar, adjectives, carcinogenic additives, tenses, cholesterol, paragraphing. But Kitty seems to be thriving on the new diet, even if Jim starts to grumble.

She starts to avoid butchers' shops, those white-tiled laboratories of death: stink of blood, sodden sawdust clotted with bits of skin and gristle, racks of cruel hooks from which dangle headless rabbits and skinny pink and yellow chickens strung up by the feet, whack of knives onto bone, onto raw flesh, sloppy piles of purple liver, dripping red hands fumbling for change in the till, dishes of tripe like white knitting, stained aprons, trays of pink trotters, glistening kidneys, tiny trussed quail, chunks of dead lamb marbled with thick fat. And oh those terrible women peering suspiciously at the corpses, picking them over, inspecting the tender morsels they will carry home and cook and eat, swallowing death: she rejects them too.

Now she spends her time in stationers' shops, gorging her eyes on sheets of marbled and hand-blocked paper, notebooks bound in satin and silvery plastic, silky purple carbons, fresh rubbers, thick-snouted felt-tips, black-eyed pencils. The white pages open under her gaze, inviting: write on us. She comes home with armfuls of A4 pads, pocket-sized notebooks, gold-beaked fountain pens. She deprives her daughter of sweets and gives her cards of coloured stencils instead. She cuts down on Jim's beer and buys him rainbow stacks of blotting paper.

Her neglected marriage starts to break down. Jim wants to lie with a woman between ironed cotton sheets not ruled paper ones. He wants a woman with powder not ink on her nose. He wants a woman who looks at him more often than she looks at a book. Who can blame him? She almost breaks down too, discovering her old desires now flourishing openly in the notes she scribbles in the bath, on the bus. Terror, and guilty joy. Will her mother still love her once she reads what she writes?

Poetry breaks back into her life, poetry written by women this time, poetry, written over the centuries, that acknowledges her submerged experience, keeps her awake at night, sends a fizz down her spine.

She has taken a woman lover and cannot write romances any more, cannot write a lesbian romance either much as she would like to. That struggle and soar and rock of body against body, mind against mind, demands less smoothness, dangles loose ends of words all over the place. She does not know how or what to do.

She stares at the onion-enfolding radiant dark blue tissue paper, and searches for words, new words, to twist the paper into the wick of a rocket and shoot her, firework scared of exploding, into the night skies high above that street in Toulouse.

21   During my librarianship training I became aware of the Woman Problem.

Leafing through the volumes of the subject index in the Reading Room, I discover, as Virginia Woolf did long before me, the hundreds of entries referring to books on Woman, most of them written by men. There are no entries for Man, which puzzles me until I think about it.

The following year, at library school, I study classification theory. The Dewey system, used in all the public libraries in Britain, places Woman in a sub-section of Sociology along with Lunatics and Gypsies. (Wanderers.) Our lecturers encourage us to criticize the rigidly hierarchical pyramidal model of knowledge favoured by Dewey (he would have approved of Origen as an Arkitect, I'm sure), to prefer the modern flexible systems based on computer programme theory which allow you to link one aspect of a subject with any other in crystalline fashion.

For my special project I design a classification system that puts Woman at its centre and allows her to relate to anything under the sun.

Here on the Ark, in my Arkive, I can connect I *want* with innumerable other words.

– But if you have a child, Noah warns me: you'll see it suffering, and be powerless to prevent it. How will you bear that? Why bring a child into a world of suffering and pain?

I search the riddle book.

Life. Sentence. Life-sentence?

132

22 We sail on, towards the next island. I'm not much of a navigator: I steer by intuition; desire my compass North, true North; and dreams my maps.

The harbour opens neatly around us, swallows us in with a single gulp, closes behind us in a belch of waves. I leave the Ark moored there, the Gaffer and the sibyls its sleepy guardians preferring shut-eye to this night excursion, and walk inland, towards the great capital.

Darkness surrounds me, a glimmer of lit boulevards ahead. This city at night is the colour of dried blood. Smell of charcoal, and pines. Whisper of my rubber soles over paved roads. The air is smoky and damp as I go down tunnels of blackness, dark green weeds of trees woven over my head. The suburbs are dull yellow and black, neon lights reflected on pavements of amber satin. I slide in just before dawn, huddle on a stone bench in the centre of the hushed city, wait for the light to irradiate the streets, for their massed buildings to take shape around me. I pick up the tattered pamphlet lying just beside me on the pink granite of my seat, and open it. This is how I practise Italian: conjugating all the verbs meaning: to produce pain.

A scream is abroad in our streets. Our city is haunted by a continuous ravaging scream, dragged out of the mouth by a sharp thin quickly coiling corkscrew of pain.

Torture: the refined systematic politically approved application of pain to the body of a man or a woman or a child. Increased reliance by the State on the extraction of a statement or a confession of guilt from the accused means increased reliance on torture in the prisons of East and West. Everybody's doing it doing it doing it the expert stamp grind hop of the

133

foxtrot of pain, yes even the smug democracies. Read all about it. Listen to the scream. Bear witness. The flesh bears witness. The cracked open mouth screams *no* while the State brands its lies on the tender body and calls this truth, calls this confession. The truth of the body uttered by poets in their struggled-for words counts for nothing here in the strip-lit hygienic cell where the police doctor stands by to monitor the pain inflicted on the body being oh so delicately torn and twisted into a rhetoric of lies. I have not had to bear this pain myself. I hear the screams of my sisters and brothers who do. They will cry so, when the torturer takes them in his arms, when the second torturer comes with his quick instruments, and Death strolls past, a glossy catalogue of sadism in his hands and a carnation in his buttonhole.

I could be one of his victims, or one of his pupils. I could be a torturer too. A woman's place is in the home. I could saw off my daughter's clitoris with a razor, my friends holding her down while she screams. To cleanse her, to rid her of that horrid little flap of excess flesh, to make her pure, to make her grateful enough to do it herself in her turn to her own daughter when the time comes. I could punish her just with words: tell her she's *nothing*, with *nothing* down there. I could, very carefully, burn her legs with glowing cigarettes, to teach her not to cry all night, not to soil herself, to be obedient when I tell her to stop crying wanting wanting wanting. I could shut her away in a drawer for the night, her mouth clogged with cotton wool so that I can't hear her choking screams. I could tie her to the bed, naughty chicken, to poke and scratch amongst her excrement. I could bind her dead body in clean white bandages, small stinking mummy, and prop her in the armchair opposite mine, perfectly behaved doll watching telly with me and no longer disrupting my nights with her crying, her intolerable wanting I can't satisfy. For who will satisfy *my* crying, *my* yearning, *my* wanting? Better to cut it out, carve it out, burn it out, batter it out. I am human; and so I can do all of these things.

I can't control the scream. I can't stop it. It withers the vines on the hillsides outside the city, so that the grape harvest is destroyed. It shrivels and blackens the olive trees in the orchards as though with frost, so that the fruit can't mature. Pregnant women miscarry, hearing the scream, while others become infertile. All the young men have lost heart, and have run away into the mountains to hide.

We don't scream back at the scream. Possessed by its echo, we have fallen silent. We can't love: we are dumb. We hide ourselves inside our homes, tidying ourselves away from the knowledge of torture and pain, and yet we cannot, however hard we try, avoid the scream.

I spend the rest of the day exploring the city. Weeds choke the public gardens. Grass grows thickly in the cracks between paving stones. The fountains are dry. A dead horse, covered in black flies, sprawls outside the State Museum.

In the late afternoon I come to a large piazza surrounded by dying palm trees. The crumbling rose and orange stucco fronts of its buildings are washed in light. I climb the rippling stone waterfall of a magnificent decaying staircase, and stand in front of the State Palace. The huge doors are open. I pass through the marble hall, honey-coloured and dim, braced by springing columns, and go through another pair of double doors and so out onto the wide terrace, set with two crouching stone lions. The stone wings of the palace open out on either side of me, long and graceful; there in front of me, stretching away like corresponding wings, are the gardens.

The neglect here is not so obvious, as though the State rulers were the last to succumb to apathy and fear. Their army of gardeners can have laid down their rakes and spades only recently: the weeds are just a pale fuzz, like a newborn baby's hair.

Directly ahead of me, beyond a gravel walk, is a huge patterned oblong of grass and earth cut by narrow paths into privet-walled boxes, the low clipped hedges twisted and curled into complicated bows and knots of dark green ribbon. To my left is a long row of tall cypresses, their inky plumes nodding and swaying against the brilliant blue of the sky. A high privet hedge runs behind them, a series of archways cut in its green thickness giving glimpses of long green corridors, the middle one lined with orange trees, a tiny white stone nymph dancing at the far end. To my right, a forest of greenery is separated by another walk of orange trees. Through this planned wilderness broad green paths pull the eye onwards towards statues set at

135

the junction of green alleys, towards a small temple crowning a moss-covered flight of steps launching steeply upwards between green walls that rustle and hold green shadows and green light.

There is no one about. The gardens are completely deserted. I walk forwards, into them.

The air is golden now, going from warm towards chill, and it smells of oranges and flowers and smoke. I go down the broad shallow steps from the terrace, and plunge through a green doorway on my left.

The walls of the privet avenue rear high above my head, so thick that I can't see through them. Marble benches are placed along it at intervals, their curved feet deep in glossy acanthus leaves. I turn, and walk, and turn corners, and walk, and am soon lost in this labyrinth of green privet rooms opening off the branching green corridors. Each garden room is a green square space, overgrown with tangling plants. Some are waist-high in brambles, some contain flowering thickets draped over trellises, some are studded with lumps of broken columns, all are carpeted with lush green grass.

The light is a deep gold now, the sun sinking lower and its radiance flooding the sky, dissolving its blue. The privet walls throw long sharp shadows, and the green darkness between them is cold and deep. A wind swishes the tops of the cypresses. I begin to shiver. I need to find the way out. I halt, uncertain which way to go, then plunge through the nearest opening.

A shock. The dead are alive, and dancing.

Facing me, at the far end of the enclosure, are white bodies glimmering against the dark green fence at their backs. Ghosts, summoned up by twilight. Half-naked ghosts, draped in fluttering white robes.

There are no birds singing. The scream I hear comes from my own mouth. The long grass smells sweet, like fresh peas, and is chilly on my ankles. I walk slowly forwards.

The group of marble statues is solid and white. Here is a nymph, her dress half torn off, her arms jerking helplessly, her mouth open in a soundless yell, being carried off by a burly male god. Here are her mother and friends mourning and gesticulating, running alongside amidst a welter of stags and dogs.

136

A sound behind me turns the back of my neck to ice. I spin round. Dark silhouette, faceless, in the privet doorway, the last gold streaks of the sun outlining his head and shoulders. My guts soften with fear.

Then his hand goes up in a greeting. I see Death there, leaning against the green wall, watching me.

23 Back on board the Ark, I tell the others what I've seen. We eat supper. I'm as hungry as usual. The food doesn't choke me, though perhaps it should. The Babble-On Sibyl has cooked *carciofi alla Giudea*, artichokes deep-fried in olive oil, crisp and golden as sunflowers.

– The sadist as gourmet? I say: take one brown or pink or black body, grill well over charcoal until the flesh blackens and peels off easily in long strips. Rub salt well in the wounds. Beat out flat with a wooden steak-hammer and lard with live electrodes. Truss well, then plunge head-down into boiling urine or oil. Garnish with gouged-out eyes and severed genitalia. Torn-off breasts may be served on a separate plate. Or cure in the sun. Tie to a stake. Smear with honey, then sprinkle with hungry live ants. Don't carrots feel pain when you pull them up? Where are you going to stop? my aunt used to say to me: the trouble with you is, you read too many books. I am Mrs Noah, and I want to be an Ark for souls. But as yet I don't dare.

– I am afraid of pain, says the Forsaken Sibyl: I am afraid of not bearing it, and afraid also of bearing it. First of all books made me cry. I cried not for my own life but for that of others. I read books in order to discover the world. I cried at what I found there. I cried when I finished a book, because it was sad, and because I had finished it, because it would never represent the unknown again. I cried when I had read all the books in my house, all the books in my school, all the books in the children's library. I joined the adult library. I wore my first pair of high-heeled shoes, winkle-pickers. I used my parents' tickets as well as my own, and carried home a basket of twenty new books. My new shoes rubbed my heels raw, pinched my toes. I refused to

138

take them off and walk home barefoot. Blisters formed and burst and bled, and the shoes rubbed up and down on the bleeding flesh. I reached home and did not cry. I discovered how much pain I could bear. I read non-stop all weekend lying on the sofa, my feet bound up with Elastoplast. Whenever my mother found me crying over a book she snatched it away. Run out into the sunshine and play with your friends.

– Most of my friends are mothers now, says the Babble-On Sibyl: with two or three young children. At college we sat up half the night talking about the books we read. Now my friends are walled in by children, tiny hands plucking at skirts. So we talk to the children or about the children. Our conversation is broken. My mother once told me: what women talk about is so boring, I prefer the conversation of men. See a mother at a party, her eyes anxiously on her children: will they break something or make a mess or be sick? Who'd choose to talk to *her*? Mothers are not available. Who mothers the mothers? If I go and baby-sit to give my friend some free time for herself, then I don't see her. How can mothers make time for women who are not? How does the friendship survive?

– The voice of the angry daughter, says the Correct Sibyl: is the only one heard in our land. What of the mother? The woman who sees her childless women friends draw back in distaste from her hands that know piss, shit, vomit, milk, blood? The woman whose women friends give her rendezvous in wine bars three miles away when she has no baby-sitter and no transport? The exhaustion. The not being understood. The rage. My mother made friends with other mothers. My mother dumped me in a carrycot and took me to Africa. My mother strapped me on the back of her bike and wheeled up the hill to Gran's. My mother plonked me in a box behind the counter while she served customers, and I played sailors. My mother brought my baby brother to Brownies: he sat on the toadstool in the middle of the fairy ring while my mother organized us hefty little girls to dance around him with our pennants; kelpies, gnomes, pixies, sprites. My mother was a great inventor. My mother doesn't believe in feeling sorry for herself.

– I don't like my children much at the moment, says the Deftly Sibyl: this makes me uncomfortable. Also I do not like

139

deodorants, sweet white wine, milk in coffee, word processors, biros, women who smile too much, hot weather, crimplene, church services, men who talk too much, chocolate cake, Wagner's music, fleas, gladioli, sleeping less than eight hours, Walter Scott's novels, single beds, nylon sheets, soap operas, reviewers, other people's dirty kitchens, people who send me unsolicited manuscripts for comment, string vests, cocktail parties, telephones, stripped pine, plastic cups, piped music in public, shopping malls, central heating, politicians, smokers carriages, cocoa, poodles, blue eye shadow.

– I used to hang onto words like hooks, says the Re-Vision Sibyl: other people's words. I was cloth cap, torn mackintosh. I was classified: a nag, shrill, strident, hysterical. I still hang myself onto hooks: I must control myself, not get drunk, not spill out my needs and desires as mess on the floor, not laugh too loud, not cry out too high, not make too many demands or be impatient. If I begin again. To choose words. In the mini-cab, sharing a lift home, after the party, with Maria. Towards our separate flats a mile apart. The radio sings, it's 3 am, net lace curtains at the back window frame a jointed model of an Alsatian dog in plush, head nodding. Scent of air freshener. Shadows and light from the streetlamps flickering over us. This is the moment, but we don't know it, you never know it, ever, at the time, only afterwards when you select it, when you're lying with your face buried in her breasts, when you think oh yes, that was it, when I suddenly realized how things were between us, how they might be, and the moment's gone, the one which changes present into future, you're not there any more, you're looking back seeing the cab speed away up the dark street, looking at her face and words stuttering out, you've already entered what will be.

– I'll never understand it, sighs the Gaffer: women loving other women. How can you love someone who is the same as yourself? Sexual *difference* is what excites *me*. Beauty: everything that I'm not. Nor do I fancy a cock up my arse, no thanks very much. I like women, you know; I always have done. I've never considered them inferior. If anything, women are *superior*. Their powers of endurance! Just look at the women characters in my novel. What puzzles me is your attitude. If, as a reader or a critic, I deny sexual difference in writers, then you

140

complain I'm treating women as pseudo-men and using a false concept of neutrality to disguise my contempt for women's work. But if I notice sexual difference and applaud women writers for their feminine style, then you assert I'm being patronizing and pushing you into a ghetto. I can't win! You're a contradictory lot, you know. You should try to be more reasonable.

– For you, *feminine* doesn't just mean different, the Forsaken Sibyl informs him: it means worse. That's why it can be a double-edged compliment. I should like to re-invent *feminine* so that it simply meant: pertaining to a woman. Then it could mean whatever the life of a particular woman made it mean. And we could keep it as a word we could use without feeling so ambivalent.

– Impossible, declares the Correct Sibyl: given the structure of language and of the unconscious. Far better to drop it.

– The *history* of women's lives, the Re-Vision Sibyl says to the Gaffer: the lives that they actually lead – that history tends to be different from men's. That's what *feminine* means to me.

– So what would a mother's history be? I ask the others: can one of you tell us a story about a mother?

24   Sending God's blessing and mine to you, my most cherished daughter whom I shall never see again, unless by God's grace the Queen's heart be softened, which is a cause I think hopeless, I write you this letter, which I have asked shall be delivered to you once you are of an age not solely to read but also to comprehend it, should you survive, by God's grace, the years of your childhood, as I pray, tonight, you may survive this present time of trouble and terror. I have charged those who will have care of you that you be taught your letters. I have sent money for that. I have said goodbye to you already, my beloved first-born, though I doubt you will remember it. Now I grant myself the indulgence of addressing you one last time.

I need to write to you more for my own sake, perhaps, than for yours. Yet I would not have you ignorant of your mother, of what made her, as she swore she would never do, send you far from her. Others will tell you, perhaps, false stories of your beginnings, of me. I pray you to forgive me if I set down my truth of it for you to read. You are my judge. When you know the story of my life, and of the first years of yours, which I shall try to record as honestly as I can, I pray you will not condemn me, but will find it in your heart to forgive your mother's weakness, and to pity her present wretchedness.

I am sending the miniature portrait in the basket I have packed for your journey to France. Do you still have it? Take it out. Look at it. I remember it well enough. Myself as I was then. The age you are now.

Two young women, dressed exactly alike. Black farthingales faced with dark pink velvet, black-sleeved gowns laced on with

142

gold cords and slashed to reveal the white lawn undersleeves, black caps, white lace collars and cuffs. Hair parted in the middle and pulled back. Long almond-shaped eyes, long noses. The eyelids lowered, half-smiles playing over the lips. Their hands tightly clasped in each other's, white skin of the long fingers set against the billowing black skirts.

The painter has lied, of course, in order to follow his patrons' whim, to flatter my parents. In fact we are not identical. Only one of us is beautiful. I'm the ugly one.

Twin sisters. Margaret and myself.

I am sitting in a garden, on the grass, with a privet hedge behind me and a long flowerbed beside me filled with lupins, hollyhocks, sweet williams, gillyflowers and roses, all mixed up in a pleasing profusion of bloom. I watch the bees dive in and out of the bright petals; their scent makes me a little sick. The orchard screens us from my father's house, and the oak trees, behind the hedge, marking the beginning of the farmlands, are a further shelter. Hard green acorns rattle occasionally into my lap, and I raise my hand to sweep them away from Margaret's face.

She lies there with me, her head on my blue stuff knees and her feet tucked up under her skirts. She wears blue too, with a black bodice just like mine, and her cap is tumbled on the grass beside her. Her hair is loose: it flows over my hands as I dip them in it, and has acorns and leaves caught in it, and smells of sun and of the rosemary wash she rinses it with. Her eyes are closed, the lashes a pale fur, and her cheek is warm to my touch.

Around us the bees swerve and drone, parting the flowers and gulping their nectar. Flies from the cows grazing in the neighbouring field circle our heads, buzzing noisily, and I flap them away. Ants creep over our ankles, nipping our stockings. Summer is ending: the edges of the oak leaves are rusty brown, and some are already fallen on the grass like tiny wrinkled books. I peer at them; then I see poems, made of stems and pebbles and dry petals. When Margaret wakes up, I will repeat them to her in the private language we share for telling each other stories and whispering secrets at table or in bed.

Margaret moves her head in my lap, opens her eyes, smiles

143

at me.

– Sister, she says: I'll make a daisy chain for you to wear at your wedding, and you make me one to wear at mine.

– Never, I cry out: never.

When we are little, I talk before she does, and have to translate her grunts and cries to our nurse. She walks before I do: when I rise, plump and wobbling, to a standing position, she pushes me over and laughs.

We sleep in the same bed, in the little room we share with our nurse behind the parlour. A dark, comfortable place like a shelf in a cupboard, with a sliding wooden door. Behind this, we curl in each other's arms on our feather bed, the tattered damask coverlet pulled up to our chins. In the morning I smell her sour breath on my face as she must smell mine. She clings to her bolster when it is time to get up, fingering the treasures she has hidden underneath it after yesterday's play outside, pretending to be asleep, her eyes tightly closed. It is our game, to see how long she can resist my rousing her with tickles and caresses. Sometimes I lose my temper, the game having turned into a task, and pinch her soft flesh through her nightgown. Then she kicks me, or cries. To punish me, she refuses to speak to me for an entire day, while I trail behind her like a whipped dog, blubbing.

As she knows how to make me suffer, so she also knows how to give me delight. Sometimes, at night, her thin fingers trace my collarbone and spine, caress my back with long slow strokes that soothe me into a grave pleasure. There are the two of us in the same bed, a fact simple as breathing, as necessary. I try to fit myself into the dent made by Margaret's body, curve myself into her part of the feather mattress, imagine I am she. Then she rolls back and repossesses the dip she has made, and I sniff at her, lick her, trace with my tongue the outline of her nose, her ear. Sometimes I want to eat her. Sometimes I dandle her like a baby. Always she is there for me.

Sometimes I wonder: how do my parents know which of us is which? Suppose that soon after birth we were turned about, in those first days before we received names? Suppose that I really am Margaret and she me? Suppose our parents were confused, right at the beginning?

144

Our father once told us: when you were born we were all so grieved that your mother had missed her mark, we prayed that at her next shot she might hit it.

I do not mind that I am not the male child they wanted, for I have Margaret. I do not mind my parents' indifference and coldness to us when we were small. I understand that too much affection cannot be wasted on children who may not thrive: it would hurt too much. Three of my mother's children have died in infancy. Can I blame her that she holds us at arm's length, watches our growth with a harsh, suspicious eye? I do not look to her for love. I am far luckier than most, for I have Margaret. We have not been sent away to school, like so many. We have not been separated. My two younger brothers, aged eight and seven, will soon leave home to begin their education, fostered out in my uncle's house in London. My mother has chosen to keep Margaret and me with her, to train us at home. We are fortunate. We have each other.

Light flashes on the blades of our knives. Nurse stands at one end of the table, scraping at the loaf of sugar. Margaret and I lean opposite, our sleeves pinned back, chopping up damsons, quinces, plums. We lick the juice of the fruit, sticky and red, off our fingers, then ladle the sweet pulp into the black iron pot hung over the fire. Belch and seethe. I poke at it with a long wooden spoon, skim off the fresh pink scum which smells of cloves and ginger. The mixture boils and boils. Our faces red and wet in its steam. Then we test it, dropping a little into a basin of water to see whether it will set. Golden strands of the sun imprisoned in a pewter dish. I cleaned that dish yesterday, scouring it well with sand. Our lady mother ordered it, a punishment to teach me humility. There is little in me this morning. I would rather be outside, lying in the long grass in the orchard, watching the wild dash of the April clouds across the sun, the shaking of the white blossom on the pear trees as the wind throws itself on the garden and the light breaks through the canopy of branches. My mother is famous for her marmalade. I am famous for my laziness.

After dinner, we bend to our sewing in the small back parlour. Little light finds its way into this low-ceilinged recess. We drag our stools over to the window, which we have set open

145

for a glimpse of blue. Cold air rinses our necks. These dark walls hung with threadbare tapestry repel me. I'd rather be surrounded by the trunks of trees. I've dusted the oak chest and brushed the stiff Turkey carpet that drapes it. I've washed the precious bowl of Venetian glass in the cupboard. Now my needle pricks in and out of linen, grubby from its daily mauling in my fingers. Margaret, opposite me, sighs in a private dream. I launch myself through the window, fly out to go riding with my brothers. My fingers canter over glazed linen fields. A glossy hedge, the raised border, to leap. The silver stab. The red line pulling through. Each stitch is a beagle with a bloody mouth. Baying. I kill the bedsheet I am supposed to be hemming. Over and over again I pierce it. Blood springs up, a row of dead birds, a string of scarlet beads. So pretty.

The birch whistles over my shoulders, not gently.

– God help me, my mother laments: how will you ever find a good husband when you resist all my efforts to teach you seemly ways? I'll beat God-fearing manners into you yet, you foolish gentlewoman.

One last whack on my shuddering neck, then she throws the birch from her, as though disgusted with it. Which I do not think she can be since she applies it so often to me.

I perform my part, as she performs hers. I understand that it is necessary. She has taught me that much. I stay kneeling on the cold flags which bruise my knees, and join my hands, keep my back straight. The needle and the birch, between them, lead me to decorum. Those harsh sisters.

– Dear madam, I growl between clenched teeth: most humbly I beg you to forgive me.

Then she's gone, her skirts rustling towards the door, a chill draught wheedling in as she opens it and passes through it. Bitterness sticks in my throat like a sour nut.

Margaret is the older of us two by half an hour. Now she is mother for me, kissing me, caressing me.

– So much trouble you make for yourself, she chides me in a whisper: can't you see how worried our mother is?

I know that my father is in the thick of arranging a marriage for the elder of our younger brothers, the heir. Young he may be, but he must be married. *We* are already fifteen. But

146

daughters matter less. Letters fly back and forth between my father and his brothers, the gods who control the estate, who secure the best interests of the family, who protect our land. I suppose they will get me a good settlement when my turn comes. I don't want to think of it.

I dream of the betrothal long before it takes place.

Time collides with us, sends the oak leaves spinning from the trees in spirals of bronze, rots the rose petals fallen on the black earth, hauls the apples from their branches, scythes the stiff corn in the yellow fields. Time is my mother in a golden gown with a wreath of oats and barley on her head, nodding and blessing me, and my new husband picking me up in his arms and carrying me away.

It surprises me, his strength, the power in his indolent limbs. He goes striding over the ploughed fields, over the long silky curls of clay under the bare oaks and elms, carrying me lightly as a bag of plums he has stolen from my father's orchard.

– I'll be your twin, he whispers: let me be your twin.

I spit into his face, so that his grip loosens. I bite his cheek, so that he stumbles. I spring from his arms and run as fast as I can back the way we have come, tripping over clods of earth and roots, holding up my skirts with both hands and jumping from furrow to furrow of the ploughed ground.

I escape him. I find Margaret high up on the hillside behind our house, beside the waterfall. She is dressed in cloth-of-silver, her hair hidden under a winged silver cap, a frosty veil streaming down her back, a silver breastplate fastened on over her glittering misty gown, and silver shoes tied around her ankles with silver wire. We stand in silence beside the waterfall, watching its thin line of water and spray plummet past us and down the hill. If I had a sword with which to defend myself I could stay here, speechless for ever, locked into this companionship of silence, of silver.

– It's no good, Margaret says, sounding troubled: it is time.

– You don't love me any more, I accuse her: you're sending me away.

I start singing then, a song of loud defiance. So of course my husband hears and finds me.

My new home is a large house. Too large, with many

147

windows and doors and innumerable suites of rooms in which I fear I shall soon get lost.

My husband takes something out of a bag and hands it to me.
– Here. Put this on.

It is a false head, like something out of a puppet show, moulded from leather, wadded with gauze inside, and painted with a sweet smiling expression. I am afraid that if I fit it over my nose and mouth I shall suffocate and die.

– No, I say, and push my husband's hand away.

He disappears then, and I am surrounded by strangers. Servants I suppose them to be, as they hurry past me, pushing and shoving me where I stand clumsily in their way. I have been set down in the middle of a play, or a masque, like those performed on summer evenings outside our old house, in which the painted and costumed performers move elegantly through dances and mime. I do not know my part; I have no idea what my character is supposed to be. I have no friend to turn to for help: my companions bustle past me, carrying steaming pots of soup, bowls of custards and fruit, platters of meat and vegetables. None of them take any notice of me; they are all too busy.

This is my life now, I tell myself: so I had better learn what do to.

I begin to copy the actions and movements of my fellow servants. Very soon I am in a line, helping to pass dishes. A fist in the small of my back makes me lurch forwards. Two hands dump a basket of plaited loaves into my grasp. I find myself going through a curtained doorway, treading carefully on the swirling patterns of the pink marble floor so as not to slip. I enter the dining room, a huge rectangular space with many doors and high windows, gold-framed paintings hung around the tops of the walls, and below them, carved wooden sideboards displaying gold plates and majolica ware. Down the centre of the room runs a long table, its damask cloth hardly visible under its array of dishes of gold. There are lamps burning, and their light dazzles back from the golden forks and spoons and plates.

There are only two people eating. The great hall is empty of other guests. I trudge to the head of the table with my offering of bread. When I am nearer, and dare raise my eyes to peep at the two seated in their carved wooden chairs, I understand from the splendour of their clothes that this is a wedding feast.

My husband is the bridegroom, dressed in a rich purple suit. He dabs at his mouth with a lace handkerchief, wiping away the grease from his lips. Beside him sits a beautiful woman, whose expression is smiling and sweet. Unchangingly so. She does not eat; she sits still, as though replete or a little bored.

I come nearer, and see that the doll-like bride wears the leather and gauze head I have refused. I throw down my basket, and tear off the head from the simpering woman who has usurped my place. My sister Margaret sits there, staring back at me.

Then I am back in the garden of our old house. The oak trees are completely bare now, curled yellowing leaves stuck to their gleaming trunks in the fine rain, mashed to a swamp at their roots. The flowerbed is empty, all its green cleared away. The rose bushes rear wizened black stumps, each thorn a shiny triangle hooking the cold air. No birds sing, and no cattle bellow in the field beyond the hedge, and the rain runs into my mouth and down my neck. But the flies are still here, a dark busy cloud of them hovering above the wet grass.

Margaret is still there too. She lies on the ground on her side, her feet tucked up under her red skirts, her long hair fallen across her face. I bend down to touch her shoulder and wake her, and she topples over onto her back. Her sockets are sightless, eyeless. Ants swarm there, and in the cavities which were formerly her nose, her mouth. Ants pick at her cheeks, unpick her bones. She is immobile, but also crazy with insect life. Her face has almost gone, her toes and fingers are vanishing fast. Her body is black with ants, as though she has grown new hair everywhere. You cannot say which is garden and which is grave: her rotting body joins them.

– There is only one marriage bed, Margaret, I say: and we cannot share it.

Daughters are a difficulty, a drain on family resources. Dowries to be found and argued over, jointures to be agreed. Luckily there are only two of us to be settled. Harder on my

149

second younger brother, I think to myself, who has to make his own way in the world, no estate at his back. Everything goes to the heir.

— You're healthy, Nurse tells Margaret: with beauty enough. You've learned all you need to know. You'll do.

Margaret preens herself, laughing. At Nurse, and at me. Alarm is a weed sprouting in me when Nurse clacks her silly tongue in my direction.

— But what shall we do with you, chick? Still so careless of your manners. So often untidy and rude. And no one could call you anything but plain. Strange how most of the goodness has gone into your sister and so little to you.

There's only so much goodness. I shouldn't have been born. My poor mother, landed with such a mistake.

— Hold your tongue, you gossiping old busybody, I shoot at her: I am a grown woman now, and shan't heed you.

— Fifty years ago, she grumbles: you could have made a fine life for yourself in a convent. Nowadays what's to be done with a girl who lacks beauty and a fat dowry, with not even a sweet temper to recommend her?

I could make do with little: a couple of rooms to call my own, enough pasture to graze a cow on. Why should Nurse imagine I want more? I disdain marriage, that race towards the marketplace, young daughters sold off like cattle into endless childbearing, sickness, early death. I start up, to box Nurse's ears for her impudence, but Margaret, suddenly my defender, restrains me. She's the only one who's allowed to tease or taunt me. Now her authority, borrowed from our mother, rat-tats in her cold voice, subduing the old woman better than any blow.

— My sister is sure to be found a good husband. In any case, that is my father's business, not yours.

Margaret is never envious, never spiteful. Why should she be? She's beautiful, she's virtuous, and therefore blessed. Sudden hatred of her is another bushy weed I find flourishing inside myself, whose head I must lop off, whose roots I must grub up. I wonder how long it has been rampant, unsuspected, in my heart. Certainly it's not a sin I'll bring to my father's attention when he reads prayers to the household tonight and asks us to lay our consciences bare before him. My little garden may be barren and bleak, but it's mine. I protect it from the

150

winds of loving paternal chastisement with high walls of sullenness and silence. If only weeds grow in it, at least I alone shall be its gardener.

Relief and rejoicing in our family. Congratulations from all our relatives. My father has secured a substantial addition to his estate; the new bride will bring a large dowry in farmland for our younger brother, the heir. My father is no great landowner. But now he has shaped a solid sufficiency for our brother to inherit. The patrimony, augmented, will survive. My father pulls off a second triumph. Margaret is married, in the spring of the year we turn eighteen, to James Grenby, whose father owns land in the north adjoining a farm brought by my mother as her dowry twenty-three years before.

I send away my nurse and the maidservants, insisting that I alone must perform this last office for my sister: to help her put on her wedding clothes.

The silver chains, the ropes of pearls, don't weigh her down. She stands tall and straight, the cloth-of-silver falling down her like moonlight.

– Sit down, I order her: and I'll do your hair.

I peer over her shoulder into the little mirror she holds up in front of herself. My reflection scowls behind hers. For so long we have been mirrors for each other: identical, if not perhaps in looks, then certainly in wishes, in friendship. Now I am not-her. The shadow; the failed copy. My eyes narrowed and hostile, my mouth turned down, a pimple bulging at the side of my nose. Beside me, in front of me, this shining stranger all expectation and triumphant looks, pearls in her ears and at her throat, a collar of starched gauze rising behind her head like a peacock's tail. She is smiling at me. She knows how I feel. That's the worst thing: her pity. That passive goodness of hers, which lets her accept her destiny, which will let her be happy.

– Be careful! she cries: be more gentle. You hurt me.

My mouth is full of pearl-headed pins. I mumble back at her, laying down the comb and starting to anchor her silver cap to her hair. Stab. Stab. Stab.

– Be quick, she counsels me: or we'll be late to the church.

I pluck the mirror from her hands and stamp on it. Bright slivers of glass crunch under my heel. The noise pleases me. I want more of it. I grind my foot on the silver shards fallen all about us. Blood blooms up through the toe of one velvet shoe. The broken glass severs my will to punish. I crouch on the floor, sobbing. Blood leaks along the hem of my new dress. Margaret gets up, pushes away her wooden stool, stands over me, rustling and silver. Cuffs me on the ear. Then she drops down beside me and is crying too, holding onto me with a grip that hurts.

I'm told I never cried for my three dead brothers. Nor, apparently, when, aged two, I was brought home from my kind wet-nurse. I didn't cry for the deaths of my aunts and grandparents. Grief only hardened me, chilled me. I'm not used to grief that's hot and runny, that tears open my body and plucks my soul out. I'm not used to crying.

My mother's two sisters and their women fetch Margaret away. All the light in the room goes out, leaving me dreary, in the dark.

One of my feet is bound with bandages; the other is free. Only one of my feet is wounded. I can walk, with a limp. I stroke the little wooden statue of the Virgin Margaret has given me, kissing me goodbye, bidding me keep it safe, in remembrance of her.

But when I put my hand out in the night, she is not there. My fist closes on emptiness. When I turn to look for her quick smile, there is only the hanging shifting in the draught from the open door. Margaret never walks through the doorway, though I sit on my stool watching it for hours each day, waiting for her. She must come back, and I must be here to attend to her. Her glance will kindle my life again, set my legs moving, give back my hunger and thirst.

Now I sew all day long. My mother, my nurse, even my father and brothers, all try to tempt me out. Fools.

– Come for a walk in the garden, my mother invites me: to see my new plan for the flowerbed.

My needle is a lance I hold in front of me. Never a tongue so sharp.

– Come for a ride, my father offers: we'll take the dogs, and my new falcon.

I am much too busy. I have these yards of linen to hem. I won't stir before I'm finished.

– Play cards with us, my brothers suggest: lay a wager with us, as you used to do.

The white material flows over my lap, and I stitch myself to it, very neatly.

– Eat, commands my nurse: you must eat. I've brought you a dish of fat quails, your favourite.

How can I eat? I don't want to get grease marks on my work. I knot and bite off the silk thread, and choose another length, licking the tip smooth so that it will pass through the eye of the needle. I, in my purity, will pass through the eye of the needle, and into the kingdom.

I need silence and stillness for this journey. And great courage. I am voyaging through a darkness beyond which lies death. I carry the knowledge of it in my eyes: I fall into their deep black pits when I look into my mirror, which I do not dare do too often. My new beauty frightens me: my flesh shrinking on my bones to bring me slenderness, my unruly hair so much neater now it is falling out and there is less of it, my wasted hands so elegant and pale. My silence is exquisite, a finely wrought music only I can hear. There are different sorts of silence, which I listen for, head cocked to one side. A silver spoon knocks on white ivory. Mist hums and vibrates just behind my head. A pebble whistles to itself before it hits the water at the bottom of the well. I offer myself to this silence. I must make myself empty in order to receive it. I must fast.

My silence, so proudly chosen, is powerful. It lets no one near me.

Sometimes, fists knuckling my lap under the heavy drift of the damask curtain I am embroidering, I allow myself clarity. I know what I am doing. Methodically, month by month, I am shoring up my defences. For I am besieged by my family, my walls attacked by their insistence that I tell them what is wrong. I stick it out. I want to die quietly, with the minimum of fuss. For aren't I the murderer? There isn't space enough for two daughters. For twins. Isn't my greedy body trying to swell up, to get fatter and fatter, despite all my care and restraint? I am the monster, the cuckoo in the nest, sucking up all the milk and

153

goodness Margaret needs. Before I remember, and spit it out. I must protect her from me. I must control my anger. Keep it inside. Where it wastes me. As I deserve.

Who can heal such a sickness of the soul? I know its name but my friends and family do not.

I am the good daughter, because no one knows I am angry. Except for Margaret. She has stolen my soul away. She knows.

In my dream I see Eve pregnant. The mother of us all wishes for sons so that she may find favour in her husband's eyes and in those of God. She picks up a fistful of yellow sand, watches the grains trickle through her fingers. Contented, her hands folded over her work, she weaves flesh, blood, bones. Absent-minded, thoughts filled with her son's future, she drops the shuttle, picks it up again, weaves her pattern twice over by mistake. Eve sits in the desert and weeps. Adam comforts her. Two sons are even better than one. They will call their sons Abel and Cain.

Margaret, born first, is Abel. I come second, and am Cain.

The mother of us all has vanished. It is my job to dig for her, to find her. I'm alone in a square room that is slowly silting up, in one corner, with sand. The angry desert has swallowed Eve, and is hungry for more deaths. My hands are spades, torn and bleeding, as I tunnel through the onslaught of grit.

It is my body that is in the way. Very well, then. A sacrifice, to appease the ravening desert-god, to stop his mouth. He doesn't want life.

The mountain of sand swells, slowly filling the room. I try to crawl up it, to stay on top of it, but it's too loose, too shifting and slippery. My hands scrabble at it. My feet find no hold. I slide down to the bottom of the travelling hill, which gathers itself up and stoops over me, prepares to dive into my mouth.

Now Margaret is crouching beside me. Her skirts are soaked in blood. The sharp skewer is in my pocket. If I stab her and throw her body down before me on the sand then the desert will pause for a second to snatch her up, and I can escape, and find my mother.

The sand has our legs fast. Is creeping higher, clutching our waists.

Margaret kisses me on the mouth, pushes her spit between

154

my lips, breathes into me. The mountain of sand engulfs us, flows over our heads. Inside the flood, we are safe, mouths glued together, the air of life passing to and fro between us. And then we breathe out, hard, a tempest that blows the sand away until it smashes the walls of our room. Our feet hobble over the golden ground. The desert lies all around us, tamed for the moment, rippled into dunes. We're still in the wilderness. But we're both alive. I know this is only a dream.

– Do you want to die? my mother shouts at me, shaking my shoulders: you will die very soon, unless you begin to eat.

So I consent, wearily, to live. I pick my way back along that hard path. I'm weak. My arms are like sticks.

My first Ark is our mother's body, the womb I shared with Margaret. Now I've jumped ship. I'm in the water, thrashing and flailing, afraid of drowning. On my own.

But it seems I shall have a companion after all. My second Ark is marriage. We enter in couples. My parents have found me a husband. The double-headed hybrid, the twins, has been cut in two. I am a woman. Not half of one. Woman: a strange name. I stretch out my hand to touch that of a stranger. I dream that my dowry is sand, ticking through an hourglass, safely contained.

I press my nose to the cold windowpane, seeing nothing but the mist of my breath. Frost has scratched the glass with a pattern of delicate fern, curly fronds. I hold a penny to the flame in the hearth to heat it, press it against the pane. I melt myself a peephole, set one eye to it, peering out. Blackened tree trunks. A few yellow leaves pasted to the withered grass. I can hear horses trotting on the road behind the garden wall. My fingers, swollen with chilblains, play with the silver chain dangling from my waist that carries my household keys. Will gave me the chain when our parents betrothed us.

Will sits behind me in the far corner of the room, playing the virginals. I settle myself on the window seat to listen, my head against the heavy blue curtain that I embroidered, in the long years of my girlhood, with animals and flowers. This is my favourite place, half in and half out. I am the room, and the garden. I am the window, and I am she who looks in and she

155

who looks out.

The music uncoils itself from Will's fingertips. His rapid hands unpick the locks of silver boxes: the notes spill out, unroll, fall into the air, liquid balls of mercury, ice petals. He at his instrument is open-mouthed: a stream of cities, pepper-pots, larks, pours from him. He is playing a dance written at the court of Spain. His fingers are slithering over a guitar, knocking on tambourines and castanets. Music that buzzes and grunts, jangles its bracelets, stamps its feet, clicks its heels together. Listening to him play, I become free: a bottle unstoppered, pouring out inarticulate sounds. I rise, and dance for him, inventing the steps I don't know, laughing.

His hair is blond and bleached as the wooden panelling of the wall. His blue eyes are intent. His hands move faster over the ivory keys. I've been for too long the silence in this room, sticky with sorrow. Now I'm the dance, a gold comb to part the air, a plait of gold wires singing. I pull the music, a gold cloud, around me, then beat it into shape with the hammer of my feet.

When the music stops, its echo rolls like a wheel into the corner. My arms chase it. I stand behind Will and bend over him, wrapping my arms around him, pressing my cheek to his. He catches my hands in his, and puts them against his breast. He's a boy only, I think suddenly. He needs comfort as much as I. Tonight, when dutifully he comes to my bed, I won't only pretend to accept his nervous skinny body. I'll dance for him again.

Will reads me the letter at dinner. I could read it myself, for he has taught me how to, but he likes to read to me. Margaret is expecting her second child. Will looks at me, loving and miserable. Three years of marriage, of managing his tiny estate, have thinned and sharpened him. God knows, I am often bad company for him. Disappointment sours my love, turns me away from his friendly hand. He never reproaches me openly, but I am convinced that in his heart he must. He needs heirs. Margaret's child is to be born in five months' time. She did not want to let us know before, the secretary writes to her dictation, in case she was mistaken.

I push back my chair, pleased at the angry scrape of wood on wood.

– I must be off to the kitchen, I tell Will: to see to things.

156

Things. I do not know what they are as I stand in the empty hall. I fill it with self-reproach. Childless. Childless. The pain is a cord twisted about my throat, choking me, a red-tipped skewer in my ribs, shrivelling my heart, a knife plunged into my belly. Ashes on my tongue. A barren woman finds no favour in the eyes of others. I have tried prayer, wringing supplication from myself like water from a cloth. I have swallowed all possible remedies and medicines, their potency sworn for by the friends who supply them, to no avail. Be patient, I tell myself: accept God's will. But I don't. I question it. Why should my sister have children, and not I?

I have grown so ashamed of myself that I do not like to meet other women's eyes, in case I see their pity, their scorn. Even facing my own serving-women has become a test of courage. I am as stern with them as I know how to be, in case they don't obey me as they should, in case they mock me. I take a deep breath before opening the kitchen door.

Smell of boiled mutton, old beer. Smoke haze. Familiar, consoling. The two maidservants are busy unwrapping several great parcels, tied up in sacking, that have been dumped on the kitchen table. Three stout barrels stand nearby, and a pile of calico bundles. Will's steward, John Whittle, is there, with a paper in one hand, a pen in the other. I suddenly remember, then. The goods I ordered to see us through the approaching Christmas season. The dried fruits. The pickled herrings. The lengths of velvet and silk. The caps and purses, the bonnets and stockings, embroidered by the nuns in Brussels with their inimitable skill, which I shall send to all the members of my family as gifts. I must stop feeling so sorry for myself. I have work to do.

John Whittle puts down his writing materials and comes to greet me. I smile at him. I like this man. He is of middle age, with bushy black hair and eyebrows, much physical vigour, simple and honest manners. I trust him. He has our interests at heart. Will pays him well, and is rewarded by his faithful service.

I stand and watch him go carefully through his inventory, checking every item against the merchandise strewn around us. I grow cheerful, feel less empty. My larders, at least, will be well stocked. My storerooms will bulge with plenty. I and my

157

household, with our lusty appetites, will not starve this winter, though many poor wretches will. I give them all the alms I can spare, then shut them out of my heart. They enter my dreams instead, an army of misery dressed in vile rags, who loot my barns and then set fire to them.

– There is one thing more, madam, John Whittle says: which my master ordered me to get for you.

He lays the knots of ribbon on my cupped hands, a soft, glittering pile. Black velvet, threaded through with gold, each one fastened at the centre with a tiny black and gold-headed pin.

– My master, John Whittle continues: told me to procure you some pretty ornament, some extra thing for the Christmas holiday. I hope they please you.

I lift my head and look at him.

– How did you guess? These are just what I need to fasten up the sleeves of my new gown.

– Madam, he replies: I commend myself to you, most earnestly. It is my joy to serve you.

Winter plods on into what should be spring. Snow drains from the sky like the watery whey from a cheese held in a cloth. Icy winds batter our doors and windows. Glass daggers hang in the porch. Will's horse slips in the snow, throwing him. John Whittle carries him home, binds up his broken ankle. He does not need much nursing. Mostly, he dozes, waking only to call fretfully, like a child, for sips of wine and water. In the intervals I can spare from my household work, I sit by his bedside, in the shadow of its drawn-back curtain, sewing or just sitting still, thinking, moving only to throw more wood on the fire. The room is dim, and warm. It is peaceful in here, sitting staring at the flames, time measured only by the scarlet heap of embers sinking slowly down, to collapse with a soft crash, or by the weak voice calling from the bed. Will is very tired. He is recovering more slowly than he should. Self-reproach flares up in me like sparks spurting in a fireplace. With all my moping and pining, I have not been a good wife to him these three years. Sometimes I take his hand in mine, very gently, and hold it, resting on the bedclothes. Sometimes he is shivering and chilled, and I heap the heavy covers about him to guard him

158

from the draughts he insists he feels. He is very young. But suppose he were to die?

One night, having sent my maidservant to bed and taken her place at Will's bedside, I wake suddenly from a heavy sleep, hurtling out of a dreamless darkness into this room ringed round with red circles of pain. I discover that the pain is inside me. I am the room, and the fire is burning me. It jabs my back, my belly. I am most uncomfortable. I want to cry, and to laugh. I can't sit still. I twist in my chair, not knowing whether I want to get up or to lie on the floor. Something is knocking inside me, seeking a way out.

I breathe deeply, trying to keep calm, to consider what to do. Will is asleep. I mustn't disturb him. But the pain disturbs me, insistent, grinding me, a grain caught between millstones.

I hobble to the door, a hand on my waist, feeling my stomach hard and swollen. My monthly time is not usually as bad as this. A glass of wine. Hot wine, with spices in it. Perhaps that will dull these pincers gripping my insides. I get myself down the stairs, step by heaving step, stumble towards the kitchen. No strength to shout for a servant to aid me. If I can reach the kitchen I will be all right. I will lie down on the cold floor and drum my heels until someone hears me.

I launch myself at the door in one last effort, knocking it open and falling inside. My glance, swinging wildly around the room as I burst into it, trips over tapers burning on the table, a litter of papers and account books, John Whittle, wrapped in his furred gown, jerking up, open-mouthed. He catches me as I reel towards him.

He won't let me lie down. He won't let me die, as I implore him to let me do. He grips my arms, marches me up and down the kitchen, from the door to the window and back again, our black shadows staggering in front of us, monstrous shapes dancing on floor and wall. The sour tallow smell of the tapers sickens me, but I need their flame, need to know that not all the fire is inside me. Sweat pours down my face, over my wrestling hands, as the pains bang my spine. All my bones yawn, regularly, a kind of music, surprising me.

– Keep walking, madam, my steward urges me: you'll be all right. Just keep on walking.

My feet slide like a broken doll's along the floor. Knees
159

buckling. An iron arm holds me up. He has driven pins through my joints so that I can't fall down. Lurching along like this with the pain, I am forced to learn its rhythm, start to lean into it, to let it pour through me and over me. Like Will's Spanish dance. The tinkle of virginals timing my breath, my hoarse gasps.

A great cramp seizes my belly, an eagle's beak picking me up and holding me over the abyss. My body is going to fall out of itself. I am opening, opening.

A high voice calling out. Mine.

– Take me to the jakes. Then leave me.

We totter together across the room. The chimney breast glistens with my sweat; I have leaned right across the kitchen and laid my wet forehead against it. I am very tall, because I am being stretched. A gold scroll unfurls in my throat. My toes are chopped-off pieces of white marble. I am paper, fire stinging my edges. Then silver scissors clip me, cut me up.

No fire in the jakes. Burned out. Cool blackness. Squatting in the blessed dark, arms outstretched, hands flat against the wall to brace me, I feel the great lump of shit leave me. I stand up then, lean on the cold wall, a sweat of lightness and relief bathing me, my dissolved bones reforming. My flesh shaped back to itself.

John Whittle hovers by the kitchen door. I sink down on the oak settle by the dead ashes of the fire and put my head in my hands until the faintness passes. My steward's voice, anxiously questioning me, plucks me back. I look up, wave my hand at him.

– I'm all right, I say between laughter and crying: this night, I know it, my sister Margaret has been delivered of her child. That's all that has been the matter with me. God be praised! My sister is well, and so am I now.

– Madam, he insists: let me leave you now. Let me fetch your woman. She should be with you.

My hands fly up, gesturing *no*.

He waits.

My mouth opens and shuts. My hips shiver. I let my eyes speak for me, compel him closer. My fingertips whirr in the air between us, searching for his.

– Madam, he whispers: command me. Only tell me what you wish me to do.

*

Three days later, the messenger on his panting horse kicks through the snow to the house. I myself see the poor brute stabled and fed, then take the letter from the messenger and despatch him to find food and warmth in the kitchen. Slowly I climb the stairs, turning over in my mind the news from London I extracted from him in the stable yard, well out of hearing of my servants, who are all Protestants. Now, to remain a Catholic is to become a traitor. The Queen has decreed it so. Therefore death. And before it who knows what agony under questioning? My knees shake. Would I be brave enough? I do not think so.

Will reads me the letter. Three days previously my sister has been brought to bed of a fine boy. Will is surprised by my calm, turns his pale face to peer at me. It annoys me to see him still so weak, to watch his thin fingers collapse on the bedclothes, his head flop back among his pillows. I need a protector for my household, not this sick child.

– God help me, I burst out: I don't wait for letters from my sister to discover how she is. I knew about this birth. I laboured through the night with her. I shared her pain. I understand her triumph.

– Hush! Will says, lowering his eyes: that's talk of witchcraft.

In nine months' time my own child will be born. I am as certain of this as I am of the sun rising tomorrow. These hands of mine can beat, brew, stitch, whip, cook, caress, embroider. This body of mine is a maker.

I stand over my husband.

– Today you must get up. Try to walk about a little. Then you can rest in your chair, by the fire. It's time you were stirring again.

Will's world has shrunk to his curtained bed. His little warm sphere where he lies lapped in warmth, cosseted, consoled for my irritable fits, taken care of. I'm impatient with him. I've other responsibilities to think of now. My child must have a future. No breath of scandal must sidle in between her and the arrangements I shall make to ensure her position and security in this world of such rapid and terrifying change.

I slip my arms around Will and lug him upright, ignoring his curses.

161

– Come on. Where's your gown? And your slippers?

I kiss him on the mouth.

– Sweet husband. You must get well for my sake. I need you in my bed again.

My bed is spread with the finest cloths in the house. New damask covers for the bolsters at my back, fresh hangings above me. I am attended by two midwives, also by three of my women neighbours and by my mother-in-law. In the intervals between pains, I play cards with them. I lose a pair of gloves, a fan, my enamelled belt. The others laugh at me, teasing me for my inattention. I don't care. It passes the time. I'd rather keep the conversation off other subjects. When they fall to fits of praying, as from time to time they do, I see them watching me slyly. Will's mother is most anxious. She and her husband have converted. Yes, I tell her, to shut her up: of course we're no longer Catholics. I ask the women to recite me some psalms.

I have hidden my little wooden Virgin deep down under my pillows. I have shut her into the dark, whispering to her that it's not safe for her to be seen. Asking her to forgive me my treachery, my lies.

In any case, Margaret is with me, her boy in her arms. She doesn't speak. Her dark eyes fasten themselves on mine, encouraging me to hold on, to endure. She has arrived in a hurry: her feet are bare, and her hair, unbound, flows down her back. Her nightgown, bordered with lynx fur, shows her white nightdress underneath, embroidered with silk thread. She floats in the darkened far corner of the room, her head brushing the ceiling. I lift my arms to her, welcoming her, as a fresh wave of pain tugs me open like a stiff gate. The child's cry in the dawn echoes mine: the sharp wail of the newborn whom I have learned, through a day and a night, how to bring out.

I bid the nurse set the cradle near the fire. My daughter is asleep, lashes like smudges of dirt on her blotched red cheeks, one tiny ear showing under her white cap slipped sideways, tiny limbs wrapped rigid and still. I have prised her from my breast, as I must, have delivered her into the arms of this sturdy woman whom I supply with plentiful meat, fish, eggs, to ensure

162

that her milk flows freely to nourish my child as well as her own. My mother-in-law has shown me how to bind my breasts tightly so that my milk stops. I have watched the babies guzzle at the nurse's fat breasts. I utter a confused prayer, silent, for Elizabeth. That she will prosper. That she won't suffer too much. That I won't need to beat her. That she will survive the calamities crowding in upon our troubled land.

– Little black thing, croons the nurse, rocking the cradle with her foot: where did you come from, you little changeling, with your father so handsome and fair?

She looks at me sideways.

My legs are wobbly. This is my first day out of bed and downstairs, and I am unused to going upright. I clutch at the back of the nurse's chair to steady myself.

– None of your old wives' tales in this house, good woman, or I'll have you dismissed. There'll be no talk of witchcraft here.

Hoity-toity, her back says to me, but she huffs into silence. That's the way to treat idle gossip. Stamp on it.

Will is the other one I have to deal with. After dinner he hands me a present. A small black bottle sealed with wax. I suppose, at first, that it is perfume. Symbol of my being churched tomorrow, of his return to my bed, of my becoming his wife again. I break the seal, raise the dark lip of the bottle to my nose. Strange odour, medicinal, of bitter herbs.

– It's for women just out of childbed, Will explains: it tightens them up again, inside.

He blushes as I stare at him.

– Who got you this? I exclaim: not your steward, surely?

He stares back at me, pale brows lifted.

– My father had it sent from France. He says that it also helps lift the breasts again. Not that you need that.

He lunges forward, pats my stiff bodice. My sharp breath constricts my bound breast even further. I walk to the fireplace and tip the contents of the bottle onto the flames. They hiss, flare up blue and smoky.

– I'll bear you fine sons yet, I declare: you wait and see what I can do. I'll prove to you what a man you are.

The flush on his cheeks spreads to the rest of his face. My cruelty doesn't even scratch him. He's too puffed up with pride

163

at the birth of his first child. Too innocent. I am not innocent. I have decided, since my husband cannot get children on me, to get them elsewhere. It's my duty to bear children. Very well then. I'm doing it.

Lying alone in my bed that night, my arms clutching at nothing, I know myself for a liar as well as an adulteress. My sin brought me a pleasure I want to taste again. I had it years ago, with Margaret, when she swept her hands along my back. Now I have it with John Whittle.

The darkness presses down on me. I give it eyes, a mouth, a name.

At midnight, laughing, I send all my household to bed, protesting that Hallowe'en is well over for this year. A pagan feast. But I couldn't resist the chance of celebration. Heated and thirsty after our long evening of dancing and singing in the hot kitchen, the servants happily take the last cup of punch I serve them. Strong ale, that brings heavy sleep, that I brewed myself against such an occasion as this. They pass the red poker from hand to hand, plunge it, hissing, into the spiced brown swirl in their pewter tankards.

I stand in the hall, yawning, bidding them each good night, Will red-eyed and unsteady at my side. I extinguish their watching eyes like the candles I snuff between wetted fingers. I pack them away into their beds like leftover cakes into the cupboard.

Now the house rattles with their snores. May their stories of hobgoblins and fairies, told in stertorous whispers around the fire in the dark, curdle their dreams. May my drug hold them fast in their beds. The neighbours have departed into the frosty night, shouting and stumbling. Pray God they don't inform against us. My husband and child are asleep. My steward has gone around the house, fastening up windows and doors.

My velvet-soled shoes hush the creak of the stairs. My gown slides after me. My straining ears catch the rub of fur on wood. I close my fingers over my little Virgin whom I carry in my pocket. Sweet Lady. Help me. Pour your grace onto me, a sinner. You're a woman like me. You understand. Don't let them catch me.

The mastiffs sprawled on a heap of sacks in the hall mutter at me, cock an ear, subside again. Why should they stir? They know me. I glide past them to the heavy door.

Too risky, we agreed, to leave it unbolted, lest someone see. I grease the great iron bar with dripping hastily scooped from the dish in the larder. I turn the bolt with both my hands, draw it back.

As the door swings open, the hinges creak. I have forgotten to smear them with the pork fat. The cold air smacks my face. I halt. No sounds from upstairs or from the servants' sleeping-place beyond the kitchen. I creep forwards, drawing my gown closely around me, shivering, pull the door to after me.

The farm dogs catch my scent, my footsteps, and set up a questioning growl. My low call quiets them. The new moon is up, thin as a silver ring. And now the night, rustling, unfolds itself around me, draws me into it. My eyes pierce holes in the blackness, see the creases of the sky thick with stars, the roofs of the outbuildings angled and sharp, the trees beyond the garden wall flattened into black paper cutouts. I pick my way across the dark puddle of the yard, drowning between cobbles. Splinter of gold light at the barn door.

I've torn the thin soles of my shoes. John holds my feet in his hands, warming them. My teeth stop chattering. I lift my legs over his and wriggle closer to him. Astride his lap, face to face, I knot my arms behind his back and hold him to me, kissing him, lolling in his mouth that tastes of sweet warm ale. Then he pushes me backwards, pillows me on straw. This is a game I like: taking turns to play master. Except that which of us is master I can't always tell. Am I master when I signal to him to undress me and he obeys me, pulling at ties and laces, opening my bodice and sliding his hand inside, setting his hands to my hips and rustling my gown slowly, so slowly, upwards? Am I master when I lie there on my back and stare at him, all my power in my eyes, pulling his hands towards me? It is a sweet power, that one, to make a man desire you just by looking at him. We call each other *master*, and we laugh.

His hands are warm and firm on my back, his caresses long and slow, moving over my spine, my shoulder blades, the curve of my waist. Straw pokes my skin through the blanket. I race with currents of water, of light. This is kindness: John soothing and waking me together, speaking to me through his capable hands. It's hard not to be quick, after we have waited for so long, but we manage it. We let the pleasure between us mount up, up, up. We follow no special path: we hang and rock in the moment. This second of touch is what matters, and this one. We're going in no particular direction. Until wanting takes me over, and I take him into me, guiding him with my mouth and hands, then riding with him on our bed of straw. The force of my wanting makes me gentle, makes me big. I swell up, happy and fat, around him, letting the sweetness inside build up, my harvest, the good grain piling up in my barns, no more starving, no need to hurry, the darkness I'm in turning blue as fire starts in my toes and ankles and swarms up inside me and I spill into him and he into me.

The gestures, the poses, the play, I learned with Margaret. Will seemed to have no such knowledge when he came to me, and I did not know how to share mine, for fear of shaming him, for fear of what he might suspect. It feels so good to be playing again. To be a woman who dances and plays and laughs. Not to be always the mother, so strong, so responsible, cradling the husband-child. To get back a bit of wildness.

We lie still, letting ourselves turn fond and silly for the few minutes more we can risk staying together. I want to lie here with him all night, contented and wet, unceasing these endearments of the farmyard, the nursery, to hear his stories and to tell him mine, to talk more of our child. But there's not time. I hoist myself onto one elbow, and sit up, and start to pick bits of straw from my sleeves.

– What's this? he asks, plucking at my knobbly pocket.

The little Virgin lies on his palm.

– My little heretic! he says, laughing: my little Catholic!

I try to hush him, but he puts his hand over my mouth instead.

– You must give her to me, he insists: as a memento of you. As a consolation during your too frequent absences from me.

I've given him the most precious thing I have. Fool. I've given him too much.

Our farewell is brief, a touching of hands and lips. I drag myself to the door.

166   *

I snatch at chances like these as they dart past me, dangerous, enticing. Also I watch over our farm and our affairs, I make marmalade the way my mother taught me, I replenish my stock of linens and hangings, I fight with our neighbours over the fishing rights to the river that flows past the boundaries of our land, I ride out with Will, I send presents of birds and game to our friends in London, I watch out for spies amongst our neighbours' servants who might betray our allegiance to the forbidden faith. I manage things. I try to keep us safe. Also I present my husband with two more bawling black-haired children. The sons he needs. I weave careful dreams around their small heads, planning their welfare.

I manage my husband too. Will is gentle, a dreamer. He is my fourth child. In this way, standing between him and the world, I come to love him. His health is frail, and, seeing my capability, my industry, he lets the reins slip from his delicate hands into mine. Increasingly he takes refuge in his collection of maps and books, his music. He writes dances and songs, and sends them, with respectful and loving dedications, to the one or two friends left to us at court. Our daughter, a fat pretty bundle tied up in stays and ribbons, perches on a stool next to him, listening as he plays. She wriggles from the arms of her nurse and bounds onto his lap, her favourite place. He loves her tenderly. I watch them tease and play with each other. I don't spend as much time as I'd like with her. I have too much to do.

My third ear keeps on listening out for Margaret, for the words unspoken in the letters passing between us.

One morning I find her in bed with me, cuddled up against me for warmth. But we're no longer girls together, playing our bittersweet games again: my sister frowns at me, in a way she never used to do.

– Why are you putting your family at risk? she whispers: why are you being such a fool?

– I never wanted anyone but you, I blurt out: I never needed marriage after our nurse explained to me that I couldn't marry you. I lost you when you were married. All my life I have been wanting you back again.

– Don't be more stupid than you can help, she retorts: and

167

don't blaspheme. Listen. You've got a kind husband, a good house, three servants, and your children. Why can't you be content with that? You're willing to lie, cheat and steal in order to have more. Think of the danger! Think of the consequences for all of you. Suppose Will puts you away, like the Queen's father did his wife? How would you live then?

I avoid her eyes. She digs her fingernail into my arm.

– Be careful, she pleads: be careful.

Then she takes my chin in her hand and forces my face round. Hissing at me now, with hot breath.

– Where is the Virgin I gave you? Where is she?

– I don't know, I mumble: I've lost her.

– And so you've lost me, says my sister: you've turned me loose.

She vanishes, and I rub my eyes, waking to a bleary grey dawn. A red crescent-shaped weal on my forearm, two dents in the pillow.

When our younger son is ten months old, Will rouses himself to make a journey to London, to visit his father, and to sue, with the help of his kind offices, for an audience with one of the powerful gentlemen in close attendance on the Queen. We have plotted this together. The masque, with songs and dances, that Will has written on the theme of Virginity Triumphant, and dedicated to Her Majesty. An additional gift of a pair of black satin gloves, marvellously embroidered with gold. We're not quite sure what we're asking for. Without giving ourselves away, we're begging not to be suspected of treachery; for a little extra time.

Not once has Will suggested that we convert in order to save ourselves. I love him for this. His courage props up mine.

For we're in great danger now. Somehow, and we don't know how it's happened, we're openly known in the neighbourhood to be Catholics. Despite all our precautions and secrecy, someone amongst the people here we thought were friends has betrayed us. News travels fast enough to court. We need to move faster. We make preparations to send the children into France, to Will's cousin at Argenteuil. Should it become necessary. Though we try to believe it will not.

– I'll take my manservant with me, Will instructs me: but I'll leave John Whittle with you. I'd rather you had him here, to keep a watch over you all.

He doesn't look up as he speaks. He is seated at his table, sorting the sheets of his music, rolling them up carefully inside a square of silk which he ties with a ribbon. I examine his profile. He can suspect nothing. I have been too discreet. With him, I am always compliant, gracious, the pattern of an obedient wife. Surely he is not laying me a trap. I make sure that my voice is unconcerned and gay.

– We could manage very well without him. Don't deprive yourself of his services, I beg you, for our sakes.

He whirls round, smashes his fist on the table. The inkwell jumps. A sheaf of parchment slithers to the floor. I dart to pick the spilled papers up. Kneeling at his feet, my skirts billowing and crackling around me, looking down so that I don't have to meet his eyes. He knows. Somehow, he knows. But as yet he has no proof. Surely he has no proof.

His hand closes on my ear, pinching it hard until I yelp with the pain. His fingers shift, jerk my earring. I don't dare to move lest the gold wire tears itself out, rips through my flesh. I crouch before him, fear rising like vomit in my throat, waiting for his blow.

– Dear wife, his voice scrapes at me: don't argue with me.

He lets go my earring. Still not daring to look at him, I feel his movement, the air pushed aside as his arm swings back and up. I dodge just in time. His knuckles catch my cheekbone as I swerve from him and fall sideways on the carpet. Tears drop down my face, of rage and surprise. My bruised cheek smarts, the flesh instantly puffing up and half closing my eye.

Now he's huddled in his chair, crying.

– You made me do it, he weeps: whereas you should mind me. Do you think I want to hit you? You should obey me.

I crawl to the door, where I'm out of his reach and he out of mine. For I'm minded to cuff him as I never do my children. I pull myself to my feet, and look back at him. My contempt dwindles him. Puny child sitting in father's chair pretending to be master. My fault, is it, for not loving him properly, not letting him grow up into a man? For certainly I've managed him. I've kept him young, protected him, I've dandled him in deceit, and coddled him with lies. I tell myself I had no choice. I

169

did what he wanted, didn't I? He let me do it, didn't he? He wanted to be weak.

Grief overcomes me for what might have been between us and never had a chance to grow, because of our fear. I'm crying like my daughter does, in great noisy gulping sobs. I can't bear it. I stumble back towards him. Wanting to babble that it's not too late. That we can start again. To begin to know each other truly this time. To find a better way of loving.

He holds his hands out to stop me.

– Who do you think has betrayed us? he shouts: if not your lover? Who else had a chance to know all your secrets, you bawd?

He wipes his snot and tears on his sleeve. I'm freezing, numb.

– It's a lie, I stutter: you know it's a lie.

– Don't think, he whimpers: that I don't know what you've been up to, you witch. You laid spells on me, to make me powerless in bed with you, to hold me fast, asleep, while you slid off to meet your lover. Of course I knew. My shame was too great. I told nobody.

He lays his head on his arms and blubs.

– You've destroyed us all.

Will is arrested while he is in London, and put into the Tower. I could not keep him at home with me. He would ride off. I disgusted him too much. John Whittle has disappeared. I know I must hurry. Soon the men will come for me too. The day after I get the news of Will's arrest, I complete my arrangements to despatch the children, in the company of the two servants left to me, to France. I make the servants swear the most terrible of oaths that they will fulfil their duty to me. I give them all the money I have, and promise them more from Will's cousin when they shall reach France. I don't send for help from my family. It's too late for that, and I fear involving them. I pack a basket with my few pieces of silver plate and jewellery, hiding them well under layers of the children's small-clothes. Then I put the children to bed one last time, and come into my room to write this letter.

Elizabeth, my first-born. It's cruel of me to make you bear all this. I should let you forget me, or invent me, in peace. For you I am a blank: absent. Dead. I want to fill in that space of your ignorance, to write my name there and offer you my history, which is yours too. I want you to inherit me. A daughter needs a mother. A daughter should know who her mother is. In order to accept her, or to reject her.

Let this letter be a bridge between your future and my past. Let this letter join the small child that you were, when I sent you away, to the young woman you have become and whom I shall never know. You're sleeping, so small and plump, as I write this. I imagine you tall and well formed and beautiful as you sit and read it. My darling, we haven't met. Writing this letter, I pretend that we have; that we might; launching it like a paper boat to carry you into your new life with a cargo of knowledge, enough strength to claim what is yours.

Conceived in such a passion of wanting, in such a joy of giving and receiving, how could you not be laid, now and for ever, at the centre of my heart?

I pray that, one day, you'll meet Margaret.

She's with me, in Will's book-lined room, as I sit writing this. Will's books and papers are strewn everywhere about us. Margaret is wearing a billowing scarlet gown, and a flat scarlet cap with black markings on it. She's my mistress. She's my perverse Mistress of Letters.

– Change all the names in your letter, she instructs me: it's safer that way. By your voice alone they'll know you.

I've thrown all her letters to me onto the fire. I don't need them any more. It's time to go with her, through the fire, up the dark tunnel behind it, and out into the sweet air of the night.

Elizabeth. I'll leave this letter behind.

25   The Correct Sibyl is looking through the racks of
clothes in the great wardrobe of the Ark that runs the
entire length of one of the decks. Instead of bookcases,
here are long rows, narrow corridors between them, of dresses,
coats, suits, arranged in no order at all but according to some
glorious carnival rule of sexual and social confusion. Dress-
suits press up to ski outfits. Policemen's uniforms are mixed up
with those of chambermaids and nurses. A judge's splendid
robes hang next to a maternity smock, a university chancellor's
scarlet gown next to a nun's habit, a businessman's sober
striped trousers and dark jacket next to a baggy harlequin
costume. Drag abounds, if that's what she wants to call it:
sequinned and beaded and feathered evening frocks, butterfly-
collared shirts with pleated starched fronts, purple cassocks,
jodhpurs, velvet smoking jackets, Boy Scout shorts, taffeta
crinolines. Racks of shoes underneath match, or mis-match:
country brogues, high boots, silver sandals, carpet slippers,
running shoes, loafing shoes, walking shoes, shoes that raise
the heel five inches or squeeze the toes into a triangular point,
shoes decorated with gold buckles, shoes that look like
Chevrolets, satin espadrilles, shoes of plaited straw, shoes of
rubber and plastic and brocade.

The Correct Sibyl has so few clothes at home that she does
not bother with a wardrobe. An old hat-stand bears her jeans,
one well-cut pair of grey flannel trousers, her one smart suit,
her few shirts, her two skirts. At a loss for words, she has
invented this wardrobe in order to enrich her vocabulary. She
is searching for inspiration. For a new voice. Her old one has
died away and left her hoarse, monosyllabic. She moves along
the closely packed rows, passing her hands over the swaying

172

hangers, parting and separating them, throwing her catch over one arm and then moving on again.

Arms overflowing, she flings the clothes she has chosen onto a big armchair, noisy heap of squabbling colours, crazy grammar of silk, linen, felt. Then she strips naked, and pauses, wondering what to try on first.

As a young girl she adores clothes. She starves in order to buy them, lies in bed in the morning for half an hour putting an outfit together, witty, stylish, irreverent, in her mind; never appears in public without making some sort of provocative and punning statement. She understands the risks a woman takes if she dresses up sexy and wild and then goes out into the street; she accepts the consequences, the wolf-whistles, loud comments, lip-smackings. Fair enough, surely. She dresses to express her own moods; she's glad when her audience responds. If she wakes up feeling happy, sensual, confident, then she dresses in revealing shapes and fabrics, in colours that suggest her gaiety, her involvement with what is around her. In this frame of mind, she's touched and pleased when men notice her as she goes by, acclaim her with rough male kindness, say hello, affirm her as person, as sexual being.

It's an exchange, she works out. Men whistle at women because they are desperate to be noticed by them. Men are babies with fragile egos, needing mother to smile and coo. Preferably a pretty and well-dressed mother. Well, she doesn't mind. She sways past the workmen and their eyes and mouths swap jokes and liking with hers.

But the babies can turn nasty if mother doesn't behave as she ought. When she is in a thoughtful, introspective mood and dresses accordingly, in something oldish and shapeless, jeans and a raincoat perhaps, the men are enraged that she is hiding herself, not noticing them, not caring that they exist. Cheer up darling! they snarl, as she drifts past in a private dream: it might never happen. And then she wakes up, shocked and irritated, and hurries past with bent head while they pursue her with irrelevant advice, new labels: she's the bad mother, the one who goes away from baby; the whore.

It's not that men can't read women's signals; it's not that they're illiterate. They prefer their own meanings, that's all, and, since the street, they have decided, belongs to them, feel

173

free to impose them. They write her in on their pavement page.

Once she's become a professional writer, more of her energy goes into composing arrangements of words than into creating flamboyant selections of clothes. Hurrying back from the supermarket she's already, in her imagination, at her desk. She doesn't care what she looks like at these times. It's irrelevant. Shiny nose and unkempt hair, laddered stockings, droopy skirt: why bother? As far as she's concerned she's invisible. Grub, not butterfly. But the men in the street don't understand. And punish her with their name-calling.

One of her pleasures is to roam the streets of her neighbourhood at night, alone with the race of clouds and moon. She's not a fool: body blanked out by her greatcoat, she's anonymous, no man's prey, scudding along dark and silent as a cat. This is freedom: to walk for hours in the city through the darkness, at peace and excited, feet flying rapid in their soft-soled shoes, unseen, her mind streaming with images, her body dissolved into shadows. This is the freedom that men enjoy without ever having to think about it, unless they're wearing drag, unless they've dressed to express their gayness. One night she walks a woman friend to the bus stop, arm in arm, and they're abused by a gang of drunken youths spilling out of the pub. She reads in the papers of a judge's comments on a rape victim being dressed up and asking for it. Stay home. Mind your baby-man.

She doesn't want to have to disguise herself, to deny her occasional, rhythmically dictated need to wear pretty clothes. She sits at her desk studying the local newspaper's report of the man who is methodically raping his way along the street in which she lives: breaking and entering by day, waiting for each woman to come home from work, then, armed with a knife, raping her. She's always thought herself inviolable, because sensible. But a rapist rapes little girls of five, old ladies of eighty, as well as women of forty. Why should she imagine she'll be spared? New locks on her windows and doors. But not always a friend to see her home. That moment between turning in at the gate and fumbling for her keys in the porch. The Ripper, according to certain male journalists, was forced to become a murderer because of his too-loving mother and dominating wife.

174

Rape, by definition, means that a woman hasn't asked for it. Except, of course, that so many men don't understand what the word means because they refuse to read a woman's signs, refuse to recognize the sign *no*. Women can't create signs, can they? Women are silenced by male speech, aren't they?

She takes to wearing dark glasses. She stops being able to write the novels she once turned out with such professional regularity. Words don't flow. She wants to spit and curse, to mourn, to write gruesome revenge stories filled with hatred and sadistic sex. Well, that won't do, doesn't fit her civilized tolerant self-image. So she shuts up. Then learns to speak a new language: dry; unfeeling; technical terms rigorously arranged; over-controlled. She reads the critics: today's high priests. They know it all.

She stands in the wardrobe of the Ark, and wrestles her way into a pair of shabby corduroys, an Aran sweater, a large pair of suede lace-ups. She picks up a pipe and waves at her reflection in the long mirror opposite her. First Deadly Sin: laziness.

– It's simply a question of self-discipline, of setting yourself a regular schedule, she declares: nothing to it. Nine o'clock every morning I'm at my desk, rain or shine, and come lunch time there's my thousand words ready for my wife to type out after she's done the washing-up. None of this fluffing about thinking up excuses to waste time, pretending you're too depressed, feeling guilty about neglecting the housework or your family. You've just got to get down to it. You've got to get used to making your work an absolute priority. You simply need to train people not to interrupt you. Let your wife answer the telephone! Your job is to be in your study, steadily writing. It's as straightforward as that. Nothing to it. If you can't handle marriage and motherhood as well as being a writer, then you shouldn't get married and have children. At least you women have that choice. Male writers don't: they have to write *and* support a family. So get on with it, why don't you?

(The First Deadly Sin has suddenly fallen in love with another man, and does not know what to do about it.)

She adds a spotted bow tie, a green velvet waistcoat, a gold fob-watch. Second Deadly Sin: intensity.

– My dear, the person in the mirror addresses her: do try to be a *little* less serious all the time. It's so fearfully boring

175

listening to you droning on and on about your deepest feelings. You seem to believe that what you say has the status of some sort of *truth*. Whereas of course we more sophisticated types know that fiction is merely a tissue of *lies*, a *game*, and that's why it works. You don't know how to *play*. You're so grim. Do strive for just a *little* more humour, just a *touch* of irony. Your writing is so *frightfully* narrow and banal without it. We've heard *quite* enough, thank you, about the agonies of the housewife frustrated in her creativity. *Try* to be a little more original, can't you? What's wrong with writing a *comic* novel, for instance? A few *jokes*?

(The Second Deadly Sin is undergoing rigorous psychoanalysis and is somewhat dismayed by the ferocity of his atavistic desires for Mum.)

She conceals these first two layers of clothes under a huge donkey-jacket, sticks on a droopy false moustache. Third Deadly Sin: lack of political bite.

– You know the trouble with your writing? she admonishes herself: it's becoming out of touch. Not what we want. Not what we like. What have your self-indulgent narcissistic musings about your interior life to do with social reality? Not much. Completely irrelevant to most working people's experience and sufferings. And this mystical religious strain that's creeping in: *ugh*. Very nasty. Reactionary. You want to be careful, girl. We're beginning to find you trite and *boring*. We like our progressive writers to be accessible, too, not relying on bourgeois forms and images meaningless to most of the population. Who weren't paid to sit around for three years at Oxford reading medieval poetry, remember? If you must write poetry, let it be ranting and rhyming. If you must write novels, for goodness sake try to remember your audience wants a *plot*. You're not angry enough, either, any more. And you've started to write about bourgeois pleasures. Tsk. Tsk. Who the hell cares what you think about breakfasts, or the colour blue?

(Last night the Third Deadly Sin had a vision of the Angel Gabriel.)

Next she throws on a tweed suit, feathered hat, sensible brogues, brown stockings, clutches a crocodile handbag in one stiffly gloved hand. Fourth Deadly Sin: arrogance.

– Who d'you think *you* are? she asks, peering scornfully at

176

herself: to think you've got the right to write? Who asked you to? What makes you think anyone wants to listen to what *you've* got to say? Giving yourself such airs. Cocky, I call it. Waste of your education, hanging around in pubs pretending to be a writer and not earning a decent living, letting the State support you while you do it. What have you got to offer that's of any value to ordinary hardworking people? Why not take up voluntary work if you want to do something useful? What's wrong with looking after your family, like decent women do? All those women who never had your chances. And you sit whining about your problems! Who *cares* about your meaningless self-inflicted problems? Mad, you are. Bad. Thank heavens no daughter of *mine* would ever *dream* of going in for such nonsense.

(The Fourth Deadly Sin knows that her husband no longer loves her.)

Now she dons a roomy suit of well-cut coffee-coloured overalls, a glittering silver belt, a pair of pink sneakers. Fifth Deadly Sin: unsisterly behaviour.

– Call yourself a feminist? Hmmm. You're not *my* idea of a feminist, I can tell you. For a start, you're much too fond of the sound of your own voice. You're too ambitious. You don't work collectively any more. You want to be a star. You've stopped caring about your struggling sisters. Women all over the world are trying to fight their oppression and you sit at home cosily writing novels. You'd never have become a writer if it wasn't for the women's movement, yet where's your gratitude? Look at you, trying to grab the limelight, wanting to pose as some sort of *leader*. Bourgeois individualism, that's called, dearie. And secondly, if you insist on writing, you might at least try to betray feminism less. All this romantic garbage you churn out about heterosexuality, real men and real women and the orgasm as every woman's fulfilment. Yuk. Nor can you even find new forms! When you're not spewing out your messy confessions you're falling back on patriarchal myths that are obsolete. Who gives a damn about the bloody Greeks or the Bible? We want *new* images, ones that suit *women*, not the men you're so anxious to impress. Take your nasty traditional feminine stories away. *And* your phallocratic psychologizing and your rubbishy religious images. You're old hat, dearie.

177

You've been left behind. We have a younger generation of writers who are *much* more interesting. And I can't say I've noticed you giving them much of a helping hand. Too busy looking out for number one, aren't you?

(The Fifth Deadly Sin works nights as a striptease artist, and is very good at it.)

She swathes herself in a black cloak, ties on a black headband, straps heavy chains around her waist and ankles. Sixth Deadly Sin: lack of avant-garde originality.

– You're not very *wild*, are you? she asks: not really weird and violent and post-modernist. You never got even as far as modernism, did you, poor thing? You're pretty middle of the road. I mean, you're still using quotation marks and narrative and conventional sentence structures and conventional ideas of character. Haven't you heard of Gertrude Stein and William Burroughs and de Sade and Bataille? Aren't you embarrassed, deep down, by the sweet safe sticky sentimental stuff you write? You should be. You've never experienced real life, of course. You've never lived in the depths. What do you know about the truth of urban survival, you babbler about nature and love? How can you expect to write a work of true passionate bitterness until you've been a hooker and gone in for S-M and been a junkie and sold your blood and refused a clear gender identity? I bet you still think of yourself as a woman, don't you? I bet you love your family. I bet you've never been to prison. You don't really *know* about much, do you?

(The Sixth Deadly Sin is a virgin. Weekends, she visits her beloved elderly aunt, and they sit and read the Bible together.)

She adds a white beard, a black gown and mortarboard, an eyeglass. Seventh Deadly Sin: lack of true artistry.

– Foolish left-wing perverted rubbish masquerading as art. Thank God there's some sanity left in this world and that books like yours don't sell, don't get reviewed, don't win prizes, and don't get taken seriously as literature. Polemical tracts, they are, not *novels*. Who wants to read banal snivelling rhetoric about ugly man-hating lesbians with herpes and dandruff raising their foul illegitimate brats on social security? You have a modicum of talent, I agree. With time, with effort, you might, if you dropped all this stridency and whining, write a second-

or third-rate book. But you prefer to grumble, don't you? It's easier than the struggle the true artist has to *transcend* his self, his personal egotism, and create an enduring work of the fullest humanity that will be recognized as *great*, as *authentic*. You just aren't in that class, dear. You never will be. Why fool yourself?

(The Seventh Deadly Sin would love to be able to write.)

She bends forward and gazes at the mirror.

– You've had it, dear, can't you see? all the Seven Deadly Sins murmur at her: you're not up to it. You lack the stamina necessary for sustained creative work. You lack imagination, confidence, originality, wit. You're too genteel. You're too hysterical. Why not give up now, gracefully, before you make a complete ass of yourself?

She is stuck to the mirror, to its definitions. She flails her arms but the layers of clothes she has assumed, one by one, swaddle her, wad her, helpless and fat as a bound baby, do not let her move away.

– I want to please everybody, she screams: I want to say the right thing and be approved of and loved by everyone and it's IMPOSSIBLE. That ideal mother, ideal listener, *doesn't exist*.

Her scream shatters the mirror. Now she can pick up a shard, cut off her clothes, piece by piece, and let them fall under her feet. Now she can be lonely, and begin to hunt for her own words.

She starts again, strolling through the racks of clothes to find something she might want to wear.

She reaches her hand into the past. The caress of memory. Her favourite clothes. Why is it that nothing she possesses now gives her an equivalent pleasure?

Here's the long white linen nightdress, tiny pleats falling heavily from the low wide neck, that she bought from the antique stall in Carnac market that summer she went on holiday with Jenny, and which she wore as a dress in the evenings, sitting in the café under the pines drinking Kirs and feeling the rough linen fall over her bare calves. As she washed it, so it frayed, went into holes, wore out. At last she had to cut it up for dusters.

Here's that cotton skirt in dull brick red, just above ankle-length, very tight and small at the waist, very full and gathered,

179

with big pockets, that she wore for years until she spilled oil on it, making mayonnaise for Paula's wedding party, and the huge dull stain would not wash out.

Here's that cotton dress cut like a French schoolchild's overall with square shoulders and a square yoke and little buttons, in the rich blue of French workmen's jackets. She left it behind in a bed-and-breakfast in Cornwall and never got around to writing to ask for it to be sent on.

Here's that tubular dress in cream linen with a cutwork yoke, wide shoulders, wide scooped neck, sleeveless, mid-calf length, that she bought for her grandmother, who wore it a couple of summers then gave it back. How she loved that dress. The dry-cleaners ruined it, marking it with pale purple dye.

Here's the black 1940s suit she bought for three pounds in Camden market in imitation of her mother, who married in wartime in sumptuous sexy black. Buttons of black jet, curved pockets and shoulder yoke outlined in overlapping rows of black silk ribbon, narrow skirt with a single kick pleat. She lent it to Laura to wear to an interview. Then Laura went to Australia and took the suit with her.

Here's that 1920s sleeveless waistcoat made entirely of sequins of mother-of-pearl, soft, gleaming, pink merging to silver. It was the most precious thing she had, so she gave it to her lover Marie. When they split up she didn't dare ask for it back. She regretted its loss more than that of Marie, she sometimes thought.

Here are the summer sandals of pale olive-green leather, with a closed toe and closed heel, woven in plaited straps, that she spent a week's earnings on one summer. They were stolen in Paris when Greta's car was broken into overnight and the cases they hadn't bothered to take into the hotel were snatched. The case was full of books mostly. It was the shoes she grieved for.

Here are those other shoes, enormous absurd platforms in bright apple-green, which she used to wear while making love with Mick. Nothing else: just the shoes. When they went out of fashion she turned them into flowerpots and grew geraniums in them until they rotted.

Here's her huge man's tweed overcoat, bought in a War-on-Want shop one autumn in Leeds for one pound. She wore it to the Guy Fawkes party at Chapeltown: the slip and hiss of fireworks, the song of bonfires, the strangers bumping against her in the dark. The sleeves became marked with wax dropped by candles at midnight Mass and at Greenham Common demonstrations; the buttons dropped off. In the end the moths got it.

Here's that pair of olive-green ex-army shorts, picked up in another market, in Aix-en-Provence. With Jenny again. Long, almost down to her knees, pleats belted tightly into her waist. Sometimes she wore them with a red forties blouse, red fishnet tights and shoes. Mostly she wore them in summer, so that she could have the deep pleasure of feeling the warm air caress her bare knees, calves, ankles, as she ran along the street or bicycled home at night through the black sweet-smelling park, and knew herself a boy again, or a boy-girl, the free rapid long-legged creature she had been before periods came with lagging steps and fear. Aged thirty-five, scampering up a hillside in Provence, she finds that boy again. She stops wearing the shorts when her daughter complains she is too old, they make her look ridiculous.

Words can be given away, lost, put out with the rubbish. Words can rot and need replacing. Loved words, favourite words. One of the pleasures of being a writer is that you can take power, please yourself and nobody else, choose your own words. So, come on, girl, get on with it: start enjoying.

26 A lot of sex used to go on in the Reading Room.
The joy of reading and researching has to be
translated into action. Like new wine in old bottles: I
understand that people may explode with excitement. Male
scholars prowl the gangways between the desks, ostensibly
tracking down obscure volumes of bibliography or lost books
delivered to the wrong seat. It is easy to allow my eye to be
caught, to find companions for lunch or coffee. Most of them
have shoulders speckled with dandruff or bad breath or
blackened teeth. That doesn't matter: they hint at sexual
matters with shining eyes.

I choose one of these scholars, a clean funny one, as my first
lover. I peel off the elastic panty girdle which is as awkward as
my virginity in a dusty cubbyhole in the bookstacks unlocked
with my bunch of keys. I lean against the scorching radiator on
which we boil up illegal kettles of tea, and lift my antique crepe
de Chine dress around my waist.

Foreplay goes on in the Reading Room, intense discussions
about Bibliography which is Ken's subject too. After half an
hour's whispering about silken headbands, rubbed and spotted
and foxed pages, laid paper, we are at such a pitch that when we
get to the cubbyhole and the radiator we are speechless,
frenzied, our pleasure increased by the need for secrecy and
speed. Downstairs again, flushed and languid, I leaf through
the letters of bibliographical enquiry from foreign scholars that
I am supposed to answer.

I don't come with Ken. It doesn't bother me. I'm a beginner,
with a lot to learn. I've got to Advanced Bibliography, and will
eventually get to Coming. But it worries Ken. Is that better? he
asks hopefully. In the end, to silence him, I begin to fake

182

orgasms. I deduce from novels in the erotica section how to act. Some people are experts at faking texts. I become an expert in faking orgasms. But I lose interest in my acquired gestures, and after a while we give it up.

Here in my Arkive on the Ark, books on sex are allowed to stand next to books on procreation.

– But the world's a poisoned place, Noah reproaches me: full of illness and death. How can you be so irresponsible as to bring a child into it?

I skim through the riddle book.

Does *to bear* mean also *to bear*?

27 The next island lifts itself, beaky and bony, from the blue seas surrounding it, two huge caverns in its white cliff. The port is on one side of the great bay, and the city straggles up the steep hills behind it.

The city is an enormous tropical fruit: a durian, yellow and rotting. The smell envelops me as soon as I step onto the quayside, and for a moment I want to turn tail back to the Ark where the others are hard at work, no time for this tourism. The smell pushes up my nostrils: moist decaying vegetable matter; urine; over-ripe fruit; dying flowers, slimy-sweet; incense; sickness; and, laid over the top, a thin vapour, the smell of chlorine and disinfectant.

It's raining. Under my feet, a brown squelch of mud, sludge of cardboard laid over potholes, dark mash of trampled litter, wet cigarette stubs, wet sand and grit. The narrow streets are tumultuous, thronged with hurrying people elbowing their way past each other, shouting and gesticulating across the heave and blare of traffic at acquaintances on the other pavement. They don't seem to mind the smell; they're armed with pomanders studded with cloves, and wear nose-masks of black cloth tied on with golden ribbons, of black silk decorated with gold lace and sequins.

Fighting my way forwards in the pushing, clamouring queue, I board a clanging tram. As it whines and sways up the steep hill I rub clear the steamed-up window next to me and gaze out at the tall shabby tenements. Traces of rich colour remain: burnt yellow, orange, dark red, grey. Palm trees, branches a bunch of untidy rags. Sodden lines of washing sagging between apartment blocks. The paint peels off windowsills in long curls. Cars hoot shrilly in the hot wet traffic

184

jam, swerve to the wrong side of the road to overtake, zip through red lights. Bruised cars; dents beaten out, panels patched up. A dump of old tyres with a handwritten notice above saying *RIP le gomme*. Stalls selling plastic baskets and sandals and necklaces. We rattle up, up, up. Craning my neck I see the bay far below, small silver crescent.

I struggle out of the crowded sweaty tram and down the folding steps. The tram swings off along its shining rail. I'm standing in a little curving piazza just below the brow of the hill. Dusk: the hour of deep transparent blue. Sharp outlines of roofs and parapets. Youths on motorbikes roar up and down, their exhaust fumes bitter in my unprotected nose. I walk away, over to the centre of the piazza where a baroque monument to some long-dead general is encircled by benches and where I can sit down, the rain slowed to a drizzle dampening my shoulders. Up here, so far above the seething fishy smells of the port, the air is a little clearer. It's possible to breathe without immediately wanting to retch.

Perhaps, once upon a time, this city smelled of chestnuts and wood-smoke, of vanilla and almonds, in those far-off days before the chemical factories made the air stink. Perhaps people used to bathe in the sea, in the time before it was used as a dump for sewage and industrial effluents and nuclear waste. You can buy expensive designer perfumes in the shops, to wipe out the disgusting natural smell of female bodies; the perfumes are processed in that factory over there, look. It's a good thing; it's meant a fall in the local unemployment figures. You can sit in a beach-side café, wearing your mask and sipping synthetic orange juice full of carcinogenic additives, and watch the sapphire-blue waves lapping on the shore littered with turds and clots of oily mud washed in from the tankers sailing by.

I read the poster stuck on the monument behind me.

Oh dear. There's been an accident at the local nuclear power station. Don't panic. Nothing to worry about. The radioactive cloud hanging over the island won't stay for long: the wind will soon blow it somewhere else.

I have the smell of death in my nostrils. Invisible death, falling gently with the rain onto the parched earth, blown with the sea breezes into the city. Death carried in the cows' milk, in

185

the new crop of spinach and lettuce, in the air I have to breathe when I go out shopping. I swallow death. I inhale it. I'm helpless in the face of it. It presses into me: a rape. Death working in my cells, against my will, to make me infertile perhaps, or to give me, or the child I want to bear, some form of cancer. I have to live with death. I can't escape it: how can you evacuate an entire nation? There are no nuclear shelters here.

The government does not wish to alarm us: no figures are released; no studies published. Jocular ministers appear on the television news programmes, telling us to take a few sensible precautions, the crisis will be over soon, as the wind shifts and bears the cloud away towards the north again, as the radioactive matter in the atmosphere and on the ground gradually decays.

One of the worst things is not knowing exactly what is happening. I can't help suspecting that in some areas the level of radioactivity is so high that the government is deliberately keeping silent, deliberately keeping us in ignorance. My fantasies grow unchecked. I can't sleep at night. The invisible dust settles on my eyes, my lips. I don't want to speak of my terrors to others and make them feel worse than they already do. We can't console each other. We are blank-faced, silent.

Oblivion is the way out for some, through sleep, drink, drugs. Some go mad, and have to be shut away. Others, with desperate gallantry, dress in their best and go out into the town to stroll up and down and chat to friends, to pretend that all is as usual. Business as usual. The shops stay open. Policemen with guns and sheafs of official papers inspect the greengrocers, to ensure that no fresh leafy vegetables are on sale, then issue the day's certificate of healthy trading. In a couple of weeks, they promise airily, we can eat raw green food again. The lettuce sown just before the cloud came, and heavy with its cargo? I am heavy with sorrow, and heavy with rage. I cry in private.

Demonstrations occur daily in front of the Ministry of Health, in front of the foreign embassies of those countries who have installed nuclear power stations. *Danger*, we cry out. *Danger*, we signal, as we don grim carnival masks and skeleton costumes and dance our dance of death. How would *you* like to dress for death? In white silk? In black tails? Here's a death cocktail, and a death dice, and a death cue.

It's too late, say the world's governments: we're already committed. They don't care, can't admit their grave mistake, refuse to reverse policy. This is just an isolated disaster. Of course further precautions will be taken to ensure such accidents never recur. Nuclear power remains clean, effective, cheap, efficient, safe. Your diseased child will be born too late to be counted as a victim. Statistics, after all, can be destroyed or lied about.

I go into the great gloomy church set back on one side of the piazza. Temporary shelter from the soft radioactive rain.

Cavern of darkness, lit with bunched sticks of glitter, trembling silver flames. I slide across the stone floor towards the high altar garrulous with coloured marbles, bronze angels, falls of lace. The chancel walls are lined with row upon row of framed cavities, like boxes in a theatre. In each one a skull set on a starched ruff, padded velvet shoulders. Sightless eye sockets gaping at the drama of death daily enacted there in front of them, on the brightly burning altar-stage, to the sound of cries and trumpets. The crucifix swings down out of the blackness. We must all die some time, the man on the cross reminds me: why make such a fuss about it?

Relics in boxes of crystal and gilt leer at me, like deformed babies, pathological specimens, swimming in stoppered glass jars.

28 We're going to have fish for supper. Caught by the Gaffer, who has spent most of the day sitting out on deck with rod and line.

I inspect the sparkling haul in his basket. Tails still flapping, until I pick up the fish and knock them out one by one, while the Gaffer flinches and looks away. Then he turns his head back towards me with a smile.

– I see you believe in mercy-killing, at least. And what about the cruel barb, dragging the throat? If you're going to continue to eat fish you should catch them yourself.

– I'm not prepared to, I say: shut up, can't you? All right, I'm a hypocrite.

Scales rippling in blue-black silver, in mother-of-pearl, in opal, shading, in gleams of light, to rose pink. The eyes stare at me, reproachful and dead.

– You'll have to de-gut them, the Gaffer says: I don't know how.

All the others watch me as I lay out the fish on a board on the kitchen table, and pick up my knife. Turn the fish belly upward. Grip the slimy corpse in one hand, slit it open with the other. The knife isn't sharp enough: I have to jab, then raggedly saw, unpicking a silver seam. Spurt of greenish goo. I reach my fingers into the red innards, curl them around the slippery entrails, squashy and yielding. Two swift tugs, my hand filled with a knot of wet sacs of jelly and white filaments, dripping blood and a dark green liquid. I scrape the innards with the knife, then rinse the empty fish under the tap. I repeat the procedure twelve times, until there's a large pile at my side of sloppy shiny guts, smelling high and raw, and two neat rows of floured fish ready for frying.

188

I hold up my reeking hands and arms, gloved in red blood up to the elbow, towards the Gaffer, and laugh.

– Easy, once you make up your mind to do it.

He shudders.

– You women! It's like some hideous pagan menstrual rite.

– A good job for a sadist who's out of work, though, I say, wiping my fishy fingers: or for a sadist who's trying to kick the habit. Keep your hand in. Displacement activity.

– I'd rather not have to read about menstruation, says the Deftly Sibyl: I quite see that it was a revolutionary topic when first introduced into women's writing, but now it's become *de rigueur* I'm bored with it. I'm also bored by throbbing wombs, moons, grandmothers, lesbians, the lost mother, nuns, witches, food, and orgasms. They're all feminist clichés. All right, no subject is inherently boring; it depends on what you do with it. But still. I'm bored with the subject of women. I'm also bored by war, tarts with a heart of gold, fathers and sons, visiting academics, bullfights, erect penises, spies, and bank accounts. But I don't suppose that will stop male writers from writing about them.

– Don't bully me, shouts the Gaffer: I'm not ready, not yet, to write as a man on taboo subjects. I need to be sure there's a market, first, for that sort of writing. I suppose sooner or later one of the women's presses is going to start a men's list. We've got spinster classics by dead spinsters, spinster modern classics by living spinsters, the spinster youth list, the spinster teenage list, the spinster children's collection. What about spinster bachelors? Spinster bachelor babies, spinster bachelor boys, spinster bachelor mature writers, spinster ageing bachelors? Somebody, sooner or later, is going to make a fortune promoting books in these categories. And then the whole bloody mess can start all over again.

– Womb envy? says the Re-Vision Sibyl: it's not a male prerogative. I've got it. A catching disease. My hands are claws curved ready to strike. Curdle of sour grapes in the stomach. Green is the colour of life, also of envy. Thwarted life, desire gone mildewy or covered in greenfly. I must hold fast to the fragile trust we build between us here on the Ark, for the winds of my envy want to blow our house down. Publishers scramble for our books, now briefly fashionable, make us compete for

189

contracts. Reviewers compare us to each other and to straw hysterics who can be knocked down, we're grateful not to be like *them*. One of you has your new novel selected for the best-twenty-books-by-women promotion: I want to lash out and hit, preferably you. One of you already has a cult following, based on only two books of stories: I want to see you fail. One of you is chosen as flavour of the month and hyped everywhere: I say I despise publicity. My envy destroys my growing love for you, shuts me up. I might kill you if the beast jumped out with her claws and teeth. I might stamp my foot on your neck. My breath is fire, and blasts you. I don't admit this; haven't men always said women are bitchy, envious and competitive? I punish myself instead. I stay away from you. The boulder of rage is stuck in my mouth, choking and silencing me. A faceted stone that fits. Gobstopper lodged in the windpipe. Breast-jet of bad milk forced at my face. Why does she hold herself so aloof, you wonder: why is she so awkward, so guilty, so distant? What shall I do. Suck on the stone, and let it dissolve, green sherbet firing my tongue. Write it all down and let you read it. Then walls of glass break, and I can touch you, and new words can come. I roll my envy lightly around my tongue, just one more taste for the palate to savour. Not bad food. Not poison. Just a part of myself. I can kiss you and not sting.

– Penis envy? says the Forsaken Sibyl: yes, that too. I envy their bodies, long and lean, patched with fur. The absence of fullness and curves, hips and breasts. Often I envy their control. My body explodes, over and over again. I open, I stream forth, urgent rhythms of blood, sweat, spittle, piss, shit, milk. I dissolve into air, then recreate myself. Stop up the exits and entrances, block the pores. Man is a signpost, one white finger pointing. Clean and lean. Less flesh to him. Less mess. Less of himself to lose. What shall I do. Go on a diet, discipline my body through weightlifting, have a sex change, wrap myself in chains so that I can't spill out. Arranging words on paper helps me to feel safe.

– I believe in God, the Father Almighty, creator of heaven and earth, says the Correct Sibyl: do I? *He* is just a word. The Word that structures difference, that structures language for everyone. *He* defines all that is not-him. What can I possibly write that does not take its shape, its bent, from accepting or rejecting *him*? Can I really write *I* and mean something else? I invent *him*, I write him in. So I can also forget him, erase him, cross him out. He's just a word. Is *she* enough by herself? The goddess worshippers say *She* made the world. Is that any better than saying *He* did? The myth starts when *he* meets *she*? Centuries of trouble, rival versions of the truth. How can I invent *she* without exploring what she touches or yearns to touch, the *not-she*, the *mother* who goes away and touches *father*? *Man* and *woman* so distant from each other in the dictionary, such a lumber of meanings in between.

– I don't like printed books, says the Babble-On Sibyl: I like a text like a letter or like a diary. Receiving the letter, snooping in the diary, I am close to the hand of the body that made it. Just one set of marks on paper, no need for duplicates. No buying and selling, the book as a commodity that circulates. Instead, the body impressed onto paper. I study the author's fingerprints. Directed towards me. I should learn to love word processors. Do I fetishize the hand that writes? Can I learn to love the brain, and print-out? Multiple copies at the flick of a switch. Just one baby? Or sextuplets? Are they all different? Do books also have souls? Now there are no more originals. Just flickering green screens.

– What about women who can't read or write? the Gaffer asks: how do they tell stories? A story, please.

29   Meg Hansey decides, after only a year in his service, to kill her master. But it's not for *his* murder that she's taken up in the end.

I visit her in Bridewell. I have a lot of sympathy for these poor women, pushed to take desperate measures in order to survive, and then cruelly punished for it. And, after all, I know Meg well, having visited her master so often at his house. Certain French books I used to bring to show him, smiling to myself to see him grow so red, so hot and so excited, and afterwards so ashamed, when his wife tripped in to lisp her compliments and to see what we were up to, and he blushed and hid the book under the tablecloth. Or when Meg came in, with a tray of wine and sweets. I take Meg wine now, when I can afford it, or beer. It comforts her. I take her bundles of bread and sausage, and I play cards with her to take her mind off her troubles. Of course she's grateful. Though at first suspicious of my motives, as she has every right to be, poor wretch. After a couple of weeks she relaxes. Then it takes only a bit of coaxing to get her to tell her story. It's a short one, an ordinary one, like her life. But I think I can do something with it.

I don't take notes. I don't want to play the journalist too obviously. I've got a good memory. I write it all down on this grubby manuscript at night, here at home in my rooms, where I'm undisturbed. My debts don't let me out too often to my old haunts, and I want to keep away from the Allens for a bit. So I shall spend my evenings writing about Meg. These rough notes, which I shall reassemble into a story. My idea is to combine the sensational details of popular novels and broadsheets with the sober nature of religious confessional tracts. I want to tell a woman's story. I want to create a woman's voice. Of course I have to invent Meg's style. In real life she's not got much of a way with words, bless her. I polish up what she tells me; I give it a shape; I make her up. You have to.

Meg's a country girl, from Kent. Not a dullard. Clever enough to snatch at the chance of a decent living, a spot of excitement, when she comes up to London to visit her aunt and sees that Mrs Penn, herself an abigail, can put her in the way of earning more than she'd ever do at home. Meg's parents are dead of the pox, and her crew of sisters and brothers hanging on by fingers and toes under the unwilling care of their grandfather. Meg abandons them, seizes her own chance. They'll end up, most likely, in the poorhouse. She tells them: I'll save money. I'll send for you. Then she flits. From far away, looking back, the house is small enough to hold in the palm of her hand. Then she drops it.

She learns fast: how to curtsey and keep her mouth shut; how to wash muslins and starch lace; how to freshen up old satin gowns rotten with sweat under the armpits; how to arrange a head, more or less; how to stir up messes fit to be carried into the chamber of one seeking to be treated as a lady. How to lie, how to look sharp, how to duck and swerve.

Mrs Penn recommends her as waiting-woman to her own mistress's cousin, concocting a neat story of Meg's former employment under a rich merchant in Bristol, now alas suddenly drowned in the West Indies with a cargo of Black slaves and his widow too distraught to furnish a testimonial. Meg's clean and sober, not pretty. She's a thin little woman. Her complexion is dark, her mouth is twisted awry. She doesn't yelp at the prospect of low wages. Her future mistress stares at her and decides she'll do.

– You'll have to sit with me at night, Mrs Allen warns her, sighing: my health is that delicate that often I can't sleep. Especially when Mr Allen is out late, or from home.

Meg likes the house, set back behind a tall brick wall from the bustle of Well Lane in the shadow of St Paul's. A small square house, solidly built of rosy red brick, with white wood casements and a fine brass knocker on the door that Meg polishes every morning. In front of the house, behind the wall, there's a garden with three lime trees and a fine flowerbed and a

193

stone bench. Meg pegs out the washing, once the washer-woman's been on a Monday, on a line she stretches between two of the trees, and draws in deep draughts of the scent of their flowers.

She makes herself indispensable to her new mistress. Mrs Allen is rising thirty-five, a faded beauty grown fretful. Yellow curls fall on a white neck. Hard eyes flicker away from too much contact. Rarely stirring out, and eating too many sweets, she's growing fatter. Her skin is still soft, but shows every mark: so many bruises. One of Meg's tasks, she discovers, is to assure her employer she's still beautiful, and this is true in the evening once the candles are lit. Then she's a pink and white girl, all dimples when she laughs at the antics of her puppy.

Mr Allen has several faces. In the morning he slouches at table in his old gown, unshaven, dipping his soft roll into his cup of chocolate and swallowing noisily, then belching. Meg, who's quickly taken on her mistress's fine manners, turns her eyes away from the slop of half-chewed bread in his open mouth, his lips slapping loosely, blocks her ears to the sounds of his chewing, to the gurgles of his stomach. He's afflicted often with indigestion, and fussy about what he eats, though not about how he appears in front of his womenfolk. In the mornings he takes it easy, with stooped shoulders and a slack belly.

Then he dresses to go out, and is transformed. He's a goldsmith, doing good business. He dresses well, to impress his clients. In his best velvet suit and his curled wig he looks a real gentleman. Not very tall, perhaps, but a fine figure of a man once he squares his shoulders and twirls his cane, his rounded stomach hidden under his purple waistcoat and his handsome calves displayed to their advantage in white stockings. He's a vain little man, pointing his toe to show off the red heels of his new shoes, pirouetting at the door for his wife's delectation. He likes her to be happy when he goes off: he chucks her under the chin and kisses her cheek before he minces down the street in a trail of lace handkerchiefs and the scent of Eau de Venus.

Mrs Allen loves him well, and sure, he's devoted to her. That first day, Meg sees what a good mood he's in when he comes home for dinner, rubbing his hands and chuckling, tweaking her ear as she stands back to let him pass her in the hall. Meg shakes out the cloth and lays the table while Mr Allen pulls his wife on to his knee: oh my pretty bird, my little popinjay; paddling his hand in her bodice, putting his mouth to her neck. She twines her arms around him and they cuddle as artlessly as a pair of children. They don't care that Meg's watching. Perhaps, she thinks: they like an audience.

– So you do love me? Mrs Allen asks, patting her tumbled hair: just a little bit?

And for answer he pecks her, and tickles her, and nips her, until she's squealing with contentment. Not entirely satisfied, though.

– Tell me you love me, she coos, caressing him with her fingertips as daintily as a sweet she'll pop into her mouth: tell me.

– My darling poppet, he says, kissing her nose: my little honey, of course I love you.

Then he leans back against the fat cushions of his chair and tells her the story of his morning, glancing away from her needy eyes, chafing at the soft bonds of her arms, holding her at arm's length while she wriggles happily on top of him. He tells her of the splendid and enticing allure of the lady he saw driving down the street in her carriage, leaning forward to look out of the window so that he saw her white uncovered bosom, her opulent mouth. He mentions his dream of the night before, too erotic to be fully revealed to his virtuous listener. He peeps at his wife sideways, to see how she's taking it. Flick, flick. Just a little stroke of the lash. Mrs Allen's eyes fill with tears. She struggles to get off his knees, while his arms, suddenly embracing her tightly, restrain her. She tries for pride, saying nothing, but her tears betray her. That satisfies him. He redoubles his pats, his kisses, soothing her back into complaisance: little chickabiddy, little silly, sweet goosie.

Then they're both ready for dinner.

Meg slams down the plates. Mrs Allen fiddles with her food and watches her maid, watches where her husband's eyes go.

– Meg, she frets: you've spilled wine on my sleeve. It's too bad. Why must you be so clumsy, you great gawk?

Her face, pouting with ill humour, is all lines. She catches sight of herself in the mirror hung over the sideboard, and crumples her napkin between her hands.

– It's my favourite gown, she weeps: and the stain won't wash out. You slattern. You wretch. You did it on purpose to annoy me.

Mr Allen covers her hand with his.

– Now then, now then. Don't cry, ducky. I'll buy you another.

Mrs Allen's sobs melt into smiles. Mr Allen's eyes meet Meg's, and she looks away quickly.

Mrs Allen does indeed have delicate health. Once a month she is confined to her bed with severe pains. Meg wraps heated bricks in sacking, then in linen towels, and places them at her mistress's feet, at her back, at her belly. She piles the covers over her, beats up the pillows, brings her hot broth and oranges and gossip.

– Don't go away, Meg, Mrs Allen pleads: I like having you here with me. You do me good.

Her washy blue eyes: frightened; watchful.

– There, my dear madam, Meg exclaims: I'll sit with you willingly.

She fetches the basket of mending and settles herself next to the big bed in a low chair.

– I miss my family, you know? Mrs Allen confides: they all live so far away, except for my cousin. And she's so often unkind to me.

She bursts into tears.

– Now then, madam, now then, Meg reproaches her: crying won't do you any good.

She speaks absent-mindedly; her mind's on her darning.

– I need a friend, Meg, Mrs Allen says: I need someone I can talk to.

Meg shifts in her chair.

– Well then, madam, I'm sure you can rely on me. I'm at your service.

Mrs Allen tells Meg of her courtship by her husband.

First there is the gravity of the flute music, and my mother's bare shoulders above the silver lace of her busk and loose gown, her white skin, seriously powdered, matt not shining in the candlelight. A summer night beyond the tall window, the long curtains flung back, the moon slides behind a flurry of cloud; a

196

dark mirror; blue-black ripples.

He sweating. Well I could see it. Hand fidgeting with the sharp-edged ruffle tickling the opposite wrist. Pleated linen, starched. Settling the plum velvet sleeve over it.

My mother's eyes are dark slits shiny as apple pips. Her skirts rise over the bolster tied around her hips and fall in thick folds of embroidered blue satin around her tiny feet in gold high-heeled shoes.

She rises, and collects the others with a gesture of fan and quick fingers. Supper laid out on tables in the room behind the folding doors. Mr Allen waits, to hand me from my chair, I suppose.

What have I to offer? A willingness to trust.

I say to him oh I've dropped my handkerchief oh what a weak ploy his eyes say oh say I thank you my eyes respond now we can talk.

There is a mole at the side of his nose that sprouts with two stiff black hairs. I don't mind, I have one too, on my inner thigh. What else do I know of him? He's as pretty and as tricksy as his clothes. Changes from sober broadcloth to bright silk in the twinkling of a mood.

Chairs in their sullen brocaded positions opposite the marble fireplace. By day this room is high-ceilinged, cold, bright, large. Tonight, the streaming fires of the branching candlesticks touch the edges of the sofa back I grip in both hands, mark out a space just big enough for we two to manoeuvre in.

Laughter from the next room, where my father turns the tap of the silver urn of wine. I'm alone here. None of those people matters to me. I curtsey to Mr Allen, have my hand kissed. The hangings shift at the window, and the moon shines in, a gold square on the carpet, and I am impatient.

Can you understand this? To stake your life on the gleam of moonlight on a man's shoulder as he holds aside a fringed curtain and waits for you to pass?

I have to make some room for my own imaginings. I need to invent him. I need to believe that I meet him naked and free as one of those nymphs in the tapestry hung on the opposite wall; and that I make my own decision. So I choose him for the way the moonlight falls on his braided coat (there are shadows thick

197

in the corner, and they scare me), for the way he looks around seeming so free. So I too could feel free.

I rise from my curtsey, and approach him, while he looks at me.

That room. Heavy with crimson on the walls, and carved doorways, and carpets. My heels clack across the parquet then the carpet muffles them. I reach him. I look at him. I hold him eye to eye. I'm drowning. If he does not respond what shall I do?

He drops the curtain and pulls it across the doorway, so that we're securely enclosed. He puts his white hand out, and takes mine, and this time he does not let go. He kisses my neck, my forehead, my lips.

Really this happens in public. All the rest of our party, ten or more persons, stand just beyond the door, talking and laughing, the clash of spoons and glasses.

I invent my own story. I need to love him. How else can I give myself away, into his keeping? I see us in the mirror, with our hands joined in an emblem of marriage, and I feel at first sick and faint, and then: that this must be so. Then we go into supper.

Afterwards he stays behind while the others crowd into the hall to say their goodbyes to my mother and father. The room is almost dark. He captures my hands again in his and whispers so low I can't hear him, then presses his mouth on mine again. This time he puts his tongue in my mouth. It is fat, like grapes. We're alone. This is how it will be. His eyes scatter me into corners. What else is there for me, besides him? I have to go forwards. What else can I do. I do not say one word. I consent to a destiny, knowing no other.

Matters run swiftly on. My body is as smooth and new for him as the sheets and towels I bring with me. I am his bed, and he slides into me. I spread myself for him. I want the treasure I have guessed at from poetry, the jokes of servants: the sweetness and the fire. Well. I learn how odd, how awkward, the way there is. Madam. He parts my thighs. Your obedient servant. He jabs a finger in, to open me up. I want to go with him, because this is what I believe I was born for, my life's summit. We're dancing a strange step. I don't know how to move, and he hasn't noticed. He is plucking at me, and I'm a

198

cold instrument, unresponding; ignorant because too innocent. Oh I'll learn won't I? Give me a few months and I'll learn this language, this music; how to answer; and joke; to bring him delight. Oh I must. I'm embarrassed. His naked body, hairy, on mine. Panting and gasping. I'm still. What has this to do with me.

This happens at night. The days are my own, when he's out on business. The days bring me duties, my power in the house to order and chastise servants, to choose dinners, to sort through my wardrobe and then select colours and stuffs for new gowns and dresses. I'm happy. Then at last the days join up with the nights, and I'm happy at night too.

After the first stillbirth I sit in the bow window in the little room upstairs, watching the birds in the garden. I wish I were a ship with three great white sails turning her prow towards unknown lands to garner a harvest of spices. I wish I could sail away and never come back.

There are no more surprises in wait. One day I will eat baked fish or stewed mutton for dinner. Another I will wear the new green satin waistcoat my husband has had made for me. Another I will touch the bricks of the passageway outside the house and wonder who touched them before me.

I don't mind this as much as I once thought I should. If only I could conceive another child, and carry it through to full term. I try not to think about it too much.

I don't like the moonlight streaming in from far across the river to fall on my bed. I close the curtains tight. The moon plays a high thin eerie music, a silver music, like a flute, and my heels lift despite themselves, my feet arch and begin to dance. I hold on to the pillow lest I'm swept across the floor by the music. I jab an elbow in my husband's ribs to wake him up, and then I dance with him. Both of us are blind in the darkness, our breaths twisting together, struggle of knees on the soft mattress. Like two rats in a cellar after our squabbles of the morning. He never takes so much pleasure in me as after I've fought with him, disobeyed him. He subdues me here in my bed, in the sweetest way. Sometimes I hate him, because he has learned how to speak to me in moon-music, in flute-language, and I can't hide from him anywhere. We understand each other too well.

*

Meg summons a polite voice.

– Poor madam. Well, we've all got our way to make in this hard world.

– Meg, Mrs Allen complains: you don't understand what I suffer.

Meg picks up the scissors to cut a fresh length of darning thread.

– No madam, she agrees: for I am not wed, and not likely to be, either. What man would take me?

She sends her wages home to the country. Bread for her brothers and sisters. This month she has kept some back, persuading herself the children will not go hungry. Scarlet ribbons to brighten her drab Sundays, to let her pretend she has a fresh petticoat. New woollen stockings. She looks with disgust at the fine silk one she is darning for her mistress. At night she hears the children crying, wails that scavenge in her heart like rats. Or she dreams of their wizened bodies strung up in the butcher's by red cords. Perhaps she will ask for a holiday. To go and see them. Her hands slacken in her lap as she considers what to do. Try Mr Allen first?

– So you see, Meg, Mrs Allen drones on: you should not speak that way of the most holy estate to which women are called. My father read to us, every night, Dr Benson's *Homily on Matrimony*. Thus I learned a wife's duties. Submission. Cheerful patience.

Her hands are fat and white as they grope for another sweet. Meg's hands fumble for the scissors. She holds up a stocking almost severed at the ankle. Oh.

She carries the bowl of slops down the back stairs, so busy fuming she doesn't see the bulky shadow looming ahead.

Her foot's on the bottom stair. The shadow comes away from the wall and embraces her, tongue pushed into her mouth, one arm about her waist, a shadow that giggles, and whispers what a fine girl she is. Not unpleasant. No one's ever praised her. And he smells warm and good. Then his hand bundles up her skirts and she panics.

She acts before she thinks. Raising the slop bowl held in her free hand. He's cursing and slipping in the wet mess in the dark while she's round the corner and safe, into the kitchen.

– You're better staying up there with the mistress, at this

200

time of the month, Alice comments: where you can keep out of his way.

She's stooping to blow up the kitchen fire with the bellows. Her face is shiny and red, and her hair dank with sweat. She smells of it, too. Old sweat. A month of unwashing.

– Hand up your petticoats as soon as look at you. Of course the mistress knows. She sent Jenny packing, didn't she? He laughs at her. Tells her she's imagining it. So you be careful. If they turn you off you won't find another place.

– Mr *Allen*, Meg marvels: but he's so old. Who'd fancy him?

In the dark, I might. Where he cannot see me either.

– Not too old to do as he likes in his own house, comes the surly reply: so don't say I didn't warn you.

Meg considers Alice's straining back and arms, and goes forward.

– Here. Let me do that.

Alice looks up, pleased.

– Thanks.

She watches Meg pump energetically, and the red flame start up amongst the wood and coals. Then she seizes a floor cloth and goes out to clear up the mess in the hall.

Meg is well scolded by Mrs Allen for her carelessness. Then the matter's dropped. Mr Allen burns a suit of old clothes in the back yard.

Six months pass. Meg deals with her mistress's moods and whims, coaxes her out on short walks to go shopping. She learns the beauty of the city, slowly revealed to her: the river slipping past in silver flashes at the bottom of a narrow street between tall buildings, the clean stone of the spires of new churches tugging upwards like kites, the tide of bodies flowing through alleys and courts, declaring their shape. She likes being a stranger, carried forward in ignorance of all the people pressing up against her and passing her. She likes the quick ring of money tilted onto counters, and the heaviness of the purse she carries for her mistress. Money stacked up to make chimneys, spread out to shingle a roof, whirling down as rain to pock the mud under her feet.

The ruts freeze to ice. Winds jerk at the kitchen window. Meg and Alice toast bread and nuts at the fire, skirts kilted up to let the heat mottle their thighs. They gossip, and tell fortunes. Mr Allen's friends sit with him, snug in the parlour upstairs, playing cards over their mulled wine, laughing. Mrs Allen sulks prettily in her room. Some nights Mr Allen sits alone, writing his diary, and shouts for Meg to bring fresh coals. Then he'll give her a kiss, a pinch or two.

When Meg catches a bad chill and falls sick, Alice accompanies their mistress to church that Sunday, wearing a big clean collar, carrying Mrs Allen's fan and gloves. Meg tosses on her little truckle-bed in the cupboard-room opening off the kitchen she shares with Alice, and hears Mr Allen's heels tapping down the stairs.

– I'm your friend, Meg. Let me be your friend. Be a good girl.

One hand over her mouth so that she can scarcely breathe, the other ripping back the blankets, hoisting her shift up over her shivering knees. Legs trembling with fever. Head boiling. Arms too weak to push him off. So she submits. He's her master, isn't he? She does not struggle. She stares at him. Yes. I need a friend. When he's finished his business and is climbing off her, she spits in his face. You should not have looked at me. I am too ugly. He slaps her lightly and goes away.

Meg's big belly is the worst insult she can offer her mistress. She understands that. Mrs Allen's outcry, followed by hysteria and fainting, doesn't surprise her.

No point in trying to defend herself. She has seduced her master, and must quit his house. The night before she is due to leave, she crouches in the dark passageway outside the privy, listening to Mr Allen grunt and strain inside. When he comes out, she springs at his throat. She flies at him with the bread knife. Their dance is silent, intimate, arms round each other, tangle of hands and feet. Then Mr Allen finds his voice. Hoarse screams. Lights along the passageway and down the stairs. Alice tearing them apart, her hands gleaming with dark red blood. Meg falls to the ground, her strength spent, and her master staggers away from her to the arms of his frantic wife, his bald head shiny with sweat, blood all over his shoulder. Alice hauls Meg to her feet, scrambles her into the kitchen. They stare for a moment. No word. No kiss. Alice shoves her out of the back door. Then Meg hears her raise her voice too in the general clamour. Murder goodbye help mercy goodbye.

It's raining. Meg lumbers along back ways in the darkness, rough breaths coming and going, enough sense left to her to know that she must keep in the shadows, and keep going. She makes for Mrs Penn's. Refuge, from which, surely, she'll not be turned away.

Standing, panting and swaying, in front of the house where her aunt works, seeing the closed shutters with no chink of light showing, she loses the courage to rouse up a house full of strangers. There's blood all down her bodice, and on her hands. She crawls into the tiny alley that opens, a black cavity, beside the house, sinks down on a heap of stinking rubbish. She must rest. In the morning she'll discover what to do.

She gives birth there, under the grey sheet of the dawn sky. The baby comes out easily, her exhausted body relaxed into the pains, no fight left in her. She dandles the baby, puny body smeared with her shit, her blood. She looks at the mewing face, and reaches out her hands. She strangles it; swiftly; cleanly. So that she won't be able to feel any more. She wrings her daughter's neck, just like a chicken's, and the head flops back on its broken stalk. Now she has cut herself off from all help. She buries the body in the rubbish, hauls herself to her feet, gasping. She dare not try Mrs Penn. She drags herself further on down the alley, deeper into the waking city where she has no home, to find a hiding place.

Mr Allen writes his account of this in the diary he will never let me read despite all my persuasions. He likes to talk of it; to tantalize me. He has some leisure for writing whereas I must make a living by my pen. I wonder what he has written of Meg. Not the truth, I daresay. I kissed her too, whenever I got the chance. I knew she liked me. Perhaps she would have let me have her. Probably glad to, poor wretch. But Allen got there first. I took care not to let him know that I made as free with his servant as he. And my story of Meg will see the light of day. Not his. I'll watch his face as he reads. And that of his dear wife. I'll change the names, but they will know. Nor will they dare admit it.

Mr Allen and I, together, compose the advertisement stating

203

his loss. I carry it myself to the *Postman* office, and thence to the printer's.

Gone away. And her mouth a little awry.

A servant girl turns her in. Found fainting behind a bale of silk in a warehouse off Cheapside.

She was hanged yesterday at Tyburn for infanticide, and is already immortalized in broadsheet ballads hawked about for a penny each. One of the oldest and commonest stories told along these streets. I'll write her life. In my hands her poor body will live again.

30 The Forsaken Sibyl's favourite place is the little flat roof, or deck, at the very top of the Ark. Here she has conjured a garden into existence: both enclosure and wilderness.

A garden compensates for loss of the countryside, not just here on the Ark, but in her life. When she is a child, her adoptive parents' back garden suffices. The inch-high doll enters the crack in the low mossy wall surrounding the lawn, moves through the towering grass, spreads her tiny fingers over the apple tree's bark, stares at the veined green hairy moons of gooseberries. Her eyes level with the earth, she peers up at the underneath of blackcurrant leaves, the strings of the net spread to keep the birds off. There are no fences around her mind; the garden is big enough to roam in for a whole afternoon without exhausting its routes. Yellow flare of peppery nasturtiums, close-packed orange dazzle of marigolds, dry crumbs of soil big as boulders springing with blue forget-me-nots.

When she's older, she likes to walk by herself out into the countryside. Ten minutes by bicycle from the university town, and she's out in a landscape of gentle hills set with woods and farms, the river winding below. Leaving the bike in a ditch, she climbs the lane white in sunshine, springs over a stile, and falls into an enormous meadow, stretching away to the horizon and tipping over it, thick with buttercups. Glossy flowers high to her knees, knocking gold pollen against her as she wades through them, the sun hot on her face, warm breeze flowing over her. She lies down in the very middle of the meadow, a grassy hump at her back, rasp of crickets, hum of bees. Her book is on her lap, but she doesn't want to study. She drowns in yellow, listens intently to the sounds of the afternoon, dissolves into it. That is joy: to be completely alone under the sky, to let go of everything, not to think, not to dream, just to be there. A part of it. Essential for this is the fact that no one is watching her.

So much chatter of birds and insects that she doesn't hear him approach. She feels him standing over her, and looks up. Middle-aged man in a grey raincoat, flies open, penis dangling.

– Please go away, she tells him.

But he's in the mood for chat, for company. So it's she who leaves, angry but also scared, all her mother's warnings ringing in her head.

Since the countryside seems to be peopled with lonely men needing girls to talk to every time she goes out for a walk by herself, she gives up her solitary adventures. She's really in prison now. The warders peer at her from behind hedges and trees. She goes walking with friends, but it's not the same, because they always want to talk. Of course she likes talking to her friends, but. Lucky Emily with the wild moors just outside her house, free to walk them alone, to lie face-down on a rock and dream for hours without fear of interruption or assault. Lucky Simone, tramping the hills of Provence, all by herself, free to think her own thoughts and boldly impervious to danger. She is a coward, lacks their courage. She reads too many newspaper reports about what happens to girls walking home by themselves.

Her circular garden on the Ark has no entrance, so that no voyeur can enter it. She sits on the close-cropped turf that she has sown with thyme and camomile and presses her bare soles against the springy stems to release the strong scent. A privet hedge surrounds her, set with arched pergolas thick with climbing roses, and in front of it the flowerbeds, a forest of delphiniums, cornflowers, irises, lupins.

Her London squat, from which she is soon to be evicted, has a garden. She's kept it wild and tangled, the way she likes it, clearing back the tall grass and weeds just enough to make a cave to sit in on long summer evenings, blue dusk above her, the pink brick wall at one side, reggae and pop drifting across the neighbours' open windows. She will obey the council's summons and move out. The house is due to be renovated and turned into flats, and she understands only too well the rage

206

and anxiety of local families waiting to be rehoused. She won't take what is theirs. She herself is not on the council waiting list, because the council does not house single people. She can't afford private rents. The housing associations have closed their lists, as have the housing coops. She'll join the drifting desperate mass of the homeless. Stupid and foolish to want to live on her own. In the past she has stayed with friends, in spare rooms, on sofas; or she has lived with others in shared houses and flats. She has no choice. That's what she'll have to go back to, just as she'll have to go back to a proper job. But she can't stop wanting her own kitchen, her own room, her own bathroom, spaces in which she can't be disturbed, in which she can practise her own secret rites.

She supposes she is mad. That's what her friends would certainly call her, if they knew what she sometimes does when she's alone. If she begins to publish what she writes, then the whole world will know she is mad too.

Very often, when she's by herself and safely invisible, she gets the urge to fall on her knees and pray. To something both inside her and outside her. The summons comes abruptly, and she lets herself obey, falling down, joining her hands together, feeling flooded with sweetness and pleasure, wanting to cry out in praise of whatever it is that suddenly opens her, inside her, and calls. In the middle of the city, the street and traffic noises bruising the window, the race of work and shopping and money-making going on just outside, she surrenders, is surrounded, opens her mouth wide and gulps in, and then a landscape of open hills, sun and cloud moving over them, enters her, and brings her joy.

Of course she tells no one. Her friends would edge away, if she admitted to having religious experiences and desires. With her friends she discusses sex, death, relationships, money, the unconscious, art, politics, books. The only taboo subject is spirituality. To be interested in this is to be priggish, neurotic, repressed and reactionary. She's done her fair share of sneering at Christians, who eat their God's flesh and drink his blood, who tend to be so depressingly unsensual and dowdy even when they try hard to be trendy with guitars in church and updated prayers and images. For her atheistical ex-Protestant friends religion means Christianity and backwardness. Other religions, foreign exotic ones, are on the other hand sympathetically respected, as being part of Third World cultures oppressed by imperialism. What hypocrites, what snobs we are, she thinks: to patronize in others what we deny in ourselves. Yet she doesn't want to be a British pagan and worship some sentimental icon of a lost Mother Goddess, she doesn't want to wear robes and sandals and be a Druid or moon about in the Celtic twilight or search for Pan, she doesn't want to be a fanatical embarrassing bore. So she keeps quiet. She wears the savage satirical costume of her peer group and generation, she goes dancing as often as she can afford it, she has her love affairs, she hopes she looks normal. The experiences keep happening, and she lets them. Deep down, she trusts them, because they bring her joy, because they allow her to let go of herself and to get lost.

Homeless, she fears being nowhere, having nowhere to go. Homeless, she starts to understand the true condition of physical existence: we are all part of one another and part of the universe. How banal that looks, written down. She ought to invent a specialist language, like the mystics did, the ones she studied at university, trying to set down their truth as precisely and scientifically as possible; rigorous systems of understanding; no despising of logical language. Concepts. Heat, sweetness, and light. To be understood by the *rational* mind.

The self can become lost, can be safely homeless. Writing is like meditation: you focus, concentrate on the breath going in and out of the body, accept the stream of images passing through. You record them, then play and pare. Not only must you let yourself be a conduit for that flow of images moving from outside to inside and then out again, crystalline and dancing; you must translate it, anchor it in your own bodily existence in society and history, bring all of yourself to bear on it as you search for metaphors.

She laughs, and tears at her hair. This is all very well, but hadn't she better get down to some writing? Enclosed in the perfect O of her garden, no exit or entrance, she is a stone, a blade of grass, a flower, a tree. It is also true that she is human, and can speak, can tell her difference from stone, grass, flower, tree. On one level she is them, knows their inaudible speech; on another, she must struggle to create her own, name herself as

208

human, find out what the hell that means. Find the way out. Find speech.

She opens her mouth.

This is the truth of it. Want.

She wants to flow out and touch that world outside herself, that m/other; surround it, merge with it. She wants to take it all into her mouth open to the air sucking biting chewing swallowing. Because she is starving. All mouth. Nothing but this wide open mouth. She is greedy, too: she'll never have enough, wants to eat the whole world, everything in sight.

The pleasure of it, on her tongue, as she eats: mother meadow mountain. That's the good moment, those few seconds of delicious taste, the juices running; before she swallows, loves the world to death, and it disappears inside her, gobbled up, inside her the corpses of beloved dead mothers bloody and chewed. Then she's all alone again, still wanting, still wanting to eat. Her mouth closes on air, on nothing. Still hungry. Unsatisfied. Desperate. Too powerful. Too destructive. If the thing she loves would only *stay*, and not vanish. If the moment of tasting it would not slip away.

She wants to disappear. She wants to let go of this greedy mouth, to flow out of her body and become part of the other, the meadow, the mountain. Will she ever come back if she lets that happen? How will she find her way back again, into the body/self that is necessary most of the time for living in this world?

She needs an umbilical cord, joining the anchored body of flesh to that other imaginary one that flows out and becomes part of what she loves. Don't cut it. Or she'll never be able to come back.

Out of this chaos inside, make a pattern. Out of the timeless perfect whole of the internal world, pluck two or three symbols at a time. Let yourself make a mess, make mistakes, fail. Laugh at yourself. Fall from paradise, from the enclosed garden, and write words. She scrabbles with her hands at the green hedge. Making a gap.

31 When I was at university I was happiest in libraries. I sit in the Bodleian, the pages of books raining through me. Books are food: I open my mouth and am filled and snort like a baby. Reading is joy felt in the body. I feast at a banquet, can feed uninterruptedly, pleasure flowing through me in wave after wave as I'm caught up out of myself into the company of poets, philosophers, mystics. I walk with them, and am one of them, and learn from them.

I remember a male student shouting at me in the courtyard: you cold virgin sitting cooped up in the library reading medieval love songs, how can you understand them when you know nothing of sex?

I join the Society of Bibliophiles. The other members are all men, booksellers and dons. Much older than I. On Sundays we take small local trains into the heart of the Cotswolds and visit shabby old homes housing famous private collections. The teas are always good: thin sandwiches filled with savoury relishes, scones and cream, walnut cake. My companions wear black overcoats rusty and greening with age, treat me with cautious courtesy, suspicious attention, unbend when they realize my passion for typefaces and paper, every aspect of printing. I learn to speak the language of my love: sheer poetry of new words precisely articulated with one another. I speak to these men, shyly, the dialect and code of books, and they let me in. It does not matter that I wear a pink mini-dress and parrot-coloured high heels: my devotion is my habit, like that of a nun in the world wearing a tiny cross on her lapel.

Here in my Arkive on the Ark, mind and body are not split.

*

– I don't *want* a child, Noah says: and there's an end to it. D'you hear me? *I don't want a child*.

I consult the riddle book.

So why does *to conceive* also mean *to conceive*?

32   I go ashore by myself. The island is all lit up, golden sparks in winter darkness. The narrow streets of dirty grey and yellow *palazzi* are choked with exhaust fumes and dogshit, webbed with gold strings, huge single crystals strung above my head on gold laces. As I look down the street, the delicate gold snowflakes stack themselves into a forest of frost; marks of the way through. The air is hoarse, dark as chocolate, smelling of petrol and cinnamon, slivers of silver shaved off it by the rasp, rasp of a plane in a carpentry workshop, door propped open. Corset shops. Wheelchair shops. Gold windows jiggle in the river. A scull, passing under the arch of the bridge, pulls a peacock tail of coloured lights.

In the early morning, the air is still clean. The winter sun falls on conical piles of yellow apples in the market, on heaps of walnuts, brazil nuts, almonds, chestnuts, dried dates and figs. Smart women in fur coats carry bouquets of artichokes and broccoli, poke at russet pears and scraped yellow potatoes, run their fingers through green peppercorns and black ones, weigh pods of carob, sausages on a string, bunches of violet onions. A warehouse, its metal front rolled up, is dense with the fires of red chillis hung from the rafters.

Smoke from the glowing embers heaped in dustbins, burning to keep the stall-holders warm. It's Christmas Eve. I want to buy a spruce tree, and shining glass balls to decorate it with, I want to buy wreaths of mistletoe and holly, and pots of scarlet flowers, and candles, and silver tinsel. I want my own children around me.

Absence of stars. Absence of joy at this midwinter festival. A dark place inside me: empty; cold ashes in the grate.

212

Plastic carrier bag heavy with grapes and oranges in one hand, I wander into a church in a side street in order to inspect its *presepio* and sit down for a rest. Crib-crawling is one of my favourite occupations at this season: every church has one, tries to out-rival its neighbours. Toys for adults, not just children, to enjoy.

The crib here dominates the whole of a side chapel. Framed by lofty serge curtains of deep blue, it presents a country landscape. Far above it and behind it the night sky, mistily blue, is pierced by stars that twinkle on and off. Regularly, every few seconds, a luminous angel with outspread wings moves across it in a steady arc, gently pulling a banner of light like the tail of a meteor. It disappears, reappears, disappears again, always on the same track. An invisible choir croons that it's dreaming of a white Christmas. On the rocky ground of crumpled brown paper in the foreground, underneath that vast blue dome of sky, innumerable peasants go about their business: small wooden models of men, women and children fish in streams of real water, boil pots over fires emitting real smoke and flames, hew wood, cart it home on their backs. Sheep, donkeys and cows are graded in neat rows according to size. Tucked away, very much on the sidelines of all these important activities, Mary and Joseph admire their new baby. He's a big boy, with fat knees, curly black hair, and a real silk nappy. I put a two hundred-lire piece in the slot below the crib. And then the sleeping baby opens his waxen eyelids, bats his long curly eyelashes at me, and jerkily lifts his wax arm up and down to bless me. Until the money runs out.

Noah's present to me is disappointment; bitter and deep, curdling my love for him, souring it to resentment, anger. I want him to want a baby too, and he doesn't: too much responsibility, too much curtailment of his freedom to roam the world. He doesn't want to be tied down by a child's needs for regular school attendance, a stable home life in one place, friends and family around. He wants to remain the child, not to become its father.

I could steal a baby from him: make love without contraception and without telling him, and so get pregnant. He never knows when I'm ovulating or when my period's due. So far I haven't done it, feeling it's wrong, that I must wait,

213

persuade him. Getting pregnant that way would be disastrous, as he has warned me: he'd be outraged, would cease to trust me, would give me scant support during the pregnancy and the birth, wouldn't help me bring up the child.

When he comes inside me, I think he is impregnating me with sterilizing fluid, or with an abortifacient. No longer that good sweet milk of his that once filled me with delight, but death. That's the way I see it now.

How long does he think I'll wait? Time's running out for me if not for him.

I could get pregnant by him and then leave him. Or leave him and get pregnant by another man. Or have A.I.D. Bring up the child by myself. Oh you selfish irresponsible girl cry all the agony aunties: deliberately to become a single mother and not give your child a father and the chance of a normal life.

Far worse: my fantasy about stealing another woman's baby. A dear friend dies, and so I adopt her baby. I kill my friend, and steal her baby. This fantasy recurs, though I try to kill it.

I'll be a single mother if I have to. Lots of women are. By necessity, when their men abandon them. Or by choice.

The Virgin Mary was a single mother. Here she is in this church, in the big oil painting hanging on the wall of the side chapel opposite the crib.

I watch the women on the canvas: the one with wings, and the one who sits under a dark green tent, eyes lowered, reading her book. The fold of a knee, the flow of a thigh; the angel insisting, making her point with a raised hand, adamant gesture of long index finger; she's thin as a boy, with a curled wi? and a tasselled cloak.

The girl opposite her grips her book, and imagines. She is reading the story of the Boat. Meditating on words, her half-shut eyes cast down, seeing nothing but the black marks on the white page, she conceives other words; new words. She creates the Word inside herself, by herself, using her *own* power.

The angel with rainbow wings represents her inspiration: the words of the other/the book, that she hears in conversation/ in reading; and takes inside. Then the alchemy: new words made out of old; new words she will offer others in her turn.

Who is she, this virgin? She who broods under her green
214

tabernacle, her dark imagination?

She is the proud hunter-goddess who walks the mountains with her companions. She has many lovers but belongs to no man. She scorns marriage, preferring freedom. She is the one who turns away her face. She is the virgin; which means the whore. She is the Ark, the maker of the Word. *She is the author*. Meditating on the Old Testament, then discarding it, she will write a new text, with herself as the subject that speaks.

This is the meaning that pushes me out of the church.

33   For supper the Deftly Sibyl has made a dish of green
ribbon noodles with *pesto* sauce. Afterwards comes a
tomato salad served with a big piece of Pecorino cheese,
and then the fruit I brought back on board with me.

– My days of discreet starvation, I tell the others: are over.
For two years, when I was living on social security while I
finished my librarianship thesis, I survived on brown bread,
carrots, apples, and cheap coffee. I paid my rent and bills; just.
When friends came, I fed them well, then starved for the rest of
the week. I was lucky: my friends could afford to lend me my
rent money when things were tight, to cook me supper
sometimes, to take me out to a restaurant occasionally. My
friends helped me survive. Other people, commenting on how
thin I was, assumed I was dieting. I knew that this period would
end; my middle-class education would help me find a job when
I needed one again. Single mothers I knew were permanently
hungry; they fed the children first. When my giro arrived every
fortnight, I transformed it instantly into my favourite food,
feasted for three days, then went back to brown bread and
carrots. Feckless, unable to budget, people like me were called
in magazine articles. A rich person can't know that pleasure:
the plate heaped high on Monday after the scanty weekend, the
delight in forgotten tastes, greediness permitted to jump out
and enjoy. Full larders amazed me. When I went out to supper I
ate more than I wanted, storing fat against a lean tomorrow.
Now I've got a job and an income, I no longer need to gobble:
the food will be there again next day. I still gobble books.
Hunger that never goes away. My body is sturdy, well rounded.
My desire is keen and lean, a paperknife cutting through pages,
slicing up the text, the book falling apart like a cut loaf. Holy

216

communion once a day was never enough. My husband feeds me well. He likes to see me eat. He courted me by cooking me supper every night for six months. *Yes*, I cried: *yes*, I'll have you. He licks me and whispers: I could eat you all up. I laugh: go ahead.

– I want to be ordinary, the Deftly Sibyl says: I want to be normal. Like other women. I believed that marriage brought me the possibility of coping with a reality shared by countless other women across the world, of sticking to a commitment, of engaging in the struggle to invent a morality I could honestly live by. Happiness: the capacity to accept reality. I did not want to be mad. I left her behind when I married, the mad girl of my early twenties. Yet she's been lying in wait in the cupboard all this time. When I'm alone, she jumps out, and gibbers. I should stay in the library, and read my book; I should control my body with contraceptive devices, not smoke, not drink too much, eat properly, get on with my writing. I don't like the story forcing itself out of my pen. I want to write a story in which the heroine does not have to leave the man she has married. She can find independence, autonomy, some freedom; by *staying*. So many women write of the necessity to *leave* men. I want to be different. For what is this freedom and self-actualization some women write about? The freedom to be selfish? To leave my children? How can it be combined with loving others and allowing their claims on me? When my friend phones to say she's sick and can I pick up her children from school, should I say: no, my time is for me? What would a man do? Would he be there to be telephoned? Are men more free? What for? To make money? Not to spend time with their children? To chase that ideal lover?

– I want to be the author of my own story, says the Forsaken Sibyl: and of my own life. I can't bear the thought of a life which finishes well before death, such as I perceive the life story of so many women to be. To be perhaps forty, or fifty, and to know: this is all. I want the power to make things go on happening. Becoming a writer protects me from happy ever after, from death before death is due, from the stopping of adventures. It's better for me not to be married, not to be tied to a lover, male or female it doesn't matter which. Yet if I become a narrator and tell a story, I'm talking about something that's over, something

217

that ends. I can't bear endings. I'll stick to the present tense. I want to be the author of my future: closed book I'll open and read, text I shall write myself.

– The dream of adultery, says the Babble-On Sibyl: the repeated desire to get away. Baby in Mum's lap, whimpering if Mum goes off, quickly finding a substitute. Is that it? I'm not sure. Certainly if you're the one playing Mum then you need to move sometimes. Often. Well, I am not pure. I have helped to make my own situation, to place myself as Mum, always available to Neil's needs. What will I have to break in order to change my situation? Will I break too?

– I'll tell you about the woman who goes away, the whore, says the Re-Vision Sibyl: it's simple as ABC. Like the ABC of Women I read about once, composed in the fifteenth century by St Antoninus as a meditation aid for his lady parishioners. Penitents. A is for Animal, B is for Beast, C is for Cupidity; and so on. Amazon, Bitch, Cunt, Devil, Fiend, Gossip, Harlot, Idiot, Jilt, Lesbian, Mollycoddler, Nymphomaniac, Nag, Pervert, Queer, Slag, Tart, Vixen, Witch. Feel free to fill in the blanks.

– You see men so crudely, cries the Gaffer: enemies to be kept at a distance, studs to be used for breeding purposes, children to be patronized. What about the men who love women yet are rejected by them? You don't care. That's *your* problem, you say scornfully. I could spend days on your picket line, helping in your crèche, servicing and protecting your peace camp, and you wouldn't bother to thank me. Haven't you lot got any men friends? Most women, normal women, would never agree with you. They like men. They don't have your problems.

– Guilty men are silent, says the Correct Sibyl: scared to say the wrong thing, scared of Big Feminist Momma beating them around the head with her stick of ideological purity. They're the worst. Holier than thou. I'd rather have you any day, Gaffer. At least you say what you think. I don't want to be any man's mother. Never again. I want men not to be scared of my power, to enjoy me, to leap at me, to play with me, talk to me, listen to me, read me, desire me ardently, notice when I'm in the mood for their company, leave me alone when I'm not. I would like men to enjoy being men: it would make life easier.

218

I like some men. Quite a lot of the time. I also like solitude, country walks, travelling, eating, drinking, reading novels at breakfast, digging the garden, all the usual things. But I have no desire to punish anybody. No, that's not always true. Let's say: no desire to act on that desire.

— I would like a story about food, the Re-Vision Sibyl says: and about punishment.

34 Already they are lost, and quarrelling.

– You're the driver, Francis accuses her: it was up to you to remember to bring the map.

– You're the navigator, Barbara snaps back: you should have thought of it.

She hunts in her bag for a cigarette, lights one, refusing to notice Francis's frown. He winds down the window, and the icy afternoon air strikes in. Barbara shivers. They are still below the snowline, but she is not adequately dressed for this weather. The cold enters her thin leather boots, her black lace stockings, her fine wool tunic, her leather jacket. She shivers again, and draws her paisley shawl around her neck. Even her hands are goose-pimpled. How disgusting.

She has pulled up on one side of the road which zigzags vertically up from the valley floor. The top of the mountain, which she can see when she cranes her neck, is a row of great jagged teeth. Thin waterfalls foam down it. The road below is a crumpled grey band, and red-roofed houses hang above them as though dangling from the sky.

– We must be on the right road, she says: that turning there can't be the right one.

The unsignposted track goes down to the left from the heart of the V of the next turn, just ahead. Crestino can't be down there. Where or how could it perch on those fluent masses of rock?

Francis runs a hand through his hair.

– You're probably right. Let's go on until we come to the next village and we can get directions.

– If we can understand them. So few people up here seem to speak English. They're so backward.

220

Barbara sighs, and stubs out her cigarette.

– Some New Year's Eve it's going to be if we can't even find our hotel. Wind up that window, can't you? I'm freezing.

She eases the car up into the next bend. They travel on in silence, climbing steeply up an interminable series of loops and bends. Twilight advances on them, the pale sun swallowed by blue mists, the edges of overhanging rock blurred by shadow. It is much colder now, and the road is glazed by ice. Snow films the crags ahead, marking their hollows, and crisps of white drift past the windscreen.

– The chains for the wheels, Francis exclaims: we didn't hire any when we got the car.

– I didn't think we'd need them, Barbara defends herself: they should have told us.

Sweat starts up in her armpits, dampening her silk camisole, probably ruining it. On the next bend, the car slithers a little. It is not dangerous yet, Barbara tells herself. She holds her breath. Concentrates.

– Careful, Francis warns her: go slower.

– Shut up! Barbara yells at him.

They emerge from their twisting ascent onto a narrow plateau, where the road, though glimmering with black ice, is mercifully flat. On their left, the mountain sheers on up, clothed in dark pinewoods, and on their right is a wide meadow edged by small pines and scrub. Tufts of grass poke up through patches of frozen snow. The meadow ends abruptly, tipping over the invisible abyss of the valley they have just climbed out of. Far beyond it, on the other side of the drop, blue mountains rear their sharp profiles like the heads of old women flung back, ready to bite, chins and noses in clear outline against the grey sky. What was that book she read recently, about a plane crash in the Alps? The survivors, lost in the vast snowslopes, huddled together under the grim needle tips of uncaring rocks, began eating their dead comrades in order to stay alive. Corpses laid out in the snow, slivers of flesh shaved off them and dried in the sun. Then the meal.

– Look, Francis exclaims: a house.

The end of the plateau widens out. On their left, between the mountain and the road, a small hill, round as a pudding, lifts itself, snow sifted onto it like sugar. A paved track, edged by low

221

stone walls, curls around it and away between tiny sloping meadows scattered with snow. The bare black branches of little thorny trees are clear as liquorice against the white and brown earth, the blue air. The house squats at the base of the hill, square and two-storeyed, a row of round windows under its sloping roof. Two stone columns, topped with leafy capitals, frame the door, and wooden shutters, painted dull yellow, are folded back. The small garden is adjoined by a pocket-handkerchief orchard, wizened apple and pear trees splayed and bent by years of wind. On the other side, a vegetable plot, sheeted by ice as clear as glass, encloses whorled turquoise cabbages, fat plaits of leeks toppling across each other, the spikes of onions.

– It's like the gingerbread house in the fairy tale, Barbara says, laughing: it's so pretty.

Looking, she can taste the earth, the cold air, the vegetables under their lid of ice. She wants to eat the little house, its cream-coloured stone, its raspberry wooden window frames, its plum-raftered roof. Her fingers itch for her notebook and camera. Later, she tells herself: first things first.

– Let's knock, she decides: and ask our way.

Even before they are out of the car, lights spring out in the house, each window an oblong of warm gold. The front door of the house opens wide, displaying the sturdy black silhouette of a woman who stands still, one hand on the latch, steadily watching them.

– There's the witch, Francis says.

– Of course you must stay here tonight, Angelina insists: we can ring your hotel. I have plenty of room. And you are too tired and cold to go any further.

– That would be wonderful, Barbara says: this is such a lovely house.

Her eyes travel round the room again, checking. The walls and ceiling are panelled in silvery pine, worn smooth by the passing of three centuries. A green-tiled stove bulges in one corner. The gleaming dark planks of the floor are scattered with woven rugs in faded primary colours, and the walls are hung with eighteenth- and nineteenth-century examples of folk art: heavily varnished and cracked holy pictures of saints

222

done on wood, scenes of country life in naïve oils, all surrounded by ornate frames of gilt and shells and tin lace.

– This house belonged to my grandparents, Angelina explains: nothing has changed since their day.

She gestures at the muslin and lace curtains hung at the two tiny square windows, the wooden benches, the porcelain jugs and bowls arranged on the shelf above the stove.

She sighs.

– Often I think of selling this house. It's too big for me now. Too much work, after my husband died so long ago.

– I'm sorry, Barbara says.

It's awkward having to converse in broken French, their only common language. Things come out clumsily, over-simply, the wrong way round. Barbara tries to work out the sentence in her head before she speaks.

– My fiancé is an antique dealer. Please. If you want to sell anything, perhaps he can help you?

Francis kicks her ankle. But Angelina does not seem upset. She sits back in her wooden chair, her palms on her thighs, smiling.

– This house has such integrity, Barbara hurries on: it's so unified, so complete.

– I am glad to have visitors who appreciate my home, Angelina answers: I shall open some wine, and we shall drink a toast to our new friendship, and then I shall cook dinner.

Barbara follows her into the kitchen. Its smoke-blackened walls are hung with copper moulds, racks of antique cooking implements, iron pots and pans. The stone fireplace is set with meat-jacks and fire dogs, a wicker basket of logs. A shallow stone sink in one corner is piled with pottery dishes. Pine shelves are stacked with earthenware jars and china. The table is spread with a red and white checked cloth.

– It's perfect! Barbara exclaims: marvellous!

Angelina smiles politely, picking up an unlabelled green bottle from the table and wiping it with a corner of her striped apron.

– I write about cookery, Barbara explains: for a magazine in London. A monthly supplement about life styles, with lots of colour pictures. I've come to Italy to do a series on Italian regional cooking. Italian food has become very important to us.

223

This kitchen is so right, so authentic. I wonder, would you mind, could I take some photographs?

– Please! Angelina says: I would be so happy.

She puts thin-stemmed wine glasses on a tray together with the bottle of wine, half a salami, a brick of pale butter, some white rolls, and picks it up with her strong hands.

– If you are interested in cooking, she says, nodding to Barbara to open the door: you must learn some of my recipes.

The salami is fresh and delicious, containing no artificial flavouring or preservative. Hard to import into England, Barbara thinks regretfully, as the *exquisite tastes of pork and pepper and garlic* burst inside her mouth. But at least she will be able to describe it in an article, give her readers a hint of the flavour of the real thing, make them salivate with longing for her recipes.

– Leave your cases downstairs, yes? Angelica suggests: let us have dinner first, and then I will show you your room. There is a little place to wash next to the kitchen. Barbara, perhaps you will like to help me? Francis, we leave you here with the wine, to do as the men do.

Dinner is served in white china dishes hand-painted with flowers and gold flecks. Francis has insisted on laying the table, despite Angelina's protests that it is not a male job. He strokes the scorched-linen tablecloth, the black-handled knives, the wrought-iron candlesticks, the silver spoons thin and sharp with age.

They eat *home-made pastry cushions stuffed with cream and spinach and nutmeg and then fried in olive oil until they puff and swell and are removed from the frying-pan to a cloth-covered basket.* Barbara has watched this operation and taken careful notes. The heel of Angelina's strong hand smiting the ball of dough, stretching it away from her across the scrubbed table top. Angelina's big fingers handling the rolled-out dough lightly, so lightly, cutting it into paper-thin diamonds with her long knife.

After this a *bollito of beef, chicken and tongue. Another simple and delicious dish, and one not sufficiently appreciated by visitors to Italy. Perhaps not even by Italians themselves. The*

*rich stock is ideal as the basis of a risotto the following day, and
can be kept for several days in the fridge.*

– How did you happen to have all this food in the house?
Barbara asks: it's as though you expected us.

– Aha, Angelina smiles: I like to eat well, that is all. A woman
on my own, I like to take care of myself and cook myself nice
things.

– I worry about putting on weight, Barbara says: I have to, in
my job. I have to look good. But tonight I'm going to forget all
about my diet!

After the bollito, *a salad of fresh green leaves tossed with
olive oil and flavoured with* rugeta, *a bittersweet herb
unfortunately unobtainable in England. Its strange taste of
walnut and egg adds the final authentic touch. No mustard in the
dressing. A drop of lemon juice may be added if wished.*

Finally, *a chocolate cake, cold, with rum in it (recipe on next
page). No cream. The plainness of the bitter dark chocolate, the
smoky rum, is quite enough. Inelegant to overdo it.*

All through the meal flow the wines Angelina insists they
must taste: *red wine earthy and strong and heavy with tannin;
white wine delicate and golden, with a dry sparkle, a hint
of petillance.*

*Black coffee, served in thimbles of white porcelain. No
saucers. That is the traditional way.*

– Why don't you stay with me tomorrow night too? Angelina
suggests: and celebrate New Year's Eve here? I can phone your
hotel for you again. There will be no trouble, I am sure.

Francis and Barbara exchange glances.

– Thank you, Barbara says: we'd love to.

– It's unbelievable, Francis declares: we've struck gold.

He and Barbara are sitting up in the high wooden bed in the
guest room upstairs, propped by square white pillows whose
cases are edged with drawn-thread work and bands of delicate
lace. The linen sheets are similarly decorated. The coverlet of
the bed, which they have folded carefully back, is made of
rubbed purple velvet threaded with stiff gold, and the quilt
beneath is of padded pink cotton stitched with a pattern of
scrolls. The panelled headboard of the bed, stretching up
almost to the ceiling, is made of the silvery pine they have seen

225

downstairs. One of the panels opens, to reveal a rosary of amethyst beads and a prayer book with gilt clasps. Francis, who has been examining the rosary as he speaks, twists round and replaces it in its tiny hiding place.

Barbara stretches and yawns.

– She can certainly cook. Her recipes will keep me going for three issues at least.

She pinches her waist.

– I'm getting so *fat*.

– Look at the pictures up here, Francis says: you can't find stuff like that any more. It'd go for a fortune.

The pictures up here are masterpieces of the intricate crafts worked by women in their homes in the eighteenth and nineteenth centuries. Framed in velvet and mother-of-pearl and beaten silvered tin, they are done in cut paper, in marquetry, in embroidered stump-work, in appliqué. Over and over again the Good Shepherd summons his flock, the Virgin holds out a stubby baby, the Son dangles from his cross.

– You'd better go carefully, Barbara warns him: don't rush it. If we want to walk away with some of Angelina's goodies we'll have to plan carefully. She's a grasping old bitch, I can tell. These peasants always are.

– I'm depending on you, Francis says, snuggling up to her: you're the interpreter.

– She's so *gross*, Barbara shudders: did you look at her neck? She's built like an ox.

She spreads her limbs out in the bed, one arm around Francis, her mind busy manipulating and discarding phrases and words. *Peasant aristocrats, sacrament of eating, ancient life of the forest, fossil shapes reflected in the forms of pasta.* She'll do better tomorrow, after talking to Angelina a little more.

– Time for a little fun and games before sleeping? says Francis, pressing closer: what d'you say?

– It's too late, surely, protests Barbara: aren't you too tired?

– I'm never too tired, he says, getting out of bed and going over to her suitcase: and besides, I want to make it up to you for being so horrid and unhelpful on the journey up here. Hmmm?

He turns round, brandishing the whip.

226   *

For breakfast they have big cups of ferocious black coffee tempered with frothy milk, fresh rolls with butter and home-made cherry jam. Barbara tries to punish her appetite, draws deeply on a cigarette. Fresh nicotine. How she loves that smell. How she loves its effect: swift laxative, voiding her of all that dangerous food. She looks around at the panelled walls of the little parlour. The polished wooden surfaces gleam back at her.

– It's like the Ark in here, she remarks in her bad French: you've rescued us and taken us on board, and the snow outside, it's like the sea.

Angelina, sitting opposite, inhales on her own cigarette, which she has rolled from coarse black tobacco taken from a tin. She holds the cigarette between thumb and forefinger. Her hands are revolting, Barbara decides: too broad, too red and coarse.

– You're a real earth-mother, she goes on: you remind me of my grandmother, you know?

She translates her comments for Francis's benefit.

– The animals went in two by two, Francis says in her ear: you've forgotten there's no Noah here.

Angelina smiles at them, visibly searches for French words.

– I just finish this cigarette, then we go for a walk. You will like to be in the snow.

Muffled in borrowed overcoats, their boots packed with layers of socks, they plod after their hostess. Up and up. The world has gone into negative: pale monochrome of peaks, the valley far below them scooped out of white blocks, speckled with the brown grains of houses. Pines bristle on the mountain's flank, each black branch lined exactly with white plush. They walk for an hour, in silence, their breath coming and going in hoarse gasps. They push up into steep woods, toecaps cutting steps in the blank ramp ahead. No path is visible. Only the walls of snow plot the curve of the vanished track. What were meadows are now full wedges of white.

The temptation is irresistible. Barbara runs heavily, floun-dering in whiteness, to the middle of a snowfield, lies down in it, waves her arms and legs carefully, in and out, in and out. When she gets up again, she has left behind the imprint of a creature

227

with a long triangular skirt and pointed wings.

– It's called a fallen angel, she tells her hostess, giggling: it's what we used to do as children, every time it snowed. It's a fallen angel, Angelina. It's like your name.

Angelina smacks her gloved hands against each other.

– It's very cold, isn't it? Perhaps it's time to go home.

The others wheel and follow her. Barbara is secretly relieved. She doesn't like walking much, and certainly not in this weather. It's much too cold. She bumps against Francis and takes his hand. Wet wool against wet wool.

They have seen no other walkers all morning. Now, the figures of three men, bulky in sweaters and padded jackets, red woollen caps on their heads, are climbing up towards them along the corridor of snow between the pine trees.

Francis drops Barbara's hand.

– Hang on a minute. I've got a lump of snow down my boot. Wait for me while I get it out.

He brushes the snow from a rock and sits down, begins to unlace his boot.

– We must hurry, Angelina announces: it will snow again very soon. Look at the sky.

She starts off again down the track, pauses, looks back.

– Barbara! Come with me, please. I need your arm. I am tired out with all this walking. I am too old.

Barbara grimaces at Francis and shrugs.

– She wants me to go on ahead with her. We'll go slowly. You catch us up. You're not going to be more than a minute.

Coming abreast with Angelina, she takes her arm. The older woman is breathing heavily, clearly in distress. She leans heavily on Barbara, who staggers a little under her weight. They set off together, Angelina maintaining a steady pace.

– I'm sorry, she pants: I just need to get home. To rest a little.

The three men meet them and pass them. Angelina turns her head away. No greeting is exchanged. Barbara, looking after them, is surprised to see them staring at her. I suppose it's because I'm a stranger, she thinks: they must know everybody around here. But the expression on the men's faces alarms her a little. Why this look of gloating contempt?

Angelina stumbles. Barbara rights her, then glances back

228

again. The three men, who have halted to watch Francis struggling with his boot, are marching away again, their backs broad and dark against the snow.

– I have a weak ankle, Angelina explains over a hearty lunch of *eggs fried with peppers and onions*: and it gets worse in the cold. I shouldn't walk on it too much. It is silly of me.

She will not let them help her wash up, shoos Francis out.

– No, she says to Barbara: let me do it. This is your holiday.

Clearly, she does not want to talk about whatever it was that upset her on the morning walk. Just as clearly, bustling about her domestic tasks is her way of soothing herself. Barbara settles herself more comfortably in her chair, watching Angelina pick up the greasy pan and begin to scour it under the tap.

– So then. Tell me what we're going to eat tonight.

Angelina ticks off the courses on her fingers. *Raw red beef carved into paper-thin slices, these delicious morsels then being salted and scattered with shavings of parmesan cheese*; next *a rich venison stew flavoured with red wine, cloves and celery*; then *a salad of curly red radicchio*; then *a dish of red lentils to symbolize good fortune in the coming year*; finally *pears cooked in red wine and served cold, with cream*.

– It's a very *red* meal, Barbara remarks.

– Quite so, says Angelina: that's how we do it here, for New Year's Eve. It's our tradition.

– What else do you do? Barbara asks: this is all so helpful for my article. I'll send you a copy, of course. I'd like you to see it, at least, even though you can't read English.

Angelina considers.

– On the stroke of midnight we open a bottle of Prosecco, that's our champagne, and sing a special song. Sometimes we yodel also. Then we all kiss one another and shake hands, and drink the wine. Always a white sparkling one, a dry one.

– Not a red one? Barbara teases her.

– No, Angelina replies: it's eating the red food that matters. The red wine we take outside and pour on the ground. Afterwards. Then we talk and dance a little.

229

She shrugs.

– For as long as we want. Then we go to bed.

She sighs.

– You can't believe how splendid it was in the old days, when my husband was still alive, before the children left home. All our neighbours and friends came for the evening, to celebrate with us. We would be twenty, thirty, for supper.

She brightens.

– But you will be here. This year it will be like it was before. When the children were here.

She peers at Barbara.

– You have children? You like children?

– No, shudders Barbara: too much mess.

Angelina smiles.

– Now I must begin my preparations. There is so much to do.

– Shall I help you? Barbara asks, fingering the notebook in her pocket: I'd love to see how you do it.

– No, no, Angelina chides her with a warm smile: go and enjoy yourself. This is your holiday.

Shouts, childish laughter, outside the window, draw Barbara's attention. She brushes past Angelina, lifts the little checked curtain, peers out. At just past three o'clock, it is already getting dark, a silvery gloom swallowing the garden, the mist beyond making it impossible to see.

– What's that noise? asks Barbara: what are those children up to?

Angelina does not cease her busy to and fro between table and stove. Her voice, when she speaks, is indifferent.

– Oh, it's just a children's game. Another tradition. On the eve of the New Year, one of the children dresses up as an old woman, to represent the Old Year. Then the other children chase him, and pretend to kill him. That way, the New Year can be born.

– How quaint, Barbara exclaims: how delightful.

– It's just a custom, Angelina says: something for your notebook, yes?

Barbara looks at the older woman's back. She shivers suddenly.

– I think, she remarks: I'll go and see what Francis is

up to.

Francis is sprawled on the bed, flicking through one of the magazines he brought with him. Barbara fiddles with the iron latch, making sure that the door is closed properly, then kicks off her shoes and curls up beside Francis on the bed.

– I'm beginning to think, she remarks: that there's more to our hostess than meets the eye. It's going to be more difficult than we thought, you know, to persuade her to sell us some of her stuff. She's pretty smart. She must know what it's worth.

Francis looks up.

– Funny you should say that. Those three men we met today, out on our walk, were talking about her. I didn't have a chance to tell you before.

– How do you know what they said? Barbara says: you don't speak Italian.

She feels quite breathless and cross.

– I understand a tiny bit, she insists: whereas you can't speak a word.

Francis rolls over onto his back, his eyes glinting.

– You'll have to take my word for it, won't you? What I *think* they said was that she used to be a film director before her husband went off, and that she's pretty rich. Hence all the bibelots. We've been idiots, you know. No simple peasant nonna could possibly possess all this stuff.

He pauses.

– They also said that she's mad. Her husband leaving her turned her brain.

He is watching her, wanting to see her get upset. She controls herself, smiles at him.

– How can you possibly know what they said?

He shrugs.

– Gestures. The expression on their faces.

– I don't believe you.

– Sweetie, you don't need to. It doesn't matter. We're off tomorrow morning. Put it down to experience.

He slides a finger along her chin.

– I know what you need. Something to take your mind off all this.

*

No more vanilla sex. Red-hot chilli. Ginger me up. Barbara finds more phrases for the recipe. *Ropes, hot wax dripped onto nipples, pincers, tongs, contract, consent, freedom, submission, cry, blood, enough, orgasm.*

Here is her own willing victim. A white backside offered like *an iced cake to be decorated.* Friend invitation tryst. Trust? Trussed. Triste? She will discover. *Athletes musclemen heroes childbirth anorexia stigmata sword-swallowers crucifixion corsets.*

– Shut up! she shouts to the cookery writer inside her brain.

She picks up the whip, and stands behind Francis. It is only a game between friends. To find out about power. Why get so het up?

She is always nervous, at first, of hurting him too much. Giggles. Feels clumsy, unschooled. Undisciplined.

– It tickles, Francis says, his voice muffled by the silk cushions of the chair.

His glossy porno mag lies open on the floor beside him. There's mummy, stuck to the page. Stapled in place. Eternally available. No whore she, going away and leaving her baby yelling and unsatisfied. Good mummy, who stays with baby. Breasts eternally on offer, legs spread wide to welcome her little man, cosy womb all ready for him, always a hot dinner on the table and a hot kiss.

Barbara sees that the twin fat cushions are Angelina's breasts. She whom the growing boy does not want to leave. Mummy mummy mummy don't make me part from you don't make me be a man.

Bad boy, Francis. Be a man, Francis. Take it like a man. Barbara takes responsibility. He is her child.

She lifts her arm again, more determined this time. She has been cheated. Her warm peasant granny is just another neurotic successful woman. Like herself. She smacks Francis harder for asking her to beat him. Your fault your fault your fault. That this is the only game we play.

Barbara is such an efficient lover. So responsive to her men's needs. She leaps springs bounces sucks. Beats when asked. Stays in control. Looks after them, holds them, brings them to orgasm, fakes her own, praises their sexual performance. Stays in control.

232

She does not know how to ask for what she wants. She does not know how to stop playing this game. Give to your baby. Give him what he wants. Beat him for wanting to stay with you. Beat him for wanting to get away.

Delicious smells, of *onions and garlic* frying, drift up from the kitchen below.

We are brother and sister, she thinks: both of us wanting the same thing. Both of us lost in the woods, and starving. Beware of the witch's house.

She puts down the whip. Francis is still moaning with pleasure.

– I would like, she begins to say: I want –

The scream beats at the window, asking for admittance. The children's voices whoop, triumphant.

Barbara runs downstairs, past the open kitchen door from which streams radio music and gusts of steam, and outside, into the blue darkness. Snow is falling. The moon is up, a slender crescent high in the sky with a single bright star at its heel. The icy air strikes her cheeks and neck. She blunders towards the garden gate, her slippered feet skidding on the glassy path, snowflakes whirling against her open mouth and melting, crisps of water, on her tongue.

She plunges across the deserted road and down the bank into the meadow. The row of pines at its far end hides the drop of the valley, and the great jagged mountains rear dimly behind, monochrome of paling blue. The meadow, deep in snow, gleams in the moonlight, the falling snow already blotting out the dents made by the children's boots. The children have vanished.

The old woman lies spreadeagled on her back, arms and legs flung wide, undignified. She is all in black, and her grey wig is askew, revealing her short grizzled hair.

Barbara kneels by the body and puts out a hand to touch it. It is Angelina's face she is looking into, and it is Angelina's hand, big and red, she is holding in her own.

Angelina's clothes are tumbled and disordered. She has torn her skirt in falling, or perhaps one of the children has slashed at it with a knife; it is spread out on either side of her like a pair of ragged black wings. Her white petticoat is similarly ripped, and her baggy bloomers. The penis pokes out sideways, limp and wrinkled.

Barbara goes on kneeling there, holding the hand of this person she does not know, while the snow falls on both of them.

This week we visit a district, famed for its peasant cuisine, in the mountainous north of Italy. Barbara Cheriton reports on fragrant ways with food and wine in the province of Adelmo, and describes rituals and festivals, unchanged for hundreds of years, in which food plays a crucial part.

35   The Gaffer sits in the Ark's Reading Room, shoulders
     hunched. He has decided that the best place to make a
     start is amongst all these writers who have come after
him, find out what they have been up to. Convinced that
his own book is the last word on the subject, he's puzzled
that others have felt able to go on stating the obvious over and
over again.

But he's depressed. There are too many books here. Too
many books by women. He's tired out already, can't stretch
open wide enough to take it all in. He can see the point of
focusing on a few new women writers: like adding salt or sugar
to porridge. A little more *crème de la crème*. Spice up the
familiar tradition. All right, he's prepared to taste books by six,
seven, even eight women writers he's never heard of, but any
more is too much. He'll be overwhelmed. They can't *all* be
good. So why should he have to read them all to find out?
He might be wasting his time. He might get bored. It's force-
feeding, that's what it is.

Surely, it stands to reason, the feminist publishers, and the
mainstream houses with women's lists, are publishing women
writers simply because they are women. An insult to any
decent writers among them. All these publishers claiming to
discover five or six brilliant new novels by women four times a
year. Surely there can't really be that many new women
writers? There isn't room for all those books in the shops. How
can all those writers become equally famous and admired? It
damages the entire concept of literary quality.

These days, he broods, male writers don't stand a chance.
You're only published if you're a woman, or Black, or gay.
Nobody's interested in white men's writing. There white men

235

have been, slogging away over the centuries to investigate meaning and enrich the pantheon, keeping the flame alight, and no one's interested any more. What's a man to do?

He strokes his chin. First of all, some research. How to define men's writing? What do men write about? What is this thing the sibyls keep banging on about called masculinity? He could start here, in the Reading Room. A man is: not-a-woman. Scan all these female texts, discover what they leave out, then plunge into that blank space and explore.

First of all he needs to transcribe these texts, make notes. He plugs in his word processor and computer. Once he's got all the women's words in his computer memory, he'll be able to search, compare, scan, index, collate. Books are such an untidy way of storing information. Better to have it all in one place, on his floppy disks. Then he'll know everything.

He plucks a book at random from the shelf beside him. An anthology of Egyptian tomb inscriptions concerning women. He laughs. Why not dogs, or camels? He'll find out eventually. He spreads his hands over the keyboard and starts to copy out the book, word by word.

By lunch time he's tapped out half a chapter. He runs his fingers through his hair. At this rate it will take him several thousand years to get every book in the archive into his memory. Better find another method of research.

He wanders over to the male author catalogue. Rows of grey metal cabinets with deep drawers. The *obvious* thing to do is to start with the great classic authors, those agreed to constitute the pantheon. Most of whom just happen to be male.

He pulls open the drawer marked SH.

Death stares up at him. Waxen embalmed face, white hands folded over velvet stomach under the cellophane wrapping, locks of grey hair, severed by decay, fallen onto the yellowed ruff propping the shrivelling head.

He slams the drawer shut. Pulls open another marked WO. Bald skull, yellow tooth sockets, one cracked tooth stump still in place, but no lips. A maggot waggles in the nose cavity. Rotten cambric of the shirt parted and rent, arch of ribs showing amidst shreds of flesh.

The metal rattles back from his fingers. He tries a third. GR. Blood dried around the nostrils, in thick clots at the side of the

236

mouth, plastered like a poultice across the chest. The wounds all smiling at him, little red lips. Fast, delicate work: knives and razors.

What about his book, then? The foundation and source for subsequent literature in the West? His name must be on a card in this catalogue. He hunts back along the drawers to GA. Pulls it open.

Oblong grey metal crib in which a dead baby is laid. Satin bonnet edged with pleats of stiff whiteish lace frames a celluloid mask, cheeks tinted bright pink. Around the head a halo of twinkling gold stars, around the neck a necklace of gilt and pearls. The tiny body is wrapped in white satin, a sausage parcel, tightly bound with ribbons of gold thread tied in a large bow on the stomach. Pearls and gold beads decorate the silk mattress on which the little corpse lies, and the sides of the casket-drawer are lined with quilted pale blue brocade.

The Gaffer shoves the catalogue drawer closed, stumbles to the nearest wastepaper bin, vomits. He's trembling and faint, in need of fresh air. His hands stink of formalin and incense when he raises them to wipe his face, and his stomach still heaves.

He leans over the rail on the roof of the Ark, strains his eyes towards the shoreline just visible in the distance. Yet another island.

Those bloody sibyls. After all his efforts at making friends. To play such a trick on him.

What *can* he write? He's no nearer an answer.

Staring at the sea tumbling past the anchored and stationary Ark, he slowly becomes aware that it is alive with mermaids, a shoal of them swimming lazily to and fro and waiting for him to notice them. Raised arms splash silver drops of water, graceful necks twist and arch from side to side, amused eyes beckon him closer. He grips the rail, and peers over it. Real women, they look like; like the topless bathing beauties on the beaches he and his companions have sailed past and which he has longed to visit. Of *course* Mrs Noah only docks the Ark at islands conspicuously lacking pretty women disporting themselves at the sea's edge. How charming, then, that these girls have let their curiosity propel them so far out from shore. Their brown skins, veiled and then revealed by the green waves curling and

237

breaking above their heads, are gleaming, their little breasts so pert, the nipples lifted, dark brown, haloed by rose. No tails visible below their skirts of green water. Not monsters, these ladies. No cold cunts, tight, rejecting. They lift their chins at him, and laugh.

The Ark is moored near a large rock. The mermaids swim up to it, loll at its foot, half out of the water and half in, on cushions of seaweed, the white spray pearling their shoulders. Each one produces a circular mirror, into which she looks while starting to comb her long salty hair. They sing now. Sweet voices tossed away on the wind, melodies of longing, of promise. Each one is lonely, and wanting a companion. Come to me, dear man, come. He smiles, tickled by their openness. It's a difficult world for women alone, he has learned that much on this voyage.

He has been broken into little pieces by lack of nourishing love. He doesn't know who he is any more, if women don't need him. Those harsh earnest sibyls. He leans over the rail, and harkens to the mermaids.

The mermaids stretch out their arms and hold up their mirrors and sing. Help me, please help me. Help me to find a kindly editor for my work. Help me to get my poems published. Please give me an introduction to a publisher. Listen to my tales of woe. Believe me, I'm not like other women. I am so much more sensitive, so much more intelligent, so much more appreciative of you.

He can be loved by all of them at once. Standing on the deck of the Ark, dazzled by their smiles and by the light flashing off their mirrors, turning round and round in an ecstasy of being looked at, held, cosseted in their regard, he can see himself reflected in all their looking-glasses at once. He is whole again. He is holy as a host.

All this nonsense, the mermaids sing: about gender and sexual difference and the oedipal moment. Don't believe it. A trap constructed by women envious of your genius. Designed to pull you down into what's falsely called reality, to drown you in cold waters of common sense. It's not necessary to enter the human world. Remain a god, laughing and playing above it. Refuse to be named in their terms, to be reduced, part not whole, man not cosmic voice. Don't let them suck you in. *Choose*: to stay outside the ugly diminished house of human

238

language, to remain androgynous; which means *omnipotent*; *free*.

The mermaids twirl their mirrors in the sunshine.

If you want stories, they call softly: listen to ours. If you want songs, we'll carol you a lullaby. We'll carry you down to an underwater bed where you can dream and never wake up. We'll take you back to Atlantis, your forgotten home, the land that existed before time began, true paradise, perfect womb where childhood never ends. Come to us, dear man, come.

The Gaffer has never been able to remember his past. Only the words he has written on paper. He started with the beginning of the world, and he was always there. Now, as the women's voices call to him, terror pokes him in the back of his knees. Where *did* I come from? How *did* I begin?

The voice of a mother. Come to me, my darling, come.

He remembers the story he told in his novel.

Then he starts to imagine a draft of a new, unauthorized version.

In the beginning there is Mother. Omnipotent, maker of everything. Her right eye is life and her left eye death. She is both beloved and terrible. Her son hangs from her breast and she loves him. She is the whole world to him and he to her. Promised land. Milk and honey. Garden of Eden. Paradise.

His childhood is filled with petticoats and soft arms, table top in the kitchen he peers over to discover his aunts shelling peas. Their arched feet in peep-toed high heels, swirls of pleated and polka-dotted skirts. They lift him up; pass him from lap to lap while they talk. Mother's hands are dusty with flour, the strong fingers kneading. Look, baby, here's how to make a pastry doll. In stalks a column of wood, very tall and smelling of coal-tar soap, hedge of hair bristling above mouth, surely he scratches mother when he bends to kiss her.

In the cool of the evening Mother abandons her son and walks in the garden with this stranger. What can he offer that Gaffer lacks? He *must* know. He eats the apple, peers round the bedroom door.

The intruder has three legs. And he has a fiery sword which he flourishes in Gaffer's face. Watch out. I could cut your head

239

off with this. Gaffer is expelled from paradise: Mother unties her apron strings and he tumbles out, no longer her treasure. He's a big boy now. Banned the lap, banned the hiding place under the kitchen table, banned the gossiping circle of aunts and best friends, banned the double bed on weekend mornings. Shut out from mother's country, of which this person called Father is king, to which only Father can command entry; country that smells of sweat masked with lily-of-the-valley talcum powder, where nylon stockings and bits of cotton wool and cut-glass bottles grow.

In the beginning there is Father. Omnipotent, maker of everything. Terrible, and wise. Far away, untouchable. Except when he chastises the son he loves and Gaffer is held in his arms across his knees. The rod that leads the chosen one across the desert, away from mother.

Gaffer resists. He likes girls, hangs around them. They do sensible things like talking to each other, reading, inventing games he enjoys. One girl shows him how to draw cartoons and do magic tricks. Her friends giggle, hostile, and she withdraws.

Mother brings home a new baby. Over and over Gaffer asks: where did it come from? How did you know to expect it? An angel told me in my sleep, mother says, smiling over his head: and babies come from God. Father is God. Father makes babies. God plants the baby in mother.

Mother? Or Father? He can't see the connection. Can't remember it: the vision through the half-open door of the wild coupling of that monster with two backs Adam-and-Eve.

His mother takes him and his two friends out into the country for a picnic tea, with her neighbour from next door. The two women loll on the tartan rug, play with the baby. Cool shade under the scrubby oak trees, yellow gorse at their backs. Tea from the thermos sipped from plastic cups, white sandwiches bulgy with marmite and fish paste and sandwich spread. The little boys tangle with the woods, bury a split ball in the roots of a hollow tree, get lost, find the way out through thickets of purple rhododendron. He buries his face in his mother's lap, and she rocks him idly while she suckles the baby and chats to her friend. Then she pushes him away: go on with you, you're much too old for that nonsense.

The postman rings early in the morning. As Gaffer runs to

open the front door his mother flies out of the kitchen and up the stairs, wrap falling open to reveal black bra and camiknickers, long white legs.

Father goes away on business. Gaffer buys a Charlie Chaplin mask in the local toyshop, a plastic pipe, practises a strutting walk, pipe waved in one hand. This week I am Father, he tells his mother: this week, let me sleep in your bed with you. The baby is asleep: non-existent. His mother snores lightly, face greasy with cold cream. Tenderly he pulls the pink satin quilt up over her. That old witch from next door comes for lunch, and he hears them laughing in the kitchen. Then the mask and pipe disappear, put out with the rubbish. They do not speak of it.

Rescued. Father. You can be like me. My power is greater than that of the female. I will show you the way out of Egypt and into the real world. I will give you a second chance. Have I not formed you in my image? I will cleanse you of the stain of the woman. I will make of you a hero; sending you forth into battle so that your blood will baptize you, redeem you, mark you as mine. Forget your knowledge of the woman, for sex means corruption and decay. I will give you eternal life; am I not the Father who makes all things? The woman's blood is the sign of death: your wounds and your blood are sacred, the signs of life.

Jam-rags and tits. Bitches in heat, stupid with giggles as he goes by. Their terrible power to reject him if he admits to needing them. The ones who do it are slags and the ones who don't are frigid. Eve is bad, and Mary is good. The terrible devouring mother glowers in the background.

He could marry one, get his mother back. Weigh her down with babies so that she can't leave him, can't leave the house. Find cosseting again. Be in control of the woman; keep her in her place. Always ready for him, permanently available. Crucify the image of the Father and get his mother back. On his terms this time. Become the Father himself. Into the Kingdom. Heterosexual male. Saved.

He could father a son on his wife. When the child asks: who made me? where did I come from? what is sex? what is death? the new Father can hand on the Christian story.

*

The Gaffer stares over the rail at the cold perfection of the mermaids, and remembers.

When she holds him in her arms. When he lies back and is still. When he does not have to prove his strength. When he does not have to do anything.

She's the one he's lost. He bears the mark of her absence. The space of loss inside him has her shape. His bawling mouth and weight of tears. His sour mouth and pricking skin. His emptiness. There is just this gap, and this crying. Parting from her is necessary. It is over. It is over.

He cries, gulping into his brown silk handkerchief. Tears break the spell. The mermaids dissolve into foam.

He stomps down the companionway. Real sob-stuff, eh? All right, sob-sisters, listen to *this*.

36 At library school I learned more about sex.

Not only am I working on the Woman Problem in classification theory, I am making a lot of women friends. I tell one of them I fear I am frigid, and she gives me Masters and Johnson to read. My imagination fills with flashing neon pictures of women strapped to machines measuring their every response to stimulation. I wonder whether machines are more effective than men. I am certainly aroused by the idea of jerking, naked, on a table, with a lot of serious white-coated male doctors watching, and envying, my multiple orgasms which apparently men don't have. I don't have them either but I like the idea. I don't tell my friend this in case she disapproves.

She lends me another book: *The Myth of the Vaginal Orgasm*. Apparently I have been doing it the wrong way. More technical information. Women are like cars, with starter buttons. All a man has to do is press the right button for long enough. I discover how to come by myself. This encourages me.

I try to put these theories into practice with my next lover, a Marxist who lends me *Das Kapital*. It's a wonderful book, full of jokes. I notice that Marxism does not attend to the Woman Problem, and have many fiery arguments with Bill about this. Extended foreplay of ritual exchanges of teasing words is followed, one afternoon, by bed. By this time I am so panting with desire that I simply lie back and open my legs and he dives into me, in and out, in and out, while we stare at each other and drown, looking. I forget all the instructions about patient stimulation of the clitoris. I just open up and suck him into me, in and out. When orgasm sweeps through me I yell with surprise, sit up and say: that was not technically possible, the

243

vaginal orgasm doesn't exist!

I decide that the pleasures of sex are like those of reading: you hunger, you yearn, you open up, you swallow, you take it in. The body, the book.

Bill leaves me the following week because I want him too often and too much. Men are not as reliable as books. I convert my suffering into something tolerable by beginning to write about classification systems. I am at the centre, and I am allowed to relate to everything under the sun. Writing is more difficult than reading, but brings the same sensation of blissful release. Oh wise nuns at my convent school who warned against lolling on sofas before lunch with novels: I understand the dangers now. Too much pleasure makes you want more.

The Ark's Arkive hums with desire. Desire off the leash and given its head, making all the books jiggle up and down on the shelves and jump out of order.

– I'm not convinced by your arguments, Noah says: it's all too pat, too simplistic.

– Part of me agrees with you, I force myself to admit: I'm beginning to think, as a result of all you've said, that perhaps I shouldn't have a baby. That perhaps I don't really want one. I'm destroying my desire. That's what you want, isn't it?

I search the riddle book.

Can he *come to terms* with my *coming to term*?

37 We creep across the bay. When the mist surrounding us
dissolves, we see the island rear up, a single mountain with
a dented peak rising sheer from the encompassing sea.

Leaving the others on board the Ark docked in the tiny
harbour thick with tourists enjoying the crowded cafés and
shops, I take the funicular railway up to the village that
constitutes the capital. Craning my neck, I see a bus launch
itself onto the road ahead and dive upwards, hang over the
precipice of the cliff at my side, zigzag further up and out
of sight.

I wander through a honeycomb of tiny *piazze* connected by
paved lanes, archways, tunnels. Over the top of the high walls
on either side of me spill bright flowering creepers: blue
campanelli, clusters of pink oleanders with stiff dark green
leaves. The houses are plastered in rainbow colours. Balconies,
terraces and exterior staircases are set with tubs of geraniums
and begonias. Trellised vines crawl across loggia ceilings;
palms and cacti grow on the flat roofs. Painted tiles are stuck
above doorways. Baskets of lemons stand on doorsteps.

The street turns, winding around a corner, into a colonnade,
the deep blue of the sea suddenly visible through a pierced
screen of white marble columns twisted about with purple
flowers. The branches of umbrella pines sweep sharply up.
Scent of basil.

I climb the steep hill. At first there are still houses on either
side, and tiny orchards planted with apricot trees, little
triangular vineyards heavy with fat blue grapes, dusky bloom
under their pointed green leaves, rows of silver and turquoise
cabbages, aubergines, asparagus. The stone passage loops
around the walled garden of an old villa, solid L-shape with

245

ultramarine shutters and white plaster dirtied to a pleasing grey, tall nodding cypresses on two sides of the courtyard framing a well surrounded by squat palms, rust-coloured urns overflowing with aspidistras and a few pink geraniums. Peering through the wrought-iron gate, I see blue-grey shadows dance along the wall as the wind rustles the leaves of a wild plantation of tall pines and holm oaks and blows through the long grass invading the paving stones.

Now the hillside opens out: steeper, stonier, less fertile. Fig and olive trees cling to the parched earth scattered with cacti and low thorny bushes. The path turns into a staircase with broad shallow steps flinging itself up and up. Cocks crow. A man whistles somewhere out of sight. The sun is pallid gold in the moist blue air, a dusted blue, a blue mist. Dry rasp of crickets, chirp and buzz of grasshoppers. The stone steps are silted with dark red pine needles. White patches of boulders stick up through the brown grass.

I reach the plateau just below the very top of the mountain: the dented space I saw from the harbour. On one side, the ruins of a once-vast villa now reduced to curving corridors of broken columns. On the other, a rustic balustrade of lashed saplings invites me to leap into the sea down a sheer drop of several thousand feet. Leaning over the flimsy paling, holding onto a palm tree for safety, I can just see a white lace of breakers around a rock a little way out from the very bottom of the cliff. Everything else is sheer blue: sea and sky are the real world up here, earth just a foothold in blue space.

I want to go further up. The way is by chair lift. I stand on the little oval platform, ducking as the iron chairs whirl up, round, and off again, never stopping. I launch myself at a chair and scramble into it as it swings past scooping me up as cargo. Two wooden slats under me, one at my back, a strut locked over my lap to keep me from slipping out.

I'm away. I'm in a flying armchair, a little spacecraft open to the sun and wind. I'm flying. I'm flying alone. Just above the tree tops, skimming up a deep green cleft in the mountain, reclaimed from desert and planted with trees. I dangle my feet over the swaying tops of chestnuts, I hover through the sunlight and the dry air, the heat branding my bare shoulders and knees, my legs hanging in the void, my arms stretched out

246

wanting to touch the mountain walls but unable to; flying gravely and slowly and silently along.

It's the only way; to step out into the empty air and trust that I will not plummet down. My wings are quill pens, and bear me up. I tiptoe on nothingness.

Then earth rushes at me and knocks me to my knees. I stumble up, and find myself on the very highest point of the mountain.

This is a lonely place. Patches of bare rock, of scrub. The wind plucks at dry grass, at the leafless branches of a black thorn tree. Up here there are no books, newspapers, pamphlets or posters to give me a clue, no rope of words to lassoo the unknown and make it tolerable.

Up here there's nothing. No one. Except myself.

That 4 am feeling, when you wake suddenly with a parched mouth and thumping heart. Troubling dream you can't remember projects itself into scrape and scrabble of mice overhead in the roof, a stranger's fingers delicately testing your front-door lock. Take it all back inside you and what have you got. Your lack of certainty about what you want and what to do. Your lack of hope. Your lack of strength, energy, commitment. Your lack of a sense of humour about yourself. Your priggishness. Your lack of kindness, generosity, warmth towards others. Your blind seeking egotism. Your lack of love. Your lack.

So that's that.

38 The Gaffer cooks supper, using some of the food I have brought back with me from the island. Fat pizza, the dough crisp and biscuity, laden with seafood. Slices of tomatoes and dripping fresh *mozzarella* decorated with basil leaves. Aubergine marinated in vinegar and chilli, and stuffed yellow peppers, rolled in breadcrumbs and fried. Two sorts of figs: purple ones that are darkly rosy inside, and green ones splitting open to reveal white flesh shaded with pink. Cold wine.

My plate clean, I lie back in my chair. Try to tell the others what I found out.

The Gaffer puts down his toothpick and grimaces at me.

– That's rather like what happened to me today. I got no writing done whatsoever. I felt really depressed.

The tears gush out of me, running warm over my face. I can't stop them. It's like slitting a sack of water. Someone's hauling me to my feet. The Gaffer puts his arms round me and I sob into his shirt that's clean and ironed and smells of fresh air. He's so big that I don't have to worry that he's not strong enough to hold me while I blub. It's comforting to lean against his plump body and feel him sturdy as a wall propping me up and letting me rain tears down him.

Then I'm back in my chair, sagging, all the tightness gone, no need to pretend.

– I had an abortion ten years ago, I tell the others: an illegal one. My period was only ten days late, but I *felt* pregnant. I was convinced. I remembered the night I got drunk and probably put my cap in wrong. I wasn't ready to become a mother: I had little money, only temporary accommodation, I was struggling to write my thesis and qualify as a librarian. Tim always

248

refused to use sheaths. He agreed I should have the abortion. He was sleeping with two other women besides me. I rang up a woman I knew who had trained in the States as a paramedic and performed safe early abortions for women who couldn't get them on the NHS. My male GP was against abortion. The woman came to my house where I was living and tickled my womb with straws until the blood came, answering the expert jiggle of her fingers. She showed me a clot of blood no bigger than a seed pearl and said: that might have been a foetus. I told no one. I hardened myself, and felt only the relief. The guilt has lain deep in me, like a bone, and the sorrow. Now, at last, I can speak of it and take responsibility for what I've done. I am not a victim. I *chose*. Inside me is a harsh female god who straddles life and destruction and tells women to *choose* what we do.

– I've had an abortion too, says the Correct Sibyl.

– And I, says the Re-Vision Sibyl.

– And I.

– And I.

– And I.

We look at one another.

– That Boat I invented in the Old Testament, says the Gaffer: floated on dark waters. Underneath its hull were all the lost cities of the world. Now I wonder: how were they found, and tested, the elect? Did God grieve for the ones he killed? I didn't think about that. I didn't make him weep.

– I want someone to tell a story, the Correct Sibyl says: about a man and a woman making friends.

39 He finds the baby only because it starts crying so hard. Otherwise it would be impossible to know it is there.

The rubbish heap leans in the darkness, a hill of darkness itself, against the corrugated-iron fence erected by the building company in a vain attempt to protect the builders' supplies against the gangs of boys who scavenge at night. It's an unofficial rubbish heap, unsanctioned by the council, patronized by the people living around the crossroads on one side of which it sits broodily, an urban compost of old prams, cider bottles, broken ironing boards, gashed sinks, black plastic sacks of discarded clothes, rotting cardboard boxes heaped with used sanitary towels, worn-out stilettos, empty make-up containers. At dusk, the women creep from the flats to chuck the rubbish out. The council vans with their grinding maws, their high whine, don't visit these streets often enough, and the dustbins get stolen. The rubbish heap functions as swap-shop, free jumble sale. Most of the local homes are furnished from it. The pickings are left to the homeless to sift through, a pecking order everybody obeys.

The boys don't bother, usually, with the spilling smelly dump. They prefer the challenge of proper stealing, leave the art of rubbish sorting to women, older vagrants, kids. They prefer to swarm over the fence at the tip's back and prowl through the deserted building site, mindful of the Alsatian dogs on guard, loose and hungry, to look for materials light enough to be carried back over the fence for re-sale. Every couple of months one of them gets savaged by a dog. Every so often the council sends its men to clear away the foetid, decaying mountain of domestic refuse, post notices warning of fines, of imprisonment.

Nobody knows what the new building will be. Mounds of earth, stacks of cement blocks, give little away. Some say it's the new district brothel. Others insist it's the council's nuclear shelter. They don't care much. They have plenty of other things to worry about.

The moon ripples silver along the corrugated-iron wall that sings and rattles in the wind. Bored with a night of no booty, Turtle stops his mooching progress to contemplate the graffiti scrawled along its undulating length. There's a new one since last night. *The daughters of Isis will eat your heart out*. The red loops of the script wobble, and the message ends in a cascade of blood red drops.

Turtle traces its syntax with difficulty, only just having learned to read. It might come in useful, Dog pointed out: for keeping one step ahead of the other gangs. Survival depends on speed and accuracy; being able to read the police posters warning of imminent clean-up campaigns will show them when to vanish, decamp to another neighbourhood a few streets away, lie low until they judge it safe to return. The Little Sisters of Liberation run a library in the nissen hut at the corner a block away. They hold evening literacy classes, after the dole-out of soup and bread, and so Dog and Turtle start to slink in at the back, hands and faces hastily washed to achieve some semblance of normality. The Little Sisters ask no questions, embarrass no one, offer their vision to any who will listen. I struggle, they spell out: I fear, I desire, I cooperate, I love. When the police raid the centre, burning the books of poetry and the novels, removing the files before tinning up the entrance and ushering the three Sisters on duty that night into an unmarked black van, Dog and Turtle, still small enough to scramble through lavatory windows, escape with pockets stuffed with bread and pamphlets. And a sketchy knowledge of how to read. The bread vanishes immediately. The tracts linger: fire-lighters, lavatory paper, shoe-wadding.

Turtle scowls, unable to comprehend the threat that bleeds across the silver barrier in front of him, worried at the idea of a new gang arrived in the neighbourhood. Possibly older and bigger. Possibly better armed. He lashes out, kicks at an abandoned box at his feet. Its fabric yields, as soft as plastic, and immediately a wail goes up from its depths. He peers down,

251

investigating. It's a suitcase, an open suitcase, squashed between a pile of empty catering tins and a torn lampshade sticking black ribs into the night. The wail deepens, steadies into an intolerable cry. Cautiously, Turtle advances his hand, touches a blanket tucked around a small breathing shape.

Shit. A baby.

He'll have to shut it up fast, before some nosey-parker warden arrives on the scene sniffing trouble, has him arrested for being out after curfew. He hesitates, then puts his hand over the baby's mouth and nose. He misses his aim in the dark, grabs its hand instead. Tiny fingers curl around his, and the anguished crying dies.

Relieved, he lets go and steps back, eyes darting along the deserted street to clear his escape. The baby begins screaming again. Enraged, he picks it up, crooning hatred into its damp woolly hat. Again, it stops crying. Gurgles. Turtle is astonished at the power he discovers in himself, and with the astonishment comes a feeling he has no name for, a clutching of the guts, his bowels softening. This frightens him, and he looks around, uncertain what to do.

There are lights flashing at the far end of the main street, the livid pink of a police beacon turning, a high scream of sirens going up. The curfew patrol. Somehow, as he gathers himself to run, Turtle forgets to drop the baby. Shoving it under one arm, he ducks around the rubbish heap and scampers into the mouth of the alley lined on one side by the building-site fence, runs head-down into safety, away from the cars, into the dark.

Dog hovers on the other side of the packing case they have laid the baby on, holding a lit candle. Its flame jumps in his uneasy hand, causing shadows to swirl and dance on the bare brick walls of the basement, hot wax to run and stick on his fingers. When he curses, Turtle, gingerly unwrapping layers of sodden yellow nappy, assumes it's with pain.

– Shit, Dog says: it's a girl.

Beneath them, the baby kicks and crows, delighted to be rid of her stinking bandages. The two boys look at one another. Turtle is short and skinny, with white freckled skin and marmalade hair. Dog has seen this expression on his face before: the snub nose wrinkled in puzzlement, the pale blue

252

eyes slitted under thick white lids, the bony jaw tense with concentration. Turtle survives street life only by a miracle, so prone is he to stop short in the middle of a thieving expedition and be thrown off course by a dahlia in the gutter, by a change in the air, by a sudden idea. Sometimes, Dog has to admit, his friend's hunches, new trains of thought, are productive, lead to an improvement in their life style, extra pickings from a fresh source hitherto unconsidered; but mostly they don't, they just root Turtle to the spot, wondering and entranced, prime victim material just begging to be picked up. Dog fears for him, tries to teach him, by dint of insult and sarcasm, the likely consequences of his carelessness, succeeds only occasionally. He ends up playing mother to the younger boy.

Mother. He glances round, as though he has spoken the taboo word aloud, as though there are great ears pinned to the sheets of brown paper they have stretched across the doors and windows to resist the draughts whistling in.

– Get rid of her, he commands: quick.

Women of Class D are subdivided into *breeders*, *feeders* and *tarts*. If they are *bleeders*. *Non-bleeders*, depending on age, are classified as *holes* (pre-pubescent) or *sacks* (post-menopausal). Women of the superior classes are called by names Dog does not know. He has never met any. They live in a different section of town. The Prime Ministress has, as one of her titles, *Big Mummy*. But these are sacred words, reserved for her alone, and rarely spoken.

Turtle's expression does not change. He goes on looking at his friend in silence. Dog, at eleven, is a year older than he is, they have worked out, but he looks older. The structure of his face is purpose congealed like rock into apparently immovable direction. His brown eyes are usually blank, carefully concentrated into a stare, and his mouth is firmly closed over his teeth. The tic at the corner of one eyelid betrays him, and the hand, which constantly goes up to push aside the flopping strands of black hair, the stubby hand with its sore cuticles, its chewed nails.

– No, Turtle decides: she's mine. I found her. I'm going to keep her.

Dog drops the candle, whose flame sputters out as it hits the wet nappy on the floor. The wick sizzles as blackness drops onto them, their little bit of bright home reduced and snuffed out, the basement once more a cavern of cold and menace. The baby screams.

– I'll manage, Turtle asserts, groping for the matches: I'll look after her.

That forbidden word roars louder than the child.

What does Turtle remember? Not much. The New Era, its dawning carefully set out in the definitions of the New Era State Dictionary, has pulled a curtain across all their pasts. Grey shapes move behind his eyes. Five children crammed into one double bed. The social worker arriving to take him into the Youth Treatment Centre. A woman bunched in desolation over a sputtering gas fire. His escape from the social worker as they emerged from the lift at the bottom of the flats and she turned aside to show her pass to the policeman on duty there.

He re-lights the candle and sets it on a saucer. What to use for nappies? He looks around. There's nothing. They sleep in a huddle of ragged blankets stolen from the Salvation Army, possess no linen. He shrugs. The baby's arse will have to go naked and unwrapped for the time being. Meanwhile, he swaddles her in his one spare jumper. In the morning he'll return to the tip and see if the suitcase is still there. Till then, his arms, the nest of blankets, will serve as a crib. He settles himself and the whimpering baby, hungry for milk they'll have to steal tomorrow, on the ground, next to the worried Dog.

– What will you call her? Dog asks: you'd better give her a name.

Turtle considers. His sisters, he suspects, once had names, now converted into numbers on state orphanage registers and therefore erased from his memory. The Little Sisters of Liberation whispered about heroines, nervous fingers covering their lips: Rosa, Eleanor, Winnie, Sylvia, Sojourner Truth. From somewhere else swim up Grace, Florence, Teresa, Joan. Impossible now. Conspicuous. Forbidden.

– She needs a name like ours, he pronounces: we'll call her Mouse.

Such is the beginning of Mouse. When she is old enough to talk, Dog and Turtle tell her where she comes from, teach her to utter their three names. By the time she is five, she knows many things: how to boil water in a can over a fire, how to scavenge

254

for fuel and rubbish, how to linger around food queues, pounce at just the right moment, escape with an egg or two, a loaf, a can of beans. She keeps her curly hair short, like Dog and Turtle do, and wears, like them, trousers kept up with string, jumpers salvaged from the dump, plimsolls lined with old newspaper taken from their steadily diminishing store. Newspapers are not printed any more. Council announcements are made through loud-hailers or pasted up on walls.

The three young vagrants keep themselves as clean as they can, in order to pass for normal, meaning Class D poor, on the street, to avoid the vigilance of social workers, community wardens, police. To the casual eye they are like any other kids on the street: Youth Treatment Centre detainees out on an afternoon's parole for Community Training. So far they have not been caught and found out. So far, like the members of the other lucky gangs, they have avoided arrest, the discovery of their lack of ID cards, classification numbers, street passes.

Mouse learns to run. Fleet and silent on her black rubber soles, she speeds behind the boys on their nightly excursions for scrap. She loves the night, being lost in it, bodiless, yet rapid as the clouds scudding overhead. She knows every brick, every windowsill, of the neighbourhood, tracks the movements of others, notes their changes of health, their acquisition of pots or weapons or bicycle tyres, can often tell by a footfall who is likely to turn a corner. Brat the dwarf en route for his evening performance at the freak show in the community hall; woolly-hatted Mr Simpkins in his three-wheeled invalid cart, being taken out for an airing by one of the social workers from the geriatric ward; Big Lucy, popping out from the brothel between shifts for a packet of fags.

Big Lucy is the only woman in the neighbourhood who dares to walk around alone at night. Any child under twelve, any old person, found wandering the streets after curfew is asking for trouble. But a woman, in addition to a heavy fine extorted by the Night Police, will be *given bliss* by any passing male. *Tarts* perform a useful social function, in channelling and containing male aggression, and are therefore reasonably well paid. They are supposed to stay inside the brothel, where the men come with their cards that are stamped weekly with red stars by the authorities to indicate that *servicing* has been achieved. Since

255

sex is organized, and legal, inside the brothel, *tarts* cannot be raped. Therefore *rape* is a concept not included in the New Era State Dictionary. *Servicing*, and *giving bliss*, are of course heavily contracepted activities. Most of the *tarts* are given sterilization. Fertility and reproduction are the tasks of a different section of the female population, controlled by a different state department. If a tart goes on the street, it's her own lookout if she gets *blissed-out* and not paid.

Big Lucy enjoys her forbidden strolls. No one dares bother her: she's too quick with her knife. So far, she's safe, and not sorry. She displays her red star, worn on the right shoulder, her long dyed yellow hair, her fat white shoulders and calves and pumpkin-bosom, with insouciance, a cold blue stare. Even the policemen leave her alone. Not their type. Too big. Too powerful. Too ugly, they tell each other.

Dog and Turtle have explained the complex street rules to Mouse. She understands. She's frightened when Lucy tries to make friends with her, coaxing her like a puppy.

– Here, babe, she croons, extending a plump palm on which lolls a square of chocolate: come to Lucy.

Mouse, who's never tasted chocolate and doesn't know what it is, backs away scowling. Big Lucy laughs, and swings on by.

It's Lucy who saves Mouse when the boys vanish.

Mouse is eleven years old. Small for her age, thin. She stays home one night with a stomach-ache after eating hard green windfalls filched from the community allotments. Crouched, wrapped in blankets, she watches Turtle don jacket and sweater, slip his knife inside his breast pocket, tie a scarf around his neck against the chill of the rainy August night.

– I wish I could come with you, she complains.

Turtle's face softens, as it always does when she addresses him, but he goes on collecting up his equipment: a plastic carrier bag, a bunch of skeleton keys, a length of chain.

– You wouldn't be able to help tonight, he says: it's a big raid. We're joining forces with the Sewer Rats. You're too young.

She watches them leave, absorbed in the coming adventure, and bolts the basement door behind them before returning to her bed in the corner. From here she can survey doors and windows, her back to the wall, eyes sweeping in arcs like

256

headlights, body tensed against possible intruders. On several occasions in the past, passing tramps have attempted to force an entry, tempted by the prospect of what looks, from the outside, like a reasonably dry shelter. So far, Dog and Turtle have always been there, armed with knives and heavy sticks, to drive the intruders off.

She cries a little, clutching her painful stomach, snuffling into the bundle of her clothes that serves as pillow. Oh, she knows. Dog and Turtle confer together in corners, whispered conspiracies that shut her out from their plans for the future. She is too young, they keep telling her, for this or that exploit, and she understands how she has outgrown her baby charm, her function as mascot, as pet. Nowadays she's a drain on their resources, a too-hungry mouth, a dragging responsibility.

When she was smaller, as recently as a year or so ago, Turtle would still sometimes take her on his lap and tell her stories. Episodes from comics and newspaper strips used in the literacy classes, flashes of video programmes winking on screens behind the plate glass of corner shops before such places were closed down. The children lined up in front of the window, impassively watching crazy axe-men, dressed in the calico smocks worn by doctors, lingeringly dismember blondes trussed like fragile quail. The New Era changed all that.

She shudders, hearing floorboards creak above, the rain driving in long gusts at the loose panes of the basement door. Her candle is burning low, and she has no other. One of the reasons for the boys' sortie tonight is to replenish their stock of candles and matches, but they didn't tell her what time they would be back.

She sucks her thumb, closes her eyes, tries to sleep. In her dreams at night she becomes many Mouses. Mice. Her dreams are filled with nothing but Mice, a clock tower with her own face telling the time, a bright palace whose wide portal is her own mouth, a galloping horse coursing on four of her legs, a river which is her own body flowing along. Tonight, Mouse has gone, replaced by jagged dark shapes running in endless pursuit of something unseen and whimpering, patterns of blood running down the basement walls, enormous mouths cackling and grinning, flecked with spittle in which she will drown.

Now the stories rise up and leer at her. Dog and Turtle have

257

told her all about the expected, the commonplace, the *asked-for-it syndrome*: the women brutally attacked on the streets at night, left to die slowly in puddles of their own blood, their bellies and vaginas gashed, gushing. A warning. A warning. Don't go out. Don't go out. Now the violent sexual murders of men have begun to happen too. The authorities pretend to know nothing about it. The neighbourhood discusses the news in whispers, inspects the corpses before the refuse cart clears them away. Ritual tortures, ritual deaths. The genitals hacked off, laid on the dead face. The killers' signature daubed in blood on the forehead. D.I. Daughters of Isis. Nobody knows who they are. They are not in the Dictionary.

As Mouse opens her eyes, her heart thumping, she hears the feet stumbling down the basement steps. A trip and a curse. Then the hand trying the bolt. Her candle has guttered out, a warm pool of wax in the saucer when she searches for it blindly. She shrinks into her corner as far as she can, pulling the thin blanket up to her chin, ready to vomit as the hard green apples of the morning rise sourly up her throat and she tries to swallow them back down again. She clenches all her muscles, but the warm piss streaks down her legs anyway.

The feet retreat from the door. Now the hands are at the window. She imagines the monster as patient, huge, able to tiptoe down the iron area steps and at the same time magically lift off the ceiling of the basement, rummage for her with a glistening scaly paw.

Hissing whispers. A giggle. The catch on the window is easily wrenched and snapped. The window is pushed up, and it, they, are in.

A match flaring spatters her briefly with light before she dives under the blanket, eyes tightly closed. Her scrabbling, her gasps, alert her guests to her presence, and they stand still by the window as the match flickers and its quick radiance dies. She can hear the pumping of her heart, the rain beating down on the steps outside, someone else's jerky breathing. The night air rushes in through the open window and coils itself, a cold tube, up her nose, down into her stomach.

– What's that? A rat?

A man's voice, hoarse, sounding as afraid as she is.

The scrape of another match, this time applied to what must

258

be a candle-end pulled from a pocket. The light lifts her eyelids.

– We'll soon see, never mind.

She knows this voice. Lucy's. She hisses and spits, fist flailing, as the blanket is torn away from her face.

– Why, it's the little boy. So this is where you live, dearie. Clever little mouse, to find such a snug hidey-hole.

She kicks and struggles, but it's useless. Lucy knows her name. Lucy's bulk overwhelms her, and Lucy's hands lift her effortlessly up.

– Isn't he sweet? Look at his curls. And his big eyes.

Lucy's deep fringe is brassy in the candlelight, which warms her pasty skin thickly coated in powder. Her lipsticked mouth dribbles tender words while her eyes watch, measure, consider.

– I haven't got all night, her companion complains: how long are you going to be messing with that bloody kid?

Lucy turns the glare of her smile onto him as well.

– Now dear, who are we to get upset? Here we've found this nice dry basement away in from the rain. And a bed, here, look. Don't go spoiling things.

Nevertheless, Mouse, watching her, can see she is annoyed, perplexed. This isn't what she hoped for, that's obvious. Her smile keeps slipping.

– All right, Lucy decides: since we're here, we may as well get on with it.

Mouse, strapped to the table leg by the man's raincoat belt, watches them. If she keeps her eye on them, perhaps they won't kill her. Who knows what they might do if she shuts them off? Despite her terror, leaking down her legs and out of the corner of her mouth, she is curious. A new lesson to learn.

It takes about five minutes. Lucy rolls her coat and dress above her waist, grunting, lowers her knickers around her ankles, kicks them away. The man unzips his fly, clambers on top of her where she lies on the bed. She heaves her plump arms around him, issues instructions.

– That's right, dear. Oh, aren't you big, aren't you a fine fellow. Oh, what a whopper. There we are. In you come. I've got you. Come along then. Come on. Hurry up. That's it. Nicely now.

The man's white arse bobs up and down several times. Lucy gazes idly at the ceiling. The man climbs off her and stands up,

259

stuffing his shirt back into his trousers.

Mouse is puzzled. A man turned into a baby. Weak and wobbly. Needing. Dog and Turtle are not like that. The male body has always been her haven. Not the other way round. Hands which pick her up and stroke her cheek. Arms that hug her. A lap that holds her. Until a year ago, when the sad Turtle told her she must grow up, stop being a baby. Does Turtle, she wonders, do this? Does Dog? Is that why they go out at night? But it's forbidden, to do this. It's dangerous.

– And now, Lucy addresses her: what shall we do with you?

Mouse drops her eyes. It's then that she sees the blood seeping through her trousers, the dark stain on her thighs.

– You little *bleeder*, Lucy curses softly: you little *bleeder*.

– Cunt! the voices cry out in chorus: cunt!

Cunt is one of the most powerful words in the language, explains the Dictionary. Whereas in former epochs in the West, backward and illiterate ones, it was used mainly by men as an insult to one another, it has now been rescued and restored to its true meaning. It denotes Woman. Whole Woman. Real Woman. What every woman should aspire to: that essential and complete female Beingness. But since the females of our civilization are still, unfortunately, in a state of only gradual evolution towards full consciousness, the title *cunt* is reserved for the Prime Ministress alone, she who, embodying female perfection, acts as an example to the weaker members of her sex. Nobody has ever seen Big Mummy. Nobody else deserves her Name. Her palace is heavily guarded. She is worshipped at a distance. A statue of her, or a portrait, stands in every home, every institution, in the country. Some of the tarts in the brothel have whispered to Mouse that Big Mummy is dead. But nobody really knows. And it doesn't matter: dead or alive, she is an allegory of virtue. Omnipotent. Eternal.

– Cunt! Cunt!

The daily reading from the Dictionary is over. The final hymn has been sung. Morning prayers are finally ending. Mouse, still on her knees, glances at the plaster figure on the bracket high above their heads. The blue eyes are both kindly and piercing, the chin thrust forwards, the hands raised in loving admonishment. The sky-blue robe, falling from chin to

260

ankle, moulds the slender girlish body, its barely perceptible breasts and hips. Over one shoulder drops a sash of white silk, inscribed with the motto of the State: Consciousness; Cleanliness; Correctness; Caring. One bare foot, slightly thrust forwards, rests on white roses. The neat blonde hairdo is crowned with a circle of stars and lilies clasped at the front by a silver crescent moon. The smile is unfalteringly sweet, with a hint of toughness. Every day, morning and evening, Mouse and the other tarts kneel in front of this image, repeating the brothel prayers, asking for forgiveness, begging that they may become more like Her.

The tarts haul themselves to their feet. Lucy slams down the lid of the piano. The first shift begins in ten minutes' time.

Lucy catches Mouse up in the corridor.

– You managing all right? Happy?

Mouse keeps on walking in the decorous line, eyes fixed on the grey overall, red star just visible on the shoulder, of the girl ahead. She tries to consider Lucy's words, what they might mean, tries to undo them, take them in one by one. She shakes her head in bewilderment. Lucy squeezes her arm.

– Cheer up, chicken. You'll get used to it soon enough. It's not a bad life, you know. No one will hurt you.

She jerks a shoulder in the direction of the uniformed male guards, guns at their hips, who are stationed at intervals along the white bare corridor. A tart has only to blow her whistle, should a client prove violent, and he is quickly dragged away and dealt with. On the other hand, any tart blowing her whistle too frequently is liable to be suspected of *non-compliance*, and had up for questioning, and possible punishment, by the superintendent.

Mouse has reached her cell door. She pushes between its minimal swinging halves and looks at Lucy over the top of them.

– Let's talk sometime soon, Lucy suggests: I could be useful to you, and you to me.

– I've got to work now, Mouse mutters: thank you for your concern.

She waits for the other woman to depart before stripping off her overall and donning her work clothes. Silver leather bra, silver leather G-string, fake tiger-fur gloves, high-heeled shoes, tiger half-mask. She checks her appearance in the mirror hung at the end of the bed. Good. Slender thighs, concave belly. Most of the tarts, Mouse included, are on permanent slimming diets, to make sure they don't become too plump. A few, like Lucy, are allowed to remain large. They cater for the special interests of certain members of the officer class. Only last week, one of these was found murdered on the wasteland just behind the brothel, beside the rubbish tip. It was hushed up, of course. But everyone knows.

Mouse yawns, applies fresh lipstick, then arranges herself carefully on the bed to await her first client of the day.

– Come to mother, she whispers to herself, very low in case she's overheard by one of the guards patrolling outside: come to mother.

Turtle stands in the queue, shivering. Jacket sleeves too short, no gloves, scarf stolen last week from the factory canteen when he went back to the serving-hatch for a clean fork and turned his back on his chair for two short minutes. He folds his arms across his thin chest, sticks his hands in his armpits. Head down, whistling to keep his courage up.

– Number. Card. Health certificates.

The queue of young men shuffles forwards, one by one sucked out of the biting wind scouring the concrete walkway into the strip-lit relative warmth of the reception area. At first Turtle can't hear what the white-uniformed woman in her plate-glass booth is saying to him. She turns up her microphone and points. He enters the steel-walled lift and is carried upwards. The automatic doors close behind him and he's in a white corridor lined with mirrors. He can't escape himself: short, skinny, hunched, carroty hair cropped short, blue eyes watering. He walks forwards, in accordance with the instructions boomed over the tannoy just beside his head, halting obediently outside a door marked Temple of Joy.

Clothes stripped off, revolve under an icy swoosh of chlorinated water in the tiny shower, don white towelling bathrobe reaching barely to his thighs. Wait, shivering uncontrollably now, in the cold cubicle walled with plastic. Lino clammy under his bare soles. Exit as his number is called.

The bearded doctor is genial, letting Turtle take his time to doff his skimpy robe, fingers trembling, climb up onto the high couch and arrange himself, lying down, on its scratchy paper sheet. Knees bent, open and apart.

The doctor waves a cheerful hand at the crowd of white-coated students pressing intently forwards at the foot of the couch.

– You don't mind them, do you? They've got to learn.

The examination would be a short one, were it not prolonged by the need of every student in turn to approach, don the thin rubber glove, probe for himself Turtle's most vulnerable places. Their fingers measure, pinch, tap, squeeze, rootle. Turtle is rolled onto his front, onto his back, onto his front again. A nurse, in the white nylon jacket and trousers of his elite profession, leans against a side wall, sardonically watching.

– They told you this examination's necessary, didn't they? soothes the doctor: just a matter of hygiene. Don't let it worry you.

He massages Turtle's penis, which has wrinkled back on itself like a snail trying to escape inside its shell.

– I tend to find that some clients even learn to enjoy this experience. A certain pleasure can be gained, a certain erotic response set up. Better to let these things out. All the more for our girls to deal with afterwards. We wouldn't like to leave any perverse fantasies lurking in the unconscious. Better to rout them out as early as possible.

From behind the students' masked male faces come their clinical questions.

– A virgin, are you then?
– Masturbate, do you?
– Masochistic fantasies, have you?
– Know what good sex should be, do you?
– Been to a tart before, have you?

Their breath smells sour. Turtle answers yes, no, no, no, no, never. They laugh at him, camaraderie. The doctor slaps his right nipple.

– You'll do. Get your blood tests and jabs from the nurse, and then have a good time.

Clothed again, arse sore, mouth dry, Turtle walks down

another white corridor, this one patrolled by uniformed armed guards and set with swinging half-doors with numbers painted on them in gold. He checks the card in his hand. Number seventeen. Nearly there.

Don't panic, Dog had counselled him before he was sent off to winter camp for retraining: there's nothing to it. The tart does it all. Once you've got her underneath you just lie there and close your eyes. Then afterwards you get your certificate and your new card, and your new set of clothes and your video recorder and your alcohol allowance, and you've done it. Done what? Turtle asked. Passed your puberty rite, Dog said, grinning: become a man, like me. You'll get used to it. We all do.

Turtle stands in front of number seventeen. The guard stationed some way down the corridor notices his hesitation, turns, begins to stroll towards him. What else had Dog told him? *Give them bliss* if they're too passive, if they don't pretend well enough. Perform. Don't let them know you're scared, the bitches.

The guard is coming closer. Turtle plunges through the swinging doors.

Huge red mouth, open, tongue playing over glistening lipstick. Eyes glittering coldly through black and yellow stripes. Thick fur, silver strappings at breast and ankle and crotch. Small furry hands playing with a heavy silver chain, links clinking against each other. Body of a half-tamed beast lying on the fur-strewn bed, ready to pounce, tear, devour. Get in there first, Dog warned him: before she springs, or bites.

Turtle approaches the bed without fear. He knows her.

– Mouse, he whispers: it's me.

Mouse adjusts the lighting with practised fingers. The strip light dims. Now the cell has shadows.

– We'll have to do it, she mutters, her breath tickling his ear: because of the camera. They give you a video of it afterwards as a souvenir. Then when we've done it they turn the camera off and we'll have a few minutes to talk before the guard comes and fetches you away.

She jerks her head towards the electronic eye above the door. Click. It tilts and swerves; they blink and brace themselves.

Turtle follows Mouse's silent instructions: the twitch of a wrist, flicker of an eyelid, grip of a knee. He remembers her. He knows her, a little. Under her savage costume she is as nervous as he: he watches the pulse beat at the base of her throat, shifts his glance towards her eyes, which are very bright. He lets go into her with a cry of grief, and her hands tighten for a second in his hair. She hasn't bothered putting on an act with him, and he's grateful.

– On the wasteland, she's whispering to him: behind the car dump. I've got a hiding place there. I'll show you. I'll meet you tomorrow night, around eleven, after lights out here. At the car dump. I'll see you.

The cab of the broken-down lorry holds them snug, a frail tent pitched against a stormy night. Outside prowl the Night Police with guns and batons, starving dogs, sleepless derelicts. Inside, they are warm, domestic. Mouse has pulled the cab's curtains, frilly cretonne stitched by some long-ago wife or girlfriend, and has lit a stub of candle. They curl on the little bunk high up behind the driving seat, faces close, under the coats they have laid on themselves as blankets. Tonight Turtle has his own smell back, undisguised by carbolic and cold water, and Mouse, sniffing him, is torn open. She has meant to be cautious, but now her hands fly free, suddenly frantic, and explore his shoulders in the half-dark, his neck, his ears. Her mouth, daring, rubs against his. This time unskilful, lingering, inventing each step of the way. His fingers slither around buttons and enter her overall. Her skin shouts out with a hundred voices: touch me. Kissing him, she is astonished by the flock of birds that rises inside her and migrates. Hasty, and confident now, they wriggle arms and legs free of clothes, pull the loose coats back over their bare shoulders.

They lie on their sides, facing each other, legs laced, and Turtle dips his fingers inside her and she holds him there, wanting more, more. Pleasure is easy, born of memory, of this comfortable liking, this hunger not held back. Turtle is light, moving beside her and on her, his hand caressing the place she has shown him, the little bud blossoming plump and wet, and they move over and against each other, intense heat at the core, that hand her anchor of sweet sensation as they ride and ride, she enclosing him, he leaping gently into her. Coming is just a continuation of this slow dance, first a tingle from the seabed,

265

then a warm current lazily pushing up and through her, finally a pouring deep inside. Mouse feels enormous, full, the long valley pulsing while she lies there and laughs, while her knees are liquid and the explosion melts calves and thighs, electric.

– Let's rewrite the bloody State Dictionary, she says, giggling: let's rewrite every single damned word in it. Let's make our own meanings.

She can talk now. So much to say, to tell. Turtle is bringing her all of himself, approaching her with heaped hands, offering his gifts, his plenty, his kindness. She has not known this. She lies wrapped up with him, while they play with words. Loud laughter as the poems spill out of them, the images they bounce back and forwards, the jokes that make them wobble, almost tearful with delight, with disobedience, with loving rudeness. They name each other, and each other's bodies, slapping each other with new names. They turn policemen into milk bottles, butter up tarts, make men soluble in tears, stick red stars onto the matt black sky.

– Mother, calls out Mouse over and over: mother.

– I've written it all down, Turtle tells her: every word. But we need a safe place to hide it in. It's treasonous to write poetry.

Mouse opens her mouth to reply. I know that, stupid. Give it to me. I'll bury it somewhere. But the cab door speaks instead, a screech of rusty hinges. Then the flashlight, blinding them for a second, zigzagging across their faces.

Lucy's face, startled and white. Lucy's other hand coming up to her mouth. A red hand. Blood, glistening and fresh, like a rubber glove. And behind her, not very far away, a play of yellow searchlights, the hunting cry of the sirens of the Night Police.

40 No island visible this morning. We're lost, becalmed in glassy green sea.

I don't know what to do once I've finished my chores. Not in the mood for reading or cooking. Too cloudy to sunbathe. I decide I need company, and go off in search of the others.

Here they all are, descending the companionway leading down from the cabin deck.

– Where are you going? I ask: can I come too?

– Sure, says the Deftly Sibyl: we're going down to the hold. Of course you can come.

Down to the hold. Down to that dark windowless place ribbed like an upturned church, where those who have upturned reason and sanity disport themselves. I've heard them. The hysterics, uttering their cries and groans, stamping their feet in bitter rhythms, beating at the walls of their wooden cage. They've kept me awake many a night, kept me tossing on my hot bunk and worrying about how securely the hatches are battened down and whether the whole mob of them won't burst out in mutiny and commandeer my ship.

I shudder.

– We can't go down there. It's dangerous. And it's filthy.

– We've been going down there regularly, the Forsaken Sibyl soothes me: we know what it's like. Don't worry. Come and see for yourself.

The hold is the one place I didn't want to design. All the Arkitects were brisk: let us take care of it; sanitation and sewage disposal, not a job for a woman. In the end I did do it myself. A large cellar-like place, to take all the rubbish. Then I locked the door and forgot about it.

– Down into the bowels of the Ark? I cry: whatever for?

I don't know how the hysterics got in there and I don't care.

– Come and see, says the Gaffer, holding out his hand: you might find it quite interesting once you get used to it.

– Why didn't you tell me? I demand: where you've been going all this time? You've never said a single word about it.

– You never asked, says the Correct Sibyl: did you?

– You'd come back on board in the evenings, says the Re-Vision Sibyl: bursting to tell us all about your adventures, and somehow we never got to telling you about ours. We assumed you weren't interested. Or that you'd disapprove. So we kept quiet.

– It's quite difficult to explain the writing process to other people, adds the Babble-On Sibyl: I always assume they'll get bored. So I tend to shut up about it.

– Come *on*, shouts the Gaffer: get a move on, girls.

I'm dumb. But I don't want to be left out this time. So I follow the others down the companionway. The iron rungs are slippery. I lose count of the steps. Down one steep ladder-like decline, then down the next, gripping the cold rails with both hands. Smell of wet tarpaulins and wet ropes. The deck slimy under my bare feet. Greasy puddles slicked with oil and smeary rainbows.

We halt outside a massive iron door. I know how the bolts work: I tested them long ago, concerned for security. I slide them back, then touch the great ring handle.

– You're the only one of us, Mrs Noah, the Deftly Sibyl tells me: who hasn't told a story yet. Yours is the one that's missing.

– But I'm not a writer, not really, I hiss at her, almost weeping: I'm a librarian. I like things to be orderly, especially on my own Ark. I'm not sure I want to go in here.

– Time you got started, the Babble-On Sibyl says.

All my companions lay their hands next to mine on the iron handle. I nod my head. Then we all pull together, and the door swings open.

I close my eyes.

What a mess I'm going to find. My mess, that I brought with me onto the Ark without knowing it. This is the room I have never entered; the last place I ever wanted to be; the junkroom of old newspapers, heaps of torn lino, old vests and underpants stained yellow; the cave alive with spiders and cockroaches; the

268

coal cellar where the bogeyman lurks.

I like to have everything neat and tidy about me. I've dusted the chapel, done out the kitchen and the sickbay and the bathroom, cleaned the big step-in wardrobe, weeded the little roof garden. So it's time to go in here.

I open my eyes, and blink.

The hold is as bright and alive as a railway station, as crowded. There seems to be some sort of party going on. The dance floor is thick with performers costumed in garish silks stepping hard under spangled spotlights, under a central twirling lantern of stained glass that scatters the dazed faces with veils of colour. To one side, a man in a periwig and a blue satin coat plays raucous organ, accompanied by a woman on tenor sax. Smell of sweat, French cigarettes, Eau Sauvage, lilacs.

No one has noticed my entrance. A breathing space. I start to make my way around the walls. A quick snoop, discreet. Then I'll make my escape. The sibyls have already vanished. I can see the Gaffer on the dance floor, shirt unbuttoned to the waist, arms flung up above his head as he tosses and stamps.

Here are my two grandmothers wedged into armchairs, hands clawing cups of tea, heads nodding over the blue flame of an oil stove.

– You should have seen this place when I moved in, Nana is exclaiming: piles of tack everywhere. Balls of fluff under the beds, no hot water, the cold tap leaking through rag bandages, layers of filth on the floor. I gave it a good going-over. Rotten as a compost heap it was. Heigh-ho, look sharp, I told them, give us a hand. Then with my spit-and-polish memory I set all straight.

– The youth of today, scoffs my other grandmother: I wonder you bothered asking them to help. Self self self, that's all they think about.

She catches sight of me and scowls.

– I want, I want, I want, she mocks: that's all you can say, isn't it? I'll tell you this much. You won't get it.

– I swept up the abuse, Nana chatters on: and I burned it. Every scrap. But there was too much work left over for one person to do. So I got sat down here to rest my old bones and left it to the young ones to finish. Ten o'clock struck at the castle gate. What, girl, you dare to thwart me thus?

She laughs at me, waving a dismissal, and I wander on.

Here's the child I aborted: a tiny girl whimpering in a corner, snot congealed round her nostrils, over-large jumper crusted with food and sick. Waaa. Waaa. The plaint winds my forehead in barbed wire. When I put out a hand to her she tries to bite it. I pick her up, calming the flying fists, patting the furious red face hot with tears. After a while she stops crying. I set her down again, and she waddles off, nappy bulging at her knees, to watch the circus acts succeeding each other in a nearby alcove. A four-legged body splits apart then re-joins itself: identical twin jugglers in glittering leotards toss batons and balls at each other in a swift strobe, mirror-reflections for each other. Which is which? I can't tell. Can they? High above our heads a Degas girl in a feathered silver bird-suit bites on a noosed plumb line, makes geometry on string loops. Here's an elephant dancing with a tambourine, a fat Tarzan in spotted nylon G-string dangling from his mouth. Down tumbles a trapeze, and now three plump male fairies in skin-tight azure trunks swing from each other's fingertips. All five sibyls reappear carrying piles of encyclopedias, edge along the silvery high wire.

I'm wearing pink satin ballet shoes, their toes blocked. I go up on points, wobble. My shoes are filled with blood. I can't stop dancing.

I pirouette through an archway into what seems the vault of a museum, or the anteroom of a hospital. Broken capitals and columns are heaped pell-mell in a corner; fragments of memorial tablets cut with Latin inscriptions are set higgledy-piggledy into the wall, an incoherent poetry; cardboard boxes of pottery shards pile one on top of the other; oil paintings are stacked two foot deep against a table bearing a jumble of smashed sculptures, torn manuscripts, worm-eaten embroideries.

Here's Snow White, Keeper of Relics, holding a hacksaw.

– I'll cut your feet off, shall I? she offers: then you won't feel a thing.

She nods at the stack of corpses behind her. Like dolls they lie, rigid, eyes staring, shrouds pulled smooth, legs ending in bloody stumps.

– It's neater, Snow White giggles: I can't afford to buy shoes for all my little ones. The sweethearts. I collected this lot from the mortuary this morning. I like to get them while they're still fresh. The Third World War is breaking out, didn't you know?

270

There's been another bombing raid in the Middle East. I can't remember where, it's not my job to bother about details.

Under my feet the plaster dust of a fallen fresco. No, the ashes of six million Jews.

– Europe's dying, Snow White sighs: such a pity. All that lovely art and culture. No one will know what it was like. Gone up in flames. Irrelevant. We're washed out, all of us.

She waves her hacksaw and grins.

– But I like to keep busy, nonetheless. It's important to occupy oneself, you know, until one's Prince shall come. Hitler, Stalin, Mussolini, they all let me down. They weren't Mr Right. But I don't give up hope.

I limp off smartish, to the jerk of piano music.

Here's a fine tea table: snow of a white cloth, tiered cake-stand bearing plates of macaroons and gingersnaps, striped black and white humbugs, cucumber sandwiches. Around it are all the sibyls of the past, those whom I have not yet met, those whose names I do not know, those whose names I have not been allowed to know. All the women who have ever used the Ark are here. A reunion. A sort of Gaudy. Lazy librarian that I am: I have not browsed sufficiently in the bookstacks, the catalogue. I know so few of these women. I peer around for familiar faces.

Charlotte Brontë in a scarlet evening frock waves her cigar at Colette, whose ears are large and wing-shaped. Emily Dickinson, her hair in curl-papers, is arguing with Virginia Woolf, whose hands are full of pink betting-slips.

– I hate dinner parties, she yells above the hubbub of the Palm Court orchestra: but a quiet get-together with friends, that's different.

Katherine Mansfield catches my eye, waves her fork at me.

– Plenty of room for everyone, she cries, her mouth full of German sausage: pull up a chair.

I slide in, in between Dorothy Richardson, who is tap-dancing in tails and top hat amidst the teacups, and Aphra Behn, who is fighting a mock duel with Sappho, teasing her with brandysnaps.

– Ha, says the Nubian Sibyl through a mouthful of ripe peach: so you got here in the end, did you?

– How did *you* get here? I ask her: I thought you were out of

271

town. You could have told me you were on board!

The Bombay Sibyl leans forward from her place beyond her friend.

– We were at a bookfair in Rome. Now we're on our way to a conference in some God-forsaken place called Gravesend. We thought we'd hitch a lift. And it seemed more fun down here.

– We took the opportunity, adds the Guatemalan Sibyl: to donate copies of our latest books to your library. Seems a little understocked in certain areas. You'll find them downstairs, in the Acquisitions Department. Better get down to some homework, girl.

– We aren't, murmurs the Kentish Town Sibyl, wiping mango juice off her fingers: merely the flavour of the month. You want to run a decent library, Mrs Noah, you'd better smarten up your act.

There are my five travelling companions munching bread pudding. There's the Gaffer pouring out tea. There's Hildegard of Bingen discussing gardening with Christine de Pisan and Marie de France. There's the Mills and Boon cohort alertly discussing structuralism with George Eliot. There's Madame de Sévigné offering the milk jug to Catherine of Siena. There's Anne Bradstreet scribbling poems on the tablecloth, Grazia Deledda playing cats-cradle with Simone de Beauvoir. There are all the other sibyls whose works I have yet to read. A feast of words. At least the table is big enough for us all: no hierarchies here; no one left out.

– It takes two to make a baby, murmurs Ahkmatova, bending forwards: why do people say literature has no sex? Meaning just one? Keep me in isolation from the male poets of my generation and you'll never understand my contribution to Russian poetry.

– Deny my friendship with Dickens, remarks Mrs Gaskell: and you'll never know what he learned from me.

– Forget the fact that Richardson read us, shout Jane Barker and Eliza Heywood in concert: and you'll never understand the origins of the English novel.

– Imagism had mothers as well as fathers, H.D. points out: and actually my name is Hilda. Ezra Pound, er, defrocked me.

The Gaffer leaps to his feet.

– History doesn't make sense without you, he cries: too many

272

so-called definitive anthologies, compiled by men of course, leave you out. The idea of the canon is a con. The great tradition is a fake. Select lists of great authors matter far less than *writing*. *Verbs* are what matter. *Doing* it.

He is radiant, ecstatic.

– It's time I told you all, he confesses: the truth about my book. I didn't write it all by myself. A group of us did. A team. I've taken all the credit all this time. My friends were so generous. They never betrayed me. I'm just a rip-off merchant.

He sits down again and hides his face behind a large meringue.

– But I like your book, Elizabeth Barrett Browning comforts him: I really do. You have real talent.

– Who is this guy? asks the Bangkok Sibyl: some sort of ageing hippy? Some sort of travelling salesman? Pass the fruitcake, will you? I'm still hungry.

– He must have been feeling a bit *lonely*, muses the Brixton Sibyl.

She leans across the table and touches the Gaffer's arm.

– I had a phone call half an hour ago, she says: from Donne and Wyatt, did I tell you? They're signing up for the next trip. That will cheer you up. You'll have some male company.

I'm confused. All the books in the Arkive bookstacks have come off their shelves and jostle as eager angry bodies in this room. Parents or writers? I can't sort them out. I can't tell one category from another. My library skills fail me. I need new words.

All this time I have been searching. All this time I have been wandering around the earth, going out, out, to look for a solution. Now at last I've found what I've been needing. Here.

Not Outsiders but Insiders.

This is the house of language. The house of words. Here, inside the Ark, the body of the mother, I find words.

The islands of faery. The blessed isles in the west. The earthly paradise. The country formed out of a single rock, surrounded by sea. With its walled garden, its precious minerals and spices, its singing streams, its beasts that talk. Here. Home.

I have darkness, I grope in darkness, I carve chunks out of it

273

which are my words.

Home is the body. The bone-house. The room of my own is inside me. Each day I build it and each day it is torn down.

Creation starts here, in the Ark. Love actively shapes the work. My mother nourishes me with words, words of such power and richness that I grow, dance, leap. But the purpose of the Ark is that I leave it. The purpose of the womb is that I be born from it. So that when I'm forced to go from her, when I lose her, I can call out after her, cry out her name. I become myself, which means not-her; with blood and tears I become not-the-mother.

She points to the rainbow, umbilical cord connecting us. The curve of light in the rain joining belly to belly, the silver rope dangling earth, that mud baby. The symbol of the symbol, denoting the separation between worlds, the one I know and the one I have lost; also their connection.

Cutting the cord, she gives me speech. Words of longing for that world I've lost, words of desire to explore this absence-of-her. I must go further into absence, and find more words.

Ark. Imagination. Body. Home. Book.

The words juggle and swap, changing places, piling up on top of each other, jumping over semi-colons, free to move and play, to puncture syntax, tilt meanings, stand them on their heads. I'm inside the classification system of the Arkive, relating to everything under the sun and related to it. I'm inside the Ark and the Ark is inside me.

I have no name: I am Noah's wife. The Ark has drawn me onwards and has set me free. The Ark has made me want. The Ark has allowed me, in my turn, to become the virgin-whore who is both the mother and the wanderer; word that's been missing for so long; word that reliably keeps going away.

Delphi, Apollo's shrine, was the *omphalos*, the navel-centre of the universe. Here, inside. Daphne's place, where the hunt for meanings starts.

The sibyls and the Gaffer have plaited a rope of stories between them. I must add mine, while the sun shines in the rain, and finish the rainbow. Add the colour that's missing. A home at last: one that dissolves, is incomplete, and vanishes. As my child, in her time, will die. As my book, in its time, will rot.

Shaped against death, in the teeth of death, out of death, returning to death when the time comes. A pause between deaths, fought for by my hands.

Writer. Mother. Two words I have linked through this voyage on the Ark, this arc of stories, a distance of so many nights, such longing. This long twist of words spun out of loss.

The tea party's over, melted into shadows. The organ has stopped, the circus has packed up. I'm lying on a bed of cushions, in a tangle of clothes. Blearily I count. Fourteen arms. Fourteen legs. My right breast groans, and detaches itself, looms above me. Looking up, I stare at the Gaffer, then back down at the five sibyls entwined in sleep, each other, and us. What a muddle. I start to laugh, and cautiously to detach myself from my collapsed companions. The Gaffer pulls me to my feet, hands me bits of clothing. My mouth is dry, and my head aches.

– I need a glass of water, I croak; and I think I'll go up on deck and get some air.

The Gaffer wriggles into creased trousers. He coughs.

– I've never attended an orgy before. Though I must say it was very pleasant.

He blushes.

– What happened? I ask him, checking I've still got both earrings: I'm afraid I don't exactly remember.

A sea-monster, that we made between us, a creature with seven mouths sucking, seven pairs of hands caressing, innumerable openings to be explored and filled, expanse of skin to be licked and stroked, tasting of salt, fish, cheese, sugar. I shake my head, to clear it.

– You could say, admits the Gaffer: that the party got a little out of hand. We decided to celebrate the end of the voyage.

– What? I shout: where are we?

He stares at me.

– Don't you remember? We sighted land at dawn. We're docked. We're back in Venice.

41 The Ark looks like any other *vaporetto*. We come ashore together, turning our backs on it. We leave it behind.

Our farewells are brief. A hug, a kiss, a promise to keep on writing. Then I walk away, my eyes full of tears, leaving the others drinking coffee on one of the large café rafts bobbing alongside the Zattere. I stride along the edge of the Giudecca canal, concentrating on the wide pale green sky, the skip and race of the waters under the great boats gliding past the distant warehouses. I turn down the Rio S. Trovaso, towards the Accademia. I'm not ready to face Noah yet. I need to walk.

Now the city closes around me, streaked with green like onyx above and below. I stand on the Accademia bridge, listening to the clang of church bells. I become a needle, pushing my sharp inquisitive head through passages and alleys, whipping around the edges of *campi* and *piazze*, pulling my bright red thread behind me, stitching stone to stone, making a track, remembering, finding my way back.

The sun comes out slowly from behind pearly mist, at first just a faint warmth on my face, a delicate light on the red roofs of houses, then dry and sparkling. The *campo* I'm crossing becomes larger. Palaces tilt backwards. People stroll, don't hurry. Three dogs in black muzzles circle a dark smear on a paving-stone. Voices murmur in French, German, Italian. Heat laps my skin, dissolves me into the city. I find a bar, stand at the counter and order coffee, a brioche. I'm starving. I feel as though I haven't eaten for a long time. Needing sweetness, I sift sugar into my tiny cup with a long-handled silver spoon. The brioche is still warm, apricot jam at its heart. I eat a second one. A good breakfast. Now that I'm pregnant I must take proper care of myself.

I walk out again. I'm alone. No husband here. No Ark. Gone my anchor and maps, gone my compass, gone my passport into the world. I'm sailing alone now. Single, my eye driving forwards, into the wind. I should find Noah. But I can't return to that old world I shared with him. Will he be here in this new one?

Is it too much coffee, or morning sickness, or anxiety, that makes me feel suddenly dizzy and faint? The sun has gone in. I shudder. The *campo* is cold and black. After that I don't remember.

42 The Deftly Sibyl has taken over the garden shed. Lawn mower, hose, fork and spade, twig broom, all are cleared away into a corner. George's carpentry bench serves as desk. Pens and pencils bunch in a flowerpot, earthy, red. Discarded drafts rest on a sack of potting compost, there to rot like dry leaves and fertilize her brain. The typewriter purrs. Small square of dusty windowpane presses her nose against dripping green bushes, slime of cuckoo-spit on white flowers, slender black branches. Invisible: the sap running inside. Rain bounces on the corrugated-iron roof, clatters down its silver tilt. She has bolted the door, hung a notice outside. Danger: Woman at Work.

She has a house. She has hung red checked gingham curtains at the window, bought herself a bentwood chair from the local junkshop, provided herself with crockery from Woolworth's, a red and yellow tablecloth. Always carry a corkscrew in your handbag, her mother instructed her once, and she does. Meals of bread and cheese in her hermitage are feasts, savoured slowly in the silence broken only by the patter of rain above her head, the wet notes of blackbirds marking out their territory in the apple tree on the patch of grass between her and the other house where George sits writing an article. She doesn't know where the children are. She doesn't know what they are doing. Half term. George is in charge.

His face when she told him. Furious, grim. A day of argument brings no change. You are ruthlessly autonomous, he spits at her. Then pouts, sulks. The children save her: something new, this, a holiday from Mum. Dad will let them eat charred black sausages for breakfast every day, won't nag about changing shoes and making beds. They swear to be good, to leave him in peace. He caves in. She refuses their help in the

278

removal, carries over her belongings herself. She doesn't want them to come into her retreat. Campbed stacked against the wooden wall. Some nights she goes back to the house to sleep, but she departs early, cherishing her dawn cup of tea alone in the chilly shed. She creeps back to piss, too, using the outside lavatory in the yard. Then slinks off rapidly before she's seen.

She sits at her desk, an old quilt padding her knees; peace enters her, slides along her bones. On the shelf she has put up in the corner by the window stand her reassembled household gods: painted wooden doll from the USSR with a tiny replica in its belly; photograph of her sister; lump of blue glass worn smooth and round, a solid bit of sea; tiny folding shrine of gilded wood from Italy whose doors open to reveal a sad Madonna flanked by spiky angels.

Living in a dolls' house. Silly woman. How pathetic. How immature. Real writers (men) can write anywhere (in the middle of a battlefield or a riot), don't need to stake out this neurotic claim to personal territory (the world is theirs to start with).

She shakes her head, and the buzz of self-hate subsides. Her fingers touch the typewriter keys, re-order her world. Tap, tap, tap. Her small hammers reconstruct what she knows: a partial vision, limited, the joins showing. So be it. You do what you can, while the dispossessed line up on the path outside and beat at the door and she opens it. All the homeless pour into her heart and squat it, their anger and despair a further hammer fragmenting her even as she strives to build sentences that will last, to do her job capably. They dictate to her: a catalogue of wild cries.

A bang on the window. She starts up out of her pain-filled trance. Her daughter's face, staring and white. Come quickly Mum Johnny's cut himself with the carving knife blood quickly Mum come.

She hurries across the sopping lawn back towards the house.

The Forsaken Sibyl has taken a month-long job in Italy, house-sitting, while roof repairs are done on their flat in Florence, for a married couple who are cousins of her adoptive parents. She needs the money; and evacuated from her squat, her possessions stored in a friend's spare room, she also needs a temporary refuge until she sorts out what to do next. The Clellands introduce her to the builders, instruct her to call on their

279

architect in case of problems, promise to despatch regular payments for building supplies and labour, then depart on their tour of Tuscany and Umbria.

She pushes open the green shutters, leans out of the study window. Below her, the impatient blaring queue of cars; the petrol fumes, rubbish heaps and dogshit of the narrow grey street; the busy shoppers; the children in pushchairs. Craning her neck one way, she can see the massive gate-arch marking the boundary of the city on its eastern side; looking the other way, she can just see the top of the Duomo, jewelled Easter egg.

But no time for sightseeing. She's here to work. She fingers her pocket dictionary, wondering whether her slender O-Level Italian will be sufficient.

The builders arrive next morning at eight, three sturdy dark brothers, wives and children left down south in Regio Calabria. They speak between themselves an impenetrable guttural code, translate for her into Italian when necessary. Eh, eh, no husband, all alone here? They laugh. It's better to be without women, wives belong in the house, a drag on a man.

She should have cleared out the big kitchen-living room last night. Frantically she packs china and glass into wicker baskets, carries the lighter furniture downstairs to the tiny storeroom, while they start knocking down the ceiling. Lumps of plaster clatter to the terracotta floor. More than dust: the kitchen is a gritty grey cloud. Next they tear down the woven cane-lining the plaster clung to, fragile basketry that has left its criss-cross print on the rubble below. Then the beams are exposed, thick logs, blackened and cracked. The large pieces of furniture huddle in the next room, widows draped in plastic veils heavy with grey powder. Fridge and cooker unplugged and hidden: she will live on fruit and water. Debris of broken bricks, ankle-deep, dust in her lungs and on her lips, her hair a stiff white wig.

Their job is to destroy, and hers to clear up after them. Noise of falling masonry as she crouches on the bed, her last oasis this one tiny room they will leave intact, trying to write. Her arms are about the house; trying to hold it up; while they huff and puff and blow her down. Beams dislodged, sawn up and vomited out of the study window into the waiting lorry, the roof can come off, heaved down in red handfuls. Women hold up half the sky? There is no sky. Just this gap. She is open-mouthed to the rain. Pigeons shit in the bath. She is walled in air. The kitchen has vanished: she stands on a bombsite under dark winds, looking up at the stars, shuddering under hammer blows, iron wedges driven into her skull, fissuring it, she tumbles across the invisible floor, a litter of broken stones.

The days batter her with anxiety. Smashed light fittings dangle from the walls. The electricity fails. Neighbours complain about noise and mess. Invoices must be haggled over. Pall of thick dirt enters every pore of the house, dissolves it, dust to dust. At night she lies sleepless in her grimy bed, ears cocked for the scrabble of birds and rats across the gaping building site on the other side of her door. Open the door: step out into nothingness; the void; half the house swinging loose from a single hinge. She is lonely. By day she feeds on brief interchanges with the builders, with shopkeepers. By night, she thinks of Londoners in the last war, emerging from bomb-shelters in the morning to find their homes toppled and smashed, of the people across the world driven by war and poverty into refugee camps, squatting under cardboard shelters to await death, watching the children sicken, their bellies swell. Count their blessings? They are alive?

Self-pity breeds revolt. On the seventh day she decides to take time off. She hires a motorbike and roars off up into the hills to see the countryside.

The Correct Sibyl stands uncertainly on the edge of the pavement, peering about her. She has already lost Tom and Jessie. Still, they are old enough to be sensible. And they'll enjoy themselves more without her dogging them.

It is raining. The world is black and white and grey, shiny as celluloid. Texture and grain in monochrome. People bunch under umbrellas, waiting.

And then the first Carnival float leaps down Westbourne Grove towards her, a tongue poking out in showers of confetti colours, a dance of bright symbols unleashed, bobbing and circling, the street suddenly lit up as though by night in neon. The force of joy breaking out in her and unfurling along the tarmac is so great that she bursts into tears, fresh rain wetting her face.

Woman-spider, world-weaver, jogs along in her huge blue

and silver crinoline web. Bumblebees with furry knees jump up. Spacemen in silver-paper suits advance their hips. Drums beat, shrill whistles blow. A long narrow ceiling of plastic is held up against the rain by the file of dancers as they sway and step beneath it, and the watching people break free from the pavement and jig forwards under their umbrellas over the mud and refuse in the gutter, and the Correct Sibyl goes with them, released into this joy. All day long she sings and dances with these unknown neighbours in the dark streets which she helps illuminate. Repression lifts: the people lift their knees to the rhythm, splash in rain and music, twirl their hats, joggle their bones and shake their flesh free and get soaked. Lifting up their hands. No cars. No more division between pavement and road. Just this tide of bodies surging through the city and claiming it as theirs. The unconscious is out. Snaking serpent that coils and doubles back, that pours forward in primary colours and glitter shedding sparks and beer cans and streamers. A stranger darts in under her twirling umbrella and clasps her waist, putting his dark face next to hers, mixing sweat, tight black curls glistening, mouth amused, and they sway on together, swallowed up in the thrashing crowd, the wet.

The Babble-On Sibyl is building a new bed. She and Neil have designed it together, squabbling, grabbing the pencil from the other's fingers, furiously crossing out.

It must be *wide*, she insists. Wide enough for her to be able to lie on her stomach and scissor her legs out before she sleeps, wide enough that they can both loll surrounded by books. Wide enough that a child can tumble in with them of a weekend morning. No more of your rules of conduct, she tells Neil: I shall sleep late as often as I want, I shall lie in this bed on Sundays uncaring that I smudge the sheets with newsprint, I shall eat breakfast in bed, you will even bring me an early morning cup of tea.

They have sawn up the pine planks, which lie stacked on the carpet. They have agreed on the height of the headboard, the lack of curves and frills. Now they start to fit it all together.

He holds the wooden parts, she wields the screwdriver. Then they swap. Slowly, the bed assembles itself. Takes shape. She has not bought enough screws, and now the shops are shut.

Impatient, she runs to the kitchen door, prises from its top hinge the two long black flat-headed screws she needs. As supper time approaches, it is done. Sturdy, low, a frame of gleaming wood onto whose supporting struts they fit the new mattress.

The bed takes up most of the space in the tiny room. They edge around it, putting on the clean cotton sheets and pillowcases, tucking in the scarlet blanket. It is ready. Plump and soft, inviting.

– I'm not hungry yet, are you? she says: let's try it *now*.

Clothes off, sweat and grime rinsed away under the feeble lukewarm shower. Shivering, dry. Padding barefoot across the litter of wood-shavings, sliding naked between deliciously cold sheets. Bodies warmed by each other, by the blankets, air blowing in from the open window to curl around their necks. They design together how their bodies will fit; they manoeuvre arms and legs in intricate joins; carefully, according to no blueprint but this second by second of shared breathing and answering gestures, they begin to build. And all the time, even as she takes her pleasure and gives it, she is watching, considering, analysing; taking notes.

The Re-Vision Sibyl and Maria sit opposite each other at a small square table in the far corner of the restaurant. They've chosen the upstairs room, liking its old-fashioned decor, mournful and plain: brown walls lined with occasional mirrors, no plants or pictures. When they arrived, the restaurant was large, echoing. Now it is packed with people. Roar of noise buffets their ears, drowns their talk. They lean close, lipread in order to hear each other. Between them the thick white tablecloth, heavy white plates, silver knives and forks, glasses of mineral water alight with tiny bubbles, a dark red bottle of wine. Their hands, teasing crusts of bread, almost touch. They are underwater, swimming in this sea of shouts and babble, their faces looming up large, not quite bumping.

Maria's mouth is wide, full, red. Playing her role for tonight with scarlet lipstick, wide-shouldered forties suit, seamed silk stockings, little high-heeled shoes of black suede. She gestures with one hand, a crumpled white napkin. The lamp above her head is a bowl of dull yellow glass, opaque like milk. Her

283

shoulders are black, severely cut. The wall behind and beside her is painted brown. Her bright head bisects this angle coloured like mud. Her face breaks up, changes, frowns, smiles, as she shapes sentences and gesticulates.

Maria loves to talk, and to eat out in restaurants. She will pay the bill. She flings herself into her pleasure, talking rapidly and intensely, then letting herself float in pools of silence while she searches for words, and the Re-Vision Sibyl listens in joyful concentration, ears spread to catch the words issuing from Maria's mouth into this larger ocean of booming sound.

Love means a conversation. These words we carefully dredge up then cut and polish, offer each other, test between our teeth. Or given raw, smelling of salt. Pearl is grit. What else is love but this language we invent then share, these words we pass back and forth. Talking with Maria is coming, the same thing not different. This moment. Brown water lapping us.

These months of talking with Maria make love solid as a house of stone built into a hill. Foundations of trust. No game of enticing then slapping down, flirtatious dance promising all then giving nothing, need for control and holding back. She can say anything. She has a sense of being set completely free. She can reveal herself without fear. Peace. No more craving. Maria fills her with her words and she takes them in and is blessed.

Wine sinks in the dark red bottle, turning it dark green. Pizza slithers across their plates, puffed and blackened at the edges, shiny with melted cheese, blue puddle of Gorgonzola. She sticks her fork in, tears at it with her teeth.

Then it's over. Table cleared, cloth whisked off, chairs scrape back on the brown floor. Into the street, cold air on flushed face, arm in arm to the tube. Walking Maria home. Impossible to spend tonight together; baby-sitters; children; but it's all right.

Down her street under the huge dark blue clouds scudding under the wind tossing the tops of trees in the square. The iron railings are wet and black. She plunges into shadows, lets the wind fist her back, push her on. The joy of this, being out at night completely alone, hardly conscious of thought, the race of the indigo sky. Freedom and solitude. This too she cannot do without. For ten minutes only, tonight; coming home to her daughter.

43 I wake to a room full of darkness, darkness flowing between invisible walls, pressing outwards to make a shape I am boxed by. Cube of solid darkness one second, of dissolving darkness the next. Comfortable, comforting. I am part of the darkness, and I swim in it. Now I separate myself from it, make out the high rolled end of the bed, the black sheen of a mirror set above the soft cavern of blackness that must be a washbasin. I put out a hand, touch the marble top of the cabinet next to the bed, the cool swell of a lamp, the fringe of a linen towel.

A clock ticks somewhere. Inside me, my heart a pendulum pushing to and fro, pushing the darkness from side to side. The clock strikes eight, loud and resonant as the beat of a gong, hammer blows smoothing out the creases my fingertips find in my puzzled forehead. I know that clock. It's the one that stands outside our room in the Pensione Seguso, in the corridor.

So I'm back, then? So I must get up. Where's the light? Where are my clothes?

I fumble my way across the cold tiled floor to the window, throw back the shutters. There's the little canal flowing past the hotel, three floors below, and there's the walled garden opposite. I remember them now.

I stand in front of the washbasin and peer into the mirror. I haven't looked into one for so long that I've forgotten what I look like. Dark brown hair chopped off at chin length, thick brown eyebrows, green eyes, big nose, big mouth. I remember liking my face. This morning it's a collection of jigsaw pieces that don't make a whole. I feel too tall, too broad-shouldered. I take up too much space in this room, which has Noah's books, files and papers piled everywhere in it.

285

Then I spot a notebook, familiar, lying on the chair standing next to the basin, and pick it up, puzzled.

I remember now. I bought it late that first afternoon we arrived in Venice, on the way to the restaurant. It's a pretty object: A5 size, cover of thick paper marbled in blue and green, red silk headband, red silk marker. Here's the clutch of felt-tips I bought, and the two Chinese brushes, and the bottles of black and red inks. I was going to write, and I was going to enjoy myself. I was so lonely on that trip, which seems so long ago now: Noah out touring hospitals all day, I needed a friend. Then we got to Venice, for Noah's medical conference. And then?

I open the diary. I've hardly written in it at all. The two first pages are scribbled over in my untidy hand. The rest are blank. *Noah died last night . . . I should ask for forgiveness. But I can't. Not yet.* That's it. Must be a dream I had. I shake my head.

The door opens. I recognize the man who enters. It's Noah, wet black hair sleeked down, towelling dressing gown tied round his middle with his trouser belt, hands full of sponge bag and toothbrush. He looks at me, uncertain.

– How are you feeling?

I sit down on the bed. I'm wearing a white cotton nightdress. How?

– All right, I think, I tell him: but I can't remember much. What happened?

He treads towards me, rubber flip-flops slapping on the floor. Halts next to the bed and dumps his things on the cabinet. Doesn't touch me.

– We had a row last night. You were very angry with me. You were saying you'd had enough. You wanted a proper home as soon as we got back to London, no more living in my flat with no room for all your possessions. You wanted a baby too, and you were fed up with waiting. You said you'd been waiting for too long.

He pushes his hair back with one hand.

– Then you ran off and jumped into the canal. I fished you out. I think you banged your head going in. You were staggering about like a drunk. I had to get your clothes back on you and you were fighting me. I had a hell of a time getting you back here, both of us sopping wet. We were lucky no one saw us and fetched the police.

– Then what? I ask him: go on.

– I told the *padrona* you'd fallen in. I don't know what she thought. She helped me get you to bed, and you went out like a light. So I decided to leave you be and just see how you were this morning.

I watch him make the decision to control his anger, to bend down and touch my hand.

– We need to have a proper talk. But not now. After lunch, after you've rested and are feeling better.

– Yes.

He throws his dressing gown onto my lap and starts to dress. I burrow my hands into the soft towelling and look at him. I've always thought him so beautiful, with his lean build and long legs, his thatch of black fur, his dark blue eyes and flopping black hair. I watch him put on his underpants, triangle of thin white cotton, lift out a clean shirt from the wardrobe. I don't iron his shirts. I do remember that.

– Noah, I tell him: you won't believe this, but –

He swings round.

– Later. Save it for later. I'm sorry, but the conference opens at nine, and I must be there. I don't like leaving you alone, but there's nothing else I can do. I'm reading my paper in the opening session. You've probably forgotten that.

He buttons his cuffs.

– We haven't talked properly for weeks, I say: you've been so busy taking notes on all the hospitals and then writing your paper. I didn't realize how difficult I'd find it, no privacy, sharing a room all this time and you having to work every night. I realize I should have told you more about how I felt. I *must* talk to you.

A knock on the door. Noah zips up his trousers.

– Here's breakfast.

44   I spend the morning in bed, dozing at first, then waking again and staring at the wall.

If this were a romance I could give myself a happy ending. Marriage means compromise, my mother said to me once: and one of you tends to compromise more than the other.

How does a woman survive?

I pick up my pen and open my diary.

I like the feel of this paper, the black wetness of this ink. I like writings that can be torn out, scribbled on a shirt cuff, chalked on a wall, drawn with a stick in the sand on the seashore and then washed away. I was taught that art is supposed to last, to be preserved in libraries and museums, to defy rotting and perishing, to contain eternal meanings that transcend history, that survive the time-span of the body. My art won't be like that. The creation of the world happened in seven days and seven nights. Writing in this diary won't be like that. My creation will be as daily as dusting, or dreaming.

My story, I write: *begins in Venice*.